Miranda and the Miner

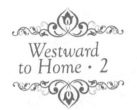

Westward to Home · 2

Miranda and the Miner

MELODY CARLSON

WhiteFire
PUBLISHING

This is a work of fiction. All characters and events portrayed in this novel are either fictitious or used fictitiously.

MIRANDA AND THE MINER

WhiteFire Publishing
13607 Bedford Rd NE
Cumberland, MD 21502

ISBN: 978-1-941720-62-2 (print)
978-1-941720-63-9 (digital)

1

August 1884
Double W Ranch, Colorado

Miranda Williams desperately longed for a change. Or perhaps she simply wanted to change herself. She wasn't even sure as she slid the peach satin gown over her head. It had been altered for her to wear at stepsister's wedding, and she had to admit it was a gorgeous garment. As she struggled to button the back of it, she wasn't sure it was possible for her to change. The past few months only seemed to reveal just how spoiled and stubborn she truly was. Not to mention just plain silly and childish. But being around Delia this summer had triggered something in Miranda. She knew that her stepsister had something that she wanted. And it wasn't just the ranch that Delia had inherited from her father.

And it wasn't Delia's fancy eastern gowns and pretty jewelry. It wasn't even Delia's handsome fiancé, Wyatt Davis. Oh, Miranda would've loved having all those things for herself. And she'd certainly tried to snatch them. But now she realized that had been very wrong…and the consequences severe. Still, she longed for something more…something she couldn't even put into words.

On Saturday, Miranda would stand by Delia as she repeated wedding vows with Wyatt before a small crowd of family, friends, and neighbors. While Miranda was honored, she knew herself well enough to know she'd being fighting back feelings of envy…and self pity. Delia's happy life just seemed to cast a dark, sad shadow across Miranda's. Just one more reminder of her own immature selfishness. Would she ever grow up?

Miranda sighed as she studied her image in her bureau mirror. With her auburn curls pinned up with a silver comb that had belonged to her deceased mother, she actually did look somewhat grown up. The problem was, despite recently turning seventeen, she felt very much like a child. And despite recent demands to be treated more like an adult, Miranda suddenly wanted to turn back the clock. And she didn't want to go back East to attend the university that both her stepfather and Delia had decided would be perfect for her. Miranda was definitely out of sorts!

"Oh, my! You look beautiful!" Delia exclaimed as she entered the bedroom. "That color is lovely on you, Miranda." She examined the bodice. "Ginger did an excellent job of altering it."

Miranda nodded. "But it'll be too short for you now."

"That's perfect since I'm giving it to you. As well as a couple of other things that you'll need in Philadelphia. Not fancy dresses, although there will be a few formal events at the university."

Miranda cringed at the word *university.* Everyone kept assuming she was glad to be sent off to a strange school in a strange place—and to be fair, this was partly her fault since she'd sort of played along. But as her departure date drew closer, her confidence shriveled.

"What's wrong?" Delia asked as she finished buttoning the back of the gown.

"I don't know…just a little out of sorts today." Miranda sighed. "Maybe it's the heat. It's been awful hot the last few days."

Delia went over to close the window. "Better shut this to keep what little cool air there is inside. It has been hot. Even the chickens looked droopy this morning." She chuckled. "But at least your bedroom is on the cool side of the house."

"One thing to be thankful for." Miranda frowned.

Now Delia peered curiously at her. "Are you upset about being moved back to your old room? Because you know—"

"No, no, that's all right." Miranda sniffed as she glanced around the small, cluttered room in need of tidying after she'd carelessly dumped her things in here. Truth be told, she had been rather miffed at getting kicked out of the master bedroom she'd claimed after her stepfather was murdered. But then she realized it rightfully belonged to Delia since she was the true heir of the Double W. And it would belong to both Delia and Wyatt after they married. Besides Miranda's attempt at squatter's rights, that room had never belonged to her. Nothing on the ranch really belonged to her…anymore. She was only the stepchild…Delia was Winston Williams' *real* daughter.

As Delia helped her out of the silky gown, Miranda felt starkly aware that she truly was the *stepchild.* Hadn't everyone gone out of their way to make that clear once Delia arrived? And with the reading of the will, it all grew crystal clear. Delia was the true heiress. She got everything. And, sure, her older stepsister had been generous enough, but it wasn't the same as if Miranda were *lady of the house* like she'd dreamed of…that was hard to let go.

"What is it then? Why are you scowling like that?" Delia sat in the wooden rocker by the window. "I've noticed you're unhappy these last few days. Please, talk to me."

Miranda tried to sort and sift her thoughts. "Oh, I don't know. It's a lot of things. I'm not even sure what…" Wearing only her chemise and bloomers, she sat on the edge of her bed and, folding her arms in front of her, tried to contain her emotion…and tears.

"Well, I'm not surprised." Delia sighed. "You've been through a lot, Miranda. We both have. And there's so much going on lately. I can understand how it might take its toll on you."

Miranda just shrugged. Delia's sympathy just made the lump in her throat become harder.

"Besides losing your mother, even though it was awhile back, you just lost your father and you—"

"You mean *your* father."

"He was your father too, Miranda. And you got to spend almost ten years with him. Years I never had." Delia's green eyes grew sad. "And, more importantly, I know how much he loved you."

"I guess so." Again, she shrugged. "But he didn't always approve of me. I know he thought I was a silly flibbertigibbet sometimes. I'm sure he would've liked me to be more like you." She looked at Delia with teary eyes. "I wish—I *wish* I were more like you."

Delia got up and, hurrying to sit next to her, put her arm around Miranda's now trembling shoulders. "Oh, darling."

"But I'm not like you," she sobbed. "I'm a selfish, spoiled brat."

"No, you're not."

"I am too. I heard Ginger and Daisy talking the other day. They said that very thing. They both think I'm a selfish, spoiled brat."

"Maybe you *used* to be like that," Delia said gently, "but you are growing up. You help out a lot more now. Remember how grown up you acted when Wyatt first arrived? Even Ginger was impressed with how you jumped in to help."

"It was only because I wanted to impress Wyatt. Because I wanted to steal him from you, Delia." Tears streamed down her cheeks. "And that's worse than selfish. It's horrible. I'm not only a spoiled brat, I'm conniving and evil and—"

"No, you're not." Delia laughed. "It's no wonder you went after Wyatt. You recognized a good man when you saw one."

"Even though I knew he was *your* man?"

"Well, that was a bit indiscriminate. But I give you credit for recognizing Wyatt was a much better choice than poor Marcus."

"*Poor* Marcus?" Miranda turned to Delia with anger. "Marcus was a murderer! He killed our father."

"I know." Delia grimly shook her head. "I still have to work to forgive him for that."

"I will never forgive him. *Never!*"

"Well, for your sake, I hope you do forgive him, Miranda. Someday...when you're ready—"

"Never!" Miranda declared with heartfelt conviction. "He ruined everything. He was a beast and a liar and a murderer. I'll hate him until the day I die. And longer!" Now she was crying harder than ever.

Delia handed Miranda a clean hanky. "Like I said, little sister, you've been through a lot. It's no wonder you're out of sorts. But have you really told me everything that's troubling you?"

Miranda wiped her nose. "No...there's one thing I haven't mentioned to you...or anyone."

"What is it?" Delia looked intently at her.

"It's about going to the university...in Philadelphia. It's frightening—it scares me to death."

Delia actually smiled. "Oh, is that all?"

"Is that all?" Miranda wadded the hanky into a tight ball. "I've never been anyplace bigger than Colorado City and Denver. I will be a fish out of water in that big city. I will be completely lost there." She bit her lip, knowing it wasn't truly the big city that disturbed her. In a way, she looked forward to that part.

"You won't feel lost there, Miranda. And I already told you that Wyatt's Aunt Lilly and Uncle George are coming to the wedding. I wrote a letter to his aunt, and she wrote back saying she looks forward to meeting you and she even offered to help you to get settled in the city and—"

"That's not really what I meant." She took in a deep breath. "I'm really worried, Miranda. To be honest I'm scared to go to the university."

"But why? It's a wonderful school. I loved it there."

Miranda bit her lip, wondering how much to disclose.... "This is the real truth, Delia. I know I'm not smart enough. I will be a complete failure, and it will be terribly humiliating for me...and a disappointment to you. I know it." She felt relieved to have thrown her cards on the table. "I'm just plain stupid."

"That's not true. I read through your school materials in our father's library files. And I realized not only was he a very good teacher, I could see that you're quite smart."

"I might be smart about some things. But not like you. Everyone talks about how intelligent you are, Delia. I'm not like that. Even though my schoolwork looks fine to you, you don't know how long it took me to complete my assignments. Father tried to be patient with my lessons after my mother passed, but I know he felt I was slower than molasses. I honestly don't think I can succeed at higher education and I don't—"

"You just need to give it a chance. There were lots of girls in college who were, well, not so academic as you'd think and, well, they just had to work a bit harder, but they—"

"No, no, that's *not* me, Delia. I can't do it. And I don't want to do it." She was crying again. "I would rather stay here and tend chickens and milk cows and scrub floors and—and—anything!"

Delia looked amused. "Interesting…since you've never been particularly interested in farm work before. And I suppose that's an option, but I can't believe you'd want to settle for that. Our father had higher hopes for your future."

"Well, then I could get married. I'm sure there are plenty of nice men around here who'd be willing to marry me. I suppose I was so stuck on stupid old Marcus I didn't pay attention to other fellows."

"But you're barely seventeen, do you really want to marry? And to just anyone?"

"I'd rather be unhappily married than lost and miserable at some Eastern college."

"You can't be serious."

"I am! I think I'd do anything not to be sent to that university."

Delia slowly nodded. "All right. I hear what you're saying. I'd like to give this some careful thought, Miranda. And some serious prayer.

I know our father wanted you educated like I was, but maybe there's another solution."

"Yes!" Miranda grabbed Delia's hands. "There has to be another solution."

Delia squeezed her hands then slowly stood. "Thank you for being honest with me about this." She picked up the peach gown, carefully hanging it on the wardrobe door before she turned to look at Miranda. "Try not to worry about it, honey. This is supposed to be an exciting week, remember? Uncle Enoch is coming on tomorrow's train. And we have a lot to keep us busy these next few days."

Miranda tried to feign enthusiasm. "Yes...I do want to enjoy the wedding preparations. And I do feel better now. Thanks."

"Somehow, we'll figure this all out. Maybe Wyatt will have some advice."

Miranda thanked her again, and after Delia left she did feel a bit better. But she still felt absolutely certain that she did not want to attend the women's university. Delia had frequently told Miranda about her schooling, trying to convince her it would be a great experience, going on about how intellectually stimulating her classes would be, and how fun it would be to live with other smart young women. But the idea of being cooped up with a bunch of bookworms scared Delia witless. She knew she'd never be able to read all those books or keep up with that kind of intense education. Furthermore, she didn't want to!

2

Delia found Wyatt out by the bunkhouse. He'd been staying out there since they'd announced their engagement. "If you're not busy, I'd like to talk to you," she said as she approached him.

"Never too busy for you. In fact, I was hoping to speak to you about something too." He laid down the halter he'd been repairing then bent down to pet Hank. The faithful dog, as usual, was right by her side. "Care for a before-dinner stroll?"

"Thank you." She linked her arm in Wyatt's. "And now I'm curious. What do you want to speak to me about?"

"Not so fast. You said you have something to tell me. Ladies first, I insist." He winked.

"Fine." Suppressing her curiosity, she quickly relayed Miranda's concerns about school. "What do you think? My father so wanted her to have the same educational opportunity as I enjoyed. And I do think it would be good for her."

"Because it was good for you?"

"Yes." She nodded as they took the trail up the hill. "I'm grateful for my education."

"But Miranda is not you."

"No, of course. I understand that."

"And, from what I can see, she's not the academic type. I've tried to get her interested in reading some good books and, well, she hasn't the slightest interest."

"That's true. But she's only been taught at home. Perhaps if she had some more formal schooling. If she just gave it a try."

"But you just said she's completely opposed to the idea."

"Yes, but I'm supposed to act as her guardian."

"Even if you forced her to go...well, you can lead a horse to water, but you can't make her drink."

Delia sighed. "I know you're right, but I do want to honor my father. He made his intentions clear in his will."

"No doubt, he wanted the best for Miranda. But maybe your university isn't the best thing. For her."

"You could be right about that." She turned to him. "Now, enough about Miranda. What did you want to talk to me about? Curiosity is killing me."

"Well, I received a telegram today. In response to a wedding invitation."

"Oh, is it your aunt and uncle? I hope they're still coming."

"As far as I know. Although I realize it's hard for Uncle George to leave his boot factory. Still, he didn't want Aunt Lilly to make the train trip alone."

"Oh, good. Then is it Uncle Enoch? He's rather elderly. But I was so looking forward to seeing him. Has something happened to prevent—"

"No, no, this isn't in regard to him. In fact, Caleb recently got a letter from Enoch. It sounded as if he's in good health and eager to return to the ranch for good. It seems the East does not agree with him."

"I'm not surprised." She glanced down at the beautiful ranch her father had so carefully created. "I bet he's missed this."

"Understandably."

"So, tell me, who sent the message? I can't think of anyone else who'd send a telegram."

"Well, I wasn't going to mention this. Not until I knew for sure." His expression looked slightly guilty. "I have a confession to make."

"A confession?" She looked intently into his mossy green eyes. Wyatt had never deceived her before. But to be fair, she'd only known him for a few months. Still, she knew him well enough to trust him implicitly.

"You see…I invited someone without consulting you, Delia. I honestly didn't think they'd come, but I thought perhaps it would be a good way to mend some fences."

"What fences? What are you talking about?"

"I invited your family."

"What?" She stared at him in horror. "My family? You mean my mother? My stepfather? My siblings?"

He nodded somberly. "Remember after we became engaged and started to plan a wedding? You mentioned how it would be sad not to have your own family here?"

"Yes, but I realized it was impossible, Wyatt."

"Well, about the time we set out wedding date, I noticed your parents' Pittsburgh address in your writing things in the library… and, well, I was so excited about everything that I took the liberty of writing to them at the same time I wrote to my aunt and uncle. So, anyway, I invited your family to come out here for our wedding."

"Well, I'm sure they must've declined your gracious invitation. Is that what the telegram said?"

"Not exactly." He rubbed his chin with a furrowed brow.

"You do remember what I told you, don't you? How enraged my parents were after I refused to marry old Henry Horton—for his wealth." She grimaced to remember the horrid disagreement. "It was an awful scene. My stepfather said he never wanted to see me again."

"But they *are* coming, Delia." He looked intently into her eyes. "Please, tell me you're not angry at me."

She blinked. "I—I'm not angry. But I am shocked. I just can't—can't believe it, Wyatt. Are you saying my whole family is coming? My mother, stepfather, and Julianne and Julius?"

"The telegram said to expect the four of them."

"But my stepfather completely disowned me. Why would *he* agree to this?"

"Maybe he's forgiven you."

"I find that hard to believe." She frowned.

"Well, perhaps your mother persuaded him."

"I've never seen my mother persuade him of anything."

"Why question this, Delia? Just be glad that you'll have family here. You did mention it was something you'd dreamt of for your wedding. I did it for your sake, darling."

"But I never dreamed it possible…." She was still trying to sort it out in her head—it sounded perfectly crazy. "Besides everything else, I don't see how they could afford such a trip. They were in bad financial straits when I left. That's the reason they were so determined I marry Mr. Horton. How could they possibly afford such a trip? Four round trip train tickets and traveling expenses?"

Wyatt rubbed his chin. "I sent them the needed funds."

"What?" She shook her head. "Why would you do that?"

"Well, it was your mother who wrote back to me, Delia. Last month. It's as you said, they were unable to come. Due to the expense."

"And…?"

"That's when I wired them the money."

"Oh, Wyatt. I can't believe you did that." She hated the thought of him wasting his gold mining profits on what would certainly turn into a fiasco.

"They're your family, Delia. I hoped it would make you happy. And if you're worried about that money, you know how well I did up in Alaska. I can afford it."

"I'm just afraid it was for nothing. Knowing my stepfather, he's probably lost it at the horse races by now."

"I don't think so, darling." He smiled. "The telegram was from your stepfather. He said to expect them on Thursday afternoon's train in Colorado City. Same as my aunt and uncle."

"Oh, my!" Her feelings were definitely mixed as she stared at the sheep grazing down below. The creek moved slowly this time of year, but at least it was moving.

"Please, tell me you're not upset." Wyatt sounded concerned. "I'd hate to think I angered you—just days before our wedding."

She knelt down to stroke Hank's sleek head and ears, trying to calm herself and to carefully sort her words before responding. "No, dear, I realize you did this for me. But…it's a lot to take in." She forced an uneasy smile, trying not to imagine what a fiasco this unexpected family reunion could evolve into.

He hugged her. "I understand. But remember you're not alone. I'm by your side now. And think about it, Delia, won't it be nice to have family here? You just told me last week that you were missing your siblings…and your mother too."

"Yes, but that was because they were far away. You know what they say about absence making the heart grow fonder." She sighed. "And my stepfather…well, to be perfectly honest, I haven't missed him at all."

"I know." He waved toward the handsome ranch house, barn, and outbuildings. "At the very least, you can show him that despite rebelling against his plans for you, it turned out quite well. For you anyway. That alone should give you a glimmer of satisfaction."

"You're probably right." Her smile grew genuine. "And I don't mind for them to see all that my father accomplished with his life. I'd like for them to respect him." She gazed down on the corral and stables, the pretty horses grazing in the back pasture, the orchards and gardens beyond the house. "And I'm sure Julius and Julianne will enjoy the country life."

"You see, it was a good idea after all. Imagine your brother and sister running around here like regular farm kids. Maybe they'll want to do some riding."

"Yes, but now I'm wondering where I'll put everyone. I'd planned to have your aunt and uncle in the master suite. And I wanted to put Uncle Enoch in the guest room and—"

"Caleb just told me that Uncle Enoch wants to be in the bunkhouse—just like old times. You know how he and Caleb go way back."

"So I could put my parents in that guest room." She thought. "And I could set up Julianne and Julius in the old nursery. It will be a full house and a lot of work for our household staff, but I suppose it will all work out."

"Of course it will. And it's only for a few days." He leaned down to kiss her. "And after our wedding supper, you and I will be off on our wedding trip to Denver. We will leave our family behind to sort things out for themselves. In the meantime, I don't want you to worry about it."

Despite his reassurance, Delia couldn't quite imagine how it would all turn out. The idea of her family making the arduous trip from Pittsburgh to Colorado City, just for her wedding—well, it was almost unimaginable. Especially considering the sour note they'd parted on. Although the twins would probably enjoy the train trip. Their visit to the "wild" West would give them something to brag about in school. But Delia's mother, who was used to all her comforts? And her difficult stepfather? Well, anything could happen. Still, she planned to take Wyatt's advice and instead of worrying, she would try to pray.

3

With all the hustle-bustle in the house, everyone preparing for the upcoming wedding, cooking and cleaning and guests beginning to arrive today, Miranda had no opportunity to ask Delia about the plans for her to attend the university in Philadelphia. Was it still on? Or had Delia decided to take Miranda's concerns seriously? She had no idea. And as a result, Miranda was on pins and needles as she rode with Caleb to town.

"Are you excited to see your Uncle Enoch?" Caleb asked as the carriage neared town.

"Yes, of course," she assured him. Not pointing out that Enoch was not truly her uncle. Certainly, he was Delia's. But not hers. "First, I want you to drop me by the mercantile. I can get a head start on shopping while you meet the train. Delia asked me to pick up a few things for the wedding."

"How about I give you an hour before I come and fetch you?" Caleb suggested. "That'll give me some time to shoot the bull with Enoch."

"That's fine." She clumsily let herself down from the carriage and, nearly tripping over her skirt, fell right into a man passing by the boardwalk.

"Oh, Miranda!" Jackson O'Neil caught her, steadying her on her feet. "Easy does it, little girl." Still holding onto her, Jackson nodded up to Caleb. The old guy just grinned then snapped the reins.

"Thank you, Jackson," Miranda said in a snippy tone. "I'm quite able to walk on my own."

"Could've fooled me." Jackson stepped back, looking more closely at her. "And I reckon I was fooled to call you a little girl. Say, how did you grow up so fast?"

"For your information, I just turned seventeen." She held her head higher.

"What're you doing in town today?" he asked with arched brows.

"Doing a little shopping." She studied him closely now. Jackson O'Neil's family had been friends with hers for as long as she could remember. But Jackson usually ignored her. Not today. "What are you doing in town?" she asked in a crisp tone. "Shouldn't you be out at your family's silver mine—striking it rich?" She knew from town gossip that the O'Neil mine wasn't producing these days. A lot of the miners had left for richer fields.

"I'm making other plans," Jackson answered with a more serious tone.

She peered curiously at him. Jackson was about five years older than her and, although she'd often admired him from a distance, she'd never managed to garner anything besides big-brotherly teasing from him. "What kind of plans?" She rearranged her shopping basket over her arm, standing a bit taller.

"Well, Wyatt told me about the gold fields in Alaska." He spoke quietly, as if concerned someone was eavesdropping. "I'm thinking I might give them a try."

"Truly?" She blinked. "You'd go all the way up to Alaska?"

"Sure." He nodded. "Wyatt told me about his friend Jake Robinson. I guess he goes by AJ these days. That's for Archibald Jake.

Anyway, I plan to look old AJ up. Wyatt said the gold vein they discovered up there together has played out, but that AJ plans to look for another. Wyatt seems to think AJ needs an experienced and trustworthy partner."

"And that would be you?" she challenged.

"Well, I've been mining since I was knee-high to a grasshopper. I reckon I know a thing or two about it. And some people think I'm trustworthy." He frowned.

Miranda regretted her snippy words. After all, Jackson was being quite forthcoming with her. She smiled brightly. "Well, I agree with Wyatt. You are experienced and trustworthy. And I'm impressed, Jackson. You have to be pretty brave to want to go up there to the Alaskan wilderness. It sounds so far away and frightening."

"Sounds like an adventure to me." He adjusted the brim of his hat against the sun.

"I wish I was as brave as that—ready to take on an adventure."

"Aw, you're a girl—I mean you're a young lady. Why do you need to be adventuresome?"

"Some people think I do." She scowled.

"So, what are you doing in town today?" he asked quickly. "Seems you'd be helping with your sister's wedding preparations. My ma is busy as a bee today. She plans to bring a dozen apple pies to your place on Saturday."

Miranda explained about Caleb fetching Enoch. "And Delia asked me to pick up a few things." She nodded to the mercantile.

"So…you probably don't have time to get a cup of tea." His dark eyes looked hopeful.

Miranda lit up. "I can make time, Jackson. It'll only take me a few minutes to get what I need here. And Caleb won't be back for an hour."

"I need to go to the bank and post office. After that, I'll meet you at the Elk Horn Restaurant. I mean, if you want."

She happily agreed then hurried into the mercantile to gather the things on Delia's last-minute list. It didn't take long to fill her basket. She could hardly believe she was about to have tea with Jackson O'Neil at the Elk Horn Hotel. As she walked down the street, she held her head high, imagining she was an independent grownup lady, not just a seventeen-year-old girl about to be shipped off to some dreadful college for egg-headed females.

Jackson politely stood as she joined him at the table, even pulling out her chair. He'd never treated her like this before. Was it because she was wearing one of Delia's altered dresses, with her hair pinned up beneath a pretty hat? Whatever the reason, she was happy to be here. And Jackson looked handsome in his dark vest and coat.

"I went ahead and ordered your tea," he said. "Since your time is limited."

"Thank you." She removed her gloves, smiling happily. "I'm so glad I ran into you."

"Yeah. You really did run into me." He chuckled.

"Now, tell me more about your Alaska plans." She knew that most men enjoyed talking about themselves. Feeling grown up and sophisticated, she carefully poured their tea.

"Well, I want to head up north before summer ends. But I promised my parents I wouldn't leave before Delia and Wyatt's wedding. Everyone's looking forward to that. I just came to town to tie up a few loose ends today. I hope to head out in about a week."

"I may be leaving next week too," she said quietly.

"Leaving?" He frowned. "Where to?"

She explained about the university in Philadelphia. "It's a women's college. And my father wanted me to go…and now Delia is bound and determined to send me."

"You don't sound too enthused."

She sighed deeply. "I don't see any reason for it." She peered closely at him, curious to gauge his take on the subject. "Most men don't think women should be overly educated."

He chuckled. "Well, that's probably because we don't want our women to be smarter than us. But truth be told, my mom's smarter than my dad about some things. She keeps all the books for the mine and does a pretty good job of it too."

"Did she go to college?"

"Well, she got her teacher's certificate. In fact, she was the schoolmarm when I was a kid."

"Oh, yes, the school at the mine. I never got to go there because my father died and we moved into town. But I do remember seeing the older children going there. I had hoped to go there too."

"So, if you went to that university back East…well, how long would you be gone?" Jackson asked.

"Delia spent two whole years there." Miranda frowned.

"Might be interesting to see Philadelphia," Jackson said. "A lot of our country's history is back East. I wouldn't mind seeing it for myself."

She blinked. "So you think I should go?"

He shrugged. "My opinion's not worth much."

"But I'm curious, Jackson. What *is* your opinion?"

"Well, it seems your dad thought it was important. And Mr. Williams was one of the smartest men I ever knew. I always had the utmost respect for him. He was always reading books and studying up on agricultural things. And the way he built up that ranch was really something." He refilled his teacup. "Then there's your sister, Miss Delia—she's an intelligent, respectable woman. My ma says she's just the person to run the Double W. Might be that schooling had something to do with that."

"I suppose that's true." Miranda grimaced. "Trouble is that I'm not as smart as Delia." She knew that was an understatement.

"Well, your sister's older. She's had more schooling so, of course, she'd be smarter. But I always thought you were pretty smart, Miranda. Or maybe you just had a smart mouth." He grinned.

"Thanks a lot."

Now his smile faded. "But, excuse me for saying so, but you

weren't too smart when you carried a torch for that Marcus Stanley. Now there was a real scoundrel."

"Worse than a scoundrel! He was a horrid beast. I can't bear to hear his name." She felt her cheeks flush to be reminded. "Trust me, that's something I will regret for the rest of my life."

"Well, like my ma says, live and learn."

"I guess so." She no longer felt very grown up...instead she felt like a very silly girl. Would she ever be able to live down her relationship with the horrible man she'd welcomed into their home and lives? Maybe going back East wasn't such a bad idea after all.

"Sorry, Miranda, I reckon I should've held my tongue about that." He refilled her cooling teacup. "But back to our traveling plans. It's interesting that I'll be heading to Alaska around the same time you'll be heading for Philadelphia. Both bound for adventures."

"In opposite directions." She sighed.

"Yes, but it's similar in a way. I think it's interesting."

"I guess so." She wondered how many miles there were between Alaska and Philadelphia.

"I hear a fellow can get lonely up north. Especially in winter. Might be nice to get letters."

"Letters?" She brightened.

He nodded. "Are you a good letter writer?"

"I haven't had much practice, but I'd be happy to try."

He smiled. "You want to try with me?"

She felt a warm happy rush. "Yes, I'd like that."

Jackson pulled out his pocket watch. "I don't want to rush you, Miranda, but you said you're supposed to meet Caleb and it looks like your hour's spent."

"Oh, yes. I nearly forgot." She reached for her gloves. "Thank you for tea."

"Thanks for joining me." He politely stood, shyly smiling. "I s'pect there'll be dancing at the wedding festivities on Saturday."

"Yes. Of course. We have musicians all lined up."

"Can I ask you to save a dance for me?"

"I'd love to." Her cheeks grew warm again, but this time it wasn't from humiliation. It was for another reason. "See you on Saturday." She picked up her basket and, once again, holding her head high, exited the restaurant, once again feeling more like a grownup.

She spotted the carriage parked in front of the mercantile and, waving to Caleb who was looking up and down the boardwalk, she hurried over. "Sorry to be late," she called. Then, eager to greet Uncle Enoch, she hopped in. After exchanging a welcoming hug, she quickly explained to the two old men about having tea with Jackson.

"We lost track of time," she said as Caleb drove the carriage through town.

"Jackson O'Neil?" Uncle Enoch sounded impressed. "Now there's a good boy for you. Comes from a good family too."

"Well worth being late for," Caleb agreed.

Miranda told them about Jackson's plans to go to Alaskan gold fields as soon as next week, which of course led to the two old men exchanging their own mining stories from days gone by. As the two chattered happily, Miranda leaned back into the seat, daydreaming about Saturday's wedding festivities and the prospects of wearing the peach colored satin gown and dancing with Jackson. It all sounded perfectly lovely.

But like the gray clouds creeping over the mountains, Miranda suddenly felt dark and gloomy. It figured—a truly nice young man finally gave her a second look, and he was getting ready to venture off into the Alaskan wilds. Just her luck! She felt foolish to remember how smitten she'd been over Marcus—the monster. So much so that she'd paid no heed to Jackson O'Neil this past year. But compared to Marcus, Jackson was a knight in shining armor. And he'd been enjoyable company this afternoon. But by next week this time, he'd probably be long gone. And in all likelihood, she would be too.

But was there another way? What if she could *really* turn Jackson's head? What if she could convince him to stick around…in order to pursue a romance with her? And if Jackson changed his plans, perhaps Delia would allow Miranda to change her plans. After all, Delia liked Jackson and his family. If this could only work out right, they might all be planning for another big wedding. Perhaps in the fall!

4

Delia hurried out to greet Uncle Enoch, happily embracing him. "I'm so glad you could make it back." She walked him up to the house, with Miranda and Caleb trailing them.

"Nobody's gladder than me to be back at the Double W." He paused to gaze around. "It's a sight for sore eyes." As they stopped in front of the porch, his expression grew grim. "But I'm so sorry that Winston is no longer with us. I can hardly believe he's departed the land of the living." He looked at Caleb. "I'm still chewing on what you told me about Winston's foreman. I can't believe the way he made us believe the Leaning R Ranch was the troublemakers behind everything. I never much liked Marcus, but I never dreamed he was that diabolical." He sent an uneasy glance Miranda's direction.

"Unfortunately, it's all true," Miranda admitted in a flat tone. "Marcus Stanley was a no-good, low-account snake in the grass. I wish we'd never met him."

"So Jerome Roswell had nothing to do with it."

"As it turns out, Jerome's ranch has water now," Delia explained to Enoch. "He put in a deep well last month. We're all on good terms with him these days. He's even coming to the wedding."

"And the whole squabble over water rights is over and done with." Caleb frowned. "Just wish he'd put that well in sooner."

"Might've saved Winston's life." Enoch sadly shook his head. "If I'd a known something like that was going to happen, I never would've left."

"If you'd never left, we wouldn't have gotten Delia here," Caleb pointed out.

"That's true enough." Enoch reached for her hand, warmly grasping it. "A lot's riding on you now, little lady. I hope you're up for it."

"She sure 'nough is," Caleb assured him. "You should see Delia on a horse. Can't remember if I told you she helped round up the cattle to the highlands?"

"I'm not surprised." Enoch grinned at Delia. "You remind me a lot of my sister Adelaide. Your grandmother was a strong, independent woman too."

"That's kind of you to say." Delia glanced at Miranda, worried that she was feeling left out right now. "You two get better get washed up," Delia told the men. "Ginger figured you'd be so worn out that she and Daisy got an early supper all ready for you. Smelled good too."

Enoch smacked his lips. "Good ol' ranch cookin'—been dreaming about it all the way out here on the train."

As soon as the old men headed for the bunkhouse, Miranda tugged Delia onto the porch. "I *have* to talk to you," she said in a hushed but urgent tone.

"Is something wrong?" Delia felt a wave of concern.

"No." Miranda smiled brightly as she set her shopping basket aside and sat in a rocker. "Something is very right."

"Oh, good. Tell me all about it." Delia sat next to her.

"I had tea at the Elk Horn Hotel. With Jackson O'Neil!"

"How interesting." Delia studied Miranda's expression. She'd never seen this girl so happy. "Do you know how pretty you look with those roses in your cheeks and such a bright smile?"

Miranda giggled. "It's because I'm happy."

"Tell me everything!"

Delia listened as Miranda relayed her impromptu tea party. Clearly the girl was smitten by young Jackson. And why not? He was a good young man. Kind and generous and thoughtful. Everything Marcus had never been.

"And the best part is that Jackson seems as interested in me as I am in him. Isn't it wonderful?"

"Yes." Delia eagerly nodded. "I don't know a nicer young man."

Now Miranda's smile faded. "There's only one fly in the ointment."

"What's that?"

Miranda told her about Jackson's plan to go to Alaska. "And it's Wyatt's fault too." Her lower lip jutted out. "If he hadn't gone up there and found all that gold, Jackson wouldn't be so determined to do the same."

"I did hear Wyatt and Jackson talking about Alaska after church about a month ago. Mostly they were talking about the adventure of that wild country. I didn't realize Jackson was seriously interested in going up there to search for gold."

"Well, he is. The O'Neil silver mine's slowed down, and Jackson is certain the Alaska gold fields are going to line his pockets."

"It might be a long shot…or he could be right." Delia remembered her doubts about Wyatt finding gold. And yet, he'd struck it rich.

"But I don't want him to go. And Jackson said that he's going to join Wyatt's minding buddy. That Wyatt is helping set it up." Miranda leaned forward. "Maybe you could talk to Wyatt. Get him to discourage Jackson about the whole thing. After all, fall is coming. Jackson shouldn't want to be up there in the winter. I've heard it's horribly cold and the sun never shines."

Delia nodded. "Yes, I've read that too."

"It's not that I'd want Wyatt to be dishonest." Miranda's blue eyes grew wide. "But if Wyatt could just warn him, make Jackson understand that it's dangerous and all that. Encourage him to, at least, wait. After all, Wyatt went up there in summertime. Wouldn't it be wiser for Jackson to do the same?"

"It does make sense. But if Jackson is really set on going...well, it might be hard to dissuade him. Especially if his family's mine has quit producing."

"But mining is like that. It comes and goes. One week, they say it's all dried up and the next week, they're striking the mother lode."

"Perhaps Jackson simply wants the adventure. I saw his eyes light up when Wyatt told him about the country up there. About bears and moose and salmon fishing."

"We have those things here," Miranda argued. "And even if his family's mine dried up, Jackson could come work for us. You were just saying we could use some dependable hands."

"I would welcome Jackson on the ranch, Miranda. And he knows that. But it's his decision."

"Yes, but if Wyatt could just discourage him." She held her thumb and forefinger apart. "Just a teeny tiny bit."

Delia laughed. "Well, I will ask Wyatt to be perfectly honest to Jackson. To paint a realistic picture of what Jackson will find in winter. And also about the realistic chances of actually finding gold. From what I heard in AJ's last letter, his gold vein gave out last month. Sure, he thinks he'll hit another, but who knows?"

"Exactly." Miranda nodded. "And Jackson needs to hear that." She sighed. "Just not from me."

"You seem very intent on keeping him here." Delia studied her closely. "Do you think you're in love, Miranda?" She wanted to add "after one little tea party," but stopped herself.

"I think I might be in love." Miranda's smile looked dreamy.

"And what about college?"

Miranda's smile vanished. "I don't want to go. I told you that already."

"And you think marriage is the way to avoid it?"

"That's not the reason I'd want get married, Delia. I swear to you. I would only want to get married because I was truly in love…and because he was in love with me. Honestly."

For some reason Delia believed her. She reached over to grasp Miranda's hand. "Well, then I'm going to pray for you and Jackson. I'm going to pray that God will direct your paths. And if it's meant to be, it will be."

Miranda hugged her. "Thank you, Delia!"

Delia reached for the shopping basket. "And did you get everything on my list?"

"I think so." She stood and smiled. "Did I tell you that Jackson asked me to save dances for him at your wedding?"

Delia laughed. "I am not surprised."

"Wait until he sees me in that peach silk gown." She sighed happily. "If that doesn't snag him, nothing will!"

Delia laughed even harder as they went inside. Part of her wanted to chide her little sister for wanting to "snag" anyone. But another part of her was glad to see Miranda happy again. Hopefully, it wouldn't be short-lived.

It wasn't until their after-dinner stroll that Delia broached the topic of Jackson going to Alaska with Wyatt. Her intent wasn't to intrude, but simply to enlighten. She started by describing Miranda's encounter with the young man earlier today. "But she is disheartened that he won't be around for long."

"So Jackson really wants to go up there?" Wyatt sounded pleased.

"So it seems." They paused at their favorite bench overlooking the meadow.

"Good for him. An adventure like that is the making of a man."

"Is that how your adventures were?"

"Yes. Each one was different, and each time I learned something new."

"I remember when you tried to convince me you were a drifter," she said with amusement. "On the train out West."

He chuckled. "I think I might've been trying to convince myself."

"What do you mean? You'd already done a lot of traveling. You seemed like a drifter to me. Especially when you switched from your city clothes to your cowboy attire. You looked like an entirely different person."

He laughed loudly now. "I remember feeling embarrassed when I had to escort you around the Chicago station. You looked like a princess, and I looked like a wrangler."

"I thought you looked rather handsome."

He leaned over to kiss her. "And that, my dear, is why I know we were made for each other."

After a moment, she pointed out that Miranda might be feeling that way about Jackson. "It could be just a passing fancy…or something more. Anyway, I told her I'd mention her concerns for Jackson's safety during an Alaskan winter."

"Valid concerns. But AJ has been there long enough to know the ropes. He can help guide Jackson. And Jackson's an experienced miner. I wouldn't be overly worried."

"Even so, perhaps you could warn Jackson about the difficulties he will encounter. Give him a realistic picture of what he'd be getting into."

"You want me to discourage him?" Wyatt frowned.

"No, dear, just enlighten him. He will obviously make up his own mind about it." She chuckled. "Well, unless Miranda has her way. She hopes to enchant him at our wedding. I'm sure she believes that if she can get him to stay here, he will want to marry her, and she will have the perfect excuse not to go back East for her education."

"What would your father think of that?"

"Well, I know my father liked the O'Neil's. I suspect he'd agree that Jackson is a good match for Miranda." Still, she wasn't absolutely sure about this. Miranda still had a childish side to her. She could be willful and stubborn and selfish at times. And she could be a handful for a kindhearted fellow like Jackson. Education could give her time to mature...season her a bit. Perhaps Delia's father knew that. Whatever the case, Delia was determined to keep her word with Miranda. She would pray for God to direct her and Jackson's paths. What would be would be.

5

Miranda was in good spirits the next day. And not only because of Jackson, although he was the top of her happy list. But it was also exciting to be preparing for the wedding. And anticipating a houseful of guests. Visitors from the East would surely perk up the place. She was most curious about Delia's mother. From what Delia had told her, she was a very stylish and citified woman. It sounded as if she was rather outspoken and opinionated, which could prove interesting. They were scheduled to arrive on the afternoon train today. As well as Wyatt's aunt and uncle from Philadelphia. Their quiet, out-of-the-way ranch was about to liven up.

"I'm dying of curiosity," Delia said as she and Miranda arranged flowers from the garden. "Wondering if my family will have made the acquaintance of Wyatt's family on the train."

"Do you think they'll like each other?"

"I can't even guess since I've never met Wyatt's aunt and uncle. Although his Aunt Lilly sounds like a darling. But my family can be, well...I've told you already. Somewhat off-putting."

"Meaning they are snobs?"

"I hate to admit it, but yes. My stepfather's family came from money. Not that he earned any himself. And as far as I know, he has little to show from it. But he still acts superior. And I'm sure he will not approve of what my mother has already called 'the wild west' or rough old ranch hands like Caleb or Uncle Enoch."

Miranda laughed. "Well, they're in for some surprises then." She nodded to where Hank was sleeping peacefully under the dining table. "And animals in the house too? Will they approve of that?"

Delia shrugged. "Hank's a member of the family."

"Father never kept him in the house." Miranda snipped a rose stem.

"Well, he's not *always* in the house," Delia defended the snoozing dog. "And I'll make sure he stays outside when our guests are here. But I plan to have him inside when winter comes. I happen to enjoy his company. And Caleb said he's more than ten years old. Maybe he's earned his right to sleep under the table."

Miranda shrugged. "Is your step-father going to walk you down the aisle?"

"What?" Delia's blue eyes flashed.

"You know, will he be the one to give you away at the wedding?"

"I already asked Uncle Enoch to escort me down the aisle."

"What will your step-father think?"

"I don't know, and I'm not concerned. Enoch is my father's uncle, my blood relation, and a dear old man."

Miranda held up a cheerful arrangement of bright pink roses, white chrysanthemums, and blue cornflowers. "How's this?"

"Perfect. Place that one in Julianne and Julius's room. Not that Julius will care. But Julianne appreciates pretty things."

"I'm excited to meet her. She sounds interesting."

Delia smiled. "She reminds me a bit of you. Younger, of course. Although for a twelve-year-old, she is rather old for her age. At times anyway."

Miranda felt a trace of sadness. "And she's your real sister. Well, half-sister anyway. A real relative."

Delia put a hand on Miranda's shoulder. "You're my sister too."

Miranda smiled. "Thanks."

"Why don't you take your arrangement up to the nursery—I mean, the other spare room?"

"It's all right." Miranda stood. "I don't think of it like that. Not as a nursery anymore."

"Good. And will you make sure it's all ready for the twins? I know Ginger turned it out, but I haven't seen it this week. And I still want to go cut flowers for the dinner table."

"Dinner will be festive tonight." Miranda picked up the ceramic vase. "I can't remember the last time we had eleven people in the dining room."

"Yes, Daisy was just complaining about that. Although Ginger's been helping her. And Rosie will be here by Friday to help in the kitchen."

"And I've been trying to help Ginger with housekeeping," Miranda reminded her. Sure, her motivation for being so helpful might have more to do with Jackson than anything else. But she wanted to prove to everyone that she was not a child…and that she was ready to become a wife.

"You've been especially helpful," Delia assured her. "I appreciate it more than you can possibly know."

"After I check on the twins' room, I can check on the other guest rooms too. Make sure they've been properly dusted and that the windows get closed before it gets too warm out."

"Perfect." Delia handed her the crystal vase with pale pink roses, blue lobelia, lavender, and ferns. "Please, put this in the room for Wyatt's family while I'll finish this last arrangement for my parents."

As Miranda carried the vases upstairs, she imagined herself as lady of the house. Oh, she knew that she would never be lady of this house, not like she'd once dreamed. But perhaps she could be lady of the house with Jackson someday. It would be fun to arrange flowers and make things pretty for him. And if all went well on Saturday, she might even get the chance.

She took the first vase to the guest room that was all set for Wyatt's family. Ginger had already dusted in here, and it seemed everything was in its place. Even the window was closed. This was the room that had been so carefully prepared for Delia's arrival and, compared to the other rooms, it was really the nicest.

Now she carried the smaller vase down the hallway toward what had once been planned for the nursery…the room where her mother had died giving birth to a tiny baby brother who had also died. Even though it happened many years ago, Miranda had always avoided the dreadful room. It wasn't that she believed in ghosts exactly, but there had always been a bad feeling in there. A coldness that was hard to shrug off.

Even when she'd seen Delia painting the faded blue walls a fresh shade of shell pink, Miranda had kept a distance and not offered any help. With a slight feeling of trepidation, she pushed the door open now. Just standing in the doorway, staring into the space, the room was unrecognizable to what she recalled from childhood. And to her relief, she no longer felt that hauntingly cold chill. Perhaps it was the new paint color or the warmth of the afternoon…or perhaps the room was truly changed.

Most of the previous furnishings had been removed and replaced with pieces Delia had gathered from here and there in the house. A pair of beds borrowed from the bunkhouse, covered in cheerful crazy quilts, with a small oak table set between them. Miranda placed the bright bouquet on the table, centered between a pair of blue glass kerosene lamps. A small dresser, equipped with a white pitcher of water and generous washbowl as well as soaps and linens, sat beneath the window, which was now curtained with white linen trimmed with a border of crocheted lace that fluttered in the warm summer breeze. Upon closer inspection, Miranda realized it was actually a pair of pillowcases that had been turned into curtains. Clever.

Three new pictures hung on the walls. One of a peaceful sheep pasture, one of a pair of horses galloping across a field, and another of a barefoot shepherdess beneath a green tree. On the recently scrubbed wood floor was a fresh pink and yellow braided rug. The only piece of furniture that hadn't been changed was the big oak wardrobe, which Miranda knew concealed the wall safe put there by her stepfather, the spot where he'd hidden his will. Not for the first time, Miranda wondered...had he known his days were numbered then? That his life was endangered? All because of her? And her foolish attachment to the monster, Marcus? Would she ever escape the guilt from that?

"Don't think about that now," she quietly chided herself as she firmly closed the window. She needed to remember the advice Delia regularly doled out. *The past is past...learn from your mistakes...*but when Miranda reached the *forgive and forget* advice, well, that was not so simple! She would never forgive Marcus. And likewise she would never forgive herself.

Delia was grateful for all that needed to be done today. Perhaps she'd even added more tasks than necessary. At least that's what Wyatt had said this morning when she'd run her chores list past him. But anything to distract her from fretting over the arrival of her family was welcome relief. As she took the bouquet up to the master bedroom, which had previously been hers, but would now be occupied by her mother and stepfather, she felt an unexpected surge of anger. Why was she going to so much trouble for the people who had planned to ruin her life and then essentially threw her out when she refused to cooperate with their selfish schemes?

Why had she uprooted herself, as well as all her clothes, personal belongings and wedding gown, from this comfortable, spacious room? Why was she now relocated to the least of the guestrooms—the only room that hadn't been cleaned and prettified and adorned with fresh flowers—in order to make her so-called parents comfortable?

She set the elegant crystal vase of red, pink, and white roses on the table by the window and let out a long, frustrated sigh. Wasn't she over this by now? Was she really this angry? And if so, was she even capable of going through the exercise of forgiving them—*again?* A part of her—and not a godly part—declared they did not deserve her forgiveness. And they certainly did not deserve this lovely room and all the attention she was giving it. She should be putting her mother and stepfather in the bunkhouse with the hired hands. Or better yet, the aromatic loft above the chicken coop! That's what they really deserved.

She went over to the big bed and, smoothing out the robin's egg blue and white coverlet and plumping the white lace-trimmed pillows—all recently laundered and smelling of sweet sunshine—she reminded herself that the same way her heavenly father forgave her, that was how she needed to forgive her parents. And like Reverend Johnson's last sermon said, she should be willing to do it seventy times seven. Well, with God's help—which she desperately needed just now—she resolved to do this.

To be honest, this exercise in forgiveness wasn't only for her family's sake, although that was part of it. But it was also to free herself from all the ill feelings and bad memories that would plague her otherwise. She was determined to keep her negative family memories from spoiling her and Wyatt's wedding day. Selfish perhaps, but true nonetheless.

Knowing this would take more than just a casual passing prayer, Delia actually knelt down next to the bed and, bowing her head, earnestly asked for God's divine help. Asking him to assist her in forgiving her mother and stepfather, she handed the frustrating parental pair over to God. She would not carry this burden with her. With God's help she would welcome them into her home with grace and dignity. And she would leave the rest to her Heavenly Father. She sealed this prayer with an enthused "Amen."

"Excuse me?"

Still on her knees, Delia turned to see Miranda peering into the room with a puzzled expression. "Oh…Miranda." Delia got to her feet.

"I didn't mean to—uh—to interrupt." Miranda's brow furrowed with confusion. "Were you just praying?"

Delia nodded, smoothing the front of her skirt.

"On your knees?"

Delia's smile felt sheepish. "I guess I needed some extra help with forgiveness."

"Forgiveness?" Miranda blinked. "For what? Did *you* do something bad?"

Delia considered this. "Well, I was having ill feelings toward my stepfather and Mother. That was wrong."

"You're not serious. You asked God to forgive you for *that?*" Miranda scowled. "Seems to me you have every right to be angry at them. You told me how they wanted you to marry that old man for his money. And then they disowned you because you refused? That would make me furious."

Delia wondered how to explain this…or if Miranda could even understand.

Miranda came into the room, surveying it with an approving expression. "Besides, I thought you were beyond all that. You seemed perfectly fine about them coming. You even gave up your room for them. I never would've done that."

"Well, it seemed right to do." Delia gave the room a last glance, reassured all was in perfect place. "But underneath it all, I just discovered I was still sort of irked at them. So I was asked God to help me forgive them."

"I would never forgive them if I were you. They don't deserve it." She pointed to the room. "And they don't deserve the best room in the house either."

"Maybe not. Do you recall last Sunday's sermon? Reverend

Johnson preached about forgiving others *seventy times seven times?* And how that actually represents an infinite number. Remember?"

Miranda shrugged. "I guess so. Not that I really understood all that."

"Well, that's probably how many times I'll have to forgive my parents. Over and over. But it's not always easy. Still, by the grace of God, I think I can." She checked her pocket watch. "They should be getting off the train about now, which means they'll be here in about an hour. And there's still lots to get done."

"I heard Wyatt telling Caleb he planned to take his aunt and uncle around Colorado City to see all the sights. So they won't be here that soon."

"That's right. They can only stay a few days and Wyatt wants to be sure they get a good look around. But Caleb's collecting my family in the large carriage, and as far as I know he planned to bring them directly home." She smiled at Miranda. "So, my dear, will you take charge of setting the dining room table? I told Ginger we'd handle that. But I still need to do some tending to the vegetable garden and get changed before our guests arrive." She looked down at her dusty and worn work dress. A part of her was tempted to just leave it on. She could imagine her mother's shocked expression.

"Do I get to use the good china and crystal and silver and everything?"

"Why not?" Delia closed the master bedroom door.

"Good! Because we want impress them." Miranda winked mischievously. "Especially your high and mighty parents. We'll show them that folks in the West can be civilized too. I'll even get out the big silver candelabras."

"Sounds lovely. But most of all, I want everyone to enjoy their visit to the Double W," Delia declared as they went downstairs. "I simply want them to feel at home here."

"Just as long as they don't try to make it *their* home."

Delia laughed. "No worries there. Wyatt's uncle has his boot factory to get back to. They're only here until Monday. And my family is very citified. I'm sure they'll be eager to escape the 'Wild West,' as my mother calls it, as quickly as possible."

"I don't know. What you said about your stepfather, Delia…well, what if he's as greedy as he sounds? Maybe you should be on guard against him. He reminds me of Marcus. You never know, he might want to take over the Double W too."

Delia balked at Miranda's insinuation. "Oh, I don't think so, Miranda. My stepfather likes his city comforts—the telephone and electricity, the newspaper on the step, men's club down the street, his horse races. He wouldn't want to give that up." Still, she wondered… why had he so easily agreed to come here? Certainly not to celebrate her wedding, especially after he'd disowned her. He was too proud for that. What if his motivation truly was greed? Perhaps Miranda had it right, maybe Delia should be on her guard.

6

MIRANDA WAS JUST PUTTING THE FINISHING TOUCHES ON THE DINing table when Delia came rushing through. "You look like a farmhand," Miranda pointed to the mantle clock. "And your family is probably almost here by now."

"The berries were coming on strong. Needed picking." Delia paused to look at the table. "Oh my, this looks beautiful, Miranda." She patted her back. "Nicely done."

"Thank you." Miranda gave her a nudge. "But you need to bathe and dress."

"Can you please meet and greet my family for me?"

Miranda nodded eagerly. "I'll play lady of the house until you come down."

"Good girl. Thanks." Delia hurried toward the stairs.

As Miranda gave the big dining table one last look, she remembered when she'd dreamed of being the true lady of the house—and the underhanded ways she attempted to achieve it. Fortunately, Delia didn't hold that against her. She wandered into the living room to look around. Her stepfather had loved this space, with its massive stone fireplace and masculine leather and wood furnishings, but it had never been her favorite room. Still, she gave had to give Delia credit. She'd softened it by removing some bulky pieces and rearranging others and generally freshening it up. Plus the pretty flower arrangements here and there added a needed feminine touch.

She continued on to the parlor, which was her favorite room. Her mother had been in complete control of this pretty space. From the rose-colored drapes with silk tassels and fringe-trimmed damask tablecloths to the ornately carved chairs and tapestry upholstery. Perhaps it was a bit crowded, but whenever Miranda came in here, she felt at home. It reminded her of Mother. And after Mother died, Miranda had made this space her own.

She adjusted the pink blooms she'd arranged in her mother's favorite crystal rose bowl, centering it on the lacy doily her mother had crocheted. It had graced the round mahogany table for as long as Miranda could remember. And, to her, it all looked perfect. She hoped their female guests would appreciate it too. She had just settled into the settee by the window when she heard the jingle of harness and the sound of horses' hooves coming up the driveway. Discretely peeking out the window, she spied the large buggy pull up to the house. A well-dressed man sat in front by Caleb with a woman and two children in back. Delia's family was here!

Smoothing her gown, a pale blue one that Delia had given her to take back East, Miranda poised herself as she went to open the front door, preparing to welcome the Blackstones. She watched as the gentleman helped his wife from the carriage. She was shorter and stouter than Delia, but dressed in a handsome burgundy velvet traveling outfit, she looked dignified. And, for her age, attractive. Next came the children. Both were towheads and, although they looked alike, the girl was taller. Also dressed in attractive traveling clothes, but not as dignified as their parents, they looked around the farm with wide-eyed wonder.

"Welcome!" Miranda called as she stepped out onto the porch.

"What?" the woman looked surprised. "I thought you were my daughter, but it seems you are someone else."

"I'm Miranda Williams." She held out her hand. "Delia's stepsister. Your daughter will be down shortly. She asked me to welcome you. You must be Delia's mother."

"Yes." She nodded, but her eyes darted around as if trying to take it all in.

"Pleased to meet you, Mrs. Blackstone." Miranda smiled. "Welcome to the Double W."

Mr. Blackstone politely dipped his head as he took Miranda's hand. "Pleased to meet you, Miss Williams. And these are my children, Julianne and Julius."

Miranda greeted the kids. "I hope you'll enjoy your time here at our ranch. We have fun places to explore. And we have horses if either of you enjoy riding."

"I want to ride a horse," Julius declared.

"Neither of you know how to ride," Mrs. Blackstone pointed out.

"Julius thinks he's going to be a cowboy here," Julianne teased.

"Well, he's in the right place." Caleb unloaded a suitcase then let out a whistle toward the corral, waving over to Cash for help.

"Come into the house," Miranda urged them. "I'm sure you're worn out from your long trip."

"Oh, yes." Mrs. Blackstone sighed. "It was exhausting."

They were just entering the house when Miranda spied Delia hurrying down the stairs. Until she saw them in the foyer. And then, almost like royalty, she held her head high and took her time to gracefully descend. She had on the green gown that made her eyes look even greener. And holding out her arms and smiling, she graciously greeted her family. She embraced the twins with enthusiasm, her mother with a bit of stiffness and then, standing straight and tall, she simply extended a hand to her stepfather. "I hope you will all feel welcome in my home."

"Thank you for inviting us here. From what I've seen, this is a handsome farm." Mr. Blackstone removed his black derby as they entered the living room, pausing to gaze up at the high ceiling. "I hadn't imagined anything quite this grand out here in the west."

"Yes, as Miranda likes to say, we're *very civilized* here," Delia teased.

Miranda giggled. "Well, we don't have electricity or a telephone... not yet anyway."

"And probably not for some time either."

"But we do have indoor plumbing, Mrs. Blackstone," Miranda said proudly.

"Since you're Delia's stepsister, why don't you call me Jane?" Delia's mother smiled at her. "I'll admit I was surprised to discover you have a stepsister," Jane said to Delia.

"Miranda is more like a real sister." Delia directed this to Julianne and Julius. "And she'll be like a big sister to you two."

"I always wanted a big family," Miranda told them.

"Would you like us to show you to your rooms so that you can relax and wash up a bit?" Delia offered.

"Yes, please," Jane murmured. And unless Miranda was mistaken, her eyes glistened a bit. Tears of gladness at seeing her daughter?

Delia turned to Miranda. "Could you get Julianne and Julius settled in their room? Do you mind?"

"Not at all. Right this way." Miranda led the twins upstairs, but Delia and her parents remained below. She could hear them speaking quietly but couldn't make out the conversation.

"This is a nice house," Julianne said politely. "Father thought we'd be staying in a log cabin."

"Mother told us not to expect much," Julius added. "She said we might even be sleeping on the floor."

Miranda laughed. "Oh, I think we can do better than that." She paused by the bathroom door. "This is the bathroom. There's another smaller one downstairs, and we also have outdoor facilities—in case this one's occupied."

"I need to use it *now,"* Julius said urgently.

"It's all yours." Miranda continued to lead Julianne down the hall. "Did you have a good train trip?"

"It was fun to see all the places along the way, but it did take a long time."

"You and your brother will share this room," Miranda opened the door.

"In the same room as Julius?" Julianne wrinkled her nose. "He's such a pest."

"Delia got the room ready for you herself. She even painted the walls."

"It is a nice color." Julianne set her little velvet bag on the bed nearest the window. "I'll claim this one before Julius gets here."

"Did you miss your sister?"

Julianne's brow creased. "I didn't really think I would. You know, because she'd been away at school for two whole years. But knowing she was so far away out here, that I might never see her again... Well, yes, I did miss her. I missed her more than I care to say." She peered curiously at Miranda. "Do you like having Delia for a sister?"

"Very much so." Miranda nodded. "I never had a sister before."

Julianne frowned.

"But she is still your sister, Julianne. And she has spoken quite fondly of you."

"Really? That's nice." Julianne brightened. "How old are you?"

"I just turned seventeen."

"You're almost a grownup."

"And you're eleven?"

"Twelve now." Julianne stood up straighter. "We just had a birthday."

Miranda turned to the sound of Julius tramping down the hallway toward them. "This is your room," she told him.

He scowled. "You mean I have to share it with my sister?"

"Sorry, it's the best we could do. We have other guests too."

"Hey, you wanted to be a cowboy, didn't you?" Julianne poked her brother in the chest. "Why don't you go sleep under the stars?"

"Can I?" His pale brows arched.

"Why not? You'd be comfortable out there with bears and rattlesnakes and crawly things," Julianne teased. "You wouldn't be scared."

"And don't forget about the cougars and coyotes." Miranda winked at Julianne than turned to Julius. "But if you really want to be a cowboy, maybe you'd rather sleep in the bunkhouse. With the other ranch hands."

"Can I?" His eyes lit up.

"We're actually a bit short of hands right now. So I'm sure there's a spare bunk. And I doubt the fellas would mind. They might even put you to work roping calves. It's almost branding time."

"Yes! I want to do that!"

"You better check with your parents first."

"I will!" He jumped up and down with excitement. "If I rope cows and sleep in a real bunkhouse, I can tell my friend George that I was a real cowboy when I get home."

"Go ask Mother and Father," Julianne urged him.

As Julius took off with a loud whoop, Julianne crossed her fingers and grinned at Miranda. "I hope they let him so I can have this room to myself. Julius's feet smell like stinky cheese."

Miranda laughed. "Well, I think you're lucky to have a brother. I always wished for one." She suddenly remembered the infant that would've been her baby brother…and that this was meant to be his room…and that he would be about five by now. She glanced around the room with growing uneasiness. "If you'll excuse me, I'll let you get settled in."

As she hurried to her room, quietly closing the door and taking in a deep breath, she reminded herself that the room was changed. It was nothing like before. And she no longer felt that old coldness there. And yet the sadness wasn't completely gone. Hopefully Julianne wouldn't be bothered by it.

Delia knew this might be the most opportune moment to clear the air with her mother and stepfather—before the other guests arrived. So, as soon as Miranda ushered the twins upstairs, Delia spoke up. "I'm so glad you decided to come to my wedding." She tried to arrange her words, praying they would be both gracious and honest.

"It was so kind of you to invite us," Jane declared with what seemed genuine sincerity. "I must admit I was quite surprised at your generosity, Delia. Thank you!"

Delia slowly nodded. Did her mother assume the invitation and travel funds had come directly from her? "I must admit to equal surprise…that you would actually make the long journey to get here."

"Did you think I'd miss my own daughter's wedding?" Jane smiled.

Delia sighed. "The last time we spoke, it was…well, rather unpleasant. You both informed me I was no longer your daughter and that I was no longer welcome in your home and that—"

"Those words were exchanged in the heat of the moment," her stepfather interrupted. "You know how I spout off sometimes. Especially when I'm upset. And you had upset me greatly that day, Delia. As you knew, I'd worked hard to do everything possible to secure an advantageous marriage for you. Henry Horton is the wealthiest man in Pittsburgh. Your mother and I had strived to cultivate a beneficial relationship with Henry and his family. All for your sake. It's perfectly understandable that we were offended by your quick dismissal of the whole affair."

"I understand your disappointment, but did that give you the right to curse and call me foul names?" Her words were quiet and calm, but she locked eyes with him. "To disown me? To make me an outcast in my own home?"

He scowled but said nothing.

"We were wrong, Delia." Jane reached for Delia's hands. "I do hope you can forgive us. It was all so sad and unfortunate. Very regrettable."

Delia looked deeply into her mother's eyes. "I do forgive you. I simply wanted to clear the air. Especially before the others arrive… before the wedding. I needed to speak my piece."

"Good. I hope you feel better." Her stepfather patted her back in what felt like condescension. "I wouldn't want to see you chastising your parents in front of your other guests, Delia. That would be in very bad taste. It appears you have matured into a sensible young woman." He paused to gaze around the room, fixing his eyes on the painting above the fireplace. It was a massive depiction of cowboys driving cattle through a canyon, and probably valuable. "It also appears you've fallen into a fine-feathered nest, daughter. I assume Winston was generous with your inheritance."

"Oh, Delia, I nearly forgot. I was so sorry to hear about your father." Jane, still grasping Delia's hands, spoke quietly. "Wyatt's aunt explained it all to me on the train trip out here. Apparently Wyatt had written to her about it. I was so shocked to hear of it. And I'm truly sad you never got to meet Winston in person. Such bad timing."

"Yes, it was very sad." Delia bristled to remember how her mother had kept her father a secret. How she hadn't wanted her to come out here. "But being here, in my father's home, on his beautiful and beloved ranch…well, it's almost like knowing him. I can feel his presence everywhere." She sighed.

"I was quite surprised by this place, Delia. It's far more impressive than I expected. Your father must've done very well." Jane's eyes were sad and, unless Delia imagined it, she seemed softer somehow.

"Yes, he worked hard to make the Double W what it is today." Delia was well aware that her father had done far more with his life than her unmotivated stepfather. Was her mother making the same observation? Did she feel any regret for giving up on her first husband so easily? Perhaps Delia would never know the answer. Perhaps that would be for the best. "My father kept up on the latest agricultural news and incorporated many modern innovations here. I hope you'll both feel free to explore the ranch and see all he accomplished here."

"I think your father hopes to wash up and have a rest," Jane said.

Delia cringed at hearing her mother calling this man her father. "I'd like to clear something up," she directed this to her stepfather. "Now that I'm well aware of who my father is and is not, I would rather not call you Father. I'm sure you must understand."

He looked irritated. "What would you prefer to call me?" he asked stiffly.

"Perhaps Mr. Blackstone," she suggested.

"Oh, Delia, you don't need to be that formal with your fath—"

"That's right," he agreed. "You're an adult now. Why not just call me Jefferson?"

Delia wasn't sure she wanted to do that, but she simply nodded. "Fine."

"And I look forward to seeing more of the Double W," Jefferson declared. "But your mother is right. I'd like to wash up and get settled first."

"Let me show you to your room," Delia told them. "I'm sure you'll both want to rest up a bit after your long journey."

"It *was* a long journey." Still holding Delia's hand, Jane spoke quietly as they went up the stairs. "Some of the countryside was quite beautiful on the first day. But it gradually became so desolate and wild. I actually felt fearful at times. I worried that the train might be robbed. You read of that sometimes. Or that Indians might attack. I've heard that happens too. I quite honestly couldn't understand why you wanted to remain out here in the wilds."

Delia opened the door to the master bedroom. "Because I love it out here, Mother. To me, this is home."

"Oh, my. What a lovely room." Jane's eyes grew wide.

"Very nice." Jefferson went over to the window, looking out toward the barn, stables, and gardens. "A very nice piece of property indeed. So green, I assume there is plenty of water. And it's well maintained and fenced. And livestock too—horses, cattle, sheep… I'm sure it must all be quite valuable. Even if it is out here in the middle of nowhere."

"Colorado is growing quickly. Some don't think of this region as the middle of nowhere."

"I must say I was impressed at the size of Colorado City. I can only assume it's the result of successful mining ventures. Did I hear that was how your father made his money?"

"That's right. And then he invested almost every penny into this land. He was very well-read regarding agriculture. He turned what had once been barren land into a modern and productive farm and ranch. When you feel up to it, I'll ask Caleb or Wyatt to give you the full tour." She turned to her mother. "Did you meet Wyatt at the train station?"

"Yes. He introduced himself when he picked up his aunt and uncle. He's an attractive young man. Younger than I'd imagined."

"He seemed very well mannered," Jefferson added. "Although perhaps a bit opportunistic."

Delia felt her emotions flare. "Opportunistic?"

Jefferson smiled, but there was coldness behind it. "My apologies. I shouldn't have said that."

"What did you mean?" she demanded.

"Oh, it's nothing. Only that I find Wyatt's timing interesting. Stepping in to wed you shortly after your father passes…the young man obviously knows about your inheritance. How fortuitous for him to marry a wealthy heiress."

"I am *not* wealthy. Did you not hear me say that my father's money is all tied up in the land? I have no *real* money."

"Well, yes, but the ranch and the land and livestock, it must be valuable."

"That's true, but the ranch has barely begun to support itself." She held up her chin. Why was he so curious about these things? Was Miranda right about his motives?

"Oh?" Jefferson's pale brows arched with what seemed disbelief. "But you were so generous to send us the traveling money that I simply assumed—"

"That was Wyatt's doing. As it turns out, my fiancé is quite wealthy. Perhaps you had not heard, but he made his fortune in the Alaskan gold fields. That is how he could afford to send you train fare. I'm sorry if you assumed it came from me. So, as you can see, Wyatt is *not* opportunistic. But perhaps you will think that I am the opportunist." She shot a challenging glare his way. "That I might marry Wyatt for *his* money."

"Oh, Delia, your father didn't mean to sound like that," Jane said quickly. "He's just tired and—"

"I'm sorry, Mother, and I don't mean to be rude, but please respect what I've tried to make clear." She pointed to Jefferson. "I respect that he's your husband, and I am trying to forgive him for his poor treatment of me back in Pittsburgh, but he is not my father."

"Well!" Jefferson turned his back to them, acting as if he were staring out the window, although Delia felt certain he was blinded with fury at the moment. And she didn't really care.

"I really do hope you will all enjoy your visit here," she said in tone that was calmer than she felt. "Like I said, I am glad you could come, but I would like to put the past behind us." She reached for the door. "The bathroom is first door to the right. Dinner will be served at seven." Without another word, she made her exit, restraining herself from slamming the door like she wanted to do. She was seriously irked at the gall of that man! And now she would heed Miranda's advice—she would stay on her guard where Jefferson was concerned.

7

Delia noticed the buggy while gathering a few herbs and tomatoes in the garden. She'd gone there on the pretext of picking more produce, but in reality it was simply to cool off. After the unpleasant encounter with her stepfather, she'd needed some fresh air. But seeing that Wyatt and his relatives were arriving, she'd hurried around the house to greet them. With her loaded basket over one arm, she eagerly waved as Wyatt pulled up to the front porch.

"We're here!" he announced as he jumped to the ground. Then while helping a gray-haired man and woman down, he excitedly introduced Delia to Uncle George and Aunt Lilly.

"I'm so pleased to meet you," Lilly told her. "You're even prettier than I expected."

"This is quite a place you have here." George nodded approval.

"I'm so glad you could come for the wedding." Delia smiled happily. Already she liked them.

"Out in the garden?" Wyatt pointed to her basket.

"What lovely vegetables." Lilly squeezed plump red tomato. "But aren't you a bit overdressed for gardening?"

"This isn't my usual work garb." Delia laughed. "But it was such a lovely day, and the garden has been so productive lately…I couldn't help myself."

"Why don't you take the folks inside?" Wyatt gave Delia a smile. "I'll unload their baggage."

"Yes, I'm sure you're weary from your travels. And I suspect Wyatt gave you the grand tour of our fair city."

George nodded. "Colorado City is bigger than I expected."

"Wyatt is trying to talk George into relocating his boot factory here," Lilly said quietly to Delia as they went inside.

"Not much chance of that," George said.

"I imagine Colorado could use a good boot factory," Delia told him. "And there are plenty of cattle around for leather resources."

"Yes, Wyatt already pointed that out." George removed his hat. "But relocating a factory from Philadelphia out here would be no small doing."

"I must say the air out here is cleaner and fresher." Lilly glanced around the house. "What a beautiful home. Wyatt wrote to me about how your father built this place up from nothing." She reached for Delia's hand. "Oh, I'm so sorry for your loss, darling. Wyatt wrote about that in his letters."

Delia thanked her and, to avoid another sad conversation, gave the couple a quick tour of the house, pausing in the atrium, where the houseplants were now flourishing. Lilly looked all around with wide eyes. "Oh, my, what a lovely, lovely room," she exclaimed. "I think I would spend all my time in here if I lived in this house."

"I enjoy it too," Delia admitted. "I expect it will be a good place when winter weather arrives, almost like being outdoors."

"You've not been here during winter?" George asked.

She explained how she'd come in early June. "So much has happened in such a short time, it sometimes feels like much longer."

"I've read a bit about Colorado recently. When I learned that Wyatt was settling here. I hear that winters can be severe," Lilly said.

"Yes, I've heard that too. But I'm not worried. We'll be well prepared for winter." As she led them upstairs, she explained a bit about the farm and the modernizations her father had implemented. "I know your visit will be short, but I hope you'll have time for a little tour." She opened the door to their room, the one her father had so beautifully renovated for her visit.

"I tried to talk George into letting us stay longer, but he worries his factory will go to pieces if he's gone too long." Lilly looked around the room. "Oh, my! What a beautiful room. I will feel like a queen in here." She nudged her husband with her elbow. "You sure you don't want to stay longer now, dear?"

He frowned. "It's not that I don't want to say, it's just that I have responsibilities.

"I understand." Delia smiled at Wyatt's uncle. "I'm just honored you were able to take the time to come here at all. I know it's quite a journey."

"Not so bad by train." He set his hat on the bureau. "Not like when my brother and his family traveled to Oregon in a wagon when Wyatt was a boy. I still cannot fathom that."

"And to think Wyatt made the same trip back East." Lilly shook her head. "On horseback."

"I'm glad he did," Delia told her. "Otherwise, we might never have met."

"And the way you met." Lilly chuckled. "Wyatt wrote to me all about it."

"He must've written you a lot of letters."

"Oh, yes, we've always corresponded regularly. Wyatt is like a son to me." Lilly sighed. "I just wish we lived closer."

"Now, Lilly." George patted her hand. "We came to celebrate our nephew's upcoming nuptials. Let's not burden his bride with your maternal concerns."

"I do want your visit here to be enjoyable." Delia glanced around the pretty room. "I hope you'll be comfortable. If you need anything, just ask. And dinner is at seven."

"That just gives us time to freshen up and rest a bit." Lilly smiled. "Thank you, dear."

As Delia left their room, she felt relieved. Wyatt's relatives were so much more comfortable than her own. Then, remembering her siblings and regretting the way she'd sent them off with Miranda, she decided to check on them. But only Julianne was in the room, carefully unpacking her things.

"Where's Julius?" Delia asked.

"He's staying in the bunkhouse with the cowboys." Julianne beamed at her. "I get this room all to myself."

"Lucky you. But did Mother agree to Julius bunking with cowhands?" Delia could just imagine her overprotective mother's reaction.

"Not at first. But Miranda promised that Julius would be perfectly safe. She assured Father that some of the older men, Enoch and Caleb I think she said, would look after him."

"He'll be in good hands." Delia sat down on a corner of the bunk not completely covered with Julianne's things. "You certainly packed a lot. I can't imagine you'll need all this for such a short visit."

"Mother packed for us." Julianne hung a pink and white calico in the wardrobe.

"Oh." Now Delia noticed the trunk at the foot of the other bed. "A whole trunk just for you? Or is that for Julius too?"

"We each brought a trunk and a valise." Julianne lifted another dress out.

"You mean you brought four trunks?" Delia blinked.

"Six. Mother and Father each packed two."

"Six trunks? For just a few days?"

"Father said we might stay longer." Julianne peered curiously at Delia. "Is that all right with you?"

"Well, I—I just didn't expect this to be a long visit. But, of course, it's all right."

"And you're glad to see us, aren't you? You're glad we came?"

"Of course, I'm glad." Delia smiled.

"Oh, good. I wasn't sure. I heard some of the things that were said, you know, right before you left home. I was worried you would hate us now."

"I would never hate you. But I'm sorry you were worried." Delia frowned. "Although that's probably your reward for eavesdropping."

Julianne made a face then lifted out a sky-blue ruffled dress. "I'm wearing this to your wedding. Do you like it?"

"Very much. It will look pretty on you. Same color as your eyes."

"And I brought the sapphire earrings." Julianne spoke quietly now, as if she thought someone was eavesdropping on her for a change. She opened up her little blue velvet bag to extract a hanky bundle. Carefully unwrapping it, she finally exposed the blue teardrop earrings. "They're so beautiful. I love them."

"Oh, Julianne." Delia had warned her she wasn't to wear them until she turned fifteen. "You know Mother will not approve."

"I'm going to sneak them into the church. I'll put them on just before your wedding." Julianne's eyes twinkled with mischief. "Mother won't see them until it's too late."

Delia couldn't help but laugh. "Same old Julianne."

"And I know that Great Aunt Adelaide isn't really my aunt now. And that's why you got all her jewelry. Because she was really your grandmother….and I know that you're really my half-sister."

"You've learned quite a lot, young lady. I hope it's not too disturbing to you."

Julianne cocked her head to one side with a twisted smile. "It took awhile for it all to sink in properly. But I think I understand it now. Mother swore me to secrecy about it. She didn't even tell Julius everything. Not fully. I doubt that he cares much anyway. He's such a silly goose. All he can think about is that he wants to be a cowboy."

"We'll have to do everything in our power to see that he does." Delia smiled. "And what can we do for you, Julianne, during your visit? Anything special you'd like to do?"

"I just want to be with you, Delia. As much as I can." Julianne sighed. "I know I used to be a brat. But I'm growing up. And I really did miss you." Her eyes sparkled with what looked like tears. "Colorado is so far away from Pittsburgh."

"That's true." Delia got up to hug her little sister. "But you're here now. And when you go, we'll stay in touch. And maybe someday, when you're old enough, you can come out for a longer visit by yourself."

"Really? You'd let me do that?"

"Of course!" She hugged her tighter. "Believe it or not, I missed you too." She felt tears in her own eyes now. It was true. She had missed Julianne. And Julius too. She'd even missed her mother. She'd missed everyone but her stepfather. In all honesty, she had never wanted to see him again. Did he really think he was going to extend his visit here? And, if so, what could she do about it?

After surprising Daisy and Ginger by offering her help in the kitchen, which they declined, Miranda went out to the front porch to sit for a while. She knew all their guests were here, but the house was quiet. She assumed they were all resting or dressing for dinner. But for some reason she didn't want to be stuck inside. She partly wondered if that was because she realized that, in all likelihood, her days here on the farm were numbered. Unless a miracle happened, and she hadn't given up hope, she would be shipped off to the East coast on the same train as Wyatt's aunt and uncle. Delia had already told Miranda that was still the general plan.

The sound of horse's hoofs made her look down the road in time to see a small trap being pulled by a roan horse and moving at a good fast clip. She watched with mild interest, wondering if the trap would continue past, on its way to the nearest farm about five miles farther up the road, but to her surprise, the driver turned it into their drive. As the trap slowed down, she peered curiously at the driver.

"Jackson?" She stood up in wonder. Was it really him or was she just daydreaming? But as the horse and trap got closer, she knew her eyes weren't tricking her. *It was Jackson.* She waved to him, running out to see why he'd come. Hopefully to propose marriage, rescue her, and take her far away!

"Hi, Miranda." He grinned as he jumped down from the sleek black buggy.

"Oh, Jackson, I'm so glad to see you." She hurried up to him, glad that she had on one of her prettiest gowns. Another hand-me-down from Delia that had been altered to fit her. "What are you doing here?"

"Ma sent me with pies."

"Pies?" She tried not to sound too disappointed.

"For the wedding. She baked a dozen apple pies this morning. Ginger is expecting 'em. Ma and Pa are staying at the Elk Horn, you know, until the wedding. And she didn't want to take the pies to her room or leave 'em at the livery stable. I guess she thought the men there might eat them. So, anyway, she asked me to bring 'em over here."

"Oh." Miranda nodded, watching as he lifted a large pasteboard box out of the back. "Want any help?"

"Nah, I can get it. You have on your pretty dress, and some of these boxes got a little sticky and drippy."

She led him around the side of the house and in through the back, explaining to Ginger and Daisy that the pies were here. Before long, they had them stowed on the back-porch pie safe and Miranda was walking Jackson back to his buggy.

"Do you want to stay for dinner?" she asked suddenly. "Or do you need to get back to the hotel?"

"I don't have to get back." He grinned. "And something smelled pretty good in the kitchen."

"Then stay with us." She linked her arm into his. "Delia won't mind." She glanced toward the house, remembering it was filled with guests. "But you'll have to go to the bunkhouse to clean up. Do you mind?"

He chuckled. "I'm quite familiar with the bunkhouse, thank you very much. Remember I was over here helping to protect you ladies during the troubles. Not that you ever paid me much heed back them."

"That's only because I was a silly fool." She sighed. "I've changed, Jackson."

"I've noticed."

She smiled at him. "Dinner is at seven."

"I'll be there with bells on."

She laughed then, feeling happier than ever, she hurried into the house to set another place. And, she told herself, as she made room at the table, it looked much more balanced now. Twelve places instead of eleven. Perfect. Very perfect!

8

Delia could see how happy Wyatt was to have his aunt and uncle safely here and, for that reason, didn't want to burden him with worries regarding her family. Particularly the nagging concern over Jefferson and the amount of trunks he'd had them bring.

"I like your aunt," she told him as they headed back to the house after a quick before-dinner stroll.

"And my uncle?" His eyes twinkled.

"Oh, I like him too."

"He can be a curmudgeon sometimes."

"I thought he seemed perfectly darling."

"Aunt Lilly told him to be on his best behavior." Wyatt chuckled. "Otherwise she would refuse to go home with him."

"She wouldn't really!"

"She's a strong woman."

Delia laughed. "Perhaps that's why I like her so much."

"Say, isn't that Jackson O'Neil over by the corral?"

Delia squinted against the brightness of the western sky. "I think you're right. Ginger mentioned that Maggie was sending a lot of pies over for Saturday. Do you suppose he brought them?"

"We'll find out." Wyatt called out to Jackson as they went to meet him and after greeting him, Jackson explained about delivering pies.

"And Miranda invited me to dinner." He smiled sheepishly at Delia. "I hope you don't mind."

"Not at all," Delia assured him. "But did she warn you we have a houseful of guests?"

His brows arched. "She didn't mention anything. Are you sure it's all right?"

"It's perfect. You will round out our dinner party to an even twelve." Delia studied him closely. "And I know Miranda must be pleased as punch to have you as her guest."

"Yeah…I reckon." His ruddy cheeks grew a bit ruddier. "I was just tending to my horse and need to clean up some. See you at dinnertime."

As Delia and Wyatt strolled back to the house, she suddenly grew curious as to Wyatt's impression of her family and decided to ask. "I know you briefly met them in the train station…but you haven't said much."

"It was only introductions." He cleared his throat. "They were polite. And everyone looked very citified. Your brother is quite taken by *cowboys.* He seemed to think every man in western wear must be a cowboy."

She laughed. "That sounds about right."

"Your mother looked a bit worn out. And your sister, well, I have a feeling that one could be a handful someday."

"That's a good observation." She looked up at the house. "And my stepfather?"

Wyatt paused by the front porch steps. "He was hard to read. Very polite, of course. But he reminded me of something."

"What's that?"

Wyatt smiled. "Well, I'm probably imagining things, and don't take this wrong, but he reminded me of a poker player named Sam up in Alaska. Sam was well-dressed and well-spoken and, according to AJ, a professional gambler. People called him Slick Sam and, well, I guess he was."

Delia grasped tighter to his arm. "I think you are the most observant man I've ever know, Wyatt." She lowered her voice. "Dinner should be, uh, interesting."

Miranda hummed happily to herself as she lit candles on the dining room table. This house hadn't hosted a big formal dinner in a long time. Not like this anyway. Her father would sometimes have ranch friends over, but the table hadn't been set with this many places or beautiful things since her mother was alive. And that seemed a lifetime ago.

"The table looks lovely," Delia said as she joined her. "And you even put out the wine glasses?"

"I hope that's all right." She pointed to bottles of burgundy on the buffet. "Ginger got those out of Father's locked wine cabinet."

"I think it's quite festive. I haven't been to a formal dinner for some time. I wonder if I can even remember the protocol."

"Protocol?" Miranda asked.

"Just little things like who gets seated first and when to serve the wine."

"Oh?" Miranda frowned. "You mean there's a right way and wrong way?"

Delia shrugged. "According to some people. As I recall, the eldest lady is escorted in first and seated. That would be Aunt Lilly. And I believe wine is served following the soup course."

"How do you know all these things?"

"My parents used to give dinner parties. And then at school, we actually had a required etiquette class." She giggled. "We even had pretend dinner parties where we played different roles and went through all the steps—but without real food."

"That could be fun."

Delia nodded toward the living room. "Sounds as if our guests are gathering in there. Why don't we join them until Ginger rings the dinner bell?"

"This is so exciting." Miranda grabbed Delia's hand. "And I'm over the moon that Jackson is here."

As everyone filled the living room, getting acquainted and visiting, Miranda made her way to where Jackson was standing beside the front window. "I'm so glad you could come," she said in a formal tone. "I do hope you enjoy yourself."

"I feel like a fish outta water," he whispered. "I didn't know this was a formal dinner. And I'm not dressed right."

"You look perfectly fine to me." She smiled up at him.

"But these folks look so doggone fancy." He grimaced.

"That's because they're from the East, where people dress for dinner."

"My ma would like it. She loves to dress up when she gets the chance."

"She'll get the chance on Saturday." Miranda paused as Julianne approached them, taking a moment to properly introduce the girl to Jackson. "Jackson's parents own a big silver mine," she told Julianne. "They were good friends with my parents. You'll meet them at the wedding."

"Will there be many young people at the wedding?" Julianne asked hopefully.

"Oh, sure." Miranda nodded. "Some of our neighboring ranchers are coming. They have kids of all ages."

"Good. I hoped it wasn't just going to be old people." Julianne looked around the room. "Like in here."

Miranda laughed. At the tinkling of the dinner bell, the room grew quiet and Delia, playing lady of the house, announced that dinner was ready.

"Wyatt will escort you in first," Delia politely told Aunt Lilly. "And I will escort in Uncle Enoch. Everyone else can proceed as they like."

Miranda hooked her arm into Jackson's. "And you will escort me."

He looked slightly embarrassed but nodded.

"I set up the dining room," she quietly told him as the others began to drift in. "I think you'll like it."

"Ready?" he asked. She nodded and he led her into the room, but unfortunately the only two chairs were a distance apart.

"I'll sit here." She nodded to the chair by Delia who was at one end of the table. Jackson politely pulled out her chair and then went to sit next to Wyatt who was seated at the head of the table. And then Wyatt, as was his habit, asked a blessing.

As they began to eat their beef consommé soup, Miranda tried to hide her disappointment at not getting to sit with Jackson. Instead, she decided to do all she could to participate in the conversation around her and appear as adult as possible. And since Delia's stepfather was next to her with only his son Julius on the other side of him, she decided to engage him.

"What sort of work do you do in Pittsburgh?" she politely asked Mr. Blackstone.

"Work?" His brow creased as if this were an impertinent question.

"I meant what do you do for employment, Mr. Blackstone?" She felt nervous now. Had she said it wrong? "What is your career?"

"I have no career."

"Oh." She nodded. "Of course." Now hoping to undo her social blunder, she asked about what he enjoyed doing in his leisure time. "Do you have hobbies or activities that you participate in?"

"I have a gentlemen's club that I enjoy." He set down his soup spoon and nodded to the wine on the buffet. "Delia, dear, would you like me to play host and serve the wine for you?"

"No, thank you," she told him. "You're our guest. Wyatt will serve the wine after we've finished our soup course."

"Oh, you're being quite proper." His tone had a teasing ring. "Very traditional."

"It's the way I was taught in school," she answered.

"Really? They taught you how to serve wine at your university? And here, all this time, I thought your education was so impractical." He chuckled.

"I've discovered my education to be quite useful." Delia's smile looked a bit forced, and Miranda's dislike of Mr. Blackstone deepened.

Now he looked across the table to where Caleb was seated. And although Caleb was in his best clothes, he still looked like a cowhand, which Miranda thought should comfort Jackson. "I'll wager you would agree with me," Mr. Blackstone directed this to Caleb. "Don't you think that educating women is a waste of money?"

Caleb pursed his lips as if considering his answer. "I mighta thought that before, Mr. Blackstone. But since I've gotten better acquainted with Miss Delia here, my opinions have changed. I reckon her pa—I mean my buddy, Winston—I reckon he knew she'd need her education. He probably hoped she'd come help him run this here ranch someday. And she's proved to me, and everyone else, that she's fit to do it too."

"Thank you, Caleb." Delia's smile warmed up.

"I'm certainly looking forward to the wedding on Saturday," Lilly said to no one in particular. Miranda suspected this was an attempt to change the subject. "I haven't heard many details yet. Where will the ceremony be held, Wyatt? And what time of day?"

"We'll be married in Colorado City. In the church. At eleven in the morning," Wyatt explained. "Reverend Johnson will officiate."

"Very nice." Aunt Lilly nodded.

"And we've got buckets of flowers out on the back porch," Miranda told her. "All ready to take to the church for decorations and to use for Delia's bouquet."

"It sounds very lovely," Jane said. "Please, let me know if you need any help, Delia. As you know, I am experienced at floral arrangements."

"Thank you, Mother. I'll keep that in mind."

"And if you need a ring bearer or flower girl, I'm sure Julius and Julianne would be happy to accommodate you." Jane smiled.

"I hadn't even considered that," Delia admitted. "But it's not a bad idea."

"I'm to be her maid of honor," Miranda announced. "And Caleb will stand up with Wyatt."

"Can I assume the honor of giving away the bride will be mine?" Mr. Blackstone smiled at Delia. "Since I've been the only father you've ever known."

The table grew quiet with all eyes on Delia, waiting for her response.

"Actually, I've already arranged for that," Delia said carefully. "Uncle Enoch is going to escort me down the aisle." Now the room became even quieter. "I do appreciate your willingness," she said to Jefferson. "But I hope you will simply enjoy being my guest at the wedding."

"After the wedding, we'll have a big luncheon." Wyatt stood as Ginger and Daisy started to clear the soup bowls. "Everyone will come out here at the ranch." He went to the buffet and picked up a wine bottle. He took it directly to Mr. Blackstone and, still talking about the wedding, generously filled his wineglass. "It should be a fun day for everyone." He continued to fill the other glasses. "We'll have barbecue and all sorts of good things. The celebration will go on all day long."

"And there'll be music and dancing later," Miranda added. "It's going to be so much fun!"

"And now I'd like to make a toast to our lovely hostess." Wyatt held his glass high, his eyes locking with Delia's. "To my beloved. May our wedding day be one that we will happily remember for years and years to come."

They all agreed to this toast and a couple more well wishes were made and suddenly the dinner was back on a congenial track. Everyone seemed to be having a good time, but Miranda couldn't help but notice Mr. Blackstone didn't seem to be participating. She tried to engage him again by asking if he liked to ride, but he answered with a curt no—and she decided to take the hint.

Finally, they were finishing up and, although Delia announced they'd serve after dinner coffee in the living room, Miranda hoped to get Jackson off to herself for a bit. So as the guests began to disperse, she went straight for Jackson, asking him if he'd enjoy a bit of fresh air. Forward perhaps, but necessary. And he seemed grateful to agree. Before long, they were settled in the front porch rockers, enjoying the colors of the sunset.

"Well, that was interesting," Jackson said quietly.

"Which part?"

"Oh, lots of it. But mostly the part where Delia told her father—"

"That man is *not* her father."

"I mean stepfather. Anyway, after she told him ol' Enoch was walking her down the aisle, well, I thought Mr. Blackstone was going to blow his stack."

She giggled. "So did I. But I'm glad Uncle Enoch gets to do it. After all, he's Delia's real blood relation." She glanced at Jackson. "I hope if I ever get married, Uncle Enoch will be around to walk me down the aisle too."

For a moment neither of them said anything and Miranda worried that she'd said too much. She knew that she could be overly pushy at times. She didn't want to scare Jackson off by talking about marriage.

"How old is Enoch anyway?" Jackson asked.

"I think he's in his seventies, but I'm not really sure."

"Oh, that's not so old. My Grandpa Jack is eighty-four and he's still kickin'."

Miranda wasn't sure how to take that. Was Jackson suggesting that she had plenty of years to go before she got married...or was he just making idle conversation?

"It's getting late." Jackson stood. "I should probably be heading back to the hotel."

"Or you could spend the night in the bunkhouse." She stood too, facing him with hopeful eyes. Couldn't he see that she was trying to communicate her feelings?

"Yeah, I reckon I could. But I still need to get back to town by morning. I got lots of errands to run there tomorrow."

"Things you need for your trip? I assume you're still planning to wander off to the wilds of Alaska…." She sighed.

"That's right. Lots to get done before I leave next week."

"I told Delia about your plans, Jackson." Miranda weighed her words. "And she said that if it's work and income you're looking for, we've got plenty here. We need good hands."

"That's encouraging, but that doesn't change anything. I want to go to Alaska for the adventure too. And I was thinking about what you said about going to school back East…maybe that's a good idea too. Like Caleb said at dinner, schooling sure helped Delia get ready for running the ranch."

"That's true." She sighed again, even louder this time. Was there nothing she could do to convince Jackson to stay in Colorado—and marry her? "But I'm not sure the university would prepare me for what I really want."

"What's that?"

"Oh, you know. It's what most women want. You know, marriage and a home and maybe children someday." Of course, that was overstating things. She still wasn't too sure about children. After losing her mother and baby brother to childbirth, it had always frightened her.

"But look at Delia, she's getting married. Education hasn't hurt that. And if you ask me, she and Wyatt seem pretty happy."

"Yes. And she did meet Wyatt on the train." Miranda put more energy into her voice. "Maybe that's what will happen to me. I'll meet a wonderful man on the train, and we'll fall in love and—"

"Oh, Miranda, is that all you think about? Love and marriage and weddings? I honestly don't see why you're so all fired up about getting yourself tied down like that. I see wives around the mine all the time. Working their fingers to the bone and looking old and worn out before their time. Doesn't seem like you'd want that." He stood up, acting as if he was getting ready to leave.

"I never said I wanted that—what you just described." She stood too, folding her arms in front of her.

"Because you're a spunky girl. Surely, you'd want something more."

"That's right." She stuck her chin out in defiance. "But you were describing those old miner's wives. I'd never be like that."

"I'm a miner, Miranda."

She turned to face him, trying to discern the meaning behind that statement. "But your family *owns* the mine, Jackson. That's different than just ordinary miners."

"Maybe. But up in Alaska I'm gonna be just an ordinary miner."

"Well, that's your choice. Besides, you told me you're going for the adventure too. You're not just an ordinary miner."

He nodded. "But I wouldn't mind if I struck it rich."

She stepped a bit closer to him. "And if you struck it rich, Jackson, would you come home to Colorado? Would you be looking for a wife then?"

"Most likely."

"And what would you want in a wife?" She asked sweetly. "What kind of woman would you choose?"

"Well, for starters…I'd like a pretty girl."

"Uh-huh." She tipped her head up, hoping that the light from the house was illuminating her in a flattering way.

"And I'd want a girl I could count on. Someone loyal and true. I'd want a goodhearted woman. Someone good and kind."

"Yes, those are important qualities."

"And…I'd like someone smart too."

"Smart? As in college educated?" She used a slightly sharp tone.

"I wouldn't object to it." He reached for his hat. "I better go,

Miranda. I think I'll stay overnight in town after all. Get me an earlier start on the day tomorrow."

"Yes, that's probably a good plan." Her smile felt pasted in place.

"But I'll see you on Saturday," he said brightly.

"I'm looking forward to it," she said politely. "Saving the best dances for you."

"Good." He stuck on his hat and then, catching her completely off guard, he leaned over and kissed her. Right on the cheek. "See you!" Before she could gather her thoughts to utter a word, he jumped off the porch and took off running toward the corral like a scared coyote.

So, maybe he was more interested in her than he had been letting on. But was he interested enough to give up Alaska? Could he be enticed to remain in Colorado? Well, she'd have to wait until Saturday to find that out. But she planned to put her full effort into it. She would try to be everything he'd just listed in a wife. Pretty wasn't so hard, lots of people thought she was pretty. Loyal and true and good and kind…she might have to work on those qualities, although they did appeal to her. And smart? Well, there had to be more than just one kind of smart. Miranda knew she'd never be book smart, but she felt fairly confident she could excel in another form of smartness.

9

As Delia set a basket of eggs on the kitchen table, Ginger scowled. "I told you I'd tend them chickens for you, Miss Delia."

Delia smiled. "I know, Ginger. But I just needed an excuse to get up and outside early. And I enjoy those noisy hens."

"But it's the day before your wedding. I hoped you wouldn't be working yourself to death. You already done too much for your guests." Ginger puckered her face. "And some of them not even grateful."

"Oh?" Delia watched Ginger carefully loading the eggs into a bowl.

"Excuse me. I wasn't going to say anything."

"Is it my family?" Delia asked quietly. "Miranda mentioned that my stepfather expected someone to unpack for them yesterday."

Ginger rolled her eyes toward the ceiling.

"I apologize for my family, Ginger. It's probably no consolation to you, but my patience toward my stepfather is wearing thin. And I'm going to tell him not to take advantage of you."

"Good. He seems to think we're a hotel!" Ginger pointed to a tray. "He asked to have breakfast taken up."

"No." Delia firmly shook her head. "I will put my foot down. If he wants breakfast, he must come downstairs. And I will let him know."

"Thank you." Ginger pushed a strand of gray hair back under her cap.

"Where's Daisy?"

"Separating cream."

"And you're going to set up breakfast like a buffet?" Delia asked. "Like I suggested. Less work for you."

"That's just what I'm doing."

"Anything I can do?"

"No!" Ginger pushed her toward the back door. "Rosie is coming to help today. Me and her and Daisy will manage just fine, thank you very much. And tomorrow Rosie's grown girls are coming to help with the big shindig."

"Sounds like you have everything under control." Delia patted her shoulder. "I bet you'll be glad when this is all over and done."

"Don't get me wrong, I enjoy the festivities." Ginger brightened. "I couldn't be more pleased about you and Wyatt. It's just I don't cater to folks who expect to be treated like kings and queens."

"I don't either." Delia sighed. "But in a few days, you'll have an empty house, Ginger. Then you can enjoy a well-deserved break."

"You go take a break yourself. Grab some more of that morning quiet. You'll have your hands full with your houseguests soon enough."

Delia suspected Ginger was right about that. And so she decided to take a little stroll and, although she hadn't planned it, she found herself going up the hill to the little family cemetery. Halfway up there she gathered a bouquet of humble but beautiful wildflowers. As she stood before her father's grave, she spoke quietly. "I wish you could see me getting married, Father. I wish you could hold my hand and walk me down the aisle. I wish you were here and could give your blessing on our marriage." She felt her eyes moistening. "But, in my heart, I believe you are here. I believe you've already given us your blessing somehow. And maybe somehow you will be looking down on us when we repeat our vows. Because I can feel your presence all over this lovely ranch you built. And I'm so very, very grateful for it." She sighed as she set the sweet bouquet down on the grave. "Thank you."

Delia turned at the sound of footsteps and was surprised to see Uncle Enoch slowly making his way up the hill. "Good morning," she called.

He returned the greeting, but his tone sounded weary. She hurried down to him and, linking her arm in his, walked him up the slope. "Would you like me to leave you alone?" She asked as they stood before the gravesite.

"No. I'm glad you're here," he said solemnly. "I just wanted to pay my respects to my boy. You know, Winston always seemed like my very own son. I still can't believe he's really gone."

"I know."

For a long moment they both stood there in silence, and then Enoch turned to her. His pale gray eyes were brimming with tears as he reached for his handkerchief. "Winston was a good man. A truly good man."

"I know. Even though I never met him face to face, I know that."

"And he'd have been mighty proud of you, Delia. I hope you know that too."

"I sure hope that's true." She tugged her hankie out of her pocket, dabbing her own eyes.

"It's hard not to feel regrets…for what might've been." He loudly blew his nose. "But like Winston liked to say, this land is for the living. And he was a man who knew how to live." Uncle Enoch smiled. "There are plenty of stories I can tell you about him, Delia. That's just one of the reasons I wanted to come back." He looked around. "And because I love this land." He nodded to the tiny cemetery. "Besides that, well, I want my own old bones buried right here when it's time."

"Let's not talk about that." She linked her arm with his again. "This is the land of the living, Uncle. Remember?"

He chuckled. "You are your father's daughter."

As they slowly walked down the hill, Enoch pointed to the pasture of contented milk cows and began to tell her about the time her father helped to birth a backwards calf. "We all told him it was impossible, that the only way to save the cow was to kill the calf. But Winston proved us wrong. Both lives were spared that day."

Delia waved down to where Wyatt was coming up the path toward them. "I haven't had the chance to ask you, Uncle Enoch, what do you think of Wyatt?" she asked quietly.

"He reminds me a lot of your father, Delia. He's a good man too."

Nothing her uncle said could have made her happier. And, after exchanging greetings, the three of them went down the hill together. "I smell bacon." Uncle Enoch smacked his lips. "So glad to be back to ranch cookin'."

Remembering her stepfather's request to have breakfast delivered to his room, Delia told them to go ahead and get started on the buffet breakfast. "I need to check on something first."

Although she wasn't eager to lock horns with Jefferson, she was determined that he respect her household workers. This was not a hotel! She tapped quietly on the master bedroom door and her mother, in her dressing gown, answered. "Oh, Delia? I expected the housekeeper with our breakfast by now. Jefferson said it was coming."

"Good morning, Mother." Delia smiled stiffly. "Sorry to disturb you, but I need to let you know that no one will be having meals delivered to their rooms. We don't have enough household staff for that kind of service."

"Oh, well, that was your father—I mean your stepfather's idea. I don't mind going downstairs to eat."

Delia explained about the buffet breakfast then excused herself.

As she went downstairs, she tried not to let it under her skin. After all, she'd grown up in a home where both her parents had put themselves ahead of everyone. Why should she expect anything different from them now?

She greeted Wyatt's aunt and uncle, already seated with Wyatt and Enoch at the dining room table, and Miranda and the twins, still at the buffet, chatted as they loaded their plates. Before long, all were seated and visiting congenially. For a moment, Delia considered how much more peaceful dining might be if her parents actually did take their meals upstairs. Not that she planned to go back on her decision.

"I understand you're not very enthused about attending the university," Aunt Lilly said to Miranda. "I wonder…have you considered other options?"

"Options? You mean like marriage?" Miranda's eyes lit up.

Aunt Lilly laughed. "Yes, well, I suppose that is an option. But I was thinking about finishing school. Have you ever thought about that?"

"What is that?"

"It's higher education for girls your age. To prepare them for womanhood. A friend of mine, Millie Madison, sent her three daughters to a fine finishing school in Philadelphia. I believe Millie's youngest girl still has a year to go. And if I'm not mistaken Millie Madison sits on the school's board."

"What do they teach at finishing school?" Miranda asked.

"According to Millie, they teach all sorts of things. From art and music and dance to the academics and homemaking skills. It's a wonderful opportunity for young women to round out their knowledge."

"I always thought finishing school was to prepare young women for marriage," Delia said. "Not that I'm opposed to that. But I'm thankful for my university education."

"Well, I'm not like you, Delia. And, if you ask me, finishing school sounds much better than a stuffy old university." Miranda stuck out her chin as she buttered a muffin.

Delia forced a tolerant smile. "I wouldn't have any objections to you attending finishing school, Miranda. Although I wonder how difficult it would be to get admitted to one with such short notice. And you are already registered at the university. What about a compromise? You attend university for a bit, see how it goes, and in the meantime we can look into finishing school as a backup."

Miranda frowned. "So my only option for not going to the university really is to get married."

"I'm not saying that." Delia refilled Aunt Lilly's coffee cup.

"I have an idea," Lilly declared. "What if I sent a wire to Millie? I'm sure she could help us with this."

Delia feelings were mixed, but she thanked her anyway. "That would be helpful."

"I will get right to it," Lilly said with enthusiasm. "Do you think that if I wrote out a message to Millie, you might get one of your hands to run it to the telegraph office in town?"

"I'm sure that could be arranged." Delia glanced at Miranda, who was looking somewhat alarmed.

"Don't get me wrong," Miranda said quickly. "I'm not agreeing to go to finishing school even if I could get into it."

"So you'd rather attend the university?" Delia asked hopefully.

"No," Miranda stated firmly. "Finishing school sounds much better than that."

"Well, I'm guessing that's easier said than done." Delia glanced at Lilly.

"Maybe so, but if anyone can make this happen, I think Millie Madison is just the one. That woman is a ball of fire."

"Thank you very much for offering to contact your friend," Miranda said primly to Lilly. "In the event I don't get a nice young man to propose marriage to me in the next few days, I expect I will be most grateful to attend finishing school."

Everyone at the table laughed as if Miranda were joking, but Delia suspected her headstrong stepsister was perfectly serious. In an effort to redirect the conversation, Delia turned to her twin siblings. "What would you two like to do today?"

"Caleb said I can help round up the cows," Julius said proudly.

"Some calves do need branding," Wyatt winked at Delia. "Caleb thought he could use help with that."

Delia looked at Julius's city-boy clothes. "Did you bring anything you can get dirty?"

Julius frowned. "I don't know."

"Don't you worry. We got some duds you can use," Uncle Enoch assured them. "Had a hand last year not much bigger than young Julius here. He left behind a few things that are too small for everyone else."

Delia smiled. "Sounds like this is your day to be a cowboy, Julius." She turned to Julianne. "What would you like to do?"

"Do you think I could ride a horse?" she asked timidly.

"Have you had any riding lessons?"

Julianne glumly shook her head.

"That's no problem." Delia grinned. "I can teach you." She looked at Julianne's light blue dress. "But you can't ride in that."

"I don't have a riding habit."

Delia imagined Julianne's dress coated in dust. "Think Mother would throw a fit if I let you ride astride?"

Julianne's eyes lit up. "Like Calamity Jane?"

"That's how I ride."

She nodded eagerly. "But what will I wear?"

"If we had time, we'd make you a split skirt. I had my riding habit reworked into one."

Julianne pointed to her brother. "I can borrow some trousers from him."

Delia chuckled to imagine her mother's reaction to this idea, but Julianne looked so hopeful that Delia simply nodded. Who should care if a twelve-year-old girl wore pants to ride a horse way out here in the "wilds" as her mother had called it? "Sounds like a plan. Wyatt, can you ask Cash to saddle my horse? And I think Dolly would be a good match for Julianne."

"Dolly sounds nice." Julianne beamed at her. "Thanks, Delia."

Delia started Julianne's riding lessons inside the corral. Dolly, as expected, was calm and easy going. And Julianne, to Delia's delight, was a good pupil. After less than an hour of instruction, she led Julianne and Dolly out to the open pasture.

"I always knew you were a smart girl," Delia told her, "but I didn't expect you to be a natural horsewoman."

"I'm like you," Julianne declared proudly. "Because we're sisters, remember?"

"That's true." Delia maneuvered Lady next to Dolly, walking the two horses side by side.

"Miranda's not like you," Julianne continued. "But that's because she's not your real sister."

"Well, Miranda is our *adopted* sister," Delia clarified. "And she needs us. So I hope you'll treat her like a real sister. We're the only family she has, and she needs us more than ever just now."

"Because she's scared about going to college?"

"That's part of it." As they walked the horses toward the creek, Delia explained about Miranda losing her father and mother and baby brother. "And then my father died. So it's natural she'd feel a bit lost. And the idea of going to Philadelphia to university, well, you heard her."

"I would love to go to university. When I'm old enough." Julianne stuck out her chin. "Because I'm smart like you, Delia."

At the creek now, Delia got off her horse. "Hopefully you'll get to go to college too, Julianne. Maybe the same one I went to." She helped sister down and allowed both horses to take a drink from the creek.

"Father won't let me." Julianne plucked up a bright orange mule's ear flower growing by the creek and stuck it in the buttonhole of the jacket borrowed from her brother.

"Oh." Delia wasn't surprised. "Well, he doesn't think girls need too much education. But maybe he'll soften up when you're older."

"That's not the only reason why Father won't let me go to college." Julianne looked intently at her. "He won't be able to pay for it. Because we are broke."

"Broke?" Delia frowned. "I know there's some financial challenges, but I don't think your father is truly broke."

"Well, he is. He is *flat* broke!"

"Flat broke?" Delia forced a laugh. "That sounds a bit extreme. Surely you're not suggesting your father is penniless?"

"Yes, I am! I overheard him talking to Mother. Just last night after dinner. They didn't know I was listening, but I was outside their bedroom door. I only wanted to borrow Mother's hairbrush since I couldn't find mine. I was about to knock, but then I heard their voices raised. I'm surprised you didn't hear them too."

"Wyatt and I took a moonlit walk last night." Delia felt a rush of concern. "You're serious? Your father really said they have *no* money? Nothing in the bank or stocks or anything?"

"He said we are broke. *Flat broke.* Those were his exact words. He said there is no more money left. And he said our house is being taken by the bank next week. And everything in it too. Mother was crying really hard." Julianne looked close to tears too.

"Oh, dear."

"What will we do?" Julianne asked.

"I, uh, I honestly don't know. Is it possible he was exaggerating the situation? He did overindulge in the wine last night. You know how that makes him get sometimes. Maybe he was just being overly dramatic for Mother's sake. You know he does that too. Makes things seem bigger and worse than they are."

"Maybe…." Julianne barely nodded.

"Anyway, it's not for you worry about. I hope you didn't mention it to Julius."

She shook her head glumly. "You're the only one I told."

"Well, I know their finances were tightened, but I can't imagine it's all gone. Maybe it's just time to scale back. Perhaps a smaller house. Not so many servants. And maybe your father will get a job." *And learn to live within his means,* she wanted to say but didn't.

Julianne sighed. "I'm just glad I'm only twelve. Otherwise Father might try to marry *me* off to old Henry Horton."

Despite herself, Delia couldn't help but laugh. And now Julianne was giggling too. As ridiculous as the idea of marrying off a twelve-year-old for money was, Delia wouldn't be surprised if, a few years from now, Jefferson would stoop to such selfish measures.

"We should probably get back to the house for lunch." Delia helped Julianne back into the saddle and was just getting on her own horse when, to her surprise, Julianne kicked her heels into Dolly's flanks, yelling an enthused "Giddy-up!" More surprising was that the old horse actually took off—in a full gallop!

"Race you to the barn!" Julianne yelled over her shoulder.

As Delia urged Lady to a gallop, she silently prayed her little sister would keep her seat! Careful not to pass Julianne and Dolly and make matters worse, Delia reined Lady back, watching with terror as Julianne bounced up and down and side to side in the slippery leather saddle. *God, please, protect her!*

10

To Delia's amazed relief, Julianne and Dolly made it safely back to the corral encircled by an impressive cloud of dust. And Julianne didn't look the least bit frightened. Still, Delia knew she needed to gently scold her reckless sister.

"My goodness." Delia shook her head with wide eyes as she got off her horse, preparing to help her sister down. "That was quite a show, Julianne."

"That was fun!" Julianne slid out of the saddle with no help.

"Fun maybe, but for your first lesson, I'd prefer you—"

"What on earth!" They both turned to see Mother storming toward the corral, her face flushed with excitement and her full skirt flapping behind her. And just a few steps behind came her husband, attempting to brush the dust from his fancy black waistcoat.

"What do you think you're doing?" He yelled angrily in her direction.

"Giving Julianne a riding lesson." Delia was determined to remain calm.

"Julianne, where did you get that ridiculous outfit?" Mother demanded.

"It's Julius's." She scuffed the toe of her boot in the dirt.

"I cannot believe this, Delia." He shook a finger at her. "We leave our children alone for a short while, and the next thing we know you have Julius out there risking life and limb to wrestle steers. And you dress your sister like a boy and try to break her neck on a wild horse. I have a mind to pack everyone up and take them home right now."

Delia looked evenly at him. "That is your choice. No one is forcing you to remain here."

Julianne grabbed Delia's arm. "But I want to stay for your wed—"

"You, hush up!" he growled at Julianne.

"And go change your clothes, young lady! Right this minute," Mother commanded. "And wash up, and get rid of those ridiculous pigtails."

"Delia braided my hair," Julianne declared. "And I like it." Then she took off running.

Seeing Cash approaching, Delia went to meet him, handing over the reins of both horses and thanking him. He stood for a moment, looking on with amused interest. Then, taking in a deep breath, she slowly turned around, preparing herself to face her mother and stepfather, bracing herself for whatever was coming next. Maybe this would be the big showdown. And maybe she was ready. But as she looked at their faces, Jefferson's withering expression gave her pause.

"I thought you'd grown up, Delia," Jefferson's tone was demeaning as he strode toward her, hands planted on his hips. "It seems I was wrong. You are still just an irresponsible child."

She stood a bit straighter, looking him squarely in the eyes. "It's obvious you're both unaccustomed to country living," she said calmly. "Apparently it's frightening to you. But, I assure you, the activities you've witnessed out here are just a normal part of ranch life. And, although I didn't encourage Julianne to race her horse like that, I'm impressed that she stayed on so well. She's quite a little horsewoman."

"And if she had fallen?" Mother demanded with a creased brow.

Delia shrugged. "We all fall off occasionally. You get up, brush yourself off, and get back on."

"We did not bring our children here so that you could put them in harm's way," Jefferson declared.

"They were simply having fun. Julius has dreamed of being a cowboy and Julianne wanted to try riding." Delia stepped away from them in order to close the corral gate and get her bearings. She wasn't ready to back down. If they still wanted a fight, she would stand her ground.

"Just because children want to do dangerous things does not mean they should be allowed." Jefferson narrowed his eyes.

"That's right," Jane agreed. "And if you and Wyatt are blessed with children, I hope you won't let them run wild and—"

"Turn into little savages," Jefferson said with mean twinkle in his eye.

"If we have children, I hope that we will bring them up to be strong young men and women, able to think for themselves." She held her head higher. "And like I said, if you find our life on the ranch too uncomfortable or feel too unsafe, no one will hold you here against your will. Wyatt assured me he sent enough money to cover your train fare back to Pittsburgh. If you truly wish to go home, please, don't let me keep you. Although I do hope you can endure our wild western ways until after the wedding." She waited but, although they still looked aggravated, neither of them responded. "And if our rustic farm life is unappealing to you, and you feel the need to be waited on, please, feel free to relocate yourselves into town. We have several fine hotels there. I highly recommend the Elk Horn."

Mother's eyes darted to her husband, but she said nothing.

He cleared his throat. "Well, I don't think we all need to fly off the handle, Delia. But you can't blame your mother and me for feeling protective of our children, can you?"

"No, by all means, you should protect your children." She locked eyes with him. "That's your responsibility as their father and the provider for your family. I would expect nothing less from you. And if you truly feel I have done anything to risk their safety or well-being, by all means, please, feel free to take them to a safer location."

"That is unnecessary."

"Or if you feel our accommodations here don't meet your expectations," she added.

"Your home is lovely," Jane murmured.

"Well, I heard that you asked for help with your unpacking and—"

"Your mother was weary from the trip."

"I understand. But as I mentioned this morning, we are a bit shorthanded. We cannot serve meals in your room or polish your shoes or do your laundry. We are not a hotel."

"Well." Jefferson's tone sounded offended.

Delia took in a deep breath, unsure if she really wanted to ask the next question but felt it the only responsible thing to do. "And I realize it's not my business, but I have heard rumors that concern me."

"Rumors?" His eyes narrowed.

"Yes. I have heard that you intend to stay here longer than I expected. I know that you packed enough clothing to stay for some length of time. I also heard that your finances are in something of, well, a crisis."

Jane's eyes grew wide, and her hand flew to her mouth.

"Where did you hear this irresponsible gossip?" he demanded.

"The source doesn't matter. I just want to know whether it's true or not?"

"Of course, not!"

"Then the bank isn't taking your house? You haven't lost everything? You didn't come out here with nothing but your trunks of fancy clothes?"

"Oh, Delia." Jane's eyes filled with tears.

"So it is true?"

"What you said earlier *is* true, Delia, it is *none* of your business!" Jefferson turned and stormed off toward the house. And now her mother was crying.

"Is it true?" Delia asked in a gentler tone.

"Yes." Mother broke into loud sobs. "It is true."

Delia hugged her mother, trying to soothe her, but wondering what she should do. Perhaps it would've been better not to know. Now it was too late.

For some reason, Miranda felt she could trust Wyatt's Aunt Lilly. And she liked that the elderly woman had taken such interest in Miranda's future. Although she wasn't overly eager to be shipped off to the Philadelphia finishing school, it did sound preferable to the university. And, after Aunt Lilly informed her that the telegram was on its way to town, Miranda invited the kind woman to join her for tea in the parlor.

"What a lovely idea." Lilly smiled. "Perhaps Delia and her mother would like to join us too."

So it was that the four women were seated in the parlor where Miranda proudly served them tea and cookies. Delia and Lilly seemed to enjoy the impromptu tea party, but Delia's mother seemed awfully quiet. Miranda wondered if something was wrong.

"This is a lovely little party," Lilly told Miranda. "Delicious sugar cookies and the tea is quite nice. You are the perfect hostess."

"Thank you." Miranda smiled proudly.

"Perhaps you're not so much in need of finishing school after all," Delia said in a slightly teasing tone.

"Truth be told, Rosie made the tea and Daisy baked the cookies," Miranda confessed. "But I set everything up all by myself."

"And a fine job you've done of it," Lilly assured her.

Miranda glanced at Delia's mother, who seemed transfixed on the side table. Was she admiring the flowers Miranda had arranged? It was a lovely bouquet and looked especially nice beside the silver framed wedding photograph of her mother and stepfather. Suddenly Miranda realized that her stepfather had once been Jane's husband. Perhaps she should've put it out of sight. Without thinking she reached for it, hoping she could stash it without anyone noticing.

"Is that your mother?" Jane asked quietly.

"Yes." Miranda picked up the photograph, unsure of what to do as the parlor grew very quiet.

"She was very beautiful." Jane sighed.

Miranda smiled down on the picture. "Yes, she was. Everyone said so. I wish I looked more like her. Apparently I take after my father's side of the family. He was Irish."

"I think you look a bit like her," Delia said. "I've studied that photograph carefully and I can definitely see you in her."

"Really?" Miranda felt hopeful.

"May I see it?" Lilly reached for it then smiled. "What a lovely couple they made. And your father, Delia, he was very handsome." She turned to Delia. "You resemble him. Through the eyes and the thick dark hair."

"Thank you." Delia looked at the photograph. "I wish I'd had a chance to know him."

"From all I've heard, Winston Williams was a very admirable man," Lilly said. "And what a beautiful ranch he's created out here in the West. That speaks quite well of him. I know that my George has been thoroughly impressed and, if you know my George, you'd realize he's not easily impressed."

Miranda turned back to Delia's mother, trying to imagine what she was thinking. "Do you ever regret that you let him go?" she asked. "Delia's explained it all to me, how you lost touch during the war and everything, but do you ever wish you'd…" Miranda suddenly knew she'd said too much. She could tell by Delia and Lilly's alarmed expressions that she'd overstepped some invisible boundary. "I mean, well, it's none of my business. But I guess I was just curious. Please, excuse me if I offended you."

"No, dear, it's understandable," Jane's voice wavered slightly. "I suppose I've asked myself that very thing. Especially after coming out here." She turned to Delia. "I do have regrets. And I regret that I didn't tell you about your father, Delia. It was wrong to keep you from him—to deceive you like that." As she stood, the lace trimmed napkin fell from her lap to the floor. "For that I'm sorry." And then she burst into tears and ran from the room.

"I'm sorry," Miranda told Delia and Lilly. "I never should've spoken like that. I wasn't thinking."

"It's understandable, dear girl," Lilly said quietly. "A confusing situation indeed."

"And maybe it was good to get the whole thing out into the open air," Delia declared. "My mother has never apologized to me like that before. It almost gives me hope." Delia retrieved a handkerchief from her pocket.

"Oh, dear, now I've made you cry too." Miranda felt terrible.

"It's all right." Delia wiped her tears. "It's a good cry."

"Maybe I do need to go to finishing school," Miranda declared. "Maybe they'd teach me how to act like a lady and how to hold my tongue."

"Ladies are allowed to speak their minds," Lilly declared. "And I'll admit that I was curious too. I wondered how Delia's mother felt to be here—in such a beautiful place that was created by her first husband."

"But you had the good manners not to ask her," Miranda said glumly. "Especially seeing that Mr. Blackstone isn't such a nice fellow. Not nearly as nice my stepfather was." She turned to Delia. "Your father too."

Delia just nodded.

"I heard them talking last night," Miranda said quietly. "Rather loudly too. Mr. Blackstone was saying some mean things."

"You heard that?" Delia blinked.

"I thought everyone on the second floor heard it," Miranda told her.

"I was walking with Wyatt, so I missed it. But Julianne filled me in." She looked at Lilly. "Shall I assume you and Uncle George heard it too?"

Lilly nodded glumly.

Delia sighed deeply. "I'm afraid they're in financial trouble. In fact, I'm wondering if they came out here expecting me to help them."

"Help them?" Miranda couldn't believe her ears. "Why on earth should you help them? After all they did to you? The way they treated you? They're lucky you even speak to them, let alone allow them to stay here."

"I don't know about that," Lilly added. "But I don't think parents should ever expect children to care for them. Of course, I never had children, so I don't suppose I should be one to talk. Although Wyatt does feel like a son to me. And I suppose if George and I were ever in need, Wyatt would want to help."

"It's not that I wouldn't want to help," Delia confessed. "Especially for the sake of my brother and sister, but I honestly don't know how I *could*. My father invested all he had in the ranch. Without Wyatt's help, we wouldn't even be able to hire the hands we've been needing. I believe that someday the ranch will make money. But I'm in no position to help my stepfather out of whatever financial mess he's gotten into."

"And no one should expect you to." Lilly patted Delia's shoulder.

Miranda set the wedding photograph back on the table and shook her head. "I feel like my tea party turned into a big fat mess. And on the day before your wedding too, Delia. I'm sorry."

Delia grasped Miranda's hand. "It was a lovely tea party, and none of this is your fault. Please, don't give it another thought." She stood. "And I should check on Julianne and Julius. I made a deal with them. If they did my garden chores for me, I'd take them up to Green Lake for a swim. Hopefully I won't get in trouble with their parents for that."

Miranda grinned. "Well, at least they shouldn't come home dirty. You should've heard your mother railing at them when they came into the house. You'd think they'd been out playing tag in the pigpen."

They all laughed, and Miranda felt better. Maybe the tea party wasn't a complete failure after all. Still, a finishing school might be a good idea. That is, if she couldn't get herself engaged before it was too late. Hopefully Jackson would come to his senses at the wedding tomorrow. Her plan was that her pretty gown and hair piled high would firmly turn his head. And that he'd change his plans about mining gold in Alaska and beg her to become his wife.

11

DELIA GOT UP EXTRA EARLY ON HER WEDDING DAY. NOT BECAUSE there was so much be done. In fact, as Ginger shooed her from the kitchen, it seemed everything was fairly well in hand for today's festivities.

"Might I beg a cup of coffee before I'm completely banished?" Delia asked Ginger. "I'll take it to the front porch and promise to remain out from under foot."

Ginger grinned. "Just like your daddy used to do."

"What's that?" Delia puzzled as she backed up to the door. "Get under your feet in here?"

"No, silly girl. He used to take his cup of coffee out to the front porch early in the morning." Ginger sighed as she filled a cup. "I sure miss that." She handed the steaming cup and saucer to Delia. "But I meant what I said, you are not to step foot in this kitchen. Rosie and Daisy and me got it all figured out. And Rosie's girls will be here in time to serve food up after the wedding."

"And you won't get so busy you'll forget to come to my wedding?"

"I wouldn't miss it for nothing. Already got my good Sunday

dress pressed and ready. Don't you worry, I'll be there with bells on." Ginger nudged Delia closer to the door.

"Me too," Daisy echoed. "We're all going to town in Rosie's wagon. And we'll slip out ahead of everyone else, and get back here in time to get the food ready."

"And my girls will already be here setting up," Rosie assured Delia.

"So don't you worry about nothing, ya hear?" Ginger closed the door behind Delia. "You just enjoy your wedding day."

As Delia went out to the front porch, she felt almost lightheaded. Was it really her wedding day? With all their guests and so much going on, topped by the troubles with her mother and Jefferson, well, she'd been somewhat distracted. She eased herself onto a rocker with a deep sigh. Dawn was just breaking on her wedding day. She wondered what Wyatt was doing. Probably chores. He usually got up before everyone else. She sipped the hot coffee and leaned back. The cool calm quiet of morning felt soothing.

"Excuse me?"

Delia looked up to see Wyatt's aunt standing in the doorway. "Good morning, Aunt Lilly." She smiled. "You're up bright and early."

"So are you." Lilly stepped out onto the porch. "Mind if I join you?"

"Not at all. Would you like a cup of coffee?"

"No, thank you. Too early for that for me." Lilly took the other rocker.

"Did you sleep well?" Delia peered curiously at Lilly. Her brow was creased as if she was troubled.

"Oh, yes. The bed in your guest room is very nice. Thank you."

"And George is well?"

"Oh, yes. He's enjoying his visit so much. He slept like a baby last night."

"I'm glad to hear that."

"I was thinking about something." Lilly's tone sounded serious. "I don't want to intrude, but I'm concerned for your family, dear."

"Oh? Because of what happened at the tea party?"

"Well, yes. And your stepfather's behavior after dinner last night."

Delia hated to remember the little scene Jefferson had created. Challenging Wyatt in front of everyone, acting as if Wyatt was usurping some sort of power of Delia by marrying her and helping to manage the ranch. Fortunately, Wyatt had been a perfect gentleman. "I apologize on my stepfather's behalf," Delia said quietly. "He can be very rude." Now, that was an understatement!

"Oh, it's not the man's bad manners that concern me, Delia. It's just that I have a bad feeling. George does too. We both suspect that Mr. Blackstone is here for the wrong reasons. We began to wonder about that when we first met him on the train. But now we're even more worried. We fear he intends to take advantage of you and Wyatt. You're both so generous and kindhearted. Well, George thinks your stepfather will ride roughshod over Wyatt and you after you return from your honeymoon."

"Well, I wouldn't disagree that my stepfather most likely will try to take advantage, but the plan was for them to leave right after the wedding. Like you and Uncle George plan to do."

"Yes, but I spoke to George about this very thing last night. He is certain that your family has no intention of leaving next week. He suspects they don't plan to go home at all."

Delia cringed to remember those trunks of clothing. "This thought has occurred to me as well."

"So, although George needs to get back to Philadelphia to manage the boot factory, I suggested that I might stay on a while longer here. That is, if it won't be a burden to you."

Delia reached for Aunt Lilly's hand. "I would love for you to stay on. As long as you like. I love having you around."

"Oh, good." Lilly looked relieved. "Perhaps I can help encourage your family to seek other living arrangements. It does seem unfair for them to foist themselves on you and Wyatt."

Delia couldn't bear to imagine her family taking up permanent residence on the ranch. It would be terrible! And poor Wyatt would probably forget his manners after a while. For that matter, she would too! But then there were the children to consider. "Oh, dear," she muttered. "The whole thing has the makings of a mess."

"Yes, that was our thinking."

"I'm sure Wyatt will appreciate you being around to help."

"Perhaps I can be of help with young Miranda as well. And if we hear something from my friend Millie, I might even accompany your dear girl back East."

"You would do that?" Delia was so pleased to hear this, she felt close to tears. "I'm very worried about Miranda. She's still so young. Sometimes she seems mature…but sometimes, well, it's hard to say."

"Well, I feel certain there's a strong young woman underneath all that uncertainty. But she's been through a lot of losses. It's taken a toll."

Delia nodded. "I agree. That's why I try to be patient with her."

"I know you do."

Delia heard voices in the house. "Sounds like others are awake." As they both stood up, Delia reached for Lilly's hand. "Thank you for your help. It's such a comfort to know you'll be around for a while longer. I know Wyatt will be happy to hear it too. He just mentioned how he's been so busy with chores and the men visitors that he hasn't gotten much time with his favorite aunt."

"And I hope I haven't troubled you with any of this. I hope you and Wyatt have a perfectly lovely wedding day. And a relaxing, worry-free honeymoon trip."

"Speaking of not worrying, I'd like to ask you a favor." Delia glanced around to be sure no one was listening. "Since you'll be here, I would greatly appreciate it if you could act as head of the household while we're gone." She sighed. "My family shouldn't be here for much longer, but I can just imagine how my stepfather might behave in my absence. Ginger probably wouldn't put up with it, but I'm afraid poor Miranda might be overwhelmed by him."

"I'd be happy to help." Lilly squeezed her hand.

"I'll let Miranda and Ginger know you'll be managing things. As usual, Caleb and Enoch will see to the rest of the ranch. They could easily put my stepfather in his place if he oversteps his boundaries."

"I'm sure they could." She chuckled.

"Aha, there's my bride." Wyatt came out onto the porch with Uncle George right behind him. "We were just about to get some breakfast. You ladies care to join us?"

Delia eagerly grasped his arm. "Thank you! We'd love to." As they went into the dining room together, Delia was relieved to see that her mother and Jefferson had not yet come down. She knew that Lilly's instincts were right when it came to her parents. And having Lilly stay on throughout next week was a huge comfort.

Miranda had attended a few weddings, including her own mother's with Winston, but she'd never stood by the bride before. And when it was all said and done, she felt Delia and Wyatt's ceremony was the most beautiful thing she'd ever witnessed. Delia in her lovely white lace and satin gown looked radiant, and Wyatt in his black suit was handsomer than ever. But it was the look in their eyes, as they exchanged their vows, that she felt she would remember forever. True love!

As she followed the happy bride and groom down the aisle of the church, she imagined that her own wedding (hopefully in the not-too-distant future) would be equally wonderful. And spotting Jackson seated with his parents, she made sure to catch his eye with a long, sweet look…and hoped he got her meaning.

Back at the ranch, there was eating and speeches and socializing and finally the four-piece band began to warm up. She'd purposely avoided Jackson during this time, hoping that he would watch her flitting from table to table, greeting friends and acting like a social butterfly. She wanted him to see her in her pretty dress with her hair piled high. She wanted him to long to be with her but to remain just out of his reach.

Finally, she came to his table, where he was sitting with his family and friends. First she greeted his parents, taking time to inquire as to their health and making pleasant small talk, before she turning her attention to their son.

"And it's good to see you too," she said politely to Jackson. "I hope you're enjoying the festivities."

"Yeah, quite the shindig." His smile looked nervous. "And good food too."

"I'm glad you're enjoying yourself." She dipped her head and hurried on her way. Hopefully, he would take a hint and follow. She went around a few more tables, greeting a few others then finally planted herself in the shade of the big willow tree, not far from the bandstand and dance floor.

Just as expected, it didn't take long for Jackson to come over and join her. Now that they were alone, he seemed nervous. She imagined it was because he was mesmerized by her appearance. In fact, he seemed to be actually stumbling over his words as he attempted some small talk. But she liked seeing him uneasy. It seemed to give her the upper hand.

"I meant to say something, uh, before. But you sure do look, uh, pretty. And grown up too. Even more than usual." He reached for his collar, running a finger around it as if it were too tight. "That was a real nice wedding."

"Wyatt and Delia seemed so in love. Didn't you think so?" She pointed toward the dance floor where a waltz was playing. "And look, there they are dancing their first dance as man and wife together. They look so happy."

He nodded. "Yeah, they do seem happy enough."

"It must be so sweet to be in love." She sighed as she watched the newlyweds dance the waltz. Now she turned back to Jackson and looked directly into his eyes. "I can almost imagine how wonderful it would feel to be them. So exciting and exhilarating—think of it—they're starting out a new life together. Can you imagine how that must feel?"

"Well, I don't know if I can imagine *that.* Like I told you, Miranda, I'm looking forward to Alaska right now. That feels mighty exhilarating and exciting to me."

Miranda suppressed the urge to stomp off. Was that all he could think about? Stupid Alaska and dumb old gold?

"Are you still going to write to me up there?" He looked genuinely hopeful.

"Well, now, I don't know. I'm not so sure you'd really care one way or another—whether I did or I didn't." She glanced away for some sort of distraction. "Seems to me gold is more important to you than little old me."

"You can't compare gold to...well, to a person, Miranda. A fellow goes looking for gold so as he can have a better life—you know, later on with someone special."

"Really? That's why you're looking for gold? To have a better life later on with someone special?" She wanted to ask him what "later on" meant, exactly.

"I reckon that's a part of it." His eyes darted sideways as he fiddled with his string tie, and nothing about his demeanor felt very encouraging.

"Well, you don't seem very sure about it." She made an exasperated sigh. "Now, if you'll excuse me." And without another word, she turned and rushed off. Was that the best Jackson could do? What happened to how smooth he'd talked to her the other night? Had he just been leading her on? Maybe he needed something to light a fire underneath his feet. How about some competition?

Just then, Miranda spotted one of the hands Wyatt had recently hired. He was a nice enough fellow, well spoken and polite, but not as good looking or interesting as Jackson. Still, young Rowdie might be useful for getting Jackson's attention.

She strolled over to the lanky lad, flashing the biggest smile he'd seen from her since he'd joined up with the Double W. "Hello there, Rowdie. Are you enjoying yourself?"

"I sure am, Miss Williams. Good food and everyone's having a good time."

"And good musicians too." She paused as Wyatt and Delia finished their dance, watching as they bowed to the crowd's enthused applause. "Hopefully the band will play some livelier numbers now."

"Yeah." He nodded eagerly.

"Because you look like a fellow who knows how to dance."

He blinked. "Why, yes, Miss Williams. I do enjoy a good dance."

"You don't have to call me Miss Williams." She gave him a flirty flicker of her eyelashes. "Not if you plan to dance with me, that is. In that case, you must call me Miranda."

"All right then, *Miranda.* Would you care to dance?" He nodded to where the dance caller was announcing a Virginia reel.

"I'd love to, thank you." She hooked her arm into his and, without checking to ensure Jackson was watching—because she felt certain he was—she let Rowdie lead her to the center of the dance floor. And to her surprise, he really was a good dancer. And, sure, he wasn't the kind of guy she'd ever be seriously interested in, but he sure knew how to twirl a girl. Hopefully Jackson was paying attention!

Delia couldn't remember a happier day, or a prouder moment than when Uncle Enoch walked her down the church aisle. But the best part of everything was seeing Wyatt's whole face light up as he took her hand in his...and the sincerity in his voice as he repeated his wedding vows. And then dancing the first dance and how the crowd all cheered and applauded when they finished. Married to the one she loved, surrounded by friends and family...well, it was a day she would never forget.

The only fly in the ointment throughout the festivities was the overall awkwardness with her parents. Fortunately, she'd managed to mostly avoid Jefferson and, based on what Caleb had just hinted at, Jefferson might be three sheets to the wind by this evening. Delia was glad that she and Wyatt would miss that. And now that the afternoon was wearing thin, although no guests had yet departed and the younger ones were really whooping it up, Delia felt weary and ready to call it a day.

"How about we make our departure?" Wyatt quietly suggested as they watched a group of younger folks dancing with vim and vigor.

She nodded. "I'd like that." She pointed out to where Julianne was happily dancing with an energetic young man. "But first tell me— who is my little sister's dance partner? I noticed you chatting with him earlier, but I don't recall meeting him. And it seems Julianne is rather infatuated with him."

"That's your attorney's son."

"Orville Stanfield has a boy?"

"That's right. Orville introduced me to young Levi. He's seventeen."

"Miranda's age? He seems younger." Delia glanced over to where Miranda and Jackson seemed deep in conversation under the aspens. Hopefully the young man wasn't proposing marriage. Somehow, she didn't think so. Miranda had already hinted her disappointment in Jackson to Delia. But things could change.

"Levi looks young to me too, but I'll tell you that boy has a good head on his shoulder. He's been away at school for several years. Orville said Levi's top of his class and plans to study law."

"Well, good for him." Delia smiled. "Julianne might only be twelve, but it seems she has good taste in boys."

"Ready to make our exit?" he asked hopefully. "I already had Rowdie load your valise and trunk in the carriage."

"Yes, I'm ready to go," she eagerly agreed. "I'll just go change into traveling clothes and we can tell everyone goodbye."

"I'll meet you on the front porch."

As Delia hurried inside, she felt a rush of happy nerves—this was truly the beginning of a brand-new life. And she was ready for it!

12

As Delia went through the front room, Aunt Lilly joined her. "I'm guessing that you and Wyatt are about to make your getaway."

Delia smiled shyly. "Yes, we're ready to call it a day and slip out."

"Would you like help changing?"

"I'd appreciate that. This gown has about a hundred buttons. I'm sure it took Miranda half an hour to fasten it all up, but then she was all thumbs this morning."

"Well, I'm very adept at buttons." Lilly chuckled as she followed Delia up the stairs, but when they reached the second floor, they were met by Delia's mother.

"Are you changing to leave—already?" she asked with a creased brow.

"Yes." Delia opened the door to her room. "Aunt Lilly is helping me."

"I'd like to help too," Jane insisted. "After all, I am your mother, Delia."

"Of course, come in." Delia held the door wide. "Although I don't know that I need two attendants, you're welcome to join us."

"I had really hoped to talk to you before you go, Delia." Her tone sounded tense as she closed the door behind them. "In private."

"Anything you say to me is safe with Aunt Lilly," Delia told her. "She is a trusted member of our family."

"If you wish to be alone, I can—"

"I want you to stay," Delia told Lilly. "Please."

Lilly simply nodded and began to unbutton the back of the wedding gown.

"Really, Mother, you can speak freely in front of Aunt Lilly. There's nothing she doesn't already know about our family…and our troubles."

"Yes, I suppose that may be somewhat true, but she doesn't know *everything*." Delia's mother sat in the chair by the window with a long weary sounding sigh.

"I probably know more than you realize," Lilly said in a kind tone.

"Fine." Jane sounded exasperated now. "Well, I know you expected that our visit would only be for the wedding, Delia. But if you don't mind, we would like to extend it some."

"Extend it?" Delia glanced at her mother.

"Yes, well, the children…they are enjoying themselves so."

"But aren't you and your husband fearful of their safety?" Delia knew she was being catty, but she couldn't help herself.

"I realize we overreacted yesterday. Julianne and Julius have assured me they were in no real danger." Jane picked at the lace trim of her gown, as if she didn't want to look up. "And the truth is, Delia, we have no place else to go for the time being. But if you want to throw us out, I will understand. You have every right to send us packing. But Jefferson begged me to ask you if we could extend our visit."

"How long would you extend it?" Delia studied her mother, whose head was still downward. "A few days?"

"I really don't know."

"Oh. What about your return train tickets?" Delia asked. "Didn't you book a date?"

Jane looked up with moist eyes. "Your father—I mean, stepfather—didn't get return tickets. To be honest, the fare for the return is used up. The truth is that we are completely out of money. We have lost our home—and everything." And now she burst into tears.

Wearing only her chemise and petticoat, Delia went over to hug her mother. "I'm sorry to hear this, Mother. But I am not surprised."

"Not surprised?" she blinked with tears running down her cheeks.

"I had, uh, heard rumors. But I'd hoped it wasn't true."

"It is true. And I don't know what will become of us. And the children—oh, Delia—can you imagine how this is going to hurt them?"

Delia couldn't. "I really don't know what to say, except that I am truly sorry. And, yes, you can remain here while Wyatt and I are on our wedding trip. Somehow we will try to sort this all out when we return."

"Oh, thank you, Delia. Thank you! You're so generous and kind." She hugged her tightly. "I thought you would be—but Jefferson was sure you'd throw us out."

Delia couldn't admit that she'd like to throw Jefferson out, but instead she just hugged her mother again. "I hope you'll enjoy your stay while I'm gone." She glanced at Lilly, who was now holding up her traveling gown. "And I'd like you to understand that we are leaving Aunt Lilly in charge of the house. If you have any questions, please, refer them to her."

"Lilly is in charge?" Jane sounded indignant. "But I thought she and George were taking the train back to Phila—"

"Aunt Lilly, like you, is extending her visit." Delia went over to Lilly, accepting her help as she slipped the dark green gown over her head.

"Oh? I didn't know." Jane scowled. "I would've been glad to take charge of your lovely house, Delia. After all, I *am* your mother."

"I appreciate that, and I'm sure if Aunt Lilly needs any help, she will ask you."

"Yes, of course." Lilly nodded.

Delia turned back to her mother. "And since you'll be staying longer, perhaps Julius and Julianne could give a hand with the chores I usually perform. I'm sure Ginger would appreciate help gathering eggs and tending the garden and such."

"Perhaps you'd like me to feed the pigs," Jane said with sharp sarcasm.

"Enoch usually takes care of that." Delia exchanged a glance with Lilly, wishing they could redirect this conversation. "I'm so relieved you'll be here to get Miranda in a better frame of mind toward school. She does need some encouragement."

"Yes, perhaps I'll hear from Millie this week. Wouldn't it be wonderful if Miranda could enroll in finishing school?"

"I'm praying that whatever is best for her will fall into place." Delia buttoned her cuffs. "But whether it's university or finishing school, it would be nice if you and Miranda could travel back to Philadelphia together."

"We will plan on it." Lilly handed Delia her gloves.

"Unless that silly girl gets married first." Delia's mother stood abruptly. "If Miranda has her way, the miner's son will be down on one knee before the night is over. Then she'll never go back East to any sort of school. Maybe that would be for the best." Now she was pacing back and forth, clearly agitated.

"And that would be her decision." Delia tugged on a glove. "I just hope and pray she makes the right one."

Lilly handed Delia her hat, helping to pin it just right and then stepping back to give an appreciative nod. "You look perfectly lovely, dear." She kissed Delia's cheek. "God bless you and Wyatt on your wedding trip."

"Yes, yes," Jane said quickly. "I do hope you have a good trip, dear." She kissed Delia's cheek too, but it somehow lacked the warmth of Lilly's kiss. "And I suppose we can finish discussing our business upon your return." She glanced at Lilly. "Maybe you and Miranda will be on your way to Philadelphia by then."

"Oh, I hope not." Delia glanced at Lilly. "I'd like more time with you before you leave, Aunt Lilly. And Miranda doesn't need to be at the university for two weeks, although I thought it wise to arrive ahead of time and get herself acclimated to the city."

"Don't you worry. I can stay here as long as I'm needed. George has given me his blessing."

Now Delia told them both goodbye and, greatly relieved to know Lilly would be here to manage things, made her way down the stairs. She had no idea how it might go between Lilly and her mother during her absence, but she felt certain Lilly was up to the task. And, as Delia saw Wyatt eagerly waiting on the front porch, she was determined not to give her mother or Aunt Lilly—or anyone back here on the ranch—a second thought.

13

By the time Jackson kissed Miranda goodnight, after the musicians had played the final number, she felt certain that he loved her and wanted her for his wife. Oh, he hadn't said as much, but she could feel it deep down inside of her. Dancing several times with Rowdie had done the trick. Jackson's jealousy had been properly stirred up, and he'd finally taken her aside and insisted she only dance with him for the remainder of the evening. She had gladly agreed.

As she got ready for bed, she realized that she no longer viewed Jackson as her get-out-of-school excuse. By now, she believed she truly loved him. More than ever, she wanted to be his wife. And she did not want him trekking off to the dangerous Alaskan wilds. When she climbed into bed, she felt almost certain that Jackson would show up at the ranch in the next day or two with a proper proposal of marriage. Even though Delia had promised to give her a bit more time, Miranda had made it clear to Jackson that it wouldn't be long before she would be shipped off to Philadelphia.

On Sunday morning, Miranda took extra care in dressing for church. She felt certain that since Jackson and his family were still in town, they would be there. But to her dismay none of the

O'Neil's were at church. She asked a mutual friend only to learn that they'd left to return to the mine. Still, she was determined not to be discouraged. Jackson loved her—she knew it. And in the next day or two, he would surely make an appearance.

For the next couple of days, Miranda tried to be cheerful and helpful around the house. Aunt Lilly was easy to get along with and seemed to appreciate Miranda's help with the chores Delia usually did. Besides that, Miranda spent time with Julianne and Julius, trying to play the big sister role. But by Tuesday evening, she was worried.

"Are you feeling well?" Aunt Lilly asked her as the two of them sat on the porch to enjoy the colorful sunset painting the sky. "You seemed very quiet at supper."

Miranda let out a long sad sigh. "It's because I'm worried about Jackson."

"Jackson?" Lilly frowned. "He hasn't left for Alaska yet, has he?"

"I don't know. He had originally planned to leave midweek. And tomorrow is midweek…so I really…I just don't know." She sniffed.

"And that's what's troubling you?"

"Yes. It is troubling. I honestly believed he'd come back to see me before running off to Alaska. That is, *if* he's going. And I'd really hoped he wasn't."

"I see."

Miranda turned to look Lilly. "I believe he loves me. And it seems that if he loves me, he wouldn't want to leave me like this. Does that make sense to you?"

Lilly slowly nodded then frowned. "It makes sense to me, but I'm a woman."

"Well, so am I."

"And what makes sense to a woman does not always make sense to a man."

Miranda let out another sigh as she remembered how Marcus had tricked her more than once. "Believe me, I know that. Some men cannot be trusted."

Lilly's brows arched. "You've had lots of experience?"

"Well, I wouldn't say that. But there was one fellow—someone I can't bear to think about, and I won't even mention his horrid name—but this monster lied and deceived and hurt me. He was a horrid, awful man. He hurt a lot of people. In fact, he was a murderer." She shuddered to think of how she'd once trusted him.

"Oh, dear. I'm sorry."

"But Jackson is nothing like him."

"I don't know Jackson very well, but I do like him. He seems like a nice young man."

"Yes, he is. He's polite and considerate. He cares about my feelings and doesn't talk down to me. But I just don't understand why he hasn't come to see me."

"Maybe he's been busy."

"That's what worries me. If he's still going to Alaska, he probably is busy. And I can't bear to think that."

For a long moment neither of them spoke. Finally Aunt Lilly broke the silence. "Well, if it turns out that Jackson is going to Alaska, what does that mean for you, Miranda?"

"I don't know." Her shoulders slumped, and she tried to blink back tears.

"Do you love him?"

She turned to look at Lilly, somehow knowing she could trust her. "Yes, I do love him. At least I think I do. To be honest, I'm not an expert on these things. But the way I feel around him, the way I miss him, the way I can't imagine him being so far away for so long...well, it feels like I love him."

"And do you believe he loves you?"

"He hasn't said as much, but I really do think he does. I really thought he was going to come here and tell me that very thing."

"So, if you love him and he loves you, do you think your love would just up and vanish if Jackson did go to Alaska? That doesn't sound like a very sturdy sort of love."

Miranda considered this.

"And Jackson doesn't plan to stay permanently in Alaska, does he?"

"No. He just wants to make his fortune and come back."

"So what would be the harm if he went to Alaska and you went back East for some schooling? You could exchange letters. Writing to a person is a wonderful way to really get to know someone. Are you a good letter writer?"

"I haven't had much experience, but I think I could write good letters to Jackson. I even told him I would write to him, but that was before I decided I loved him and didn't want him to go at all."

"So now you wouldn't want to write to him?"

"No, I'd still want to write to him. Well, if he wanted to write to me." She frowned. "But if he can't at least come by here and tell me a decent goodbye...I don't know."

"Maybe he'll come tomorrow. After all, it is midweek. Maybe he's needed this time to really think about this thing."

"You mean he might've been deciding whether or not to go? Maybe he's had second thoughts about Alaska?"

"I don't know."

"That could be it." Miranda felt hopeful.

"I suppose time will tell. You know what I'd be doing if I were you?"

"No. Tell me," she said eagerly.

"I'd be praying about this. Love and marriage are big commitments. If I were you, I'd be asking God to guide me in this big decision. And to guide Jackson too. If you ask God, he will answer."

Miranda considered this. "So if I asked God to let me marry Jackson, you think he'd say yes?"

Lilly laughed. "I'm afraid that's not how God works. You have to ask God to lead you on the path that's right for you. Sometimes it's not that path we think we want. But ultimately, God's path is always the best one."

"Oh." Miranda wasn't sure about that, but she did like the idea that Jackson might've needed more time to think about his decision to go to Alaska. That seemed to lean in her favor. Whatever the case, she would find out soon—one way or another.

Wednesday came and went, and Jackson never showed. But Miranda thought perhaps this simply meant he'd changed his mind. She just couldn't imagine him taking off on his big trip without at least stopping by to say farewell.

"Did you see that you got a letter, Miss Miranda?" Ginger asked as they cleared off the supper dishes. "I slid it under your door this afternoon."

"A letter? Under my door? I haven't been in my room since this morning."

"Oh, well, it should still be up there."

"From Delia? She said she might send a card from Denver."

"I didn't mean to snoop but I noticed it was from Jackson O'Neil and—"

"Jackson?" Miranda clumsily set the stack of plates by the sink. "I have to see it."

Ginger stopped the teetering pile from falling. "By all means. Go see it."

Miranda hurried up the stairs and to her room, instantly spotting the white envelope on the floor. She eagerly tore it open and hungrily read.

Tuesday Morning

Dearest Miranda,

I had really hoped to see you before leaving for Alaska, but it looks like that can't happen now. So I hope this letter will make up for it. I am all packed and ready to go and, like I keep telling you, I still believe that I need to go have this adventure. On this adventure, I hope to make my fortune or at least enough to come back and invest into my family's mine since it's in need of improvements.

I know you are probably angry at me for leaving like this without talking to you again, but it cannot be helped. If I don't leave on today's train, I will miss the boat out of San Francisco. Already I'm getting a late start in the season, but I'm eager to go. I hope you will enjoy your adventure back East. I also hope you will write to me about all you see and do there.

I can't make you any promises just yet, Miranda. Except that I will say you are the finest girl I have ever known. And the prettiest one too! You looked so beautiful at Delia's wedding that I almost couldn't breathe for a little bit. I love how your hair shines like polished copper in the sun, and how your eyes are the same color as the summer skies. You have the sweetest smile, and your laughter always makes my heart happy. When I saw you dancing with Rowdie the other day, I thought I was going to explode. I'm glad I didn't.

I hope you will be patient with me and that, in time, you will forgive me for not saying goodbye in person. And I really do hope you will write to me at the Juneau Post Office address I gave you. I know I'm not much of a letter writer, but I promise I will do my best.

Yours Very Truly,
Jackson Kelly O'Neil

Part of her was angry and wanted to tear the letter to shreds. But a bigger part of her held the dear note close to her heart and then read it again. More slowly this time. Maybe Jackson hadn't come right out and proclaimed his love for her or proposed marriage, but he sure said a lot of really sweet things. Still, he was gone. On yesterday's train. Probably in San Francisco by now.

She sat down and read the letter one more time. Some might accuse her of reading between the lines now, but this time she knew that he did love her—she had no doubt. And just because he'd gone to Alaska didn't mean otherwise. Jackson had simply set off to find his fortune so that he could come back here and marry her! Just like Wyatt did for Delia. And like her stepfather had done with Miranda's mother. Jackson was a good man, and he would do the same. She just knew it.

Her only problem now was that she had no excuse not to go back East for her schooling, and she might as well accept it. But maybe Jackson would get lucky and find his fortune quickly. Then she could quit the stupid university and come home and marry him. Maybe by Christmas. Or even if it took a whole year...she was willing to wait for him. Wasn't she? Really, it wasn't so terrible. Then why was she crying?

By the next day, Miranda was resolved to her fate. She knew Delia would not back down from fulfilling the stipulations in her father's will now that it was obvious Miranda would not be getting married. And so after lunch, Miranda went up to her room and began to meticulously pack her trunk. She was just placing the wedding photo of Mother and Winston inside, since Delia had said she could take it, when someone tapped on her door.

"Miranda?" Lilly called sweetly. "I have some news for you."

Miranda opened the door, momentarily hoping that the letter from Jackson had gotten it all wrong and that he was actually waiting downstairs for her right now. "What?" she asked brightly.

Lilly waved what looked like a telegram. "Good news."

"From Jackson?" Miranda reached for the paper.

"No, it's from my friend Millie. She says the finishing school has unexpected openings from two sisters who were supposed to attend this fall. And based on my recommendation of you, she submitted your name for admission, and she is happy to report you have been accepted. Isn't that wonderful?"

Miranda slowly nodded, glumly handing the paper back. "Yes, I suppose so."

"Oh?" Lilly frowned. "Does this mean you'd prefer to go to the university after all?"

"No, that's not it. I guess I just hoped the telegram was from Jackson. You know, saying he'd changed his mind."

"Oh, dear. Hope springs eternal." She patted Miranda's shoulder. "But isn't this good news? I know you were dreading the university. And the training you get from the finishing school will be useful if you and Jackson eventually do marry. Wouldn't he be proud to have a wife who's been educated with so many practical skills?"

She brightened. "Yes, I think Jackson would approve."

"Well, Wyatt and Delia are coming home on the Friday train. I think we should stay throughout the weekend and take the Monday train East. That will get us back to Philadelphia with a bit of time to spare before your classes start up. How does that sound?"

"Will I just be at the school while I'm waiting for the classes to begin?"

"No, you'll stay with Uncle George and me, of course. I will show you the sights of Philadelphia. Goodness, there's so much to see and do, so much of our country's history is there. Well, I don't know if we'll even have time for everything."

"Thank you." Miranda smiled. "That does sound nice."

"And you can spend holidays with us too," Lilly continued. "Uncle George and I will become your family, Miranda. That is, if you'll have us."

Miranda threw her arms around Lilly. "I would absolutely love that. Thank you so much!"

After Lilly left, Miranda closed her partially packed trunk and sat down to write Jackson a letter that she would send to him care of the Post Office in Juneau. Instead of lamenting over the fact that he'd left without a proper farewell, she told him of her decision to go back East with "Aunt Lilly." That was what she intended to call the kind woman from now on. She also told him about how Aunt Lilly was going to show her Philadelphia, and she promised to write Jackson about the interesting things she saw. Finally she told him the "good news" about getting into finishing school where she would learn practical things that would help her to someday run her own household and be a good wife. Hopefully he'd appreciate that. And hopefully he'd strike it rich quickly and perhaps they would be reunited before the year's end. That was what she was praying for!

14

Although Delia was happy to come home to the Double W after their delightful wedding trip, she didn't know quite what to expect. Oh, she knew her parents and siblings would still be there. And Aunt Lilly too. Hopefully Jefferson hadn't made things too miserable for anyone. The biggest question on her mind was Miranda.

"Do you think there's any chance that Miranda eloped with Jackson while we were gone?" Delia asked Wyatt as he helped her down from the wagon.

He laughed. "Not by the looks of it." He nodded toward the house. "There she is now."

"Oh, good." Delia reached for her satchel as Wyatt unloaded the bigger pieces. "Hopefully, she didn't get him to propose marriage."

"If you ask me, that young man was bound and determined to get himself up to Alaska." Wyatt set a valise on the ground. "He cornered me during our wedding celebration several times to talk about it."

"Welcome home," Miranda called out cheerfully.

"Thank you." Delia hurried over to embrace her. "I'm so glad you're still here."

"Why wouldn't I be?" Miranda frowned.

"Well, I noticed how enchanted Jackson was last Saturday. I thought perhaps...." Miranda shrugged.

"Oh, well, I understand." Miranda held her head high. "Jackson needed to go to Alaska. He's doing it for us."

"For us?"

"For him and me. He'll make his fortune then come back for me."

"Oh?"

"Yes. He wrote me a letter and said as much." She grinned. "Or nearly. I suppose I might've read some of it between the lines. But I do believe he loves me, Delia."

Delia smiled as she touched Miranda's cheek. "And why not? You're very loveable."

Miranda laughed as they walked up to the porch. "Not always."

"So tell me, how goes it here?" Delia asked quietly. "Has my stepfather behaved himself?"

Miranda scowled. "Depends on what you mean. According to Uncle Enoch, he's been overly nosy about the ranch, acting like he has a right to know everything."

"Oh, dear. Sounds like he's made a nuisance of himself." She grimaced. "And my mother?"

"She's mostly stayed in her room. I think something's wrong with her, Miranda. I tried to get her to join Aunt Lilly and me for tea a couple of times, but she always has a headache. And she locks her door. Do you think it's because she's sad?"

"No doubt." Miranda paused on the porch. "And the twins?"

"They've been running wild." Miranda laughed. "Your parents don't even seem to care anymore. Julianne's been riding Dolly a lot. And Julius acts like he's a real ranch hand now."

"Well, I like the sound of that." Delia looked intently at Miranda. "And how about you? Are you all ready to go to university?"

"That's the best news." Miranda beamed as she explained that she had been accepted into finishing school. "Aunt Lilly is taking me with her. And I'll stay at their house until school starts. She's going to show me Philadelphia and everything."

"Oh, Miranda, that's wonderful."

"We got our train tickets and will leave on Friday."

Delia grasped Miranda's hand as they went inside. "I'm very proud of you," she said quietly. "I think you've grown up a lot in the last week."

"Aunt Lilly has helped a lot."

"And there she is! Hello, Aunt Lilly," Delia called out as Lilly descended the stairs.

"Welcome home!" Lilly came over to greet Delia. "Did you have an enjoyable trip?"

"Yes. Everything was wonderful." Delia looked around. "But I'm so glad to be home."

Lilly looked uneasy. "May I have a word with you? In the parlor?"

"Yes, of course." Delia frowned. "Is something wrong?"

"Not really." Lilly lowered her voice. "It's about your mother."

"Oh?"

"I'll take your satchel upstairs," Miranda offered with a knowing look.

Delia followed Lilly into the parlor then closed the doors. She knew this needed to be a private conversation. "What is it?" she asked. "Miranda hinted that my mother's been very unhappy."

"Yes. I can understand that. Her life has been turned upside down. But I reminded her, just a couple of days ago, that you and Wyatt would be home today. I suggested she might want to start moving their things into the room you'd been using. Ginger has already gotten your things ready to move into the master bedroom. We wanted to surprise you by having it all ready for your homecoming."

"Thank you so much." Delia nodded. "Wyatt and I look forward to having the master bedroom."

"Of course." Lilly pursed her lips. "Unfortunately, your mother has not packed nor moved a single thing from that room. So I asked her again this morning, and she complained of a headache. That's when Ginger and I offered to move their belongings for them. But she wouldn't hear of it. Now she won't even allow us into the room."

"Oh, dear."

"I don't know what to do. It doesn't seem right for them to force you out while they commandeer your room. I saw the room you'd been using, and it's the smallest one up there. In fact, I was just about to move myself into that room. At least you and Wyatt could have the room I'm using, it's a nice room and I don't mind—"

"No, no. I don't want you to do that."

"Miranda even suggested they take her room since she and I will be leaving in a couple of days."

Delia considered the situation. Part of her felt inhospitable to insist her parents relocate to another room, and yet they were already overstaying their welcome. And who knew how much longer they would stay. "I would like to discuss this with Wyatt, Aunt Lilly. Thank you for bringing it to my attention. I'm sorry my mother was being so difficult."

"I'm sorry too." Lilly shook her head.

As they exited the parlor, Wyatt and Caleb were just bringing a trunk into the house. "Please, leave that down here for the time being," Delia told them. "Leave everything down here until we figure things out." She waved Wyatt into the parlor and quickly explained the situation.

"This is a conundrum." He scratched his head. "What would you like to do, Delia? This is your house."

"This is *our* house."

He smiled. "What would *we* like to do?"

"I, for one, would like the master bedroom for us," she declared.

He nodded. "I concur."

"But it sounds like my mother is not cooperating."

"Maybe it's time I stepped in."

Delia blinked. "Really? Do you honestly want to confront her on this? She might break into tears or claim she's got a horrible headache. My mother is good at making excuses when she wants to get her way."

"Perhaps I should talk to Jefferson instead."

Delia frowned. "I don't know. He can be just as bad."

"Don't worry, darling." He pecked her on the cheek. "If I can wrestle steers, it seems I should be able to handle him."

"Well, it can't hurt to try."

"Which room would you prefer they relocate to?"

She considered this. "Well, I'd rather not put Aunt Lilly or Miranda out of their rooms, so I think the little spare room I'd been occupying will be just fine for now."

He chuckled. "If they don't like that, they could always go elsewhere."

She sighed sadly. If only that were true. She glanced up the stairs. "And I think while you speak to Jefferson, I should at least attempt to speak to my mother. Hopefully she will let me in."

As they parted ways, Delia silently prayed that she'd say the right words to her mother. She didn't want to be cruel, but she knew she needed to be firm. This was probably the best time to draw a line. Her parents needed to respect that this was her home—hers and Wyatt's. If they wanted to remain here, it would have to be on her and Wyatt's terms.

Realizing it wouldn't hurt to have backup, Delia went in to say hello to Ginger then quickly explained her mission. "If you could just help me get started on moving their things moved out, I think it might go easier."

"Come on, Daisy," Ginger said. "Let's get them squatters outta there."

The two women followed her upstairs, but first Delia stopped to retrieve a spare key from her jewelry box. Then she knocked on the master bedroom door, and not surprisingly no one answered.

"Mother, it's me," she called out in a cheerful tone. "Wyatt and I are home now. I'd like to talk to you." Still no answer, so she knocked again, calling out in a louder voice. "Please, let me in."

"I have a headache," Jane moaned. "I can't make it to the door."

Ginger rolled her eyes, nudging Delia to keep going.

Delia tried the door, but found it locked. So without any verbal warning to her mother, she slipped in the key and opened the door wide. Her mother was not in bed, but sitting in the easy chair by the window. Still wearing her dressing gown, her hair looked as if it hadn't been brushed in days. On the table by the chair was what looked like a luncheon tray.

"I hear you haven't been feeling well." Delia studied her mother carefully. Although disheveled, she had color in her cheeks and her eyes sparked with anger.

"Looks like you felt good enough to eat your lunch." Ginger picked up the emptied dishes, putting them on the tray and handing it to Daisy.

"What are you doing in here?" Mother growled.

"We just want to help. I can understand your inability to pack up your things while you're under the weather, so you just sit there and we will take care of—"

"Don't touch my things." Mother stood, glaring at Ginger, who was gathering up an armful of clothes that were heaped on the other easy chair.

"We're simply moving them to another room, Mother." Delia opened one of the trunks, tossing some loose items into it. "Naturally, Wyatt and I will be occupying this room. It is the master bedroom, and we are the masters of this house. Surely, you understand."

"You are throwing your mother and father out—"

"We are only moving you to another room," Delia said firmly. "When Wyatt invited you to visit, he never expected you to remain this long. I gave up my room for you, but now that my husband is living in the house, I want it back." She tossed some shoes into the trunk and shook her head at how messy her mother had allowed this lovely room to become. Even the flowers Delia had arranged before the wedding now looked sad, with wilted blooms and petals covering the table. "As I mentioned, we do not have maid service here, Mother. You might want to take more care in the room you're moving into since it's smaller and does not have as many places to toss your things."

Ginger snickered as she tossed a shawl on top the trunk. "Come here, Daisy, let's get this trunk moved to the other room."

"Thank you." Delia watched as they lifted the trunk.

"And how about we set your things in the hallway, Miss Delia? Just for the time being," Ginger called out as they headed for the door. "Because this room's gonna need a good turning over and airing out before it'll be fit for you and Mister Wyatt to occupy."

"Well, I never!" Mother turned her back to Delia, facing the window with arms folded across her front in a defiant stance.

"I'm sorry if this offends you, Mother." Delia went over to stand by her. "And I know you're upset. But I suspect you are more disturbed by the fact that your husband has failed to provide for you in the manner you're accustomed to than by simply changing rooms."

"I am disturbed to be treated in such a manner. I thought I was a guest in my daughter's home."

"You *are* a guest. But as the hostess and lady of the house, I see the need to move you to another room. As a guest, I would think you would understand."

"Humph."

"Please, Mother." Delia softened her tone. "Wouldn't it be better to simply make the best of it and try to—"

"Make the best of it?" She whirled around with fire in her blue eyes. "As you so kindly pointed out, we are penniless—and you suggest I make the best of it?"

"Your financial situation doesn't have to be permanent. Your husband isn't too old to get some kind of work."

"Jefferson, work?" She laughed in that sarcastic way that always irritated Delia. "He has never held a job. He doesn't even know how to *work*. What on earth would he do?"

"Well, there's lots of work around here. That is, if he's willing to get his hands dirty. And, frankly, Mother, if he and you and the twins plan to remain here, I will have to insist that you all pitch in. Just like Wyatt and I do. Just because we own this ranch and manage our employees, we don't use it as an excuse to be lazy. In fact, I venture to say we often work just as hard as our employees." She scooped up a load of clothes that appeared to need laundering, but tossed them into another trunk anyway.

"Can you imagine Jefferson out there plowing a field or slopping hogs?"

Delia shrugged. "Why not? Might be good for him. And for you too. Hard work never hurt anyone." She removed clothes from the wardrobe, laying them into the trunk.

"It's just not fair." Jane actually whimpered now.

Delia stood, locking eyes with her mother. *"Fair?* How do you determine what is or isn't fair? Was it fair that you kept me from knowing that my real father lived out here in Colorado? Was it fair that someone shot him before I got the chance to meet him? Was it fair the way you and Jefferson disowned me? How do you describe fair, Mother? I'd really like to know."

Jane's hands curled into fists. "It's not fair that we lived so comfortably for so many years, Delia. And now we are destitute. That's what's not fair!"

"Fair?" Delia questioned again.

"How are supposed to live, Delia? I just don't understand how this all happened. How we went from there…to here. How did it happen?"

Delia shrugged as she tossed Jefferson's boots into an opened trunk. "I think I know how it happened."

"Really?" She scowled. "How would you possibly?"

"Are you saying you were unaware of how wastefully you lived?

You spent money on clothes and things to impress your friends. And your husband probably spent even more, trying to keep up with his gentlemen friends at his club, which was probably expensive. And were you unaware that he bet on horses? Were you really blind to all those things?"

She shrugged and turned away.

"You know, I think there could be a hidden blessing in all this." Delia heaped more things into the trunk as Ginger and Daisy returned. "This one's ready to go too," she told them.

"What do you mean?" Jane asked after they left. "A hidden blessing?"

"Well, the twins seem to be enjoying themselves. And maybe you and your husband will learn how to appreciate the simple things in life." She sighed as she cleared the top of the bureau, setting the toiletries in her mother's valise. "I don't know. But it seems to me that if you could change your outlook, well, things would have to get better."

"That's easy for you to say." She sank back down into the easy chair with a long, defeated sigh. "You're young and healthy and just starting out in your adult life. But your stepfather and I are old and weary and—"

"And you are the parents of two young children that still need your attention. And, as for being old, Enoch and Caleb are much older than you and Jefferson, but you don't see them complaining." She angrily emptied the bureau drawers into another trunk. "They're out there right now, working hard and enjoying life. And Ginger is older than you. Daisy might be too. So don't say you're old, Mother." She paused to look around the room, which, although nearly emptied, looked messier than ever now. "And the fact that you weren't even able to pack your own things and move into another room is, in my opinion, inexcusable and—" She stopped herself as Daisy and Ginger returned for another trunk.

Then she picked up a loaded valise and satchel and carried it down the hall to the spare room and, in spite of herself, laughed at how packed it looked with all the trunks and things. "Oh, my," she said to Ginger. "They will be rather cozy in here."

"Serves 'em right." Ginger and Daisy set the valises on the trunk at the foot of the bed. Then they all went back to the master bedroom to collect what little was left there.

"I think we got the last of it," Delia told Ginger and Daisy. "Thank you both for helping me."

"Happy to." Daisy picked up a satchel.

Meanwhile, Ginger approached Delia's mother, ignoring her glowering expression. "And now, Mrs. Blackstone, if you'll come with me, I'll show you your new room. Might take you a bit to get yourself all settled in there, but I'm sure you can do it." She winked at Delia.

Delia sighed in relief as the pair led her mother out of the room. Ginger was right, this room did need a full turning out before it would be fit for Wyatt and her to share. She had no idea her mother's housekeeping skills were so lacking. But then, there'd always been servants in the home. Delia's mother had never done a thing but order the servants around—and not always very kindly. Well, things were going to change, and the sooner the better!

15

Delia opened the master bedroom window, pushing back the curtains to allow light and air into this stuffy room. Next she stripped the bed, piling all the linens onto a throw rug that needed to be shaken and aired. Then with Ginger's help, they removed all the bedding and pillows and carried them outside to get some afternoon sunshine.

"Now, I don't want you to lift another finger in that room," Ginger insisted as they hung the quilt on the clothesline. "I intend to get everything all ready for you and Mister Wyatt."

"Don't you need to help in the kitchen?"

"No, I don't. I already arranged for Rosie to come help with supper tonight. She and Daisy have it all under control. And Miss Miranda is setting up the dining room real nice. And Miss Lilly even baked a real pretty cake. We all wanted your homecoming to be special, Miss Delia. For you and your groom. And I don't want your parents spoiling it."

Delia put a hand on the older woman's shoulder. "You're a treasure, Ginger. Thank you."

Ginger grinned. "I probably shouldn't admit as much, but I sure did enjoy myself."

"Enjoyed yourself?" Delia felt confused.

"Throwing your ma outta your room like that. That was the most fun I've had in a coon's age." The older woman chuckled as she gave a feather pillow a hard shake.

Delia couldn't help but smile. As Ginger continued beating the pillows, Delia grabbed up a produce basket and headed for the gardens. She could at least gather some things for the kitchen, as well as fresh flowers for the master suite.

As she clipped lavender, peony, and roses, she sighed. It had felt slightly painful to roust her mother out like that, but she knew it was the right thing to do. To allow Mother to have her way would only lead to more troubles down the line. And who knew how long her family planned to remain here?

Delia was curious as to how Wyatt's talk with Jefferson went but knew that she'd hear the details later. As she created a lovely aromatic arrangement on the back porch, she didn't even feel too guilty about how crowded her parents would be in the smaller room now packed with all their belongings. Perhaps the inconvenience would motivate them to reconsider a thing or two in regard to their future.

As Delia put the final touches on her flower arrangement, she was surprised to feel a pair of arms grab her from behind, but judging the child-sized hands, she knew she wasn't in danger. "Julianne?" she guessed, turning around to see her little sister wearing her brother's clothes. "Looks like you've been riding."

Julianne grinned. "Wait until you see me, Delia." She hugged her tightly. "I'm so glad you're home. I missed you."

Delia tugged a golden braid. "Looks like you're doing your own hair these days."

"My braids are almost as good as the ones you did. Mother and Father hate them, but I don't care." She scowled. "Mother and Father make me so mad, Delia. I'm glad you're here."

"Why are you so mad at them? I heard you and Julius have been getting to do whatever you like."

"That's not exactly true." Julianne frowned. "For starters, Mother won't come out of her room. She tells everyone she's sick and can't keep down food, but she makes me sneak up a tray after every meal."

Delia pursed her lips. "Well, that changes right now. No more food trays. If Mother is hungry, she'll have to come down to eat. Not only that, I expect her to help with the some of the work around here."

"I've been helping." Julianne held her head with pride. "Aunt Lilly told me I had to do chores before I could ride Dolly. So I feed the chickens and gather eggs. And I tend the garden too. I weed and water and pick ripe produce."

"Good for you!" Delia patted her head. "I was pleasantly surprised that the garden looked so well-tended."

Julianne's smile grew wider. "And Julius has to feed the pigs and clean stalls. And he even knows how to milk a cow. Uncle Enoch taught him. Julius hated doing chores at first, but Caleb said, 'no chores, no cow-boying.' And that did it."

"That's good to hear. I'm proud of both of you." Delia glanced toward the corral, hoping to spot Wyatt and wondering how his chat with Jefferson went. "And why does, uh, Father make you mad?" she quietly asked.

"He goes around acting like he's better than everyone. He tells the hands what to do, like he's the boss. But they all know he doesn't know a thing about ranching and farming. Father can't even ride a horse." She folded her arms in front of her.

Delia shook her head. "I'm not too surprised. After all, Father is used to giving orders." She didn't like calling him "father" but did so for Julianne's sake.

"I wish Caleb would make Father do chores." Julianne chuckled. "That'd teach him."

Delia agreed but didn't want to encourage Julianne to disrespect her parents. "Well, you need to remember that ranch life is all new to our parents. You and Julius seem to have taken to it more naturally. We might have to give our parents more time to figure things out."

"That's what Aunt Lilly says too." Julianne shrugged. "Well, I have to go take care of Dolly. I know how to saddle and unsaddle her all by myself now. And I brush her down and give her a few oats after every ride. And you know what, Delia?"

Delia couldn't help but smile. Julianne was turning into a very likeable little sister. Nothing like the pesky nuisance she used to be. "What?"

"I think Dolly really likes me. She sees me coming and her ears perk up and she lets out this whinny. It's like she's happy to see me. Do you think horses are like that?"

"I definitely do. Right now, you're Dolly's best friend."

"I want to be her best friend forever." Julianne hugged Delia again. "And I'm really glad you're home."

"I'm glad too." But Delia's feelings were mixed as Julianne galloped back to the corral. It was sweet seeing her young sibling so happy here, as if she'd already made this ranch her home. But what would happen when it was time for them to go their way? Because that seemed inevitable. Still, Delia didn't need to think about that now.

Instead she carried the produce she'd picked and her bouquet into the house, pausing in the dining room where Miranda was setting the table.

"I already got flowers for the dining table," Miranda informed her.

"I see that." Delia smiled at the crystal rose bowl filled with pink roses. "Very pretty too. This is for my bedroom."

Miranda nodded as she set down a plate. "I heard you kicked your parents out of your room," she said in hushed tones. "I wish I'd seen it."

"Let's say I helped relocate them," Delia said quietly.

"Good for you."

"Have you seen either of them around?"

"Mr. Blackstone just went upstairs. By the way he was stomping, he didn't sound too happy."

Delia nodded grimly. "I'll take these flowers up." She paused to look at the place settings. "Nine for dinner?"

Miranda started to count on her fingers. "You and Wyatt, Aunt Lilly and me. Uncle Enoch and Caleb. Your stepfather and the kids." She held up nine fingers.

"Let's make it ten. I'm going to inform my mother that she's no longer getting food trays delivered to her room."

Miranda rolled her eyes. "Aunt Lilly already put her foot down, but your mother still gets Julianne to sneak food up after we've eaten."

"Well, I told Julianne we're done with that."

Miranda chuckled. "Remember when I wanted meals delivered to my room and you refused?"

Delia patted Miranda's back. "But you got over it. And look at us now."

"Just like real sisters."

"We are real sisters." Delia looked into her eyes. "Remember?"

Miranda smiled. "Good luck with your parents."

"Thanks." Delia braced herself for what was to come as she went up the stairs. First she took the flower arrangement to her room. Ginger was just finishing up her cleaning. "Looks so much better," Delia quietly told her. "Thanks."

"Daisy will help me move all yours and Mister Wyatt's things in here," Ginger told her as she gave the round mahogany table one last polish. "Then we'll get the bed made up."

"Thank you." Delia inhaled the bouquet then set it on the table. "Now I'm going to let my mother know no more meals will be brought up to her."

Ginger laughed then winked. "Good for you."

Delia walked quietly down the hall to the little spare room where she could hear her parents talking, and in rather loud voices. Not wanting to eavesdrop, she knocked firmly on the door.

"Oh, it's you." Jefferson narrowed his eyes as he opened the door wider. "I heard you kicked us out of our room, Delia. Not very hospitable, if I do say so."

"I'm sorry you feel kicked out." She frowned. "That wasn't my intention. I let you have my room upon your arrival, but quite honestly, I didn't expect you to remain here this long. I fully expected to have my room back when Wyatt and I returned from our wedding trip. And surely you must understand that Wyatt and I would like to be comfortable in our home." She glanced past him to the small, cluttered room. Her mother was sitting in the only chair, amidst a heap of clothing. "I do hope you'll be able to make yourselves comfortable in here."

He laughed, but not with humor. "Shall I assume this is only a temporary arrangement?"

"I suppose that's up to you. Were you planning on leaving anytime soon?"

He scowled then turned to Jane. "I thought you said we could move into larger rooms after Lilly and Miranda leave."

"Well, I—I simply suggested that might be a possibility." Jane looked down.

Delia considered this. "I'll have to give it some thought."

"Some thought?" Jefferson challenged. "You will have two empty bedrooms, surely you could spare one of them. Perhaps Jane could remain in this room and I could move myself into the other guest room."

"You want two rooms?" Delia frowned.

"You see how small this room is for two people to occupy. I assume the other guest rooms are similar size."

"They're a bit larger. But I do like to keep one room ready for guests."

"And we are not guests?" he demanded.

"I welcomed you as guests when you came for my wedding. Now I'm not so sure."

"We are your parents," he declared. "We deserve some respect."

Delia pursed her lips, trying to think.

"Is asking for the use of two rooms too much?"

"It depends."

"Depends on what?"

"Well, if you were to help out here…if you took responsibility for some chores or helped with housework…well, I might be inclined to agree to letting you have the use of another room. But you must understand this is only a temporary arrangement."

"You are going to make us work for our room and board?" he asked with a creased brow. "You cannot be serious."

"I am absolutely serious." She pointed to the messy room. "To begin with I expect you to do your own housekeeping. I don't think that's too much to ask. And, Mother, I expect you to do your own laundry. Ginger mentioned you asked her."

"I thought Ginger was the housekeeper. And now that the wedding is—"

"Ginger has more than enough to do. I don't expect her to wait on both of you. If you want to remain here at the ranch, you need to pitch in and help. And if you expect me to give you the use of three bedrooms—"

"But we're only asking for two," Jane protested.

"Julianne has a room too." Delia sighed. "Perhaps you'd like to share that room with her, Mother. It has an extra bed."

"Oh, dear." Jane sounded close to tears as she wrung her hands. "I just don't know how we've come to this." She looked at Jefferson with angry eyes. "It's all your fault!"

"I don't have to take this abuse." He pushed past Delia and exited the room, and now Jane was sobbing loudly.

"I'm sorry you're in such desperate straits." Delia put a hand on her mother's shoulder. "But I will stand by what I just said. If you and Jefferson want room and board here, I expect you both to help out." She knelt down, looking into her mother's eyes. "And I really believe you will feel better for doing so. We're having lovely summer weather, and fresh air would do you good. Please, get yourself dressed and go outside for a walk. I'm sure it will improve your perspective, Mother."

Jane just let out a low groan.

"By the way, we are having a celebration dinner tonight. Everyone has gone to a lot of trouble for Wyatt's and my homecoming. So I expect to see you and father dressed and wearing sunny smiles." Delia started to leave then stopped. "One more thing, Mother. Julianne has been instructed not to bring food up here to you anymore. So please do not ask her."

"What about the other room, Delia? You know that Jefferson and I had our own rooms back in Pittsburgh, that we're accustomed to more space. Even in your nice master suite, it felt crowded to share it. So I do hope you'll be able to let us use another room."

"Well, Lilly and Miranda aren't leaving for a couple of days. Why don't we see how helpful you and Jefferson can make yourselves until then?" Delia forced a smile. "You might want to start with this room."

Her mother grumbled something inaudible as Delia closed the door. Not that she'd expected anything more. As she went down the hallway, she spied Lilly peeking out of her room. "How is it going?" she asked quietly.

Delia went over to Lilly, noticing with satisfaction that her room looked as lovely as the day she and George first arrived. "I have been laying down the law," Delia whispered. "I'm afraid they're not very happy with me."

Lilly chuckled. "That doesn't surprise me in the least."

"But I plan to stick to my guns."

"Good for you." Lilly pointed to the bags still in the hallway. "Would you like help unpacking from your trip?"

"I would love your help, Aunt Lilly." They both picked up a bag and took them into the master bedroom. Mostly she just wanted Aunt Lilly's pleasant company. Too bad she wasn't the one extending her stay. As she opened her valise, Delia wondered just how long her family really planned to remain here. Indefinitely? She hoped not!

16

Miranda knew that tonight's celebratory supper was to honor the newlyweds, but as she looked around the full table, it felt like something more. It felt like she was part of a real family. A much bigger family than she'd ever known before. She imagined how she would carry this memory with her while she was away at finishing school. And how she would plant this image like a seed...toward the family she would someday share with Jackson. At least she hoped so.

As toasts were made to Wyatt and Delia, she imagined how it would be when, someday, these toasts would be for her and Jackson. And his family would be sitting around this table too.

"Miranda," Delia nudged her with an elbow. "Caleb just asked you a question."

"I'm sorry." Miranda smiled at the old cow hand. "I guess I was daydreaming."

"Thinking about your big trip to Philadelphie, I reckon." He winked. "I was just asking if you were all packed and ready to go?"

"Mostly." She nodded.

"You'll have to write to us," Uncle Enoch told her. "Tell us what you think of the big city." He rubbed his chin. "So modern nowadays. I was surprised at how much it'd changed. Hardly recognize it."

"Well, Miranda has never been there," Lilly reminded him, "so she'll have nothing to compare it to."

"I think Pittsburgh has changed even more than Philadelphia," Delia said. "But not for the better. In the past ten years, the steel mills have turned Pittsburgh into a dark, dreary, smelly place."

"Those steel mills you complain about are making some people very rich," Jefferson said sharply.

"Not you," Julianne said to her father, and suddenly the table got very quiet.

"Watch yourself," Jane warned her daughter.

"Sorry." Julianne's cheeks flushed with embarrassment, and Miranda felt sorry for her.

"Well, I bet none of your eastern places have grown as fast as Colorado," Caleb said suddenly. "When me and Enoch and Winston first come out here, there was nothing but wilderness. Then we hit gold. And not long after that there was the silver strike. Next thing you knew, the railroad come through and, well, ain't never been the same since."

"I remember the big celebrations when we got statehood," Miranda added. "The fireworks and parties! I was only nine, but I'll always remember that day." She turned to Julius and Julianne. "Did you know that we became a state the same year America turned a hundred?"

"That was a big day for sure," Uncle Enoch agreed.

Once again, the conversation at the table was light and congenial, everyone taking turns to put in their bits and pieces. Everyone except Delia's stepfather. He sat silently glowering down at his plate. Miranda wished he'd just excuse himself from the table. What was the point of sitting there like a big old sourpuss? She glanced at Delia and could tell she felt it too. Poor Delia, what would life be like for her after Miranda and Lilly were gone? She'd have to put up with her parents without them. But at least she had Wyatt. And, of course, Caleb and Uncle Enoch could step in if needed. Still, it probably wasn't going to be easy.

Delia was happy to wake up in her own room the next morning. And thanks to Ginger, everything in the room felt fresh and clean and the morning sun was streaming through the window. But where was Wyatt? He must've gotten an early start on chores. As she pulled on her dressing gown, she realized it was past seven. That was late for her. Still, it had been so nice to sleep in her own bed, she didn't even feel guilty.

As she leisurely got dressed, she considered the day ahead of her. Happy to be home again, and anticipating a lovely summer day on the ranch, she was eager to get at it. Yet she knew she'd eventually have to cross paths with her mother and Jefferson, and that cast a gloomy shadow over the clear sunny day.

Still, she reminded herself, she planned to spend time with Miranda this morning, and Miranda had promised to help with chores. And this afternoon she looked forward to riding with Julianne. Her little sister was eager to show off her new riding skills. So perhaps she'd manage to avoid her mother and Jefferson after all.

Her hope was to keep as far from them as possible until after Aunt Lilly and Miranda left. Then she'd have to figure things out.

Delia went quietly past her parents' room and downstairs. If she was lucky, they might still be sleeping. In the dining room, Lilly and Miranda were still eating breakfast. "Sleeping beauty has risen," Miranda teased as Delia filled a coffee cup.

"I was surprised at how late I slept," Delia admitted sheepishly.

"You probably needed it." Lilly buttered her toast.

"Well, I'm glad to see both of you this morning." Delia sat down. "I can't believe you'll be leaving tomorrow." She looked at Miranda. "Are you excited?"

"Excited, scared, nervous...but mostly excited, I guess. It will be an adventure."

"Wyatt and the men were just talking about an adventure," Lilly said.

"What's that?" Delia forked a bacon strip.

"It's time to bring the cows down from the highland pasture," Miranda informed her.

"Oh, that's right. I nearly forgot about that."

"Did you know Delia did the trail drive to take the cattle up there?" Miranda said to Lilly. "She was like a real cowhand."

"Really?" Aunt Lilly looked both surprised and impressed.

"You should've seen her when she got home, Aunt Lilly. Mud from head to toe. She looked ridiculous." Miranda pointed her spoon at Delia. "You're the one who should've been sent to finishing school." She giggled.

"Maybe so." Delia tipped her head to Lilly as she reached for the berry preserves. "But while I was out there in that nasty rainstorm, Miranda was dressed in one of my finest gowns and best jewelry. Hosting my beau right here."

Miranda looked sheepish. "Yes, well, that wasn't one of my finest moments."

Aunt Lilly laughed. "I wish I'd seen that."

After breakfast, the three of them went out to the orchard where lots of fruit was coming on. By noon they had filled numerous bushel baskets and were working at an outside harvest table to cut up and prepare fruit for canned preserves.

"I'm so glad you could help with this," Delia told them. "Ginger and Daisy are appreciative too."

"I'd rather be out here than in the kitchen," Miranda said. "It's like a steam bath in there."

"Ginger said they've already canned three dozen jars today." Delia waved her knife toward the quickly filling bowls and pots. "By the end of the day, it will probably be three times that. Ginger said it will be a record."

"Many hands make light work." Lilly reached for another apple.

"And I asked Daisy to fix you up a box of preserves to take back on the train with you," Delia told Lilly.

"Oh, wonderful. George will be thrilled." Lilly looked out toward the garden and trees. "I am feeling a bit sad about having to leave this beautiful place, Delia. Do you realize it's like a slice of heaven?"

Delia nodded. "Now you know where we are and how to get here. I hope you and Uncle George will make the trip again."

"Maybe they can come home with me when I get done with my classes in the springtime. Aunt Lilly said they finish up the first week of June and then I get the whole summer to be back here."

"That's a perfect plan," Aunt Lilly agreed.

Delia nodded. She just hoped that her mother and stepfather would be moved on by then. But she didn't want to say as much—didn't want to even think it.

"Will you be going with the men to get the cows?" Aunt Lilly asked her.

"I'm not sure. I'd like to hear Wyatt's thoughts on it." She considered it. "It was sort of fun, but the truth was I went because I felt I needed to prove myself. Some of the hands had challenged my authority to run this ranch."

"But she showed them." Miranda lobbed a peach stone into the bucket. "You'd never get me up there. Sleeping outside in the wilds like that, with cougar and bear and rattlesnakes."

"Sounds exciting." Lilly wrinkled her nose. "Not everyone's cup of tea."

"If I had to choose between rounding up cattle or finishing school, I'd definitely go with finishing school."

Lilly and Delia laughed. But Delia's humor evaporated to see her mother and stepfather approaching. As usual, of late, their expressions looked rather grim. But Delia pretended not to notice as Lilly and Miranda greeted them.

"I'm glad to see you outside," Delia told them. "It's such a lovely day. The fresh air will do you good."

"I've been outside every day," Jefferson said sharply.

"Good for you. I meant for Mother. I think it'll improve her health."

"Yes, that's what I told her and why we are taking a walk," he said crisply.

Delia explained where some of the best walking trails were located, but Jefferson seemed to have a lighter stroll in mind. They headed through the gardens and, as soon as they were out of earshot, Miranda spoke up.

"I wish you weren't going to be stuck here with them," she told Delia. "Can't you just send them on their way?"

Delia sighed. "I'm afraid they don't have any place to go."

"Don't worry." Lilly patted Delia's hand. "Things have a way of working themselves out. And I will be praying for the best outcome for you and them."

"Yes, that's probably about all we can do for now." Delia changed the subject, asking Miranda about whether she had everything packed yet and offering to help her with it.

Miranda never realized how sad she would be to say goodbye to the ranch and everyone there. Not until she and Aunt Lilly were all loaded up into the carriage, waving their final farewell to Delia and Wyatt and the others, standing out on the porch. As the carriage trundled on down the road, a few tears trickled down Miranda's cheeks.

"Oh, poor dear." Lilly reached for Miranda's gloved hand, giving it a squeeze.

"I didn't expect to be sad," she confessed. "So many times I used to say I wanted to get away from this place. And now that I am, well, it just feels so sad. Like maybe I'll never be back here again."

"Oh, you'll be back. Remember, you and George and I are planning for next summer. I'm already looking forward to it."

As they rode toward town, Lilly continued to chatter in an encouraging way, and after a while, Miranda's thoughts focused on the adventure ahead of them. First there was the train ride, all the way back East. That alone sounded exciting. Dressed in her best traveling clothes, complete with an attractive hat from Delia, Miranda felt more grownup than ever. She really was starting out on a new life. She wondered where Jackson was right now. Was he enjoying his big adventure?

17

Jackson had only been in Juneau a couple of weeks, but already he felt comfortable there. It helped having AJ to show him around, pointing out who was trustworthy and who was not. And it helped that Jackson had grown up in the silver mines. That alone seemed to garner some respect among the rugged men up here. He wasn't just another greenhorn hoping to get rich quick. Oh, sure, he wouldn't mind an easy strike, but he didn't expect it. He knew he'd have to work for it and, even then, it might not pay out.

And according to AJ, who seemed way down on his luck, the gold strike that Wyatt and he'd found was all run out now. Worse than that, AJ looked to be all run out too. It didn't take long for Jackson to figure out that AJ seemed to have wasted his fortune. And that wasn't all that surprising, since lots of miners were rich one day and dirt poor the next. But Jackson just hadn't expected that of Wyatt's good friend.

"So you're saying you mined a lot more gold after Wyatt left?" Jackson asked AJ as he warmed up beans and bacon for supper. He was trying not to feel irked at AJ for acting like Jackson's provisions were his provisions. But at this rate, Jackson would be feeling the pinch before springtime, which was why they'd been eating a lot of beans and bacon the past few days.

"That's right." AJ glumly poured a cup of coffee.

"So you were a lot richer than Wyatt? And it's really all gone now?"

"Yeah, it was the smaller stuff, and plenty of work to dig out. But I reckon it was worth about half of what Wyatt and I got out before he went home."

Jackson did the math. "Meaning you got double of what Wyatt got?"

"That's about right." AJ handed Jackson his tin plate.

"And it's all gone?" Jackson filled the plate and handed it back.

"That's what I said, isn't it?" AJ scowled down at the beans. Hopefully he didn't plan to complain about the free meal.

"I just can't figure it." As Jackson sat down on a stone, balancing his own plate on his knees, he felt renewed respect for Wyatt. He'd come home with a small fortune, while AJ had stuck it out up here, expecting to get even richer. But now AJ had nothing.

"Well, like I already told you, I'm not proud of myself." AJ forked into his beans.

Jackson said nothing. Just quietly ate, wondering what he'd gotten himself into with this guy. Maybe he'd be better off on his own.

"If nothing else, you ought to learn from my mistakes, Jackson." AJ's tone softened a little. "If I'd known then what I know now…"

"Meaning what?" Jackson tried to keep the judgment out of his voice.

"Well, like I already told you. There are folks up here who make it their business to get rich off of us miners who're working ourselves to death. There are wolves and cheats and thieves in this town."

"That's nothing new." Jackson poured some coffee. "My pa always says that crooks follow money."

"True enough. Guess my pa never taught me that." AJ shook his head. "Wyatt used to warn me about tricksters. He wanted me to go home with him when he left, but I thought he was crazy to leave for a stupid girl."

"Delia's not a stupid girl."

"Yeah, I reckon she's not. But aside from that, I knew there was more gold to be found. That's why I stayed. I never figured that not having Wyatt around would be trouble. But I can admit it now. Wyatt helped keep me on the straight and narrow."

Jackson wondered if that was why Wyatt encouraged him to come here—to help rescue his friend. He sure hoped not.

"After Wyatt left, I worked real hard to get the rest of the gold out. Only took a couple of weeks before it was dried up. After that, I got lonely. It was still summer, and I got to spending more time in town. I had plenty of money so I could eat where I wanted and buy anything I liked. It was fun...at first." He sighed in a way that suggested he wanted to go back to that time.

"Then what happened?" Jackson probably could guess the rest of the story. He hadn't been blind while growing up in a mining town. But maybe AJ needed to talk. Like Ma sometimes said, "Confession is good for the soul." And so he listened.

"I s'pose I looked like a real easy target," AJ admitted. "Going around with a wad of cash on me, and spending like there was no tomorrow. A pretty yellow-haired gal named Starla warmed right up to me. She made me believe I was special to her. Oh, sure, she was a dancehall gal, but the way she talked to me, like I was the only fellow in the world, well, I really believed she wanted something more." He laughed as he helped himself to more beans. "I was right about that. She sure did want something more."

"Your money?" Jackson warmed his coffee.

"Starla like me to buy her things. And she sure liked pretty things. She told me it was from growing up poor. And she said her family mistreated her. She claimed she came up here with her cousin in order to earn enough money to stand on her own two feet. But seems she wanted to stomp on mine along the way."

"Sorry to hear that. So did this Starla gal take *all* your money?"

"No, but she sure did help. Remember I pointed out Slick Sam in town the other day?"

"The gambler?"

"Yep. Slick Sam really emptied out my pockets. With Starla's help." He drained the last of his coffee. "And some strong whiskey too." He shook his head. "I reckon I was a first-class fool."

Despite feeling somewhat used by AJ, Jackson felt sorry for him. "Sounds like you learned your lessons the hard way." He slowly stood, stretching his tired back. "But do you think you really learned, AJ?"

"What are you suggesting?"

"Well, I grew up around miners. Some of them just kept making the same mistakes over and over. And some learned from 'em and made better choices. I'm just curious about you. Say we hit a big vein tomorrow—do you think you'd be running to town for dancehall gals and drinking and gambling?"

AJ laughed. "Here's the honest truth, Jackson—the thought of those things just makes me feel sick now. Reminds me of a time when I was a kid and my ma got a bag of sugar from the store and left it sitting on the table. Well, we never had much sugar in the house and when Ma wasn't looking, I sneaked a big old bowl of it and took it outside and ate the whole thing."

"Make you sick?"

"I still don't like sugar or sweets too much."

Jackson chuckled. "Well, I hope that's how you feel about gambling, drinking, and dancehall gals."

"Starla and her cousin moved to Fairbanks. Not that I'd be tempted. But I reckon I'm glad she's gone."

Jackson wondered if AJ had cared more for her than he let on but didn't want to ask.

"What about your girl, Jackson? I noticed you got another letter from her. Don't that make two now?"

"Yeah. The first one was sent from Colorado. And the next one she wrote while riding on the train. She'd be in Philadelphia now. In school."

"Going to college like Wyatt's girl did? I sure wouldn't want to marry an overly educated woman myself. But maybe that's because I just told you how dumb I am."

"Well, it's a different kind of school. Miranda says this school is good preparation for becoming a wife."

"So you do plan to marry her?"

"Like I already told you, I don't know. She's a good girl. Pretty and smart. But sometimes she's a little bit, well, conniving." Jackson knew that sounded wrong, but he couldn't think of the right word.

"Ah-hah—like Starla?"

"No, no, not like that. I just mean Miranda likes to get her way. And I s'pose I'm a little wary of that. I reckon time'll tell."

"Will you read me her letters again?"

Jackson smiled. "I guess I could." He reached inside his jacket pocket and extracted the two well-worn letters and proceeded to read. Miranda did write a nice letter, and he didn't blame AJ for wanting something better to think on than all his misfortunes. Jackson just hoped that AJ really was putting those vices behind him.

Miranda thoroughly enjoyed her time in Philadelphia with Aunt Lilly. Being a guest in their home, seeing the city's sights, visiting museums, shopping, being entertained by Aunt Lilly's friends, even visiting Uncle George's boot factory…she loved it all! So much so that it was a bit of a letdown to be dropped off at school.

Oh, she'd been excited at first. The idea of meeting girls her age, making friends, and learning how to be a good wife all held a certain appeal. But when she realized they were required to wear scratchy brown woolen uniforms, which in her opinion were quite ugly, and that she had to share a drafty dormitory room with nineteen other girls, her enthusiasm waned considerably. It felt more like a prison than a school.

Her only friend so far was Lottie Thompson, a spunky sixteen-year-old from Baltimore. Lottie's older sister Dorothea had spent three years in the academy, graduating with honors last spring. "Dorothea turned out so well that she got engaged to Grover Flanders last summer. And he's one of the most sought-after bachelors in Baltimore," Lottie whispered to Miranda as they got into the dinner line. It was only the third day of school, and Miranda already regretted her choice to come here.

"Girls really do this for *three years?*" Miranda muttered half to herself, cringing to imagine serving such a sentence.

"Don't worry, Miranda. It gets better each year." Lottie nudged her forward in line.

"How is that possible?" she asked quietly.

"Well, for starters, second- and third-year students get to wear their own clothes."

"So that's why I've seen some girls in nice dresses."

"And they don't have to line up to get their own food like we do. They sit at tables and are served their meals."

"I heard it's served by first-year students," Miranda glumly admitted. "I'm assigned to kitchen duty next month."

"So am I. Maybe we'll get to work together."

"Maybe." Despite Lottie's optimism, Miranda didn't look forward to it.

"And there are other privileges too. Third-year students get to host teas, and they hold socials and dances where the boys from the military academy are invited to attend."

"That sounds fun, but that's two years from now." Miranda frowned.

"That's because we have to prove ourselves in our first year. You know they don't just let anyone in here."

"Oh." Miranda picked up a tray. She couldn't help but wonder if she would've been let in if she hadn't gotten help from Aunt Lilly.

"And some girls don't even make it all the way through the first year." Lottie lowered her voice. "Dorothea called it *spring weeding*, and Mother warned me I better not be one of the weeds getting pulled."

"Well, spring's still a ways off." Miranda didn't want to think about that. "At least the food's not too bad," she whispered.

"That's because we're supposed to learn to appreciate French cuisine and how to prepare fancy dishes and confections and whatnot. But from what I hear, most of the girls already know how to cook."

"I don't." Miranda regretted this confession when she saw Lottie's brows arch.

"You don't know how to cook at all?"

"Well, I know a few things." Miranda felt defensive as they went through the line and on to their assigned table. It wasn't as if she couldn't boil water or peel an apple. "I was just starting to learn to cook before I came out here," she quietly confessed.

"My mother made sure that Dorothea and I knew how to cook. She still believes the way to a man's heart is through his stomach. But Dorothea's fiancé is so wealthy, I doubt she'll ever set foot in a kitchen. I hope to follow her example."

As they'd been instructed on the first day, the first-year students all sat up straight with hands in laps as they waited for other classmates to be seated. After that, the dean of the academy, Mrs. Grampton, would stand to read a scripture and ask the blessing. With that done, they were expected to gracefully unfold their napkins, neatly lay them in their laps, and eat their meal in the proper order, with the manners and decorum of lovely, well-bred young ladies. Talking was allowed, as long as it was quiet and polite—and no food in the mouth. And if you broke any of these rules, you could expect a sharp rap on a shoulder from a manners monitor wielding a twelve inch stick that stung. Miranda knew because she'd already received a shoulder whack for not properly opening her napkin.

She had felt so grown-up last week. It was as if she was a real adult while she spent time with Aunt Lilly. She was spoken to and respected as an equal. Even more so than when she was at home and often treated like a child. But here at the academy, she felt more like a child than ever before in her entire life. How girls could survive three years of this treatment was a mystery. She feared she might not make it through one.

But the thought of Delia or Aunt Lilly's disappointment if she failed was motivation. Plus she really did want to learn how to be a better wife. Jackson deserved it. For the sake of those three, Miranda was determined to do her best. For at least a year. Perhaps she would be polished enough for wifehood by then. After all, she didn't want to marry a wealthy aristocrat. She would be happy with a miner like Jackson. Well, as long as he had some money. That would help.

After dinner, the girls were encouraged to take a "constitutional" stroll around the school grounds. And then they were welcome to socialize in the fireside room, but only certain "ladylike" activities were allowed. They could sit and read or draw or do needlework or quietly visit. They could also do jigsaw puzzles or play Anagrams at the game tables. And if a girl was musically talented, she could take a turn on the grand piano—as long as the music wasn't too lively. A redheaded girl named Sadie McGuire had been reprimanded for playing a lively song about pirates a few nights ago. Apparently, pirate tunes were not acceptable for dignified young ladies. But Miranda had thoroughly enjoyed it and now hoped to get to know Sadie better. The only problem was that Sadie seemed a bit elusive. Especially after getting reprimanded for her music.

"Let's go to the jigsaw puzzle table," Lottie urged Miranda after they finished their walk. "That's Beatrice Phillips sitting there. The Phillips of Boston are a very influential family." She lowered her voice. "And I heard that Beatrice has an older brother."

Miranda wasn't sure why this was of interest, since first-year students weren't allowed to interact with any males of any social standing. But she didn't protest as Lottie led her over to the jigsaw table where a rather plain looking girl with light brown hair was peering down at the puzzle pieces.

"Care for some help?" Lottie offered cheerfully.

"Thank you." Beatrice nodded, but her expression seemed bored. Or perhaps it was just superior. Miranda remembered a time or two when Delia's mother had acted that way, looking down her nose at some of the people who lived on the ranch.

But Lottie simply introduced herself and sat down. "I'm from Baltimore." Lottie nodded to Miranda as she picked up a puzzle piece. "And this is Miranda Williams from Colorado."

"Colorado?" Beatrice blinked as if Lottie had said Miranda had come from the moon. "Are you serious?"

"Yes, I'm from Colorado." Miranda suddenly felt defiant. It wasn't the first time a girl questioned her home state, but it was growing more and more irritating. It was as if everyone assumed Colorado was only inhabited by mountain men and Indians.

"I didn't believe civilized people lived in Colorado." Beatrice narrowed her eyes at Miranda.

"Then you are wrong." Miranda picked up a puzzle piece that looked like part of a tree and popped it into place. "Colorado got its statehood eight years ago, and we are surprisingly civilized." She knew that might be a stretch in some circles, but she was weary of the subtle putdowns.

"What does your father *do* out there in the Wild West?" Beatrice cocked her head to one side. "Does he shoot bears?"

Miranda had already made the mistake of admitting both her parents were deceased to a girl who'd assumed she was writing home, when she'd actually been writing to Jackson. But her answer had brought a disturbing mix of sympathy followed by suspicion. "My family has a large ranch," Miranda told Beatrice. Perhaps that was a bit misleading, but wasn't Delia her family? She often said so.

"Is that like a *farm?*" Beatrice made a face. "With cows and chickens and pigs?"

Miranda grimaced. "We do have livestock on our ranch."

"If you live on a farm, why are you at the academy?" Beatrice wrinkled her nose as if she'd had a whiff of an overripe chicken coop. "Seems you'd be better off learning to sew your own clothes and bake bread. Isn't that what a farmer's wife does?"

"I plan to become a miner's wife," Miranda answered too quickly and instantly regretted it. Why should she tell this obnoxious girl about anything personal?

"A miner's wife?" Beatrice laughed. "Goodness gracious, that's even worse. You can't be serious. You are going to marry a miner?"

"Actually, his family *owns* the silver mine," Miranda clarified. "They are quite well off." She had no intention of admitting the O'Neil mine was failing or that the miners were threatening to strike. That was none of this nosy girl's business!

"Well, that's a bit better. But mining is such dirty work, *Miranda from the Wild West.* Being a miner's wife sounds very undignified to me. And I certainly don't see why you need the academy. But perhaps you will be a very *refined* miner's wife."

"Do you think refinement is limited to wealthy people?" Miranda challenged hotly. "Because judging by your manners, I would suppose your family runs the slaughterhouse down by the railroad tracks."

"Well!" Beatrice's pale blue eyes flashed.

Miranda stood. "Please, excuse me." And without another word, she hurried off to the dormitory. It was too early for bed, but she no longer wanted to be in a room filled with haughty rich girls. She wished she knew where that Sadie girl was because she suspected she might feel the same.

Instead of feeling sorry for herself, Miranda decided to sit down and write Jackson a nice long letter. Although she wanted to lament about how much she disliked this stupid finishing school and how she wanted to be finished with it, she decided it would be better—and more mature—to simply describe her studies. What was the point of worrying Jackson? Especially since, more than ever, she wanted to convince him that she was maturing…and would soon be ready for matrimony. Maybe even sooner than he expected.

So she wrote about how she was enjoying her drawing and music classes, and how she could already say a few things in French. She wrote about how her math skills were improving and how she looked forward to becoming a better cook. And as usual, she sent him "all her love." Hopefully Jackson would reciprocate in a similar vein sometime soon. And if he struck it rich, perhaps he'd send her a real proposal of marriage. That's what she was praying for!

18

Mid October, 1884 Colorado

Delia felt she was at a stalemate with her stepfather. Although he would talk himself up to her and Wyatt, and claim he was doing "more than his part" to help out on the ranch, she knew better. Not only that, he continued to try to take advantage of others and often acted as if the ranch hands were there to serve him. As if they should drop everything just to drive him to town. And after the scene in her father's den just a few minutes ago, she was more than just a little irked at the situation.

It had started in the front room after supper. Jefferson had been lecturing everyone about why their favorite candidate for governor was unfit for the job. Uncle Enoch got so exasperated he slipped off, but Caleb had stood his ground. Meanwhile, Delia and Wyatt had snuck off to the den, and even closed the door, just to escape Jefferson's rant over something he knew little about. But when Jefferson confronted the two of them in the den, Delia had said a cool and crisp goodnight. Wyatt departed Jefferson's company a few minutes later.

"I'm sick and tired of him," she confessed to Wyatt as they sat in their bedroom together. "And feeling like I cannot relax in my own home without being subject to Jefferson's self-centered speeches, well, it has gotten more than just a little old."

Wyatt smiled as he watched her vigorously brushing her hair. "Careful there, Delia, your hair is too beautiful to go ripping it all out over this." He reached for her hairbrush and gently took over for her. "And I agree, Jefferson is aggravating and oversteps his bounds. Trust me, I see it outside all the time."

"So do I." She took in a slow deep breath. "But it's easier to distance myself from him out there. What will we do when winter sets in and we're in the house more? Already my mother seems to have taken over the parlor. And to be honest, I don't mind. That room has never felt comfortable to me. It's far too fussy and over-furnished. But I hate to change anything in there since Miranda adores it. It's like a shrine to her mother. And, frankly, I'm glad my mother likes it."

Wyatt set her hairbrush on her dressing table then looked around the bedroom. "Well, this is a pleasant enough place to hide out in. No complaints from me." He gently rubbed her shoulders.

"I agree, Wyatt, but I've had a thought." She told him her idea about connecting their room to what used to be Miranda's room next door. "It could be like a sitting room for just you and me."

"Where would Miranda stay when she came home?"

"She could have the lovely guest room that I used to stay in," Delia said. "She likes it better anyway."

"The room your parents have been hinting should be theirs to use." Wyatt looked amused.

"But I never promised that room to them. I only said if they started to help out around here, I would consider letting them have another room to use. I had imagined they would use Miranda's room so that we could keep the guest room for real guests. But to be fair, they've done little these past few weeks to convince me they deserve another room. My mother attempts to lend a hand at times, but her idea of helping leaves a lot to be desired. Poor Ginger was fit to be tied after Mother ruined a whole load of clean laundry. And Jefferson, well, he doesn't even try. That man can't stand to get his hands dirty."

Wyatt chuckled. "Yes, I know." He rubbed his chin as he stared at the wall separating the two rooms. "You know, Delia, it's not a bad idea to connect these rooms for our use. It wouldn't be too difficult to knock a doorway through the wall right there. And it would give us a nice little getaway—a reprieve from your family."

"That's what I was thinking." She stood up, wrapping her arms around him. "Want to figure it out?"

"I'll start tomorrow." He grinned down at her. "And this will give you a perfectly good excuse for not giving in to Jefferson's demands for an additional room."

"Yes," she agreed. "We don't have the room. After all, my family is already occupying two rooms up here. We can't give up our only guest room. There's Miranda to consider."

Miranda quickly discovered who her real friends at the academy were. And they were few. Lottie had acted like a best friend at first, but whenever someone of more influence came along, she had no problem leaving Miranda in the dust. As a result, Miranda didn't fully trust her. But Jericho LaSalle, a soft-spoken southern girl, seemed trustworthy. Perhaps it was because Jericho, like Miranda, was a bit of an outcast here. Just because she was a southerner—and it wasn't something she could hide since every time she opened her mouth, her heavy accent gave her away.

"What made you come to the academy?" Miranda asked her as they were getting acquainted on their way back to the dormitory one evening.

"It was my grandmother in Philadelphia. She talked Mama into bringing me up here. Mama went to this academy when she was my age. In fact, that's how she met my daddy. He was a cadet at the military academy. They met at a Christmas cotillion."

"Sounds romantic." Miranda sighed. She wished she and Jackson could attend a cotillion together.

"I s'pect it was romantic. Well, until their parents heard the news. The war hadn't started, but North and South were at odds back then. And my daddy was a born and bred southerner, but Mama was from up here. They were kind of like Romeo and Juliet. And my mama's parents got real upset when Mama married and went to live in New Orleans."

"That's where my parents came from!" Miranda felt even closer to Jericho now.

"Then you must know how hot southern blood runs. Big Papa, that's Daddy's father, well, he acts like the War Between the States is still going on sometimes. He did not like me coming up here. Not one little bit. And I swear if you ever got my northern Grandmama and Big Papa in the same room, it would be like the War Between the States, only worse. Why, I'm sure someone would get killed. Probably Big Papa too." Jericho giggled. "Because Grandmama is a rather stout lady. She could just sit on him and that would be the end of it."

Miranda laughed. "I'm so glad to know you're from New Orleans, Jericho. It makes me feel closer to you. We could be related."

"Maybe we are. What's your family name?"

Miranda told her all the names she could think of, which weren't many. But Jericho didn't recognize any. Still, Miranda felt a sisterhood with Jericho. More than that, she felt she could trust her. But the bell rang, signaling it was time to be inside the dormitory and preparing for bed.

The next evening after supper, Miranda and Jericho did their constitutional stroll together, and Miranda explained how her parents had come from the south too. "After the war, they went to Colorado. My daddy wanted to strike it rich, but he died in the mines. After that my mother married a northerner. So I'm kind of like you."

"So is that where you came from? Colorado?"

Miranda explained about her deceased stepfather's wish for her to get an education. "It was all arranged in his will. Although he wanted me to go to the university. But I don't think I'm smart enough for that. So I came here."

"Grandmama said she wanted me to have some proper schooling," Jericho explained. "But I think she wanted to get me away from the South. I think she hopes I'll marry a northerner and stay up here."

"Would you do that?"

Jericho firmly shook her head. "I cannot imagine living up here. I love my home in New Orleans."

"Even if you fell in love with a northerner?"

Jericho pursed her lips. "Well, now I don't know. I suppose if I loved him dearly, I'd have to consider it. Like my mama tells me, if you love your man, you follow him wherever he wants you to go."

Miranda nodded. "My mother followed my father to Colorado." She almost added that she would follow Jackson to where he wanted to go but stopped herself. Beatrice had already teased her for talking about Jackson. And Lottie now warned her to keep her mouth shut about marrying anyone because first-year students weren't allowed to be engaged.

It wasn't long before Miranda managed to befriend Sadie McGuire, the musician who liked pirate songs. Jericho liked Sadie too, but for some reason she seemed suspicious about her. Miranda thought it was probably because Sadie kept everyone at arm's length. Especially when it came to disclosing any information about her family heritage or where she came from or why she'd come here.

Of course, this only made Sadie more mysterious and, consequently, Miranda more curious. But Jericho pestered her for information anyway. And that just aggravated Sadie.

"What difference does it make?" she asked Jericho hotly. "I am who I am. What does it matter about my parents?"

"Excuse me for being interested," Jericho said in a hurt tone. "I like to get to know people. Where I come from, it's acceptable to ask about one's heritage."

"Well, I can understand just how Sadie feels," Miranda said in her defense. "Not everyone wants to talk about themselves. I don't see anything wrong with that." After all, Miranda didn't care to disclose all the information about her family. Some things truly were better left unsaid. Even if she was curious about Sadie, she didn't plan to aggravate her by poking around. It seemed obvious that Sadie's father was wealthy. Unless she was fabricating stories, Sadie had lived in opulent homes and visited many places.

Miranda had hinted that perhaps Sadie's family got rich with gold or silver mines, but Sadie quickly dismissed that theory. Sometimes Miranda wondered if Sadie's father was a pirate. Silly perhaps, but it was fun to imagine Sadie sailing around the world on a pirate ship. Naturally, Miranda kept her musings private. For one thing, she didn't want to frighten off Jericho. More than that, she didn't want to alienate Sadie. Because truth be told, she valued Sadie's friendship more than anyone's at the academy.

Sadie was so much fun that dreary classes and schoolwork felt tolerable. Besides being pretty with her flamboyant red hair and sapphire eyes, Sadie was creative and funny, and a natural musician with a good singing voice. As the three girls would stroll the grounds after supper each night, Sadie liked to entertain Miranda and Jericho with her antics. And she had an appreciative audience—particularly with Miranda.

Sometimes Sadie told amusing stories of faraway places. Whether she'd been there or not remained a mystery, but she was good at making her tales come to life. And if they begged her, Sadie would sing them songs. She knew dozens of them. Ballads to make you cry, love songs to make your dream, or lively little ditties to make you laugh. But the forbidden pirate ditties were Miranda's favorites. And she loved learning the lyrics and singing along with Sadie.

Lottie walked with them a couple of times, but she seemed quite wary of Sadie. And she warned Miranda to be careful, reminding her that first-year students could be dismissed for such frivolities and silliness. But Sadie's influence was strong, and before long, both Jericho and Miranda were singing all her songs right along with her. Although Jericho was more careful, always on the watch to be sure none of their supervisors or certain untrustworthy classmates were within earshot.

Thanks to Jericho and Sadie and the occasional letter from Jackson, the days at the academy were passing surprisingly quickly. Miranda had always longed to make friends with girls her own age, and she couldn't imagine better ones.

When Thanksgiving week came, Miranda had already agreed to spend the weekend with Aunt Lilly and Uncle George but, discovering that Sadie's family was in some far off place, Miranda telephoned Aunt Lilly to see if she could join them.

"Of course," Aunt Lilly agreed. "We'd love to meet your new friend. Uncle George will pick you both up on his way home from the factory this afternoon."

"I wish I could go with you two," Jericho told Miranda as they all waited outside the academy for their rides. "I'll be stuck with my grandparents for the whole holiday."

"Well, you have my aunt and uncle's telephone number," Miranda reminded her. "Maybe we could get together with you on the weekend." She waved to the familiar carriage now pulling up, watching as Uncle George climbed out to greet them. Before long, the driver had their bags loaded in back and they were on their way.

After Miranda introduced Sadie to Uncle George, Sadie graciously thanked him. "It's such a treat to be in a real home for Thanksgiving."

"Well, Lilly has been busily making pies and what have you these past few days. I'm sure she thinks she's feeding an army. But last I heard there will only be twelve at our table this year."

"Twelve?" Miranda was impressed.

"Yes. Friends and family. The usual ones we have on these

occasions. Although not as many as last year. So we're even more pleased you could join us," he told Sadie. "I hope you will feel at home."

"I already do." Sadie beamed at him. "Thank you very much."

When they got to the house, Uncle George helped them move their luggage into the guest room. "Sorry you girls have to share a room," he said. "Lilly's sister and husband are here, as well as my cousin Margaret. So we are a full house."

Sadie politely assured him that was fine. "I'm just grateful for your hospitality." She looked a little uneasy. "This will be my first Thanksgiving celebration in a real home."

Uncle George looked surprised. "How can that be, child? Are you from another country?"

"Not exactly." She smiled. "My family does travel a lot. And often we're in hotels. We've had Thanksgiving in restaurants before. So, really, this will be a first for me."

"Well, I do hope you enjoy it."

Miranda removed her coat and hat. "I'm going to find Aunt Lilly," she told Sadie. "Go ahead and start unpacking if you like."

Miranda hurried downstairs, locating Aunt Lilly in the kitchen where she and their cook Maggie were discussing whether or not what looked like a very large turkey would fit in the roasting pan.

"Aunt Lilly!" Miranda ran up from behind.

"There's my girl." Lilly hugged her. "Welcome home."

"Thank you. Sadie is upstairs unpacking. But I thought I should come see if you need any help."

"I appreciate that, but I think Maggie and I have things under control." She nodded to the turkey. "Except for this bird. We're not sure he'll fit in the oven."

"I think we got it," Maggie called out as she slid the roasting pan into the space. "His wings and legs might need to be tied in, but I think he'll fit."

"Wonderful." Lilly clapped her hands. "Now go put it in the brine until tomorrow, Maggie, and we'll be set."

Miranda looked at the row of pies on the counter and smiled. "Everything looks beautiful, Aunt Lilly." She explained how this was Sadie's first Thanksgiving in a real home. "Can I bring her down here to see the pies and everything?"

Aunt Lilly laughed. "Of course."

As Miranda ran upstairs to get Sadie, she felt like this was going to be the best Thanksgiving she'd ever celebrated. Being here with Aunt Lilly and Uncle George and their family and friends—and having Sadie here as well. The only thing that would make it better was if Jackson would show up. But she knew that wasn't going to happen.

19

Juneau, Alaska
Thanksgiving 1884

After more than a month, Jackson felt relieved that AJ had remained true to his word. They did have one near mishap in mid-October—while Jackson was getting supplies at the Mercantile, AJ had wandered into a tavern and was about to buy a drink when Jackson had caught him red-handed. It was one of those times when Jackson was grateful for being a large man with a strong grip. He'd grabbed AJ by the collar, dragged him out of the bar, and right there on the boardwalk, he'd forced AJ to swear never to shadow the door of one of those establishments again. He even made him hold up his hand while he pledged to "abstain from strong drink, shady ladies, and gambling." And if he'd had a Bible handy, Jackson would've forced AJ's hand on it.

Since then, they'd been to town one other time with no incidents. And being that today was Thanksgiving and they'd had a little bit of luck scraping out some bullion last week, they planned to celebrate by having a real Thanksgiving dinner at Beulah's Restaurant down below the Kodiak Hotel.

While AJ took his mule, Rosie, to the livery stable, Jackson stopped by the post office and was pleasantly surprised to have a letter from Miranda. He read it slowly outside, then went into the hotel lobby where AJ was waiting for their table at Beulah's to open up.

"So you going to tell me what your girl said?" AJ asked eagerly as Jackson joined him. "What's the East Coast news?"

Jackson opened his letter, glancing over it again. "Oh, there wasn't much news. Mostly it's about her school. She seems to like it well enough. And she's made a couple of friends. One girl is Jericho, and she's from New Orleans. The other girl sounds pretty interesting." He scanned down the letter. "Her name is Sadie McGuire, and she has bright red hair and is a good singer. Miranda thinks her father is a pirate."

"What makes her think that?"

"She says Sadie is mysterious, has traveled all over the world, and her father is very rich."

"Maybe Miranda's onto something." AJ chuckled. "Ya think there are any real pirates out on the high seas these days?"

Jackson shrugged. "I've heard stories of blackbirders, buccaneers, crimps. Who knows?"

"Yeah, and what about *Shanghai Kelly*?"

"I read about that guy. He had a birthday party aboard his ship then served whiskey laced with opium." Jackson frowned at AJ. Hopefully, he wouldn't ever fall for something like that.

"Yeah, in just one night, he shanghaied about a hundred men out of San Francisco."

Jackson tapped AJ's chest. "Just one more reason for you to stay away from hard drink, buddy."

"Nobody gets shanghaied in Alaska."

"What makes you so sure?" Jackson challenged. "There's a lot of lawlessness up here that no one ever talks about. I don't think a man can be too careful."

"The host is waving to us." AJ stood. "Looks like our table's ready."

As Jackson followed his partner across the dining room, he

wondered just how safe AJ would remain. Town was crawling with folks today. Some just looking to celebrate Thanksgiving. And many looking for a "good time." But a few predators would be looking for trouble.

Jackson didn't like the idea of being his "brother's keeper." But he'd gotten fond of AJ these past few months and didn't care to see his buddy go downhill again. Besides that, he felt they were getting close. If the tiny vein they'd just discovered played out, they would have plenty to keep them busy in the upcoming months. And it wouldn't be something Jackson could do very easily on his own. It was a two-man job. And that meant AJ needed to stay on the high road, which probably meant Jackson would have to make sure he did.

Miranda was pleasantly surprised how, in just two days, Sadie easily won over both Aunt Lilly and Uncle George, as well as their Thanksgiving guests. Whether she was playing piano or singing or telling stories, she was just as charming to the older crowd as she'd been to Miranda and Jericho. When Sadie invited Miranda to accompany her in song on Friday evening, performing for a few guests that had gathered for pie and coffee, Miranda couldn't have been more pleased. And, according to Cousin Margaret—who considered herself something of an expert on music—their voices had blended together beautifully.

The next morning, Aunt Lilly invited the girls to go to town with her. "We can do some shopping and have afternoon tea," she suggested, and they eagerly agreed.

As they strolled through town, Sadie pointed out a poster for a Harvest Faire and Dance at a local meeting hall. "Look, this is for this evening." She read the notice aloud. "Doesn't that sound fun?"

"Would you girls like to go?" Aunt Lilly asked.

Naturally, they both eagerly said yes. So it was agreed. Uncle George and Aunt Lilly would accompany the girls to the dance tonight. But back at the house, as the girls were getting dressed for the big evening, Sadie seemed a bit out of sorts. "I wish you aunt and uncle didn't have to go with us," she said in a somber tone.

"Oh, they'll probably just sit on the sidelines," Miranda assured her.

"But doesn't it make you feel like a child?" Sadie slid another hairpin into Miranda's hair, helping to pin it up. "As if they have to watch you every minute, like chaperones?"

Miranda shrugged. "I figured they just wanted to go to the dance for the fun of it."

"Maybe so. But I think they feel a responsibility to keep an eye on you." Sadie frowned. "Of course, you're only seventeen. I suppose they still think you're a little girl."

"No, I don't think so. I mean, they usually treat me like I'm grownup." Miranda considered this. "But you know, they never had children. So I suppose they don't quite understand how to do it. Maybe they just feel extra protective of me."

"Maybe. But you know I'm eighteen and—"

"You're eighteen?"

"Eighteen going on nineteen in February." Sadie held her head high.

"I thought first-year girls were my age or younger," Miranda admitted.

"I suspect my father may have lied about my age, in order to get me enrolled," Sadie tucked a curl behind Miranda's ear. "Plus he donated a bucket of money."

"Oh." Miranda considered this. "Does it really matter that you're older than the other first-year girls? It doesn't matter to me. And Jericho is only sixteen, but I don't mind that."

"I guess it doesn't matter. It might if I had to go all three years."

"You're not?"

"No." She firmly shook her head. "I only agreed to attend the academy for one year. And that's only because my father threatened to cut me off from my allowance if I didn't."

"Why is that?"

"Because he didn't think I was old enough to be out in the world on my own."

"And did you think you were?"

"Of course. But not if I was penniless. So my father forced my hand."

Miranda nodded. "That's sort of how it was with me too. My stepfather put it in his will. I was supposed to go to the university. But the academy is hard enough." She hated to think of how she could've been floundering in even harder classes right now.

"The academy isn't so hard." Sadie twisted one of her own curls around her finger, letting it fall down beside her cheek.

"Maybe not for you." Miranda had no illusions. She knew Sadie was smarter than her. Not just in worldly things, although that was true, but academically as well.

"You do fine in your classes, Miranda. I think your French is really coming along nicely."

"Thank you."

"Anyway, I'm just doing my time at the academy until the end of the school year. By next summer, I will be free as a bird and get my allowance. In the meantime, it's hard to be treated like a child *all* the time. I sort of wished we could be like grownups this weekend. You know?"

"Yes. I understand. I like being treated like a grownup too. I keep wishing Jackson would strike it rich and send for me, and we could get married and live however we like." Miranda sighed. "And if he doesn't do something by the end of the school year, well, I might just take the bull by the horns, so to speak."

"What do you mean?" Sadie put on a sparkling earring.

"I mean I might just go to him."

"You'd go to Alaska?" Sadie looked impressed.

"I've thought about it."

"By yourself?"

Miranda nodded, although she wondered if she was really that brave. And she wondered what Jackson would do if she actually did. Still, it was fun to dream about.

"And what would you do up in Alaska? Pressure Jackson to propose marriage to you? That doesn't sound very romantic."

"No, I wouldn't pressure him, that doesn't sound very nice. But I might entice him." Miranda smiled dreamily.

Sadie laughed. "Ever the romantic."

"Maybe. But I'm pretty sure he loves me."

"And you're sure you love him?" Sadie looked skeptical.

"Oh, yes, I am. I think about him all the time. I dream about him at night. I'm certain I love him."

"That's nice for you." Sadie sighed. "Well, I suppose we'll just have to settle for being treated like little girls for this evening."

"You don't look like a little girl." Miranda blinked to see how grownup Sadie actually looked with her red hair piled high and her well-fitting sapphire blue gown. "You look like an extremely pretty young woman."

"Why, thank you. And so do you." She moved next to Miranda so they could see themselves in the bureau mirror together. Sadie's sapphire blue looked lovely besides Miranda's lavender gown. "We sort of look like sisters," Sadie said suddenly. "We're the same height and our coloring is similar. Only I have freckles. You're lucky you don't."

"And your hair is redder." Miranda looked at her own auburn curls. "I wish mine was more like yours."

"And I wish mine was more like yours." Sadie threw back her head and laughed. "We always want what we don't have."

"Maybe so." Miranda remembered how often she'd longed to look more like Delia.

"Anyway, we will just have to make the best of it tonight, won't we?" Sadie reached for her fur trimmed wrap.

Miranda agreed as she reached for a woolen shawl.

"You can't use that granny shawl," Sadie told her. She went over to one of her bags and removed a fringe trimmed purple velveteen wrap. "This is much better."

"It's beautiful." Miranda pulled it on.

"Perfect with your gown." Sadie was tugging on her gloves.

"We'll be the belles of the ball." Miranda laughed.

"We will dance the night away," Sadie proclaimed.

And when they got to the festivities, thanks to Sadie's outgoing personality, that's exactly what happened. While Lilly and George joined some friends at a corner table, barely paying notice to Miranda and Sadie, the two girls proceeded to happily dance with a number of local boys and young men. Miranda would never had had so much confidence at a big dance like this, but she followed Sadie's lead, imitating her every move. And it was really fun!

All in all, it was one of the most delightful evenings Miranda had ever experienced. The only thing that could've made it better was if Jackson had been her partner. That would've been perfection.

By the time the girls were home and falling into bed exhausted, Miranda was convinced that she would never have a better friend than Sadie McGuire. She just wished she could find out more about her mysterious friend. And as Miranda drifted to sleep, she wondered...wouldn't it be exciting if Sadie's father truly was a pirate?

20

Mid-December
Colorado

Wyatt's idea to converge Miranda's old bedroom into theirs to create a sitting room turned out to be perfect. Now if Julius and Julianne were occupying the den, as they often did since there were more interesting activities to be found in there, or if Mother was crocheting in the parlor, an activity she classified as "work," or if Jefferson was simply roaming the house like a lion, eager to jump on any unsuspecting victim in order to "discuss" politics or any other controversial topics, Wyatt and Miranda could escape.

"As much as I appreciate having our little getaway, I am disturbed by the idea that we could be doing this indefinitely," Delia confessed one evening in early December.

"To be honest, I feel a little guilty sometimes." Wyatt laid his book in his lap.

"What do you have to feel guilty for?"

"Well, they are your parents. I realize Jefferson is your stepfather, but they did raise you, Delia. Perhaps we owe them more than just two rooms in this house."

"Two rooms and board for four people," she reminded him.

"Well, I have another idea…something I'd like to run by you." He stood, rubbing his chin with a thoughtful expression.

"What is it?"

"I was thinking about building a little guest cottage. Out by the orchard there's a good flat spot that even has a good view. We don't know how long your family plans to remain with us, and I thought having a small house for—"

"That's very generous of you, Wyatt. But it seems too much."

"So you wouldn't like a guest cottage?"

"A guest cottage that my stepfather will take over?" She knit even faster now, probably from frustration. "Just now you made it seem as if I owed him something. And perhaps I do, I'm not quite sure. But there's something I never told you about. In fact, it's something I never knew until I came out to Colorado. But it was my father's money—Winston Williams—that helped to support my family while I was growing up. Money that my stepfather helped squander. My real father sent money by way of his mother, a lovely woman I knew as Aunt Adelaide."

"Yes, I remember the elderly aunt who helped your family. She was actually your grandmother, right?"

"That's right. I always assumed she was Mother's aunt, a wealthy widow with no children and so she was generous to our family." Delia sighed. "I suppose it's because of that, combined with the way they deceived me…well, I don't like to sound miserly, but I honestly don't feel I owe my parents anything."

"I understand."

"Besides that, Wyatt, it's your money keeping the ranch going right now. But your gold mining assets can't last forever. Hopefully the ranch will be self-supporting soon. But if not for you, I probably would've had to sell this place by now."

"I like to think it's *our* money, Delia. And I like to believe God is the one providing for us. So even if the coffers run low, we can trust He will continue to provide. After all, he owns the cattle on a thousand hills."

"I agree, but do you really think it would be wise to invest in a guest cottage right now? Just for my family?"

"To be honest, I was thinking about Aunt Lilly and Uncle George too. We invited them to return with Miranda next summer. Wouldn't you like to have a lovely guest cottage for them to use?"

"You mean if my parents hadn't taken it over for good by then?"

"Well, in that case, we'd have more room here in the house." He grinned. "And I know you like being hospitable. No one's as good a hostess as you. Think how you would enjoy hosting family members or friends in a nice little guest cottage."

Delia laid down her knitting and went over to wrap her arms around him. "You always manage to bring me around, Wyatt. And you're right, I would love to have a guest cottage on our property. It's a wonderful idea." She paused at the sound of her siblings running up and down the stairs. "Goodness, if those two are already this antsy, with winter barely begun, I can't imagine how it'll be in January."

"Maybe we'll have a guest cottage by then." His eyes twinkled. "I already started to draw out some plans, and I've walked off the space. I think it could work. And I know we can afford it."

"It would be nice to have our home to ourselves." She sighed to imagine it.

"It's too bad we don't have a school out here for the twins. I think they miss that."

"I'm not sure about Julius, but I know Julianne does. I felt sorry for her when she got so sad about missing her friends at supper tonight. I know it's hard on her." She returned to the rocker and picked up her knitting.

"Do you think Jefferson is doing a good job with their studies?" he asked. "Your mother suggested you take over as their teacher."

"Yes, I know, but I have my ranch work to do."

"That's true. But not as much with winter here."

"Yes. And I do feel sorry for Julianne and Julius when I hear them doing their lessons with Jefferson. That man knows how to lecture, but he's not much of a teacher." She made an exasperated sigh "I couldn't help but overhear him this morning. He was ranting and raving about why Grover Cleveland was going to be the best president ever and what a horrible candidate Blaine had been."

"As if we hadn't heard enough of that already from him." Wyatt shook his head. "Does he never tire of politics?"

"Apparently not. According to Mother, political debate was his most popular activity at his men's club in Pittsburgh. I suppose he misses those lively discussions." She chuckled. "So I stupidly stuck my head into the den and stood up for James G. Blaine. I pointed out that Blaine had been an early supporter of Lincoln and Negro suffrage, as well as a few other things I thought my siblings should know about."

"How did that go?"

"You can probably imagine. The way Jefferson took me to task, going on and on about Cleveland as if he was defending himself, well, it made me wonder. Do you think Jefferson could possibly have more than a passing interest in politics?"

"You mean, would he run?"

"To hear him talk, one might think he was campaigning."

"Well, he's certainly longwinded enough to be a politician."

"And unscrupulous." Delia grimaced to imagine Jefferson in leadership position. He sure wouldn't get her vote!

"We've seen how he devours our newspapers. He reads every single page before I get a chance to see the headlines."

"That's because he thinks it's his responsibility to regurgitate the news stories back to us at mealtimes." Delia giggled. "Sorry, that wasn't very ladylike."

"But an accurate depiction." Wyatt laughed. "And think about it, Delia. His name is suited to politics. Jefferson Blackstone. Doesn't it sound like someone running for office?"

"It would go straight to his head if he were elected." She moaned. "There'd be no living with him. Not that I want him living here."

"I wouldn't worry about him being elected. Even if he did have those ideas, a man without resources or an address would be hard pressed to run for anything. Especially in his home state Pennsylvania. Competition there would be stiff."

"That's true enough." Still, she wondered. What if Jefferson Blackstone had aspirations for holding a position in Colorado? That might not even be too farfetched, given that this was such a young state and most of the folks here were relatively new. Still, it seemed unlikely. Like Wyatt had just said, Jefferson had neither funds nor address. Neither in Pennsylvania nor Colorado.

"Say, Delia, have you given much thought to Christmas?"

"What do you mean?"

"Well, I overheard Julianne talking to her mother about what she hoped to get for Christmas. She might as well have been asking for the moon."

"Oh, dear." Delia cringed. "The children are used to being spoiled at Christmastime. My mother always went overboard. She used to love to go shopping and having things wrapped up beautifully and delivered right before Christmas."

"I got that impression."

"I'm afraid Christmas will be disappointing to Julianne and Julius this year."

"But there must be things we can do, ways to make it special for them," he said eagerly. "Wouldn't it be fun?"

She considered this. "Well, I wouldn't want to go to a great expense. But it would be fun to do something festive. Something they could remember years from now."

"Good." He picked up his book again. "I'll leave the arrangements to you then."

"Will you bring us home a tree?" she asked hopefully.

"You tell me how tall and when you want it, and I'll fetch off the north hill. I saw some good ones up there."

"I'd like it one week before Christmas."

"That's just a few days from now."

"I know. But that's the way my mother always did it. And I liked that we got to enjoy it longer. Some of my friends didn't get their trees until Christmas Eve and then they took them down right after Christmas. It seemed a waste to me." Suddenly her mind was whirling. "I'll get the kids to help me make decorations. And they can help with baking."

"Great. They might need something to keep them busy when the weather's bad. Uncle Enoch told me we're going to get a big dump of snow in a day or two."

"How does he know?"

"His bones were aching."

She laughed. "Speaking of Christmas, that reminds me I wanted to get this sent to Miranda." She held up the lacy rose-colored shawl she was almost finished knitting. "I know she'll be with Lilly and George for Christmas, but I wanted to send her something from here. The letter that came yesterday sounded a bit homesick."

"Homesick?" He frowned. "Sounded to me she was having too much fun. She went to that dance with her friend Sadie at Thanksgiving. I was surprised Aunt Lilly and Uncle George condoned it."

"Yes, it did sound like she had fun. But she also seemed a little sad or overwhelmed. I worry that the school's classes are too hard for her."

"Time will tell."

"Anyway, I want to finish this shawl tonight and get it sent out care of Aunt Lilly tomorrow."

"You're sweet." He set his book aside and came over to give her a hug. "And I'm a lucky man to have you, my bride." He kissed her cheek. "I can hardly wait to see what you do for our Christmas."

"It would be fun to really decorate this house. Do you think you'd have time to gather up some greens for garlands when you go up to get the tree?"

"Of course." He pointed a finger in the air. "In fact, it gives me an idea. Let's you and me invite the kids to go on the tree hunt with us. We'll take a wagon, or a sled if it's snowing. I saw that one in back of the barn. You can pack us a lunch, and we'll make a day of it."

"I love that idea! The kids will too." She frowned. "Is it all right if we don't invite my parents?"

He chuckled. "It's all right with me."

Delia felt a tiny bit guilty, except that she knew her mother wouldn't want to go outside in the cold weather. And if her stepfather went, he'd probably just get on his political soapbox and spoil everything anyway. No, this would be a time for just her and Wyatt and the children—what a fun way to get Christmas started!

21

Jackson was pleasantly surprised by how hard AJ had been working the mine. His slump over losing everything seemed to have been replaced with an unexpected optimistic outlook on life and luck and everything. Fortunate…since Jackson's spirits were drooping considerably.

"I know we're getting close," AJ declared after they'd finished a long dark day in their cave-like claim. "I can *feel* it!"

"All I feel is tired, sore, and cold," Jackson confessed as he attempted to poke the campfire coals to life. He knelt down to blow onto the fire they tried to keep going at the mouth of the cave, catching his breath just as red embers started to glow.

"You know what they say, Jackson, it's always darkest before the dawn." AJ set a cast iron pan on the grate.

Jackson stood up, stretching his back. "It feels like nothing but darkness here to me, and I can't even remember the last time I saw dawn."

"Well, sure. We're working underground," AJ reached for their canvas bag of biscuit mix. "If it makes you feel any better, the days will start getting longer after today."

"Really?" Jackson felt doubtful as he threw some fresh coffee grounds into the pot that still held leftover coffee from morning.

"You bet. Today's December 21st. Shortest day of the year. Tomorrow will be longer."

Jackson considered this. "That means Christmas is this week?"

"That's right."

Jackson frowned at AJ. "You think we'd be safe to go to town for a few days?"

"Safe? What'd'ya mean? You think someone'll jump our claim?" AJ measured biscuit mix into a tin bowl.

"I mean would you be able to keep your pledge?" Jackson diverted his eyes as he set the coffee pot on the grate.

"I told you, Jackson. I'm done with that stupidity for good." AJ vigorously stirred water into the biscuit batter.

"Well, we both got some bullion to sell." Jackson patted the little leather pouch down deep in his jeans pocket. "And a hot bath and steak dinner sure sounds good to me."

"And sleeping in a real bed?" AJ's eyes lit up.

"You think there'll be rooms anywhere?"

"Might be." AJ dropped messy globs of biscuit dough onto the greased cast iron griddle. "If we got an early start on the holiday, we might beat others to the punch."

"Want to leave tomorrow?" Jackson suddenly hoped he'd find a letter from Miranda. Last time in town, there'd been nothing. And that got him worried.

"No arguments from me."

As they ate their usual dinner of biscuits and beans and bacon, Jackson hoped this town trip during holidays wouldn't backfire on him. All he needed was for AJ to sample some "Christmas cheer"—everything he'd been working for might be ruined. He wondered if he even had enough gold bullion to make it home at this time... or if there'd even be a ship sailing. He knew that winter sea travel was patchy at best. But if he didn't hear from Miranda, he might be tempted to call it quits up here. He hated to admit that she'd gotten that much of a hold on him, but it seemed undeniable.

After they called it a night, Jackson continued to feel fretful. The darkness, the cold, the disappointment of not getting that big strike…it all was running through his head. On top of that was his worries over AJ. What would he do if his partner did return to his wayward path while in town? He knew he couldn't safely work the claim on his own. Not this time of year and not this deep into the mine they'd been carving out. Besides that, it was legally both of theirs. So if Jackson really struck the mother lode, it would be half AJ's whether he'd helped or not. That didn't seem fair.

As sleep continued to evade his tire bones, Jackson realized his anxiety wasn't as much over the long Alaskan winter, or AJ falling off the wagon, as it was about Miranda. What if she'd given up on him? It was hard to admit, even to himself, how much he'd come to rely on her bright cheerful letters…or of how often he dreamt of taking the girl he loved into his arms. Wasn't that just natural?

But what if Miranda had found someone else in Philadelphia? Some citified young fellow with lots of money? It could happen. She'd written to him about her best friend Sadie McGuire. Jackson wasn't sure why, but he was certain that Sadie wasn't the best influence for Miranda. Even if her pa wasn't a pirate.

Mostly he hoped and prayed that Miranda would remain safe and sound…and still in love with him. She had been, hadn't she? Could a girl like her fall as easily out of love as she'd seemed to have fallen into it? These were questions he had no answers to. He wondered what Ma would say? Probably she'd say, "If it's meant to be, it'll be." But those words were about as comforting as the hard rock surface his bedroll was laid out on.

It was a few days before Christmas break, and all the girls in the academy were antsy. For the most part the teachers and supervisors seemed to tolerate their whispers and giggles and lightheartedness.

But when Sadie McGuire let loose with a swear word after burning her hand in cooking class, Miss Spencer lost her patience.

"Straight to the office, Miss McGuire," she ordered Sadie. "Confess your bad language to the dean and take the consequences, young lady."

As Sadie removed her apron, she exchanged a mischievous glance with Miranda and then, holding her head high as if she hadn't a concern in the world, she was on her way.

"Can you believe she was so silly?" Lottie whispered to Miranda. "Didn't she realize Miss Spencer was listening?"

"I don't know." Miranda shrugged, but lowered her voice. "Our cowhands say 'blast it' a lot, and I never thought it was all that terrible."

"What did you say?" Beatrice Phillips demanded loudly from behind Miranda.

"Nothing." Miranda felt her cheeks grow warm as the class grew quiet and Miss Spencer's eyes narrowed.

"You did too," Beatrice insisted. "I heard you swear, Miranda Williams." She pointed at Lottie. "You heard her too, didn't you?"

Lottie looked uneasy, but barely nodded.

"Is this true?" Miss Spencer asked Miranda.

"I didn't actually swear." Miranda wanted a way to explain. "I merely admitted that our ranch hands sometimes use, uh, what some people call bad language."

"It was worse than that. She said the actual curse words," Beatrice tattled. "I heard her say the exact same thing as Sadie. And it figures, they're best friends. Birds of a feather flock together."

Miss Spencer frowned. "Then you go to the office too, Miss Williams. Tell the dean what you did and accept your punishment."

Miranda swallowed hard as she untied her apron. What was the punishment for using bad language? Based on Miss Spencer's reaction, it was excessive. What if the school revoked Christmas vacation? That would be truly terrible. She'd looked forward to it since Thanksgiving. Even though Sadie would spend the holidays with her family at the fancy Continental Hotel, the two girls had made plans to meet up during their time off. Sadie had invited Miranda to join her family for a meal as well as to attend a formal ball at the hotel on New Year's Eve. For a full week, Miranda had been dreaming of what fun they would have.

As she slowly walked across campus, Miranda hoped and prayed their infraction, which seemed so minor, wouldn't change any plans for Christmas. How could anyone be that unfair? As she entered the administration building, she spied Sadie sitting on the bench outside of Mrs. Grampton's office.

"What are *you* doing here?" Sadie's auburn brows arched.

Miranda explained, and for some reason, Sadie found this to be highly amusing. She giggled so loudly, Miranda felt certain Mrs. Grampton would pop out of her office and throw both of them into detention until next year. Miranda had only been to the dean's office once before, and that was for not completing her arithmetic homework. But she'd politely explained that she'd had an awful headache the night before and thought she was coming down with something. And maybe she hadn't felt too well, but it wasn't completely honest. The truth was, she'd been writing a long letter to Jackson. A letter that stupid Beatrice had stolen the next morning—at least that's what Lottie claimed when Miranda had discovered it missing after their midday meal. But Mrs. Grampton had been surprisingly understanding about the whole thing. She'd simply scolded Miranda then sent her off to complete the homework. However, this felt more serious.

"I can't believe it," Sadie whispered. "You actually said what I said? Out loud so everyone could hear?"

Miranda just nodded.

"How could you be so dumb?"

"I was talking to Lottie. And all I said was that our cow hands say words like that all the time. Sometimes worse. I didn't think *blast it* was so terrible."

Sadie threw back her head and laughed loudly now. "You slay me!"

Just then the door to the dean's office door flew open. With her glasses balanced on her long narrow nose and her gray hair pulled into a severe bun, she always looked intimidating. That combined with her supreme authority made all the girls fear her. "What, may I ask, is going on out here?" She scowled at the girls. "Why are you sitting outside my door creating a ruckus?"

"Miss Spencer sent us to you," Sadie spoke up. "We're supposed to confess that we used bad language."

"*Both* of you?" Mrs. Grampton's brow creased even deeper.

Sadie confirmed this and Miranda mutely nodded.

"Into my office," the old woman grimly commanded.

Sadie led the way proudly and Miranda, head hung low in embarrassment, followed. Mrs. Grampton pointed to a pair of chairs, instructing them to sit. For a long moment, she simply studied them.

"Well, bad language is a serious infringement of academy rules. I'm sure you're both aware of this. You've read the student manual, have you not?"

"I read it," Sadie answered.

"Yes," Miranda muttered. "Me too."

"I have also," Mrs. Grampton corrected Miranda.

"Yes, I have also." Miranda stared at her hands in her lap.

"So you both understand that we expect our young ladies to speak graciously with polite decorum. You both understand that your words betray the thoughts of your hearts? Good begets good and evil begets evil."

Sadie said nothing, but Miranda nodded.

"And yet you allowed a curse to pass over your lips?"

"Yes," Sadie somberly admitted. "I said it first." She held up a red finger. "But it was only because I burnt myself on the soufflé pan. It hurt a lot."

"That does look painful." Mrs. Grampton sounded almost sympathetic. "But just because you injure yourself is no excuse to speak profanely, Miss McGuire."

"I know." Sadie nodded glumly. "And I do apologize for uttering a curse like that. Truth be told, I've heard my father say the same thing. A lot. I guess I didn't think."

"Well, from now on, you must learn to think before you speak." She turned her attention to Miranda. "And, you, what have you to say for yourself? It seems to me if you witnessed your friend's consequences for using offensive language, you would've watched your tongue more carefully. Or did you burn your finger as well?" Her expression was skeptical.

"No, no, I didn't burn my finger. I simply told my friend that I've heard the cow hands on our ranch use those same words. And I guess I used the words when I explained it to her. But I didn't say them as a curse. I was just—"

"It seems to me you were even more disrespectful, Miss Williams. You didn't express that curse out of pain or shock. You simply said it in matter-of-fact conversation. Even though you'd just seen Miss McGuire reprimanded."

"Yes, I suppose I was very stupid."

"That's not a pretty word for a young lady to use either." Mrs. Grampton shook her head. "I realize you grew up on a ranch out west, Miss Williams. But that is no excuse to flaunt our rules." She looked back at Sadie. "And just because your father uses bad language does not make it right for you to do so."

"I know." Sadie apologized again, even more profusely this time. And once again Miranda followed her example. Then they took turns promising to be more prudent in the future.

"Well, you both need to understand this infraction goes into your record. It's a demerit against your name. And you both already have one violation." She shook her head. "This is only your fourth month here. You do know that first-year students can be terminated on the third infringement? You realize it's in the contract your parents or guardians have agreed to? So you both fully understand what this means?"

They both nodded somberly.

"One more demerit of disobedience and we may have to dismiss you."

They both nodded again.

"For your punishment, you will both be assigned to the kitchen. You will perform chores before and after supper. You will continue your kitchen duties every day from now until Christmas break begins. You may report directly to the head cook."

Miranda cringed to imagine spending the next few nights peeling potatoes and washing dishes, but she was relieved that Mrs. Grampton hadn't taken away their Christmas break.

"At least we get to be punished together," Sadie said once they were safely away from the office. "Is that why you cursed too? So you could be with me?" She reached for Miranda's hand. "You really are my best friend. Don't worry, we can make it fun. Maybe the cook won't mind if we sing while we work."

Suddenly the punishment didn't feel too severe. Maybe that was why Miranda had spoken the curse out loud like that earlier… maybe she had wanted to be punished with her best friend. Wasn't it sort of noble? Still, she was concerned about how Aunt Lilly would react if she were ever to hear about this. She had kindly taken the role of Miranda's guardian in regard to the academy. And the last time Miranda had seen Aunt Lilly, she'd seemed genuinely proud of Miranda. But what would she say if she found out Miranda had two infractions against her? Hopefully, she would never know.

The next few days felt long and tiring. Besides the usual schoolwork and exams, Miranda had kitchen duty to look forward to every afternoon. That mean no free time. As much as she wanted to write Jackson a nice long letter, she was too tired by the end of the day. It was all she could do not to fall too far behind in her studies.

"Are you worried about failing?" she quietly asked Sadie as they walked toward the dormitories on the last day of school before Christmas vacation.

"Failing what?"

"Your classes." Miranda let out a sigh. "I feel sure that I made a mess of my arithmetic exam this morning."

"Oh, I don't worry about those things," Sadie said lightly.

"But we only have one more demerit before we're ousted."

Sadie shrugged. "So."

"So?" Miranda looked curiously at her. "What will happen to you if you are kicked out? Won't your father be upset?"

"Maybe. But I could figure something out." Sadie held her head high. "I'm eighteen, Miranda. I'm not a baby. If I have to make my own way in this world, I can. In fact, I think it would be exciting."

Miranda wished she felt that brave. "Well, if I failed here, I suppose I'd just have to go home to Colorado. And I'm sure they'd all be terribly disappointed in me."

"Jackson too?"

Miranda wondered.

"Why worry about something you can do nothing about?" Sadie asked as they went into the dormitory.

She considered this. "I guess that makes sense."

"Tomorrow we will be free of this oppressive place, Miranda. Why not think about your Christmas vacation plans?"

"Good idea." Miranda nodded. "I can't wait to see Aunt Lilly and Uncle George." That is, unless they knew about her two demerits....

"And you're going to visit Papa and me at the Continental. And we will go shopping. And then there's the New Year's Eve dance to plan for. We have so much to look forward to, Miranda. So please do not be such a dark, gloomy cloud."

Miranda hugged Sadie. "You're right. Sorry about being so glum. I think I'm just worn out from all that work."

Sadie hugged her back. "Don't worry. A couple of days from now, you'll be having so much fun you won't even remember our stint at kitchen duty. We have all of Christmas vacation to live like grownup and independent young women. I am sick and tired of being treated like an infant."

As she got ready for bed, Miranda hoped Sadie was right about their upcoming time off from school. Because she was tired of being treated like a child too. Hopefully Aunt Lilly and Uncle George would realize that and respect her as an adult.

22

JACKSON TRIED TO HIDE HIS DISAPPOINTMENT AS HE LEFT THE Juneau Post Office. "Ready for that steak dinner?" he asked AJ with a forced smile. "I'm starved."

"Me too. But let's get Rosie to the livery and secure some beds first," AJ suggested. "I just heard that the Kodiak is already booked full, and they're the cheapest hotel in town."

"How about boarding houses?"

"Good luck with that," an old, grisly-looking miner growled at them. "I already been to most all of 'em, and there's not a room to be had nowhere. Well, 'ceptin' the Nugget, but they're asking a fortune. Take me a year to pay for a week in that place."

Jackson and AJ exchanged glances as the old guy tottered off. "Wonder what he considers a fortune," Jackson muttered as he fingered his leather pouch. They'd already exchanged most of their bullion for what they felt was enough cash for their little holiday stay in Juneau. What little Jackson had left, he wanted to hold onto.

"Maybe the old fella's had a bad year." AJ jerked his thumb toward the Nugget. "Only one way to find out how much it'll set us back."

Even though Jackson didn't like the idea of staying at the pricey

Nugget, since he knew the reputation it had for dance girls, drinking, and gambling, he'd been looking forward to a hot bath and a few nights in a warm bed. Still, they couldn't afford to waste all their funds on just a few days. "Don't forget we need to replenish our supplies and I need a new pickax," he reminded AJ as they entered the fancy hotel lobby.

Fortunately, although the price of a room was pretty steep, it wasn't as bad as the old miner had insinuated. And, as AJ pointed out, they would save some money on a bathhouse since the Nugget had plumbed bathrooms. "Let's live it up for a change," AJ said as they went into their room. "Woo-hoo!"

"We can live it up, as long as you don't live it up too much," Jackson warned.

"You got my word on that." AJ dropped his bag on the floor. "Toss ya for who gets the first bath."

Jackson wasn't too disappointed when AJ won the toss. "How 'bout I take Rosie to the livery and pick up supplies while you get cleaned up? Might be better selection now than after the town really fills up for Christmas."

"Might get better prices too." AJ dug into his pocket then handed over his cash. "Don't forget to get us some new hickory shovel handles. And I could use some new gloves."

"You got it." Jackson reached for his hat. "I'll be back in an hour or so."

"Why don't you make us a reservation for supper?" AJ suggested. "I heard that man in the lobby saying that was the only way to get a table tonight."

"Good idea." As Jackson went downstairs, he felt a wave of relief to have AJ's extra cash in hand. At least this would secure their supplies. Now if AJ fell off the bandwagon, the worst he could do was blow his food money. And if he did that, Jackson was determined to enjoy his big steak dinner just the same. AJ could dine in the room on their food supplies if he broke his promise. Just deserts.

Town was already getting busier, and it turned out to be a good thing that Jackson was gathering supplies early. Already they were running out of a few things and some prices were going up right before his eyes.

"Seems like the only ones getting rich 'round here are the shysters selling us supplies," a short, stocky miner grumbled as he slapped his cash on the counter of the general store.

"Ya can always take your business elsewhere," the storekeeper shot back at him with a sly grin directed to Jackson, who was next in line.

"And where'd that be?" another man challenged from behind.

"Look, I don't have to serve any of you," the storekeeper yelled. "If ya'll can't act civilized, get on outta my store."

Jackson forced a smile as he handed the storekeeper his list. "I'd be grateful if you could fill this order for me, sir."

"Now that's what I like." The storekeeper nodded. "A mannerly miner."

There were a few snickers that Jackson suspected were at his expense, but as the storekeeper measured his flour, coffee, sugar, and things, it appeared he was being more fair than he'd been with the customer ahead of him.

"There ya go, young man." He announced the total, and although it was surprisingly high, Jackson counted out the money without complaint.

"Thank you, sir. Now you have a Merry Christmas." Jackson smiled as he picked up the wooden box.

"You too, young man." The storekeeper dropped a couple of candy-canes on top of the dry goods. "Thank you for your business."

Jackson politely dipped his head at the waiting customers as he left, and unless he imagined it, they looked slightly bewildered, as if pondering the possibility of attaining better service if one was courteous. What an idea!

Jackson whistled as he strolled through the busy town. Sure, Miranda hadn't written to him like he hoped, but that was probably because she was busy with her studies. And she'd told him how restrictive the academy was, and how it was very protective over the girls, and how no males were allowed on the campus. In the last letter he'd gotten from her, she'd compared it to a nunnery and a prison. Really, he assured himself as he went into the hotel, she was in very good hands. Learning to be a good wife and being educated. What more could he ask for?

The hotel lobby was busier now, and he could hear jovial voices coming from the attached barroom. Probably just miners starting their celebrations early…and those in the lobby seemed to be cleaned up and dressed nicer than earlier. Also, there were a number of young women loitering about. Jackson could tell by their colorful, fancy dresses and painted lips they were dance girls and to be avoided at all cost, lest they empty out a fellow's pockets and rob him of his self-respect. Like they'd done with AJ.

Despite their flirtatious smiles, these young women were not going to get the best of Jackson O'Neil. He was no fool. He paused on the staircase and balancing his loaded box on the banister, removed his hat, and mentally compared his Miranda to these flashy women. Many of them had hair that appeared to have been dyed or tinted. But Miranda's curly auburn locks were her own. And their painted lips didn't compare to Miranda's full, youthful ones. And her figure was better too. No, their temptations were not tempting to him. The only thing they had over Miranda was that they were here and she was thousands of miles away. But someday they would be together again. He just knew it.

Miranda's Christmas with Aunt Lilly and Uncle George was not nearly as jolly as she'd hoped. To begin with, Mrs. Grampton had telephoned Aunt Lilly with the news that Miranda had already attained two demerits at the academy. Not surprisingly, this did not sit well with Uncle George. And it hurt to see his disappointment in her.

But Aunt Lilly seemed even more scandalized by the news. Probably because she worried her friend Millie would hear of it.

On her first day of vacation, Miranda attempted to explain the two situations at suppertime. "The academy is a good school, but they treat first-year students like we are infants. And I'm going on eighteen. A lot of girls get married by my age."

"The school is trying to train up their girls to be respectable young women," Aunt Lilly reminded her. "How can you fault them for enforcing honest and good character?"

"Well, I made up my arithmetic with a passable grade the very next day. And I didn't actually swear. I simply mentioned that, back on the ranch where I grew up, certain words aren't considered to be profane." Miranda sighed. "I thought it was unfair that Sadie got in trouble for saying *blast it.*" She covered her mouth. "Sorry. Mrs. Grampton warned me I need to think before I speak."

Uncle George almost looked amused by this confession, but Aunt Lilly seemed truly disturbed. "Mrs. Grampton is right, Miranda. A young lady should be able to control her tongue. Even if you don't find a word offensive, it's possible that others do. For instance, if we'd had guests here and you explained yourself like that, well, some ladies would be offended."

"I understand." Miranda nodded somberly. "And I do want to control my tongue, I really do. But I suppose I grew up with so much freedom on the ranch…well, acting ladylike doesn't come naturally."

"I think we've gone on about this long enough," Uncle George said to his wife. "Let's trust that Miranda has learned her lesson and won't get any more demerits against her."

"I hope you're right." Aunt Lilly's brow creased as she turned back to Miranda. "It's just that Mrs. Grampton told me how many first-year students don't make it into the second year. The second-year class is smaller for that very reason. And it seems the third-year class is the most exclusive, yet girls who graduate—"

"I don't want to be there for more than one year," Miranda said quickly. "That's plenty for me."

"Well, let's just hope you make it for the whole year." Aunt Lilly sighed. "I'd rather not have Millie reminding me of the favor she did…and how it turned out."

"I'll try to do better," Miranda promised.

And although she thought that was the end of that discussion, the topic came up again a couple days after Christmas when Miranda wanted to visit Sadie at the Continental.

"I'm not sure that Sadie is a good influence on you," Aunt Lilly told her.

"She's my best friend." Miranda frowned. "I thought you and Uncle George liked her."

"Well, she's a likeable girl. But according to Mrs. Grampton, she has a bit of a wild streak in her. Mrs. Grampton confided to me that she will be surprised if Sadie lasts a full year at the academy."

Miranda considered this. Without Sadie there, Miranda would feel lost. Already, she'd felt her other friends, Lottie and Jericho, both distancing themselves from her and Sadie. At first they'd complained about them singing and laughing and cutting up, then they'd stepped even further away after the cursing incident. It was as if they thought Miranda and Sadie could contaminate them somehow.

"Uncle George and I feel it's best for you to refrain from spending too much time with Sadie," Aunt Lilly explained. "For your own sake, dear."

"But I was only going to have dinner with her at the hotel. I'd love to see the Continental, Aunt Lilly."

Aunt Lilly frowned. "I understand…and I have an idea. How about if you and I meet Sadie and her mother for tea?"

Miranda bit her lip. "I don't think her mother is there."

"I thought you said Sadie was there with her family?"

"To be honest, I don't know if Sadie even has a mother. But I do know her father will be there."

"So you really don't know that much about Sadie's family, do you?" Aunt Lilly looked concerned.

"I guess not. She doesn't really talk about them much. I mean, she talks about places they've been and all that. But I don't even know if she has brothers or sisters. And she's never mentioned her mother. But she does talk about her father. She calls him Papa."

"The one you thought might be a pirate?" Aunt Lilly's brows arched.

"Oh, I was only joking about that. I'm sure he's not a real pirate. But maybe a sea captain. Sadie said something about Papa's ship once, and I asked if he was a captain."

"And what did she say?"

"Just one of her mysterious answers. Sadie is very mysterious."

Aunt Lilly shook her head. "Well, unless I accompany you to the Continental to meet with Sadie's family, whoever they may be, I'm afraid I'll have to put my foot down. Delia specifically asked me to watch out for your welfare and, although I've never had children of my own, I feel a very maternal responsibility for you, dear." She patted Miranda's back. "I do hope you'll understand."

"So I don't get to see Sadie at all?" Miranda tried to hide her anger. Was it possible that Aunt Lilly was going to treat her even more like a child than the academy?

"Like I said, I'm happy to go with you. We could have a lovely tea party with Sadie and—"

"But I don't want a tea party. I want to feel like a grownup and dine with them at the hotel. Without being accompanied by a chaperone." Miranda stuck out her chin. "I don't mean to hurt your feelings, Aunt Lilly. But I've been looking forward to this."

"I'm sorry, dear. That's the best I can offer."

Miranda pursed her lips and took in a deep breath. She was about to bring up the New Year's Eve dance, but she knew that Aunt Lilly's stance on that would probably be even stronger than the dinner invitation. So perhaps Miranda had learned something in all of this after all. She could hold her tongue. And somehow, she planned to sneak out and go to that celebration on New Year's Eve. She just needed to figure out a foolproof plan.

For the next few days, Miranda tried to appear the model of good, ladylike behavior. Although she telephoned Sadie at the hotel a couple of times, she never brought up her name to Aunt Lilly or Uncle George. She made herself helpful and congenial in their home, and when New Year's Eve day came, she complained of a headache.

"But we're all invited to the Sampsons' tonight," Aunt Lilly reminded Miranda that afternoon. "They have the best New Year's Eve parties."

Miranda let out a sad sigh, pulling the rose-colored shawl that Delia had sent for Christmas more tightly around her shoulders. "That sounds nice…but my headache is pounding. A roomful of noisy merrymakers sounds torturous to me. I'd rather just go to bed early."

Aunt Lilly touched her forehead. "You don't feel feverish."

"I don't think I'm sick. Just this silly headache." Miranda smiled weakly. "If I feel better, I might sit down and write Jackson a nice, long letter. I'm afraid I'm overdue. But I do hope you and Uncle George will have a good evening seeing in the New Year. And please, don't worry about me."

"If you're sure you're not really ill." Aunt Lilly squeezed her hand.

"I'll be just fine," she assured her. "Maybe we could have that tea party you mentioned tomorrow."

Aunt Lilly brightened. "Yes, I would love that. We will plan on it." Now she frowned. "But what about your supper? I gave the cook the night off."

"I can find something, Aunt Lilly. Don't worry. I'll just fix something to take up to my room."

So it was settled. Not only had Miranda gotten herself excused from the Sampsons' party, she would have the whole house to herself.

But first she took to her room and, wearing her dressing gown, she meekly told Aunt Lilly goodnight when she came to check on her.

"You get a good night's rest, and we will have a lovely little tea party tomorrow."

"I'll look forward to it." Miranda complimented Aunt Lilly's gown then leaned back in the chair with a weary sigh. "You have fun."

As soon as Lilly and George left the house, Miranda peeled off her dressing gown and finished getting ready for her big night. She'd decided to wear the peach-colored gown that she'd worn for Delia's wedding. As she pinned her hair up high, she thought of that day… and how she'd danced with Jackson. If only he were here now. She wondered if he was sleeping outside in the cold—how cold did it get up there in Alaska?

She glanced at the clock to see it was getting late and Sadie had promised to send a carriage by eight. But she still needed to make it look as if her bed was being slept in. She quickly rolled up an extra blanket and pillow and created what she hoped would pass for her sleeping self if anyone decided to check on her. Then, feeling a bit like Cinderella sneaking off to the ball, Miranda hurried downstairs and stood in the foyer, watching for her ride.

When she saw the shiny black coach pull up, she was pleasantly surprised to see that Sadie was waving from inside. "I'm so happy to see you." Miranda hugged her friend as she got in.

"We are going to have the time of our lives," Sadie promised as the coach took off. "Wait until you see the Continental. It's all decorated and full of partiers. I've never seen such a crowd."

The two girls chattered happily as the coach rattled toward town. And soon they were getting out of the coach and entering the well-lit hotel. Miranda felt grownup and excited. Everything was as Sadie had described and better.

Soon the girls were dancing the night away with well-dressed gentlemen of varying ages and backgrounds and, as Sadie had predicted, having the time of their lives. As they took a refreshment break, Miranda inquired about Sadie's father.

"Oh, Papa? Good grief, he's probably three sheets to the wind by now."

"Oh?" Miranda felt a bit uneasy. "So he's not attending this party?"

"Sure. He was over there." She tipped her head to where some tables were set up by the bar. "Swapping stories and drinking rum, acting like the old man of the sea. Why?"

"I, uh, I was hoping to meet him." Actually Miranda's conscience had been comforted to think Sadie's father was nearby. Like an unseen chaperone should they need him. It was a bit disconcerting to realize they were completely on their own.

"Oh, there he is." Sadie pointed toward the bar. "See that old fellow with the bushy white hair and beard? That's Papa."

Miranda's eyes grew wide. "He looks old."

"He *is* old. Sixty-five." Sadie laughed. "Come on, I'll introduce you." She led Miranda over to where a lot of older men were gathered at tables and drinking. "Papa, meet my best friend, Miranda." She winked at Miranda. "And this is Captain Mac."

"Pleased to make your acquaintance." Captain Mac took Miranda's hand and actually kissed it. "Any friend of Sadie's is a friend of mine. You girls could pass as sisters." He tweaked one of Miranda's loose curls. "And your hair's almost as red as Sadie's too."

"No, Papa, her hair is auburn." Sadie corrected.

"Are you really a captain?" Miranda asked him.

"You bet I am." He nodded vigorously. "Got me own fleet too."

"You're down to one ship, Papa." Sadie narrowed her eyes. "Remember?"

"Well, I *had* me own fleet. Not so long ago." He reached for a tumbler of what was probably rum and took a sip then got a grim expression. "Not so long ago, but another lifetime…another world."

Miranda was curious what that meant, but Sadie seemed intent on getting her back to the dance floor. "Nice to meet you," Miranda called out as Sadie tugged her away.

"Don't take his prattle too seriously," Sadie told Miranda. "He goes on and on when he's drinking."

"He seems interesting," Miranda said as a pair of young men approached them. And soon they were dancing again. But after a few dances, Miranda's right heel seemed to be developing a blister. So she decided to take a break and, seeing Captain Mac sitting by himself at a table, she decided to join him.

"Oh, good. You're back." He lifted his tumbler to her. "I'd offer you a drink, but I know you're too young because my Sadie's too young. But I could order you a sarsaparilla."

Before she could decline his offer, he was waving to a barmaid, yelling out to "Bring a sarsaparilla for the little lady."

She thanked him then politely inquired about his travels around the world. "Sadie seems to have been everywhere and seen everything," she said. "But I never realized you really were a ship's captain." She giggled. "I thought maybe you were a pirate."

He laughed then got serious. "Worse than a pirate, little lady."

The barmaid set down the sarsaparilla with an exasperated expression, as if Miranda had no business sitting over here. And maybe she didn't, but Captain Mac didn't seem concerned. "How could you be worse than a pirate?" Miranda quietly asked.

"There's seamen worse than pirates," he growled. "And there's things better left unsaid. Things no man is proud of."

"Oh?" Miranda felt more than a little curious as she sipped her sarsaparilla.

"My papa was a seaman. A captain too. Made his fortune in shipping. Started with one rat infested boat and ended up with a fleet of five vessels." He stared down at his drink.

"And so that's how you became a captain?" she gently prodded. "You followed in your father's footsteps?" She sipped her drink.

He looked at her with teary eyes. "My papa didn't know t'was wrong. There weren't no laws back then."

"No laws?" She felt confused.

"Just the laws of the high seas."

"Was your father a pirate?"

"Miranda Williams!" Sadie grabbed her by the forearm, glaring down at her. "What are you doing here?"

"I got a blister on my heel. I just wanted a rest."

Sadie narrowed her eyes. "So you're questioning my papa?"

"We're just talking, Sadie." His smile looked a bit sloppy and his speech sounded slurred. "Miranda's a good girl. You been telling me she's a good girl. Now I believe you. She's a good girl and a good friend."

"She's a good girl who's snooping." Sadie pulled Miranda to her feet. "I thought you came here to dance."

Miranda's heel still burned, but she nodded, allowing Sadie to escort her back to the dance floor. But as she danced with a short, pudgy man who smelled like beer, she thought she was getting a real headache now. And then, as the ballroom got noisier and people were yelling "Happy New Year!" she began to feel dizzy and wobbly, as if she were about to faint.

"What's wrong with you?" Sadie asked her.

"I don't know." Miranda clung to Sadie.

"Have you been drinking?" Sadie demanded.

"Just sarsaparilla," she muttered. "But I don't feel good."

"I think someone put something stronger in your drink." Sadie linked her arm in Miranda's and led her through the noisy crowd. But as they walked, everything grew blurry and fuzzy…and after that, nothing.

23

By the time Miranda woke up, the room was light. But it was not her room at Aunt Lilly's and it was not her dorm room. She sat up and looked around the luxurious room, trying to remember how she'd come to be here.

"You're awake." Sadie came to the bed and set a tray in Miranda's lap. "Here's some tea and toast."

"Where am I?"

"My room. In the Continental." Sadie sat down with a concerned expression. "I think someone slipped something into your sarsaparilla. I asked Papa and he doesn't remember. But that's not surprising."

"What time is it?"

"It's almost nine." Sadie frowned. "I thought about calling your aunt and uncle but wanted to check with you first since I know you sneaked out."

Miranda let out a low groan. "They're going to be very upset."

"Maybe they don't know. They might think you're sleeping in."

Miranda considered this.

"I thought we could sneak you home and you could just say you went out for a walk," Sadie suggested. "Of course, you couldn't wear your gown. But you could borrow something of mine."

"Do you think it would work?" She gulped down her tea then pushed the tray aside.

"It's worth a try." Sadie laid a blue woolen suit across the bed. "You'll have to leave your evening things with me. I can bring them to school with me on Monday."

So with Sadie's help, Miranda got dressed and they were soon on their way. "I'm sorry I got angry at you last night," Sadie told Miranda. "I shouldn't have said you were snooping. Papa said you were just having a polite conversation."

Miranda was so worried about Aunt Lilly's reaction that she could barely remember what had been said last night.

"Papa has things in his life that shame him," Sadie explained in a tone that was strangely serious. "Things he doesn't talk about unless he's been drinking. And he was definitely drinking last night."

"Yes, I remember that." Miranda studied her friend closely. Were those unshed tears in Sadie's eyes?

"Most of the time Papa lives like a respectable sea captain. But he has—" Her voice cracked with emotion. "He has his demons, Miranda. Oh, he's never been mean or wicked or anything. But his father was...."

"Your father mentioned something," Miranda offered.

Sadie blinked. "You might as well know that my grandfather was not a good man. He did some shameful things to get wealthy. And my papa, well, he feels guilty about it sometimes. Especially if he's been drinking."

Miranda simply nodded. Had Sadie's grandfather been a pirate?

"Papa wants me to be respectable. That's why we made the deal for me to spend one full year at the academy. And Papa likes you, Miranda. He thinks you're a good influence on me." Sadie grasped her hand. "And you are! You are truly my best friend. The best friend I've ever had."

"You're my best friend too, Sadie." Miranda paused as Aunt Lilly and Uncle George's house came in sight. "And I'm grateful you took care of me last night and are helping me now."

"Of course, I would take care of you. I could never let anything bad happen to you." Sadie hugged her. "I hope it goes well with your aunt and uncle." She peeked out the window. "If they see the carriage, you can just say you bumped into me, and I gave you a ride home."

"Uh-huh." Miranda nodded nervously as the coach rolled to a stop. "I guess I'll see you back at school." She climbed down then, after a feeble wave, hurried up to the house. Could she possibly pull this off? She hated the idea of lying to Aunt Lilly.

"Miranda!" Aunt Lilly rushed to her as she came into the house. "Where on earth have you been? I was worried sick."

Miranda started to tell the story Sadie had concocted then stopped herself. And with tears pouring down, she poured out a confession of her transgressions. "I'm so sorry. I just so wanted to go to that dance with Sadie last night. I wanted to feel like a grownup for once. I know I'm a terribly wicked, silly flibbertigibbet of a girl and I don't blame you if you locked me out of your house and never spoke to me again."

Aunt Lilly hugged her tightly. "Oh, dear! I'll admit I was upset and worried when I found you missing this morning. But it's only because I love you, Miranda."

"I wish I'd never done it," Miranda confessed. "I didn't even have much fun. Oh, maybe a little at first. But I got a blister on my heel. And then my head started to hurt—for real. And then I felt really sick. Sadie let me sleep in her room last night."

"That Sadie. I knew she was a bad influence. I warned you about her."

Miranda wanted to defend her best friend but knew that wouldn't help. So she simply remained silent as Aunt Lilly lectured her about the importance of good friends and how the wrong ones could lead her astray.

"Do you know who your best friend is, Miranda?"

Miranda didn't know what to answer since she knew Aunt Lilly wouldn't like to hear the truth.

"Your best friend is Jesus, dear. At least he wants to be."

"Oh." Miranda barely nodded. "Delia told me something like that too. But I'm not sure I fully understand that. I mean, I do believe in God. And I even pray sometimes. But I'm not so sure about Jesus. Delia told me that Jesus is all about forgiveness. But I guess I have a problem with that."

"A problem?" Aunt Lilly looked confused. "You don't want His forgiveness?"

"Well, Delia says we can only be forgiven if we forgive others. And there are people I will *never* forgive." Miranda cringed to remember Marcus and the ruin he'd brought to the ranch. Things she still partially blamed herself for too.

Aunt Lilly frowned. "Delia is right about forgiveness, Miranda. But I see it a bit differently. I think we make it impossible for God to forgive us when we refuse to forgive others. Because unforgiveness makes our hearts hard. And He can't penetrate a hardened heart."

"Oh." Miranda tried to comprehend this.

"What I'm trying to tell you, Miranda, is that Jesus wants to be your friend. And He's a friend you can trust completely. And I just think you need a friend like that."

"Meaning Jesus is a better friend than Sadie?" Miranda couldn't really believe this. How could an invisible friend be better than one who was right by your side?

Aunt Lilly just nodded. "I pray that you figure that out, Miranda."

Miranda nodded, but she knew that Aunt Lilly just didn't understand Sadie. And after hearing Sadie talking about a wicked grandfather, combined with the strange things from Sadie's father last night, well, Miranda just knew there was still a lot more to Sadie's story than she was telling.

If anyone ever needed a good best friend, it was Sadie McGuire. And Miranda was determined to stand by her side. Perhaps Miranda could be a good influence on her. Together they would be on their best behavior at the academy and, somehow, they would make it through the rest of the year without getting one more demerit. After that...freedom!

24

Before leaving Juneau after Christmas, Jackson had checked the Post Office one more time in the hopes a letter from Miranda might've made its way up North. Although there'd been a nice letter from his mother, there had been nothing from Miranda. And for that reason, he had mailed her a short letter he'd written at the hotel. On the fancy Nugget Hotel stationary. In that letter, he'd painted a more colorful picture of their holiday visit in Juneau. He'd described the dancehall girls and how they flirted with him. Oh, he knew it was silly, but he wanted to see if Miranda would care. He hoped she would.

Back at the mine, he and AJ went to work harder than before. Jackson was glad to go to bed exhausted every night. It helped him to block out dark concerns over Miranda. During the day, while pounding away on the mine, he'd reassure himself there were all kinds of reasonable explanations. Miranda had to keep up with her studies. Hadn't she been concerned the academics might be too challenging? Or perhaps the East Coast mail had been extra slow due to winter weather. Or maybe Miranda had gotten sick with some seasonal influenza. Oh, he hoped not. He prayed not!

In a way, Miranda's silent spell just made him work all the harder. More than ever, he wanted to find gold. He *needed* to find gold. Not just for Miranda's sake. He and AJ needed to hit color soon just to survive. They had enough supplies to get them through six more weeks, and then they'd need to replenish in order to make it through the rest of winter. And if spring came without hitting something good, well, Jackson might just have to give up and go home with empty pockets.

So when they made another trip to Juneau for supplies during a warming spell in late February, he felt certain there'd be a nice long letter or two…or more. Miranda couldn't have forgotten him.

"Think your girl wrote you?" AJ asked as town came into view.

Jackson shrugged. "Hope so."

"What if she didn't?" AJ pressed. "Would you just forget about her?"

"Forget about her?" Jackson wasn't sure he could ever forget about her.

"You know. Pick up your tent, shake off your boots, move on? Could you do that?"

"I don't honestly know." Jackson frowned. "Anyway, what would be the point?"

"The point? How about the girls in town?" AJ nodded to where some fancy dance girls were loitering outside the Nugget Hotel, soaking up the short spell of winter sun.

"Whoa, buddy." Jackson turned to eye AJ. "You haven't forgotten our agreement, have you?"

"You mean about avoiding gambling, drinking, and wayward women?" AJ teased.

"Yeah. You did great during Christmas. You still on board?"

AJ shrugged. "I reckon. But there are girls in town who aren't dancehall girls, Jackson. Maybe I meant one of them."

"If there are such things, and I doubt it, I sure haven't seen any."

"There's the preacher's wife."

Jackson punched AJ's arm. "Yeah, and she's married. But there's always Beulah." He chuckled. "She's old enough to be your ma, but at least she can cook."

"What about Margaret Stinson?"

"Who's that?"

"You know, the old lady who owns the Nugget. She's a widow."

Jackson laughed. "And she could be your grandma."

"Well, there might be some respectable girls 'round here," AJ argued. "We don't know that there aren't."

"And we don't know that there are." Jackson removed his pack from Rosie's back. "I'm heading to the post office. Want me to check for your mail too?"

"Sure. Not that I ever get anything. I'll get Rosie to the livery then meet you at the mercantile."

At the post office, Jackson was pleased to see he had two letters. One from Miranda and one from his mom. Although he wanted to save the best for last, curiosity got the best of him. He opened Miranda's first and, leaning against the hitching post, quickly read it through once. Then more slowly the second time.

January 20, 1885

Dear Jackson,

Please forgive me for not writing to you more. It is not because I don't think about you all the time, because I really do. And I miss you every day. I did not like hearing about those dancehall girls in your last letter. I hope you know better than to give girls like that the time of day. I believe you do.

The main reason I haven't written more is only because I've been very busy. First there was Christmas with Aunt Lilly and Uncle George. That is a long story that I will tell you someday in person. Maybe we will laugh about it.

After the holidays, it was back to school and classes.

If you ask me, the academics are getting harder and harder. The other girls have had proper education. They say this school is easy, so I try to hide how it's a challenge for me. I'm sure they all think I'm very stupid. Truth be told, they are not very nice about it, either. Sometimes I hate them.

Even the girls I thought were my friends seem to shun me because I'm not rich or smart, and because I come from the "wild west," as a very mean and homely girl named Beatrice likes to call it. She also calls me Farmer Girl and make jokes about slopping the pigs. She seems to have me in her crosshairs constantly. She only does these things when no one is around to catch her. I'd try to get back at her, but that would get me kicked out of school, and I really want to stick it out for a full year.

Dear Sadie McGuire remains my very best friend. We spend all our free time together. Mostly we like to sing silly songs, as long as no one can hear us. And now I know her secret, Jackson. I will tell you since there's no one you can tell that will matter up there in Alaska. Sadie and her father are very ashamed over this secret, but since I'm her best friend and she can trust me, she confessed that her grandfather made his fortune by shipping slaves from Africa to America. I was very shocked and saddened to hear it, but as I told Sadie, it is not her fault, and she shouldn't feel guilty for it. Please, don't tell anyone. I know what it's like to feel guilty for something you couldn't help, but you shouldn't let it ruin your life.

Well, it's almost lights out so I better finish this so I can put it safely in an envelope and hide it under my pillow. Beatrice might steal it from me otherwise. She is really a sidewinder!

Please, write to me and tell me how you're doing. But no more talk of dancehall girls, please! Every night, I pray you find the mother lode, Jackson. I love you. I really do! I hope you still love me.

Yours Truly,
Miranda Williams

Jackson carefully refolded Miranda's letter, slid it into the envelope, and tucked it safely into his jacket pocket. Next he read his mother's letter. He hoped to hear some good news about the mine, but it seemed nothing had changed. It was possible the family silver mine truly was mined out. And miners no longer threatened to strike, they simply left to go work another mine. He felt guilty to think of his father struggling to keep the mine alive and going, but he didn't know how his presence could make any difference. Possibly the best way he could help would be to really strike the mother lode up here. If that was possible. As he walked to the mercantile, he felt glad to know Miranda had not forgotten him, but worried that her school experience wasn't going too well. And he wished he could give that awful Beatrice a piece of his mind!

Miranda had an awful feeling as she walked toward the administration office. It wasn't that she'd broken any rules. Not that she was aware of anyway. But she'd gotten a notice from Mrs. Grampton just the same.

"Where are you going in such an all-fired rush?" Sadie hurried to catch up with her. "Didn't you hear me yelling for you?"

Miranda held up the note. "Mrs. Grampton wants me in her office. I'm supposed to report after my last class today."

"Uh-oh." Sadie grabbed her hand with wide eyes. "What did you do?"

"Nothing. I don't think so anyway. Old Beatrice is always trying to get me in trouble."

"I know, but we've both been trying to keep our noses clean, Miranda. Why would you get called in?"

"I don't know." Miranda glanced at the trees just starting to bud. "And I was just thinking how it's almost spring now, and only a few more months till summer. I really hoped I'd make it to the end." She felt close to tears. "I wanted my family to be proud of me."

"Maybe it's not bad news," Sadie suggested as they neared the building.

"Maybe." Miranda grimaced to think of facing Mrs. Grampton's cold stare.

"Want me to go with you?"

"No, no." Miranda let go of Sadie's hand. "That would probably just make things worse."

"Do you think Mrs. Grampton could've possibly heard about New Year's?" Sadie's blue eyes grew wide with concern as they paused by the front steps.

"Oh, dear, I hope not. I don't see how."

"Well, I'll wait over in the courtyard for you. Come tell me what happened as soon as you're done." Sadie crossed fingers on both hands. "Good luck."

"Thanks." Miranda thought she'd probably need it as she went inside the building. Before long she was sitting across from Mrs. Grampton and trying not to look overly frightened.

"I'm sure you wonder why I called you in here." The dean removed her glasses, rubbing the narrow bridge of her nose. "Rest assured, Miranda, you are not in trouble."

"Oh." Miranda tried to relax.

"It's just that I've heard you struggle in some of your classes." She peered curiously at her.

Miranda slowly nodded. "My education was, well, not like the other girls'."

"So I gathered."

"Is it that I'm failing?" Miranda asked in a mouse-like tone.

"No. You're not failing. But I have decided to give you what is called an aptitude test."

"What's that?"

"It's a way to measure what you know. A tool to help us to understand you better. Perhaps to help you."

"Oh." Miranda wondered if it was simply a means to prove that she was too stupid to be in this school. And, if that was the case, so be it.

"I'd like you to take it now." Mrs. Grampton took out a booklet and a writing tablet. "If you don't mind."

"Now?" Miranda would prefer to go outside and breathe in the fresh spring air, to walk with Sadie and sing songs.

"Is that a problem?" Mrs. Grampton's eyes narrowed.

"No, of course not."

And so it was that, there in Mrs. Grampton's office, Miranda took an aptitude test. Some of the questions were so silly it felt like it was designed for a seven-year-old. If this was to measure what she knew, she felt certain that everyone must assume it was very little. Even so, she persevered, working as fast as she could to get the stupid test behind her. It took nearly two hours, and by then she really felt like her head wanted to explode, but she tried to act natural as she handed the tablet back to Mrs. Grampton.

"Do you want to wait while I score this, or would you prefer to go?"

Miranda considered this. Part of her wanted to run free...but another part was curious. "I suppose I'll sleep better tonight if I know the results," she confessed. Even if they decided to kick her out, wouldn't it be better to simply know?

"It won't take long." Mrs. Grampton put her glasses on and using another book, started to go over the tablet Miranda had written in. A couple of times she smiled and once she almost laughed. Of course, this didn't make Miranda feel better as she sank down into the chair.

"Well." Mrs. Grampton laid the book and tablet down. "It seems there is nothing wrong with your mind, Miss Williams."

"Really? Did I pass the test?"

"Oh, it's not really like that. But, yes, you did just fine. I suspect it's as you said, your education wasn't like the other girls' here. But your intellect seems to be perfectly intact."

"Really?" Miranda felt slightly teary. "So I'm not stupid?"

"Stupid?" Mrs. Grampton frowned. "Why would you think that?"

"Oh…you know…some of the girls act like I am."

"Well, perhaps it's because you haven't always used the best sense, Miss Williams. Getting two demerits in the first semester was not too bright."

"I know. But I've been trying hard since then." Miranda tried not to think about the New Year's fiasco.

"Well, you are certainly not stupid, Miss Williams. In fact, I suspect you are much smarter than you realize. Much smarter than average. I hope you will begin to think of yourself in such a way."

Above average? Her? Miranda nodded, a bit dazed at the words. "I will. I promise I will."

"Good." Mrs. Grampton checked the clock. "You have just enough time to get cleaned up for supper."

Miranda thanked her and hurried outside to where Sadie quickly caught up with her. "I waited and waited," she said. "Until I got cold and went inside. What happened?"

As they both cleaned up for supper, Miranda quickly explained about the test and the results. But Sadie didn't seem the least bit surprised. "I always knew you were smart, Miranda. Isn't that what I've told you? It's just those stupid other girls who try to make you think you're not."

"You know, I didn't want to take that test, but I'm glad I did,"

Miranda said as they hurried toward the dining hall. "It's as if I feel smarter now."

They both laughed as they went through the door, but quickly settled down as they entered the dining hall. They knew that decorum was important and that they were being watched. But as they took their places, Miranda held her head higher than usual. She would no longer let anyone make her feel stupid!

Although Jackson had wanted to reply directly to Miranda's letter and get it sent in the mail, he just couldn't force himself while they were in Juneau. For one thing, they'd only spent one night there, and he hadn't really had time enough to write a proper letter. At least that was what he told himself when they got back to camp. But as they returned to digging in the mine, he knew the real reason. It was that he could think of nothing encouraging to write to Miranda. And he refused to lie to her.

Several times in the next few weeks, he'd attempted to write to her before bedtime, but each time he came up empty. Just like the mine. If he were to write honestly to her, he might have to admit that it looked hopeless. Not only had they failed to strike anything substantial, his parents' mine was failing as well. What could he possibly have to offer her now? He'd be lucky if he saved up enough bullion to make his way home. If they didn't starve first. Beans and cornbread might fill your belly, but they didn't really keep a man going. Jackson questioned why he'd ever come up here in the first place. Oh, he'd claimed it was as much for adventure as it was to find his fortune. But he'd come up short on both. With spring rapidly approaching he wondered…was it time to quit?

25

Spirits at the academy rose high during the week preceding Easter vacation. Spring was definitely in the air, and Miranda, like the other students, was eager for a break from the dreary drudgery of school. However, since discovering she was smarter than she previously thought, her interest in academics had increased, and as a result her grades had improved.

Perhaps her most remarkable accomplishment was that both she and Sadie had managed to avoid any more demerits in the past three months. Despite her good behavior, Miranda's friendships with Lottie and Jericho seemed to have completely evaporated. Probably because both those girls were under the control of Beatrice Phillips nowadays. Not that Miranda particularly cared, since she still had Sadie's companionship.

"One more day until we are freed from this prison," Sadie announced as the two of them paraded around the school grounds after supper.

"Then one glorious week of living like grown women." Miranda hoped Aunt Lilly would treat her like an adult again. Otherwise, her week of freedom might be rather boring. Miranda knew Sadie was going up to Massachusetts for the week. Although she would miss her best friend and envied her journey by ship, Miranda felt slightly relieved. There would be no temptations to do anything upsetting to Aunt Lilly and Uncle George during this vacation.

"I wish you could come to Boston with me," Sadie said for what must've been the twentieth time this week.

"I do too." Miranda sighed. "I've never been aboard a ship before."

"Well, someday you will be," Sadie declared. "You have my word on it. Maybe after we finish school in June. Could you take a trip with me and Papa before you go home to Colorado?"

Miranda considered this. "I don't see why not."

"Then it's all settled. I'll let Papa know so he can make all the arrangements for us. Maybe it could be a long one!" Sadie broke into a song about the South Seas, and Miranda joined in, singing even more lustily as Phoebe and her tribe of stuck-up followers walked toward them on the path. Nothing about the song lyrics was objectionable, but the pair sang it in such a way as to suggest it might be.

"So unfortunately lower class," Beatrice said in her usual snobbish tone, but loud enough to be heard by all.

"It's a wonder those two are still in school," another girl said.

"I bet they don't make it to the year's end," Beatrice declared as the two groups met in the path. Not surprisingly, Beatrice and her friends refused to yield so that Miranda and Sadie had to step aside.

"Scurvy dog," Sadie hissed into Beatrice's ear as they passed by with their noses in the air, as if the smell was offensive.

"Did you hear that?" Beatrice said to her friends. "Sadie swore at me."

"That is *not* swearing," Sadie defended herself. "It's just a saying."

"We'll see about that," Beatrice retorted.

"Blast her," Sadie said after the group was out of earshot.

"Be careful," Miranda warned. "And you're sure that *scurvy dog* isn't swearing?"

"I don't know if I care," Sadie growled. "I haven't even told you what Beatrice did in drawing class today. I'm still fuming." Sadie quickly explained how she was working on a watercolor. "It was a sailing ship with three masts, and I was nearly done. Then Beatrice whisked by with a large stretched canvas in her hands. Of course, it knocked over my water jar, which completely ruined my painting."

"Oh, dear." Miranda shook her head.

"I wanted to give it to Papa for Easter." Sadie frowned.

"I'm sorry." Miranda patted her back. "That's awful."

"And Beatrice acted all sorry, pretending it was an accident while Miss Forbes was watching. Then Beatrice had the audacity to say 'oh, the painting looks so much better now, like a ship in the fog.' And she even got Mrs. Forbes to agree with her."

"Beatrice *is* a scurvy dog," Miranda declared.

"Wouldn't it be fun to get her into trouble?"

"Of course, but I don't know how. She's always surrounded by her minions." Miranda felt proud of herself for using a word she'd just learned in history class.

"I have an idea." Sadie reached into the pocket of her dress and removed a small box with the image of a pretty woman on the front.

"Playing cards?"

"Nope."

"Soap?"

"No. These are cigarettes."

Miranda's eyes grew wide, and she glanced around to be sure no one was looking their way. "Where did you get them?"

"I've had them since Christmas. I got them at the Continental."

"Do you smoke them?"

"No. That's not why I got them." Sadie giggled. "Although I wouldn't mind trying it…someday."

"Then why did you get them?" Miranda felt seriously worried. "And why do you have them here at school?"

"I'm not sure why I got them in the first place," Sadie confessed.

"I guess it seemed exciting. I've had them hidden all this time, but after Beatrice ruined my painting, I got an idea." She described an intricate plan for how they could plant the package on Beatrice. "I'll do it during cooking class tomorrow morning. But I might need your help to distract her while I'm at it."

"Oh, I don't know, Sadie. It sounds—"

"Are you afraid?" Sadie demanded. "I thought you were brave, Miranda."

"I'm not afraid. I just don't want you to get caught. It would be your third demerit, and I'd be lost without you here."

"I won't get caught. It's a foolproof plan." She grinned as she pocketed the pretty package. "Just imagine how great it will be when Beatrice gets caught with cigarettes. You've read the rules. Any student caught with alcohol or tobacco is automatically expelled from school. For the rest of the school year, no more Beatrice."

Miranda didn't know what to say. As badly as she wanted to see the last of Beatrice, Sadie's plan sounded dangerous. But there was no time to discuss it further since it was nearly curfew. All she could hope for was that Sadie would cool off from the art class incident and reconsider her plot against Beatrice.

But when morning came and Miranda met with Sadie after breakfast, her determination was clear. "All I need you to do is distract any of Beatrice's friends from watching me," Sadie quietly told her.

"How am I supposed to distract them?" Miranda pondered aloud.

"I don't know. Drop a bowl on the floor. Pretend to burn yourself. There must be a dozen ways you can cause a little commotion." She grabbed Miranda's hand. "I need your help to pull this off. That's what best friends are for, right?"

"Yes, I'm sure you're right." Miranda nodded. "But I still don't understand how you're going to make sure Beatrice gets caught."

"You don't need to know the details, Miranda. I have a plan, and it's up to me to carry it out. And to make everything more believable, let's not even go into cooking class together."

Miranda felt relieved. The less she knew the better she would feel. As she went into the cooking classroom, she tried not to act uneasy as she thought up a good distraction plan. They were just finishing up on sauces today. If she let out a shriek as she "accidentally" spilled her sauce all over the place, the class would be all eyes on her.

Today she was making Allemande Sauce and, because she still wasn't terribly adept in the kitchen, having an accident wasn't completely out of character. While the veal broth heated on the stove, she whipped the egg yolk into the cream. The next step was to mix the heated broth into the cream mixture. Her hands were already trembling as she used a potholder to remove the heavy saucepan then attempted to pour and simultaneously stir the liquids together. Whether it was truly an accident or premeditated, she couldn't even be sure, but when the heavy pot slipped from her hand, crashing into the ceramic bowl, she let out a loud scream and the mixture of broth, cream, and eggs splattered all over her apron and dress. "I'm so clumsy," she muttered as she peeled off the soaked apron then grabbed up a dishtowel to mop up the sticky mess. "I'm just a clumsy ox."

"Oh, dear." Miss Spencer was by her side now. "Don't be so hard on yourself, Miss Williams. Your sauce is certainly ruined, but so are you. Go change your dress and come back. You can give me an oral report on how to make your sauce."

"I'm so sorry for my clumsiness." Miranda laid down the dishtowel. As she hurried toward the door, she could hear classmates giggling and making quiet remarks at her expense, but she didn't look back. She didn't try to see Sadie or whether she'd accomplished her sabotage. Miranda just wanted out of there, and out of her stinking, soggy woolen uniform dress.

By the time she was cleaned up returned to cooking class, the other students were just finishing up their sauces. Still not wanting to look around, Miranda went straight to Miss Spencer. Her voice trembled a bit as explained the steps she would take to make the

Allemande sauce and even remembered to call the veal broth *velouté*. "And then salt and pepper," she finally added.

"That's right." Miss Spencer nodded with a hard-to-read expression. "Despite your clumsiness, you do know the recipe. So I will give you a passing grade." She looked up at the clock. "And now class is over. I wish all you young ladies a lovely Easter vacation. Hopefully, you will impress your parents with some excellent cooking during your time at home."

Miranda took in a deep breath and, as the others were all moving about the room, some leaving, some visiting with Miss Spencer, two students were conspicuously missing. Both Beatrice and Sadie. Not wanting to ask about this, Miranda simply picked up her books and proceeded out the door. But in the hallway, she overheard Jericho whispering to another girl. Even though she knew Jericho hadn't been on friendly terms, she decided to approach her. "Is something wrong?" she asked with her best innocent expression.

"You don't know?" Jericho asked with a suspicious expression.

"Know what?"

"That your best friend Sadie McGuire got caught with *cigarettes!*"

"What?" Miranda didn't have to pretend to be shocked.

"Yes. She was trying to sneak them into Beatrice's pocket. But Lottie saw her and told Miss Spencer."

"Really?"

"So Miss Spencer sent all three of them to Mrs. Grampton. But Sadie is in for it now." Jericho grimly shook her head. "We tried to tell you she was trouble, Miranda."

"She'll be expelled for sure," the other girl said.

Miranda felt sick as she slowly walked to her next class. Sadie expelled? What did that mean for Miranda? The rest of the school year with no best friend? And now Beatrice and her bunch would be worse than ever. She could imagine them taunting her. Even worse, she could be partially blamed for the cigarette fiasco. But as she went into her history class, she thought she didn't care. If Sadie was expelled, perhaps Miranda would want to be expelled as well. Except there was her family to consider. What would they say?

She didn't cross paths with Sadie until midday. Because it was the last day of school before vacation, classes were ending early. Miranda found Sadie sitting by herself in front of the academy. With all her bags around her, she looked as if she'd lost her best friend. But Miranda was determined to convince her otherwise.

"Did they kick you out?" Miranda asked as she set down her own valise.

Sadie merely nodded. "But I don't care. I'm done with this prison."

"What will I do without you?" Miranda muttered hopelessly.

Sadie shrugged. "I don't know. Furthermore, I don't know what I'll do without you."

"What will your father say?"

"He won't be happy." She sighed. "And he won't allow me to be financially independent now. That's what he threatened, and I know he'll stick to his guns."

"So what will you do?" Miranda studied her friend closely.

"Papa will expect me to stay with him. To sail where he sails."

"That sounds exciting."

"It's not as exciting as it sounds. Not when you've done it all your life. Besides, he will probably treat me like an infant again."

"Oh."

Sadie turned to Miranda with an excited expression. "But now I'm getting another plan. In fact, it's a very adventurous plan." She began to describe how she would take the next train West. "And from there I'll take a ship up to Alaska and—"

"Alaska?" Miranda's eyes grew wide. "But that's where Jackson is."

"Yes. Isn't he in Juneau? Maybe I'll see him. I can send him your regards." Her blue eyes twinkled with mischief. "I can give him a kiss for you."

"You're really going to Alaska?" Miranda blinked, trying to make sense of this. "But how can you afford it?"

"I have some money. And I have jewelry I can sell. From my mother."

"And when you get up there? What will you do?"

"I'll have fun. If I need to, I'll get a job. And I'll look for an exciting, rich gold miner to marry. Isn't that what you wanted to do?"

"Yes, but—"

"Come with me, Miranda."

"Come with you?"

"Yes! It's only a matter of time before you're kicked out of school too."

"How do you know that?"

"Beatrice told Mrs. Grampton that you helped me by dropping the pan so I could sneak the cigarettes."

"Mrs. Grampton believed her?"

"I don't know. She made note of it and said she's speak to Miss Spencer. I'm surprised you weren't called in today."

"Blast it!" Miranda covered her mouth, but Sadie just laughed.

"See, you don't belong here. Come with me, Miranda. We'll have such fun."

"But I don't have money for train fare or ship fare. I can't—"

"Yes, you can." Suddenly Sadie was putting together a plan. "You will go home to get your things. While you do that, I will sell my jewelry. Then we will meet at the Continental. I'm supposed to stay there one night before Papa comes to get me tomorrow afternoon. But we will book a trip on the first train heading west. Maybe as soon as this evening."

Miranda felt short of breath and could barely think.

"You have to come with me," Sadie insisted. "We will have such an adventure. And we will be free. Completely free."

"I don't know."

"Are you saying you don't want to see Jackson?" Sadie tipped her head with a coy smile. "Because I can certainly send him your regards."

"I do want to see him." Miranda frowned. "Do you really think Mrs. Grampton knows I helped you?"

"If she's talked to Miss Spencer...."

Miranda imagined the humiliation of a phone call to Aunt Lilly. The disappointment in Uncle George's eyes. "All right, I'll go with you," she declared.

"You won't be sorry. We will finally be living, Miranda. No more prison school for us." Sadie hugged her. "And just imagine Jackson's face when he sees you!"

Miranda wondered about that. She hadn't had a letter from Jackson for so long she'd started to wonder if he'd forgotten all about her. And in the last letter he'd written, three months ago, he'd talked about the dancehall girls and how much they'd admired him. What if one of those girls had gotten her claws into him? Suddenly, Miranda was more motivated than ever to do this. Not only for Sadie's sake, since she felt her friend needed a companion, but she would do it for Jackson as well. Surely, when it was all said and done, her family would understand. At least she hoped they would.

26

It was Delia's first time to experience springtime at the ranch and, although it came later than spring in Pennsylvania, seeing fruit tree blossoms budding, calves and lambs being born, hearing happy birds singing...it was all rather miraculous. But not quite as miraculous as the fact that Jefferson had moved to town two weeks ago—and remained there. The parting had been a somewhat dramatic turn of events and left her mother in hysterical tears. But the aftermath had left the environment inside and outside the house almost as warm as the fresh spring air.

"Father sent Mother a note from town," Julianne informed Delia as they saddled their horses for an afternoon ride.

"Oh?" Delia was curious but didn't want to press.

"Mother doesn't know I sneaked a peek at it." Julianne's grin was mischievous.

"My little snooping sister strikes again?"

Julianne giggled as she adjusted the cinch. "Someone has to keep track of these things. Otherwise we'd never know what was going on."

Delia suppressed a chuckle as she swung up into the saddle.

"Don't you want to know what he said?" Julianne let down the stirrup and peered up at Delia.

"I suppose I'm curious, but is it any of my business?"

Julianne stuck her foot in the stirrup and slid into her saddle. "Well, if you don't want to know..." She nudged Dolly, steering her toward the open corral gate.

"Is it anything you think I should know?" Delia asked as she caught up with her. "Is there anything wrong?"

"No, it was rather a cheerful letter. Father has rented a room in a boarding house and taken a job at the newspaper."

"At the newspaper?"

"Yes. You know Father always fancied himself to be clever with the pen." Julianne shook her head. "And as we all know, he has plenty of opinions to go around."

"That's true, but newspapers are supposed to be about news, not personal views."

"Do you think Father knows how to separate the two?" Julianne giggled, and Delia couldn't help but laugh. For a twelve-year-old, Julianne was quite smart. Maybe too smart.

"You've done well in your studies lately," Delia said as they rode through the open field.

"You mean better since Father isn't tutoring us anymore?" Julianne tossed her a sideways glance. "You're a much better teacher than him, Delia. It doesn't make up for not being back at school with my friends, but it's far better than listening to Father. Even Julius is improving."

"I wish there were a way for you to be at school with girls your own age, Julianne. I know how much you miss it. I've talked to Mother about you and Julius going to town for school. They have quite a large school there. But it would require a bit of a drive every day. I'm afraid it's too far to walk. Especially in winter."

"Mother mentioned it. But she said we have to wait until next year to see."

"Well, that makes sense. The school year will soon be over. And as far as I can tell, you're not behind in your studies."

"And having school with you allows me to ride Dolly in the afternoon." Julianne nudged her horse into a trot. "Race you to the creek."

Sometimes Delia let Julianne win and sometimes she didn't. Today, she decided to take it easy, watching as the young girl and older horse made a beeline through the meadow, stopping by the big oak tree next to the creek where Julianne waved victoriously with both arms.

Delia took her time, gazing over to where Caleb and Enoch were herding the sheep into a different pasture. Then the other direction where some of the hands were working with the cattle. Wyatt was there with them. Springtime on the ranch…did life get any better than this?

She urged Lady to a trot then gallop, quickly making her way over to Julianne, who'd just gotten down from her horse.

Delia got off too. "Isn't this a beautiful time of year?" She picked up a fallen stick, poking it into the fast-moving creek.

"I really do love it here, Delia. And I love living in the little cottage with Mother and Julius. Mother likes it too." She frowned. "If Father ever made us go back to our old lives in Pittsburgh…I don't know what I'd do."

Delia was surprised. "But you're always saying how you miss your friends."

"I just say that." She tossed a rock in the creek. "And, sure, I miss kids my own age sometimes. But I wouldn't trade that for this."

Delia slipped an arm around Julianne's shoulders. "And I wouldn't want you to."

Julianne looked up hopefully. "So even if Father starts to make money, and if he gets a house like Mother says he will, are you saying I could still stay here with you on the ranch?"

Delia considered this. "Well, that would sort of be out of my hands. Your parents get to make those decisions. But, yes, you would always be welcome."

"Is someone calling your name?" Julianne asked.

Delia strained her ears to hear. "It sounds like Wyatt." She quickly got back into her saddle. "I hope nothing's wrong." Soon she had Lady in a full-blown gallop, hurrying over to where Wyatt was standing next to a fence with her mother on the opposite side. Everyone seemed excited. Even Hank was barking.

"What is it?" Delia demanded as she dismounted her horse.

"A telegram from Philadelphia." Her mother waved the envelope in the air. "It's for you, Delia. Just came."

Delia took the envelope. "It's from your uncle," Delia told Wyatt.

"Must be concerning Miranda." Wyatt bent down to hush Hank. "Read it."

Delia removed her gloves, nervously opening the envelope. "I hope she's all right." She quickly read the short message then, feeling shocked, she handed it to Wyatt, waiting for him to read.

"She's run off?" Wyatt said to Delia. "Just like that."

"Sounds like it." Delia sighed.

"She ran away?" Jane frowned. "What would make her do that?"

Julianne joined them, curiously listening in. "Did Miranda run away from her finishing school?"

"So it seems." Delia reread the message. "Uncle George says she came home for Easter Vacation on Thursday afternoon and went missing the next morning."

"That's all it says?" Jane persisted. "No explanation or anything?"

"Just that her bags were gone too." Delia shook her head.

Jane snatched the telegram, reading the brief message aloud. "Miranda arrived home Thursday. Went missing Good Friday. Took everything with her. Please inform. Uncle George."

"She *must* be headed home," Delia said. "That's the only logical explanation. She didn't sound too happy in her last letter. But I thought it was because Christmas vacation was over and she was back in school."

"Is that the last you heard from her?" Jane asked.

Delia just nodded. "I figured she's been busy with studies."

Wyatt scratched his head. "Well, today is Monday. If Miranda left Philadelphia on Friday, and if she's coming home, she should be here soon."

"She could be here as soon as today," Delia pointed out.

"Maybe she's there now," Julianne said.

"I wish we had a telephone." Delia checked her watch. "The afternoon train has already come and gone. Should we send someone in to look for her?"

"I'll go," Wyatt offered.

"I'll go too," Julianne said eagerly.

"Thank you, but I think I'll go with him." Delia smiled at Julianne. "You can give Ginger a hand. If Miranda is coming, we will need to get ready for her arrival."

"Silas, you take Delia's horse and get the buggy ready," Wyatt called out as he grabbed Delia's hand, hurrying her toward the house. "Don't you worry about it," he said calmly. "We'll figure this out. You get yourself changed, and I'll go help Silas with the buggy."

"And if Miranda's not there, I'll let the station master know to look for her tomorrow and ask him send us a message," Delia said as they stood on the back porch.

"And I'll send a wire my aunt and uncle," he said.

"What's going on here?" Ginger asked as she joined them by the backdoor. "What's all the ruckus about?"

Delia quickly explained. "Hopefully, Miranda's at the train station right now. So why don't you get the guest room ready just in case?"

"Will do." Ginger nodded grimly. "Sure hope that child is all right."

"We all do." As Delia hurried upstairs, she remembered what a headstrong girl Miranda could be. But Delia had hoped finishing school would smooth some of the rough edges. And now she'd run away from it—and from Aunt Lilly and Uncle George too! How must they feel? Had Delia been wrong to send Miranda to school back there? Except it had been her father's wishes. As she quickly changed from her riding clothes, she prayed that Miranda would make it safely home—and soon! Hopefully that was where she'd headed. And hopefully she knew she was always welcome here.

Miranda had never been so sick before. But she'd never been aboard a ship before. Sadie had assured her she'd get her sea legs shortly after they departed San Francisco. But this was the third day of rocking and rolling on the high seas, and Miranda was ready to jump overboard. Drowning would be better than this!

"Just sip some broth," Sadie urged her.

"I can't." Miranda turned toward the wall with a weak moan.

"You have too," Sadie insisted. She grabbed Miranda's arm and turned her back around on the narrow bunk. "Come on, just a little. I'll spoon it into you."

Miranda barely opened her mouth, allowing Sadie to slide the spoon with lukewarm liquid in. It took all her will to swallow it, but somehow it went down. Several spoonfuls later she felt slightly better and was actually able to sit up.

"How long till we get there?" she asked in a whisper of a voice.

"Depends on the weather."

Miranda closed her eyes and slumped back into the bunk.

"If you would just come outside with me, you'd feel better." Sadie held out another spoonful of broth.

"I—I can't."

"It's the only way," Sadie declared. She'd been saying this very thing ever since Miranda had taken refuge down here. "It's a beautiful clear day with a good southerly wind."

Miranda swallowed a few more spoonfuls of broth then sat up. "I just want this to be over with, Sadie." She felt tears coming again. "It's as if I'm being punished for running away."

"You're being punished for staying below like this." Sadie stood. "I'm used to the sea, but being down here with you almost makes me feel sick."

"I'm sorry."

"Come on," Sadie urged. "I promise you it's better out there. Fresh air and sunshine is what you need. I know what I'm talking about." Now Sadie was pulling Miranda's rose-colored shawl around her and tugging her to her feet.

"I can't." Miranda swayed with the ship's movement. "It's too—"

"Hold onto me, I'll steady you." Sadie was already moving her toward the door. "We're getting you out of here."

It was a struggle to make it up the steep steps, but somehow Sadie managed to drag and pull Miranda to the upper deck. Miranda grasped a brass rail, looking out to where an endless band of blue spanned out from all directions.

"At least I can throw myself overboard up here," Miranda muttered as Sadie continued to push and pull her across the upper deck.

"Hush! We're going to the bowsprit." Sadie practically dragged her toward the front of the ship. Some of the sailors paused from their tasks, pointing and laughing, as if Miranda with her knitted pink shawl over her cotton nightgown and wild auburn hair was their personal entertainment. And she didn't even care. She felt too horrible to even be humiliated.

At the very front of the ship, with Sadie's arms securely around her, Miranda watched as the bow moved up and down, cutting into the ocean in front of them. She fully expected to upchuck what little broth she'd managed to swallow, but a curious thing was happening. She was feeling better. She took in a deep breath of fresh air and held it in for a moment. Then she slowly released it. She turned to look at Sadie, who was grinning from ear to ear. "You feel better, don't you?"

Miranda barely nodded, unsure if this would last.

"See! I told you. You should listen to a sea captain's daughter."

"Thank you," she mumbled.

For the next couple of hours, the two girls remained on deck, and Miranda felt better and better. She was able to drink tea and consumed a full bowl of chicken broth and two pieces of bread. "I feel silly being in my nightgown," she finally confessed, "but I'm afraid to go below to get dressed. What if I get sick again?"

"We'll go down really quickly," Sadie suggested. "I'll help you get dressed and then we'll get right back up here."

Miranda reluctantly agreed, and before long she was properly dressed and none the worse for wear. Still, she had no desire to go back down to the stuffy berth and even asked Sadie if it was possible to sleep on the deck. "These deck chairs aren't too uncomfortable." She pulled the wool blanket higher, imagining how it would feel to sleep out here under the stars.

"No, we can't do that." Sadie firmly shook her head. "Some sailors have no scruples. But I do have an idea. You stay here while I ask the captain about another option." While Sadie spoke to the captain, Miranda felt grateful to have a traveling companion like Sadie McGuire. Sadie seemed to instinctively know how to handle almost anything—and to fear almost nothing. She had covered all their traveling expenses so far, and she hadn't scrimped on anything. They'd traveled in style on the train. And their week in San Francisco, while waiting for this ship to sail, they had stayed in a fancy hotel, gone shopping, and dined at expensive restaurants. Miranda couldn't remember when she'd ever had such fun. Of course, she did feel a bit guilty for the way she'd left Philadelphia…and for not getting in touch with Delia. But the plan, Sadie and Miranda had agreed, was to tell no one of their whereabouts until they were safely in Juneau. Then they would send telegrams.

Sadie hadn't even seemed sorry that she'd had to sell all her jewelry for their trip—valuables she'd inherited from her mother when she'd passed away. Miranda now knew that Sadie had lost her mother at an even younger age than Miranda. Still, there was some sort of mystery connected with her mother's death. Something Sadie didn't care to talk about…yet.

"I got us a stateroom on this deck," Sadie announced when she returned. "It costs more, but it's worth it to keep you from getting seasick again. The captain's having some shipmates move all our things for us right now."

Miranda hugged her. "Thank you, Sadie! For everything!"

"Well, I didn't want to see you jump overboard before we even get there," Sadie teased.

After sunset, the two girls retired to their stateroom. Much bigger and better than where they'd stayed down below, but now Miranda felt guilty for the added expense. "It's so nice up here, Sadie, but it must be costly. I hope it didn't set you back too much."

"No worries. If I'd known about your seasick tendency, I'd have gotten it in the first place." Sadie set a tea tray on the little table by the window. "We still have plenty of money to enjoy our time in Juneau. One of the deckhands told me the best hotel there is called the Nugget. I've decided that's where we'll be staying."

"Sounds lovely." And the idea of being on solid ground sounded even lovelier.

"We'll leave the window open." Sadie cracked the round window slightly. "The fresh air will keep you feeling better."

"It sure feels good to feel good again." Miranda poured the steaming tea. "Maybe I'll actually sleep tonight. Perhaps have a sweet dream…about Jackson."

"That Jackson. I can't wait to meet him. Do you suppose he's struck it rich by now?"

"I guess that could explain why he didn't write the past few months. If he were too busing mining gold…." But Miranda wondered if it was something else. What if Jackson wouldn't be glad to see her? What if his silence meant he'd forgotten her? What if her long journey was in vain? And what if he'd married some Juneau girl? It was all too torturous to imagine, and she was too tired to think about it tonight.

27

Jackson threw down his pick and somehow managed to bite his tongue before some bad words spilled out. "I'm finished, AJ."

"Quitting already?" AJ called. "It's early still, man."

"I mean I'm quitting for good," Jackson yelled back. "I've had it."

AJ dropped his shovel and carried his lantern over to where Jackson was sitting on a large stone, wiping his forehead with a grimy bandana. "What do you mean you're quitting for good?" He held the lantern up to peer into Jackson's face.

"Just what it sounds like. I'm done with this." He pointed to the slender vein he'd been working. "I worked a solid week on this vein to extract a few crumbs of bullion." He held out his nearly empty leather pouch like proof.

AJ took it, bouncing it in his hand to gauge its weight. "I bet you got close to two ounces in there. Probably worth about thirty bucks. Enough to get us some supplies."

"From almost a month of picking away. I could make better wages working in my dad's mine. Not only that, but money goes farther down there. Really, AJ, I'm done with this." He kicked the wall he'd been working. "And this vein's all petered out. The last few days have been nothing but slate."

"But slate's good," AJ reminded him.

"And unstable. The deeper we dig, the greater the chance of a cave in."

"I think you need a break, Jackson. We're almost out of supplies. How about we plan a trip to town? Give me a few more days to follow the vein I'm working, and we can go. Is Friday soon enough?"

"Fine. But when I get to town, I'll look into booking a ship back to the States."

"You got enough saved up for that?" AJ frowned.

"I don't know. Maybe I can hire on as a deck hand. Or maybe I'll wire my parents for money. Somehow I gotta get outta here." He shoved his bandana into his jeans pocket. "How about I sell you back my half of the claim?"

AJ laughed, but not with real humor. "And what'll I use for money? I haven't even got a full ounce of gold at the moment. I was even considering selling old Rosie if we don't hit something good soon."

"Why don't you give up too? We could sell our claim to some bright-eyed newcomer and have enough to get us home."

"I'm not giving up." AJ shook his head. "I got a good feeling about this claim. I think we're going to hit color soon."

"You keep saying that." Jackson took up his pick again. "I'll give this mine the rest of the week to prove it then I'm outta here."

Jackson continued to work, but his heart wasn't in it. His back wasn't either. He was done with this foolish dream. And he was done with his dream of someday marrying Miranda Williams. He hadn't heard from that silly girl in months, and he doubted there'd be a letter for him in Juneau when they went to town on Friday. Tonight he would write her a letter. If she was done with him, he was done with her. End of story.

It wasn't until they got checked into the Nugget Hotel, which Miranda felt was rather disappointing, especially compared to the Continental in Philadelphia, that Sadie made a grim discovery. "Miranda!" she yelled from the bedroom. "Blast it! Blast it!"

"What is it?" Miranda halted her inspection of the little parlor section of their suite.

"Come here!" Sadie sounded desperate.

Miranda hurried to the bedroom where Sadie had poured out the contents of her trunk and all her bags. Clothes and shoes were strewn across the bed and chairs and floor. "What on earth are you doing?"

"Blast it, Miranda! I'm searching for my money!"

"Your money?" Miranda frowned. "I thought you carried it in that money belt you've worn religiously ever since we left Philadelphia. You had it on down there in the lobby and—"

"That was *traveling* money." Sadie's eyes were bright with what looked like unshed tears. "I mean our *Alaska* money. Most of our money. It was hidden in the bottom of my big trunk. In a little beaded purse that used to be my mother's. Both the purse and money are gone."

"Gone?" Miranda stared at the heaps of clothes and shoes and things. "Are you certain?"

"I've gone through everything." Sadie grabbed Miranda's arm. "Did you take it? Oh, please, tell me you did. I won't be mad."

"No, of course, I didn't take it." Miranda pointed to Sadie's slender midsection. "But you still have some money, don't you?"

"I just paid for three nights in this suite," Sadie lifted her traveling jacket and peeled off her white linen money belt, removing a few bills. "We have enough left for food. But only a few days at most. And then we are broke."

"Broke?" Miranda bit her lip.

Sadie collapsed in the pile of clothing heaped on a chair and let out a loud sob. "Blast it! Blast it! I can't believe I let this happen. Oh, Miranda, I'm so stupid. To lose all our money—"

"How did it happen?" Miranda asked. "How could it have just disappeared?"

Sadie looked up with bright blue eyes, tears streaming down her flushed cheeks. "It didn't disappear, Miranda. It was stolen. The shipmate that moved our baggage to the state room must've gone through our things. That bilge sucking scurvy-dog who took it should be keelhauled."

"Is there anything we can do? Go back to the ship and—"

"The captain told me they were only in Juneau to drop off cargo then heading north to Anchorage. I'm sure they've sailed by now."

"Oh, dear." Miranda cleared the other chair and, sinking down with a loud sigh, wondered what they would do.

"To think I sold all my mother's jewelry. For nothing! Nothing. Just gone." Sadie used some colorful language to describe the dishonest sailor. "He even took my mother's little beaded bag." She choked back a sob. "I loved that little bag. Mother did too."

Miranda looked curiously at Sadie. She didn't usually speak of her mother like this. "What happened to your mother, Sadie?" she asked gently. "I've told you about how my mother died in childbirth, but you've never said how your mother died."

Sadie looked at Miranda with tear filled eyes. "She killed herself."

"Oh." Miranda felt bad for asking now.

"I heard someone say she was insane," Sadie said in a wooden tone. "That she took her life because she was out of her mind. But Papa never said that. He doesn't talk of it, but if someone demands to know, he just says she was sick and died."

"I'm sorry." Miranda went over and placed a hand on Sadie's shoulder. "Thanks for telling me."

"I wanted to keep that beaded bag forever." Sadie leaned over and, holding her head in her hands, sobbed loudly.

Miranda didn't know what to say or do. She'd never seen Sadie like this before. Always, she'd been the strong one, the one with all the answers...and now she seemed truly broken. And they were broke.

"It's going to be all right," Miranda declared. "We are going to be fine, Sadie." She started to pick up articles of clothing, laying them on the bed. And then she was packing. "First of all, we have to get jobs. We knew we'd need to find work eventually—we'll just get started sooner now. But we'll be all right."

Sadie looked up with a slightly lost expression. "But how? How will we get jobs? What can we do? Who would hire us? It's useless."

"I don't know for sure. But we can't give up hope. You go wash your face and clean up for supper. I'm sure we'll both feel better after we have a good meal. In the meantime, I'm going downstairs. I'll ask around. Maybe I can locate Jackson and ask him to help us. Or else I'll figure out a way for us to get jobs." She pinned her hat back on and reached for her gloves. "We have three days to figure this all out. A lot can happen in three days. So don't despair." She went over to hug Sadie. "You took care of me on the train and on the ship, it's my turn to help you."

Sadie just shook her head as if everything was hopeless, but Miranda was determined as she left their suite. There had to be something out there. After all, the town had been bustling. Surely there were jobs for two able-bodied girls who wanted to work. As she went downstairs, she considered the cost of their room. They didn't really need a suite. Perhaps she could ask to switch to a less expensive room. Or even a cheaper hotel.

But when Miranda presented her case to the man at the reception desk, he just grimly shook his head. "Our less expensive rooms are booked for a full week. We won't have a cheaper room until next Monday. But you can change rooms then if you like."

"But we will be out of funds several days before that," she said desperately. "Please, can't you help us?"

"What's going on here, Charlie?" a white-haired woman demanded from behind him. He turned around and quickly relayed what Miranda had just told him and then the woman came over to peer curiously at Miranda.

"I'm Mrs. Stinson. I own this hotel."

"Oh." Miranda nodded then introduced herself.

"So are you saying that you and your friend just arrived in Juneau, you booked our most expensive suite, and now you are completely out of money?" Mrs. Stinson frowned.

Miranda quickly explained about Sadie's beaded bag and how it was stolen on the ship when they moved to the stateroom. "We didn't realize it was gone until we unpacked in our room just now. But it had all our money. So if we could just switch over to a cheaper room, or a cheaper hotel…that way we could save money and have more time to secure some employment."

"Employment?" Mrs. Stinson's eyebrows arched as she motioned for Miranda to come around to the other side of the reception desk. "Why don't we step into my office to talk."

Miranda followed her. "My friend and I will be seeking jobs. Probably starting tomorrow morning."

"Why not start now? Have you or your friend had any housekeeping experience?"

Miranda explained about finishing school, without mentioning that they didn't complete their first year. "Besides academics, we learned French cooking, some sewing and tapestry, music and art." She hoped that might impress her.

"Finishing school girls?" Mrs. Stinson chuckled. "Well, that's different. But what I'm looking for are maids. Do you know how to make a bed?"

"Yes. Of course." Miranda nodded.

"Well, if you girls are interested in maid work, I can offer you room and board and a small salary. You won't have a nice room like you're in now, but I do have maid quarters on the upper floor." She shook her head. "I ran shorthanded with maids all winter, and our busy season is just starting. So I need girls who can start right now."

"We can start right now," Miranda said eagerly. "Well, tomorrow anyway. You see, my friend, she's very upset over being robbed, and I think she needs a good meal and good night's sleep."

Mrs. Stinson looked amused. "Well, you girls enjoy your night in the suite. I'll have Charlie refund your money for the other two days, and we'll get you set up in the maids' quarters tomorrow morning."

Miranda felt strangely victorious as she presented Sadie with the refunded money. She quickly explained about Mrs. Stinson's employment offer. "I know it's not much, but at least we'll have free room and board and a bit of money. Maybe we can figure out something better later on."

"Oh, Miranda, that is good news!" Sadie hugged her. "And, really, I don't mind being a maid. For a while anyway. Just until we figure things out."

"And how about if we live it up tonight?" Miranda suggested. "We can dress up for dinner and act like rich tourists."

"Yes." Sadie eagerly agreed. "Tonight we will be princesses—and paupers tomorrow."

As they carefully dressed, Miranda wondered just how long they'd really last as hotel maids. It wasn't that they were lazy. But they both came from slightly privileged backgrounds. Truth be told, they were more used to being served than serving. Still, the experience might be good for them. Especially if it was short-lived! And as soon as she had time, Miranda planned to write a letter to Jackson, as well as to inquire around regarding his whereabouts.

As the two young women walked into the hotel restaurant, they could feel people looking at them. Perhaps they were overdressed, but Miranda didn't care. This might be the last time for a while. After they were seated at a table, she discretely glanced around, hoping that she might spot Jackson. Perhaps he'd struck it rich and had come here to celebrate. Then he could show up like her knight in shining armor and rescue her. Well, unless he'd found someone else.

The next day, Miranda and Sadie were moved from the suite to the maids' quarters, which reminded them of the dormitory back at the academy. But not as nice. Because of the lack of space, their repacked trunks and most of their luggage was placed in storage. A stern-faced woman named Harriet gave them maid uniforms and instructions for how to clean a guest room and then they were each partnered with a more experienced maid and set to work.

By the end of the day, Miranda was so tired that she didn't even care if she ate supper or not. But Sadie insisted she needed to eat to keep up her strength. "My partner Pricilla promised it'll be easier tomorrow," Sadie assured her as they went down to the employees' dining room. "The first couple days are the hardest."

"Oh. All my partner ever did was grumble. Nothing I did was good enough, and I was too slow and too lazy." Miranda paused at the entrance, lowering her voice. "And I'm sure Ruth made me do a lot of her work too."

"That's too bad. Pricilla was nice," Sadie said as she pushed open the door. "Maybe tomorrow will be better."

Miranda hoped so, but she wasn't holding her breath. Ruth was bossy and mean and just plain rude. She seemed to resent anyone whose station in life was higher than hers, which seemed to include almost everyone. The best Miranda could probably do about Ruth would be to become an expert on housekeeping and then work on her own.

"There's Pricilla now." Sadie waved to a stocky blonde woman. She looked to be in her thirties or older, but when she smiled, she looked younger.

After they got their food, Sadie introduced Miranda to Pricilla. "I was just telling Miranda how I enjoyed working with you." Sadie sat down beside her.

"That's because you were a hoot," Pricilla told her. "I never laughed so hard while working."

"Maybe have more fun with Ruth, Miranda. Might go better," Sadie suggested.

"You got stuck with Ruth?" Pricilla grimaced. "Don't expect any fun." She glanced around, but Ruth wasn't in the room. Even so, she kept her voice low. "Ruth's husband, Bentley, was a miner. He brought her and their son up here with him last year. Bentley struck gold and, just like that, found himself a new woman. More likely the woman found him. Anyway, he took off with Florence and left Ruth and her boy here with nothing. She's been mad at the whole world ever since."

"Poor Ruth." Miranda glumly shook her head. "I'll try to be nicer to her."

"Miranda's beau is a miner," Sadie told Pricilla. "Maybe you know him."

"His name is Jackson O'Neil," Miranda said hopefully. "He's tall and strong. With dark curly hair and blue eyes and—"

"Sorry." Pricilla shrugged. "Lots of miners come and go here, but I never get to know them. Naturally, they like the younger women. Especially the fancy ones like Florence."

"Yeah, we saw some of those last night," Miranda said glumly. "Jackson wrote to me about them. But I never imagined they'd be so colorful."

"Thanks to dyed hair and painted lips." Pricilla chuckled. "You girls may not believe it, but that was me when I come up here about six years ago. A dancehall girl."

Sadie's eyes grew wide. "You were?"

"For a spell. But when the real gold rush started, miners came up here in droves. And money flowed like water. Naturally, that's when the younger, prettier girls showed up. I reckon I was getting a little long in the tooth. So I took a job with Mrs. Stinson here. Thought I'd only be here a year or so. But here I am, still cleaning and scrubbing." She shrugged. "Guess that's about all I'm good for anymore."

"That's not true," Sadie argued. "You're good company. You're a good-hearted woman, and you're good for some good laughs."

Pricilla grinned. "That's only cuz you know how to get a body laughing." She turned to Miranda. "I s'pose you've heard her funny jokes and tall tales."

"Of course." Miranda felt a tinge of jealousy.

"And can the girl sing!" Pricilla winked at Sadie. "Honest to goodness, Sadie McGuire, you should consider the stage. What with your pretty face and nice voice, why you could make a lot more money than a chambermaid does."

Sadie laughed. "I wish."

"And I heard that Bertha Beaumont just quit the Nugget to get married." Pricilla's eyes lit up. "She was the main entertainment. I wonder if Mrs. Stinson has got someone else yet." She poked Sadie. "Why don't you speak to her about it?"

"You can't be serious."

"Better yet, I'll talk to her." Pricilla nodded. "She listens to me. Do you mind?"

Sadie laughed. "What have I got to lose?"

Suddenly Pricilla and Sadie were exchanging ideas and excitedly planning a stunning stage career for Sadie. Miranda didn't even know what to think about it. Besides that, she was too tired to think very clearly. But when Sadie suggested that Miranda could perform with her, Miranda had held up her hands. "You're the entertainer, Sadie. Not me." She picked up her now empty plate. "And if you'll excuse me, I'm exhausted. I want to write Jackson a letter…that is, if I'm not too tired to grasp a pen."

They excused her, but by the time she trudged back upstairs, she really was too tired to write to Jackson. That would have to wait. All she wanted right now was sleep. Hopefully she'd wake up to discover that being an overworked hotel maid in Alaska was just a very realistic yet unpleasant dream.

28

MIRANDA WAS DETERMINED TO TRY HARDER WITH RUTH THE NEXT day. But after several more sharp reprimands for "not doing it right," she was fed up. "Look, Ruth," she said hotly. "I'm sorry I don't meet up to your high housekeeping standards, but I'm trying. And it doesn't help anything for you to yell at me."

Ruth looked surprised.

"I realize you've had some hard knocks in your life," Miranda said a bit more gently. "And I understand how that can make a person unhappy. But I wish you wouldn't take it all out on me."

"Well!" Ruth set down her stack of fresh linens with fire in her eyes.

"Truth be told, my life hasn't been a bed of roses either," Miranda told her. "But I'm trying to make the best of it."

Ruth seemed to study Miranda more closely now. "I s'pose I been a little hard on you. My apologies."

Miranda felt surprised. "Thank you." She smiled as she hung the linens in the bathroom. "I hear you have a son, Ruth. How old is he? What's his name?"

Ruth's face lit up, and she almost looked like a different person. "My boy's name's Thomas. He'll be eight in June."

"Eight? That must be a fun age."

"Oh, yes. He's a sweetheart." Ruth handed her some washcloths. "The bright spot in my life."

"Where do you and Thomas live?" Miranda asked. "I know you don't stay in the maids' quarters."

"We stay in Mrs. Denning's boarding house. Next door to the church."

"And does Thomas attend school while you work?" Miranda neatly stacked the washcloths by the sink, the rounded fold facing out like Ruth had shown her.

"Yeah. Not a real school exactly. Pastor Gregg's wife, Polly, started it to keep the kids from running the streets. She's got about thirty pupils last count. Almost too much for the little church. I don't rightly know how Polly does it all on her own."

"That seems like a lot of children for one teacher." Miranda couldn't even imagine.

"That's for certain. Polly loves every one of 'em, but she's sixty if she's a day, and I s'pect all them rambunctious kids wear her out some."

"I can imagine." Miranda sighed. "I never got to attend a proper school when I was growing up. I always missed that."

"But you seem real smart to me." Ruth unwrapped a fresh bar of soap. "You talk good and proper."

"My parents taught me at home and tried to get me to use good grammar." As they finished up the room, Miranda even told Ruth about the academy. "I'm afraid I wasn't cut out for that. The other girls treated me like a country bumpkin."

Ruth actually laughed. "You don't seem like no bumpkin to me."

"Compared to them I was."

"Well then." She shook her head as she closed the door. "You just never know." She smiled at Miranda. "I do appreciate you telling me about yourself."

For the remainder of the day, the two women worked together with true congeniality. The second day really was better. Still, by the time Miranda went to change out of her uniform, she was dog tired. She wondered how long it would take her to get accustomed to this much work.

"There you are," Sadie said cheerfully as she came into the maids' quarters. "I've been looking all over for you."

"Ruth and I just finished up. And you were right, Sadie. Today was easier, and Ruth is really sweet. She has a little boy and—"

"That can wait." Sadie grabbed both of Miranda's hands. "Right now I have some really good news."

"Did you get your money back from the—"

"No. But it's good news just the same. I got us a chance at a better job."

"What do you mean?" Miranda unbuttoned her apron.

"Pricilla talked to Margaret—that's Mrs. Stinson, but she said I can call her Margaret when I went to see her. Anyway, she had me sing and dance and everything, Miranda. In my maid uniform. It was pretty hilarious. But she likes me."

"Oh?" Miranda nodded. "Why wouldn't she?"

"And she wants to see you now. I told her you know all my songs and that—"

"Wait a minute." Miranda frowned. "You're the one with the—"

"I told her we're a team, Miranda. I need you by my side." She was already tugging Miranda toward the door. "We have to go see Margaret right now."

"But I—"

"Don't worry about the uniform. Margaret can see past that. And here's the really good part, Miranda. If we really do this, if she agrees to both of us, we'll get to have a real hotel room. Not that fancy suite, but it'll be better than this." She tipped her head to the rows of narrow cots. "And we'll get paid much better." She lowered her voice. "Maybe fifteen dollars a week to share between us. And that's only performing for four nights a week. And of course, that's only if we can hold a crowd's attention. Margaret said that'll be the real test. But I think we can."

"I'm sure you can, Sadie. But I don't know if I—"

"Don't you understand, Miranda? I need you. I can't do this alone." She continued to rattle on and on as they went downstairs, and finally they were standing in front of Mrs. Stinson—or Margaret, as Sadie called her.

"Show me what you got, girls," the older woman said from behind her big desk.

Sadie whispered a song title in Miranda's ear then winked. "I'll start it up. You join in." And just like that Sadie was singing at the top of her voice and doing a little two-step shuffle dance. She locked eyes with Miranda, as if to say, *Do not let me down.* And despite her misgivings, Miranda jumped in. Pretending they were back at school just horsing around outside, she sang and danced, and when they finished, Margaret was grinning.

"Well, I'm willing to give you girls a try. But bear in mind, it's up to the audience. If you can't keep them happy, you'll be back to cleaning. And I'll warn you, miners can be a pretty rough crowd." She placed a finger alongside her cheek. "But they do love burlesque. We had three young women last summer. Their burlesque show kept the place packed. So, that's it. You girls will be our new burlesque show. This is perfect."

Miranda was too stunned to speak. Burlesque? Wasn't that very risqué?

"Yes." Sadie's eyes were bright. "We will be the best burlesque show the Nugget has ever seen."

Margaret laughed. "Well, don't set your sights too high. We'll be content if the miners don't boo or throw things at you." She stood up and, still talking about burlesque shows and how much fun they were, she led the girls through the lobby and through the saloon, where a few miners were starting to trickle in. "We have a roomful of costumes and props and things." She led them up the stage and behind the purple velvet curtain, showing them the dressing room and everything. "I don't know when you'll be ready for your first performance, but I say the sooner the better. Being that today is only Wednesday, you wouldn't have a real big crowd yet. It's the weekends that get busy."

"Then we'll try it out tonight," Sadie declared.

Miranda gaped. "You can't be—"

"Margaret is right," Sadie cut Miranda off. "It'll be a good practice run. Maybe by the weekend we'll have a real act ready."

"I'll let Ronald know," Mrs. Stinson told Sadie. "He's the piano player. He's been trying to keep things going out there, but I'm sure he'll be relieved to have some pretty girls to help him out." She pulled out a little writing pad and pencil and handed it to Sadie. "Just let him know which songs you plan to use. The show can start at eight. I'll put out a sign. Should I put your names on it? Sadie and Miranda's Burlesque Show?"

"We need a stage name," Sadie said suddenly. "Something with some pizzazz."

"You two look like sisters," Margaret said. "Maybe we could book it as a sister act. Something with some zing. Let's see…you seem to know a lot of ship songs and you said your father was a sea captain. How about the Sailor Sisters?"

"Why not?" Sadie agreed. "That's got a nice ring to it."

Sadie thanked Margaret then dragged Miranda into the dressing room. "Isn't this exciting? We're about to become famous. The Sailor Sisters."

Miranda didn't even have words.

"I know, I know. You're having a little bit of stage fright right now. But you can do this, Miranda. I know you can. Just follow my lead." She was already writing down song titles.

"Sadie!" Miranda finally sputtered. "Margaret said *burlesque show!* I cannot be part of a burlesque show! This is crazy."

Sadie frowned. "What exactly do you think a burlesque show is, Miranda?"

"It's *risqué.* Girls doing, well, you know. Shameful and disgusting—and I refuse to participate—"

"That just shows how little you know. Oh, sure, there are probably some gritty shows like you're thinking. But a true burlesque show is about singing and dancing and telling jokes. Papa's taken me to many—all over the world. It's just good fun, lots of laughter, fun costumes, and good music. It's not dishonorable or shameful. It's *theater.*"

Miranda felt confused.

"I promise you, Miranda, we won't do anything disgraceful. Come on, let's go pick out a costume. But I'll warn you, they won't be the kind of clothes we would wear on the street, but you have to understand we are actresses now. We are entertainers. The Sailor Sisters. We have to be flamboyant." She pointed to the clock on the wall. "We have about three hours to practice."

Miranda felt like the lamb being led to the slaughter, but as usual, Sadie's silver tongue seemed to work its magic. Before long, they were trying on outlandish outfits and laughing and singing, and by the time eight o'clock rolled around, Miranda was almost ready to take the stage. That is, if she didn't lose her supper first.

By Friday morning, Miranda knew two things. First, it wasn't that hard to entertain a roomful of miners. Especially when they were imbibing. A pair of gaudily attired girls, who could sing and dance fairly well, seemed to do the trick. "It doesn't hurt that you're both quite pretty," Margaret had told them last night. "But the weekend crowd will be more demanding. So get ready to give it all you got."

The second thing Miranda knew was that she didn't want to make a career of this. Oh, it might be fine for Sadie, since she seemed to honestly love performing. It was amazing how her friend sprang to life on the stage. Miranda had seen Sadie ham it up before, but never for a big crowd. Still, as Miranda walked through the quiet hotel lobby in the late morning, she knew she was only doing this for Sadie's sake. As soon as Sadie had confidence to go solo, Miranda would gladly step out.

And if she didn't hear something from Jackson by then, hopefully she'd have saved up enough money to get her home to Colorado. That was what she wanted more than anything now. She missed Delia and Wyatt and Enoch and Caleb…and the ranch. She only hoped that they would let her come back.

Miranda sighed as she laid three letters in the hotel's outgoing mailbox. It had taken her most of the morning to write them. One was to Delia, an attempt to explain what had happened in Philadelphia. Another was for Aunt Lilly, to apologize for running away. And the third was to Jackson, informing him that she was here in Juneau. Although she'd begun to wonder if he was even still in Alaska. She hadn't seen him, although she was always on the lookout. And no one seemed to know of him.

"Miranda." Ruth, in her maid uniform, came up from behind her. "I hear you and your friend took to the stage, but I couldn't hardly believe it. Is it true?"

Miranda sighed. "Yes, it's true. But it's mostly my friend's doing. Sadie is the talented one. I'm just sort of her backup."

"Well, I never." Ruth shook her head. "I was sorely disappointed. I did like working with you, Miranda. But I do wish you well."

"You too." Miranda grasped her hand. "And your little boy too."

They both noticed Charlie at the reception desk staring at Ruth. "S'cuse me," she said. "I better get to work."

Miranda nodded. But she felt slightly guilty as she headed out the door. It didn't seem fair that she could sing silly songs and dance goofy jigs for a few hours in the evenings and make so much more money than Ruth, who worked hard all day. Especially since she knew Ruth was also supporting her son.

Outside, the sun was shining brightly overhead, and Miranda was determined to see a bit of the town. Dressed in normal clothes and with her hat low on her brow, she wondered if any of the men on the street would recognize her from the stage last night. She hoped not. And when she saw dancehall girls loitering outside the saloons and hotels, with their colorful hair, fancy dresses, and painted lips, she reassured herself she was not like them. What she and Sadie did was different. Wasn't it? At least that's what Sadie kept telling her. Right now, Sadie was up in their room making adjustments to tonight's costumes. For a girl who hated sewing class at the academy, Sadie was proving to be fairly nimble with a needle.

At the end of the town was a small white clapboard church. Was this where Ruth's boy went to school? Curious to see more, Miranda walked to the church and, hearing children's voices playing outside, she went around back to take a peek.

"Hello?" A gray-haired woman hurried over to her. "You must be Marion's mother."

"What?" Miranda blinked. "No. I'm not anyone's mother."

"Oh, I'm sorry. Little Marion told me her mother was collecting her early today. I hadn't met her yet and just assumed." She smiled and stuck out her hand. "I'm Polly Gregg, and I run our little school."

"The pastor's wife," Miranda said. "My friend Ruth told me about you. Her boy Thomas attends your school."

"That's right." Polly frowned. "Do you work with Ruth at the hotel?"

"I was a maid for a couple of days." Miranda gazed out over the children playing in the green grass. "Looks like they're having fun."

"Yes. First sunny day we've had this week. I'm letting them enjoy a longer noontime recess."

"And you manage all these children by yourself?"

"I do my best. My husband, Pastor Gregg, helps out when he can, but he's busy with his own work." She sighed. "I keep asking God to send a helper to—" The shriek of a child stopped her, and they both looked to see a little girl who appeared to have tumbled from the teeter-totter.

"I'll help her." Miranda took off toward the crying child. Kneeling down, she could see the girl was probably more scared than hurt. "Are you all right?" she asked.

"Who are you?" The little girl sat up.

"I'm Miranda." She helped the girl to her feet, brushing dirt from her blue calico dress. "What's your name?"

"Belinda." The girl smiled. "You're pretty."

"Thank you. So are you."

The little girl took her hand. "I want to show you something."

"All right." Miranda let Belinda lead her across the yard and over to where some bright yellow blooms grew next to a tree.

"These are daffodils," Belinda said.

"Yes, I know. Aren't they pretty?"

"We can't pick them. Or else there won't be any to look at."

"Yes, that makes sense."

Belinda continued to walk Miranda around the yard, pointing out childish items of interest and introducing her to other curious girls until a small cluster of them were walking around the yard. Finally a bell rang, and the children all ran toward the church.

"Recess is over," Belinda told Miranda. "I have to go."

Miranda just nodded, but as she followed the children who were running toward the church, she felt an odd stirring inside her. Almost as if she wished she was a little girl again, going to a school like this. Silly, of course, but it was there just the same.

She went over to where Polly Gregg was standing by the door as children filed in. "Thanks for helping," she told Miranda. "I was about to say I've been praying for God to send me a helper. Any chance that prayer has been answered?"

Miranda didn't know what to say. "Well, I'm happy to help you. I don't work during the day. I have time."

"Wonderful. Come in and join us."

Just like that Miranda was standing on the sidelines of the church, which was set up like a classroom, and watching as Polly spoke to the class. Before long, Polly assigned a group of primary readers to take turns reading to Miranda in the back. Both Belinda and Thomas were in this group. After reading, Miranda helped an older group of children with their arithmetic. And the next thing she knew, Polly was ringing the bell again and class was dismissed.

"Oh, Miranda, you truly are a godsend," Polly declared. "The children seem to like you, and you fit right in. You mentioned you worked as a maid for a couple of days. But you're not doing that now?"

"No." Miranda considered her answer. "I, uh, I work in the evenings now."

"So your days are free?" Polly asked hopefully.

"Yes."

"I can't pay much, but I would love to hire you. You seemed to fit in so nicely today. Would you accept the job?"

"Don't you want to know more about me?" Miranda asked.

"Yes, of course. I was going to ask you to join me for tea." She pointed to house out behind the church. "Do you have time?"

"Sure." Miranda nodded nervously. What would Polly say when Miranda confessed to her that she and Sadie were being paid to entertain drunken miners in the evenings? Surely, that would put a damper on the job offer. But after they sat down for tea and Miranda explained how she and Sadie came to be in Juneau, Polly didn't seem the least bit concerned. Finally, Miranda confessed about their burlesque show in the saloon. "But it's not a shameful, disrespectful act," she said quickly. "We sing funny songs and dance—and Sadie, she's the real talent, she tells jokes and stories."

"How interesting."

Miranda blinked. "And you'd still want me to help at your school?"

"Of course. Like I said, I think you're a godsend. And since you're a good singer, maybe you could take over music lessons. Like my dear husband likes to remind me, I can't carry a tune in a bucket."

Miranda was tempted to ask Polly once again if she really had no qualms about Miranda's evening job. But Polly seemed so completely happy about having a teacher's helper that Miranda just couldn't bring herself to burst the poor woman's bubble. Instead, she agreed to work from ten to two every day, starting Monday. They even shook on it. And Miranda promised to attend their church on Sunday.

As she walked back to the hotel, Miranda felt better about herself. Maybe she was performing in a burlesque show by night, but in the daytime she would be doing something respectable, something of real value.

29

By Friday afternoon, Jackson's mind was made up. Despite AJ's guilt-inducing persuasion and cajoling, Jackson was done with Alaska. Even though AJ couldn't buy out his half share of the mine, Jackson resolved to work as a ship hand in order to get back to the States. He missed Colorado more than ever right now.

"I'm going to mail this letter," he told AJ as they came into town.

"To Miranda?" AJ guessed.

Jackson shrugged. "Just letting her know I'm done here. I doubt I'll ever hear from her again anyway." For all he knew, Miranda could be married to a wealthy city slicker by now. That would explain her lack of communication. And, although there was a letter from his mother, nothing from Miranda. He wasn't surprised. He shoved his mother's letter into his jacket pocket then went over to where AJ and the mule were waiting.

"I just asked about ships. Nothing coming this way until late next week."

Jackson sighed. "Reckon I'll just have to wait then."

"Here in town?" AJ frowned. "That'll run you out of money fast."

"I can camp."

"Or you can go back with me and keep plugging away for a few more days. Who knows, we might get lucky?"

Jackson looked upward. "When have I heard that before?"

"Tell you what," AJ said suddenly. "You promise to go back with me, for one more week, and I'll pay to put us up at the Nugget for tonight, including a steak supper."

Jackson considered this. "Sounds like a good deal."

"Then I better make sure they got us a room." He handed Rosie's reins to Jackson. "You get her settled at the livery then meet me at the Nugget."

Miranda decided not to mention her new day job to Sadie. She suspected Sadie would not approve. Sometimes she acted like Miranda was her own personal property. "Did you get the alterations done?" Miranda picked up a royal blue dress trimmed with gold braid and brass buttons to give it a slightly nautical look, except for the low neckline and bright pink petticoat beneath.

"Almost done." She held up a similar looking dress. "This is yours."

"Uh huh." Miranda flipped a ruffle of the fluffy petticoat beneath it. "The sailor collars are interesting."

"We're the Sailor Sisters," Sadie reminded her. "Seemed like a fun touch."

Miranda frowned at the strange looking garment. "But seems a little short. And the front is pretty low."

"I already tried them both on. They fit me perfectly, so you'll be fine." Sadie slid the needle into the fabric, pulling it through a big brass button.

Miranda picked up Sadie's dress, holding it up to herself. "This one is awfully short too. It's clear above my knees."

"Margaret said we need to show more legs. She brought up some hosiery for us." She nodded to the bed.

Miranda looked at the strange looking stockings. "Stripes?"

"They are the latest thing." Sadie laughed. "All the rage in Paris."

"Won't we look like clowns?"

"We're the entertainment. We're supposed to make the miners laugh and forget their troubles." Sadie laid the dress aside and stretched her neck. "I ordered room service for dinner. They'll bring it up at six."

"How *elegant*." Miranda's tone was sarcastic as she sat down.

"Seems you'd be more grateful." Sadie frowned. "So where were you all afternoon?"

"In town."

"The whole time?"

"Yes. Did you know there's a sweet little school? It's in the church at the end of town. The pastor's wife runs it. Her name is Polly. And Ruth's boy Thomas goes there and I—"

"Fascinating." Sadie shook her head with a perplexed expression. "Anyway, I put together tonight's songs without you. I gave Ronald his list, and yours is on the table. You should look it over to see if there's anything you're not familiar with."

Miranda read the list and saw she knew the tunes by heart. But even if she forgot a line or two, it wouldn't matter. Sadie could belt them out so loudly no one would even notice if Miranda mouthed the words. As long as she smiled and danced and followed Sadie's lead, they would be fine.

Sometimes she wondered why Sadie even needed her. In some ways it seemed she'd be better off on her own. She claimed Miranda was her support—as if she might crumble on the stage without Miranda by her side. But Miranda knew Sadie was strong. Well, mostly. She'd gone to pieces after her money was stolen, it was true. Sadie was hard to figure.

If anyone had told Jackson he'd be sitting in the Nugget Hotel's fancy saloon with AJ, or about to watch *The Sailor Sisters' Burlesque Show* tonight, he never would've believed it. But since AJ had already sprung for a big dinner and nice hotel room, Jackson was trying to be congenial. He drew the line at drinking a beer, though. Not because he was a teetotaler, but because he didn't want to give AJ any excuses to stumble. Of course, that made him wonder…what would happen after Jackson left Alaska? Well, that was AJ's problem.

Jackson looked around the crowded, smoky room. Most of the men were drinking. Some were already feeling the effects. A skinny man with an oversized mustache was playing the piano, and a few dancehall girls moseyed about, flirting and chatting, probably looking for the miner with the fullest pockets.

"When's this big show supposed to start?" Jackson as AJ.

"Sign in the lobby said eight o'clock." AJ sipped his coffee then frowned. "You sure you don't want a beer, Jackson? Just for old time's sake?"

Jackson firmly shook his head. Then the piano player played some loud notes. "May I have your attention," he yelled to be heard over the noisy room. "I want to introduce tonight's entertainment, a new burlesque act all the way from the East Coast—" He was interrupted by some loud whoops and whistles. "I present to you tonight, *the stupendous Sailor Sisters*. Let's all give 'em a big hand!"

The gas lanterns in the saloon were lowered a bit as the piano player sat back down to play a lively tune. And a spotlight was lit and shone onto the little stage. The audience of mostly men was clapping energetically and stomping their feet. And then the purple velvet curtains opened, and a pair of scantily clad girls danced out onto the stage. Apparently they were trying to resemble sailors. Strange looking sailors! Both women had reddish hair and were enthusiastically singing a robust sea shanty tune and kicking their legs high so that their pink petticoats were easily visible. Naturally, the men seemed to love it.

As the women got closer to the edge of the stage, Jackson realized that one of them resembled Miranda. A lot! Was it just his imagination? Was he just missing her so much that his imagination had run amuck on him? How could he imagine this fancy floozy woman with the red painted lips was anything like his Miranda? Then, as the girl moved more fully into the spotlight, Jackson blinked and looked again. If that girl wasn't Miranda, she was her identical twin!

After the first song, the other girl told a joke and asked a riddle, which Miranda's twin answered, making everyone laugh. Her voice was the same too! Jackson looked down at his coffee, wondering if someone had slipped something into it—something to cause him delusions. Because, crazy as it seemed, he felt certain that girl was Miranda Williams. They broke into a lively round of "Blow the Man Down," and the miners joined in the singing.

"These Sailor Sisters are great," AJ said to Jackson after they finished that song.

"Yeah…great," Jackson muttered with his eyes locked onto the Miranda look-alike. Was it really her? And if so, how was that even possible? As they started their next number, Jackson awkwardly stood and hurried out of the noisy room. He went through the lobby and leaned against a wall, feeling like he could barely catch his breath. There was the glitzy poster announcing *The Sailor Sisters Burlesque Show starts at Eight.*

"Are you all right?" the man behind the reception desk asked.

Jackson nodded. "Just a little close there in the saloon."

"Yeah. That Sailor Sisters act is really bringing 'em in."

"How long have they been playing here?" Jackson didn't even know why he was asking, probably just to make conversation.

"Just a few days. Believe it or not, those girls started out as maids. But someone figured out they can sing. Well, mostly it's that Sadie who can sing. But Miranda tries to keep—"

"Miranda Williams?" Jackson gasped.

"Yep. That's her name. You know her?"

"I used to." Jackson felt physically sick now. "I'm going up to my room."

"Yeah, sure." He nodded. "G'night."

Jackson barely remembered the trip up the stairs or how he managed to collapse onto the bed. But as he lay there in the dark room, he felt like someone had reached into his chest and extracted his heart. How could Miranda do something like this? It just made no sense. Absolutely no sense. He tried not to think about Miranda's revealing outfit or those awful painted lips…or the way the men were hooting and whooping over the girls. But it was an image that felt burnt into his brain. And it sickened him to the core.

30

It wasn't until they were a few miles out of Juneau that Jackson finally answered AJ's persistent questioning about what was bothering him and why he'd run off last night.

"All right, I'll tell you," Jackson growled at his nosy partner. "You might as well know. You'd probably find out sooner or later anyway." He kicked a stone with the toe of his boot, and a bad word slipped out.

"What is going on with you?" AJ demanded. "I've never seen you act like this."

"Those girls last night. The Sailor Sisters," he spat the words out. "That was Miranda. And her friend Sadie."

AJ laughed loudly as he socked Jackson in the shoulder. "You're punchy, man. What was in your coffee last night?"

"It's true." Jackson felt sick to his stomach again. Why did he have to revisit all this again? He wanted to forget the whole thing… just let it go.

AJ stopped walking to peer curiously at Jackson. "Are you all right?"

"No, I'm not all right," Jackson shouted. "Didn't you hear what

I said? Those girls! On that stage last night! Dressed like that! Acting like that! One of them was my Miranda. No, no, no! She's not mine anymore. I wouldn't have anything to do with her if she were the last living girl on—"

"Calm down," AJ said firmly. "You must be imagining things. And now I agree with you—you should go home, Jackson. Alaska is getting to you. I've heard stories of miners who lost their minds up here. But it's usually in winter."

"I haven't lost my mind," Jackson yelled. "I lost my girl."

"All right, all right." AJ patted his back. "You lost your girl. I'm sorry."

"You don't believe me, do you?" Jackson growled. "You think I'm making this all up? What would be the point? Can't you see it's making me sick?"

"I agree. You're not well." AJ actually looked slightly scared now. "We should get you back to town. You need to see a doctor and—"

"I'm not sick! Not like that."

"Come on," AJ urged him as he turned Rosie around. "Let's go back to town."

"NO!"

"Look, Jackson, if that really is your girl—I mean if it really is Miranda, you should talk to her."

"Never!"

"Fine." AJ stuck out his chin. "Then I'll go back."

"What're you doing?"

"I'm going back to town to talk to those girls. The Sailor Sisters. You go on back to the mine by yourself." AJ and Rosie kept walking, headed for town.

Jackson was so flummoxed he didn't know what to do. He sure didn't want to talk to Miranda. But he didn't want AJ talking to her either. He wished he'd never told him. More than that, he wished there was a ship in the harbor about to set sail. He didn't even care where it would be going, he'd get on it. Anything to get away from here! He watched as AJ and Rosie got smaller on the road back to town. And then he turned around and marched back toward the mine. It wasn't until he was nearly there that he realized all their replenished supplies and food were still strapped to Rosie's back.

"Well, fine," he growled as he sat down by their fire pit. "I'd rather starve out here than be forced to speak to Miranda." Now if he could just forget about her, wipe her name and her image permanently from his brain.

Miranda and Sadie had just finished their lunch and were about to take a Saturday stroll through town when a young man waved to them from across the street, where he was tying up a mule. Next he eagerly called out their names and started across the street.

"Do you know him?" Miranda whispered to Sadie.

"No, but he's good looking," Sadie teased. "I might like to get to know him."

"Looks like a miner," Miranda quietly observed as he waited for a wagon to go past.

"Maybe he knows your Jackson," Sadie suggested as she waved to the sandy-haired man coming their way.

"Excuse me for being so bold," he told them. "But I was eager to make your acquaintance. I saw your show last night. You girls were wonderful."

"Thank you." Sadie smiled. "So, you know our names, but we don't know you."

"Right. My apologies." He removed his felt hat. "I'm Archibald Robinson. But my friends call me AJ."

"AJ?" Miranda repeated the familiar sounding name. "Do you happen to know a miner named Jackson O'Neil? He was in Juneau, but I think he's gone back to Colorado."

"Jackson is my partner."

"Is he here now?" Miranda looked eagerly down the street.

"No, I'm sorry. He's not. He, uh, he wasn't feeling too well."

"Oh, no!" She gasped. "Is he sick?"

"Not exactly. Well, sort of." He nodded toward the hotel. "Could we go sit in the lobby there and talk?"

"Yes, of course." Sadie grabbed Miranda's hand. "Let's do that."

As they went into the lobby, Miranda felt her knees shaking. Something was wrong with Jackson. She just knew it. That's why he'd quit writing to her. He was sick or injured or something.

After they sat down, AJ explained how he and Jackson had stayed at the hotel last night. "And we took in your show." AJ's smile was slightly crooked. "And when Jackson realized it was you up there, Miranda, well, he didn't take it too good."

"Oh, no." Miranda looked at Sadie.

"So Jackson didn't like the show?" Sadie sounded a bit indignant.

"He didn't like that Miranda was in it," AJ said quietly. "But don't get me wrong, I thought you ladies were just great up there. But Jackson, well…he's a mite bit old-fashioned. A really straight stick, if you know what I mean. And I don't fault him for it none. He's managed to keep me on the straight and narrow for going on a year now. I'm most grateful for that."

Miranda felt sick inside. And her eyes were filling with tears. "I'm sorry," she mumbled. "Please, excuse me. I, uh, I don't feel too well myself." And before Sadie could stop her, Miranda hurried to the stairs and up to her room. And once there, she threw herself onto the bed and just sobbed. Why hadn't she considered the fact that Jackson might still be around, or that he wouldn't approve of her performing with Sadie? She cried even harder. To think that Jackson had been so nearby, but she never got to see him. And now she'd ruined everything!

AJ and Rosie didn't make it into camp until well after dark. By then, despite his empty stomach, Jackson had gone to bed. And when AJ nudged his bedroll, Jackson pretended to be asleep. But it was the most sleepless night of his life. By the time the sun was coming up,

Jackson felt like he'd been wrestling the meanest of demons all night long. Every bone in his body seemed to ache from it. Since AJ was still sleeping, Jackson quietly started a fire and put on the coffee.

Out of habit, he started to fix some breakfast, but even though he hadn't eaten since yesterday, he no longer felt hunger pains. Instead, his stomach felt like he'd swallowed a bag of rocks. Even the scent of bacon didn't seem to stir up any hunger.

"You're up," AJ said cheerfully.

"Yeah," Jackson mumbled as he sat on a stump, his tin coffee cup warming his hands.

AJ helped himself to coffee, poked the bacon, then sat across from him. "I met Miranda and Sadie," he said simply.

"So." Jackson shrugged.

"So, I thought you might want to hear—"

"All I want is to never hear that name again," he said gruffly.

"Really?" AJ glumly shook his head. "That's too bad."

"Maybe. But that's how it is." Jackson dished out his bacon and biscuits and, although they weren't quite done, he proceeded to eat them, but like the bag of rocks, the food just seemed to sit there. "I'm going to work." He stood and, picking up his tools and lantern, went into the cave. Mostly he just wanted to be alone. He didn't want to hear anything AJ had to say about those girls—*the Sailor Sisters indeed!*

Despite all of Sadie's reassurances, Miranda felt certain her romance with Jackson was over. She performed with Sadie on Saturday night, but her heart had not been in it. And according to Margaret, Miranda's forced smiles hadn't impressed the rowdy crowd.

"You must try harder," Margaret told Miranda on Sunday afternoon. "Otherwise you'll drag Sadie down. Your act was such a success the first three nights. But last night was disappointing. I'd hate to shut you girls down, but the Sailor Sisters is a two-girl act."

"Miranda will do better on Wednesday," Sadie assured her. "Just wait, you'll see. We'll practice every day. And I have some new ideas I want to try. We can do this, Margaret."

"I hope so." Margaret frowned. "Otherwise, I'll have to look for a new act."

After Margaret left, Sadie turned to Miranda with a creased brow. "Are you going to let Jackson ruin everything?"

"I'm sorry." Miranda sighed. "But it's hard to hide my sadness."

"Why do you have to be sad?" Sadie asked. "I told you that AJ said that Jackson had been true to you. He never looked at another girl. And the reason he didn't write was because he was waiting to strike gold. He wanted to send you a happy letter."

"Yes, yes, I know all about that. But that was *before*."

"Before he saw our act." Sadie sat down on the bed. "But AJ said it was probably just because he was shocked to see you."

"Jackson had high ideals for his wife. His mother is a wonderful woman. Everyone looks up to her. And my stepsister Delia too. Jackson greatly admires her. I'm a complete disappointment to him. I know it. I don't blame him either." She sank into the chair. "I know we needed the money, but I wish I'd stuck with being a maid. It wasn't so bad."

"We wouldn't have this room, or good meals. We wouldn't make nearly as much money."

"I know. But if I could, I'd trade all that. In order to get Jackson back."

"Well, AJ was going to talk to him. He promised to tell him our story. About leaving school to come here—just because Jackson was here. And he knows about how we lost our money. How we had to work. AJ was very understanding about it." Sadie smiled. "In fact, he was quite nice about everything. He's such a gentleman. If Jackson is anything like AJ, I'd think he'd set his judgment aside and come running to you."

Miranda wished he would, but she knew that Jackson had his pride.

"And if Jackson wants to act like a stubborn old mule, I think you should just forget about him." Sadie stood with a defiant look. "AJ said that Jackson plans to go back to the States anyway."

"He's leaving?"

"That was his plan. AJ said Jackson came to Juneau to book passage on the next ship to the mainland. He's sick of Alaska. And he's given up on ever striking gold. Even though AJ thinks they could be close, Jackson's determined to go home."

"Oh." Miranda wished she could go home too. But it would take weeks, maybe months, to save up enough fare money.

"So maybe it's all for the best." Sadie grabbed Miranda's hands, pulling her to her feet with a bright smile. "Why not just forget Jackson? Put all your energy into our act. Like my papa says, there are more fish in the sea. Just meeting AJ gives me hope. You need a fresh start too, Miranda. So just put Jackson out of your mind."

Miranda didn't think that was possible.

"Maybe we should practice today. After all, we promised Margaret we'd give our best."

Miranda studied Sadie for a long moment. "Do you think you'd be able to perform alone?"

Sadie released her hands with raised brows. "What are you saying?"

"You're so talented, Sadie. I just don't see why you couldn't do the show on your own. No one would miss me up there. All eyes are probably on you anyway."

"That's not true, Sadie. I need you! You're the reason I can do what I do. Having you there to encourage me and—"

"What if I encouraged you from the audience?" Miranda suggested quickly. "And what if I helped with your costumes? I can sew. And I could do your hair. I could study new styles in magazines. And I could help you with new props and things. I'd be like your manager or assistant or something behind the scenes. But you would be the one bright and shining star!"

"No." Sadie's eyes flashed in anger. "I need you beside me, Miranda. We're a team, and I refuse to let you break up the act."

Miranda felt trapped and on the verge of tears again. She tried to remember the sermon she'd heard this morning. It had been so encouraging…it had made her believe there was a way out of her mess. But now, she felt stuck. Hopelessly stuck.

Even though Miranda had carefully explained about her commitment to help out at the school, Sadie acted surprised when Miranda prepared to leave on Monday morning. "We have to practice our act," she insisted.

"That will have to wait. I promised to work from ten until two." Miranda reminded her. "We can have as much time as you want after two."

Sadie frowned. "Do the pastor and his wife know you're part of a burlesque show?"

Miranda sighed as she pinned on her hat. "I told Polly that we sing together to entertain. I didn't say anything about a burlesque show."

"Well, it seems to me that parents might not approve of having a *burlesque* performer teaching their children."

Miranda suppressed her anger. "You told me that burlesque was perfectly respectable," she reminded her.

"Well, yes…but not everyone would agree." Sadie was tugging on a shoe.

Miranda reached for her gloves. "Like Jackson for instance."

"You were supposed to forget about him." Sadie threw her other shoe, barely missing Miranda's head. Without another word, Miranda made her exit.

As she walked to school, she wondered if she should ask Polly exactly what her wages would be. Polly had warned that it wouldn't be much. But surely it would be more than a maid's wages. What if it was enough for Miranda to part ways with Sadie? Of course, then she'd have to find a place to live. Room and board would probably make it impossible to save. Then she could end up like so many other women who'd gotten stuck in this town. As much as she wanted to be free from the Sailor Sisters Burlesque Show, she knew it might be her only chance at affording a ticket home. And if Jackson was unable to forgive her for being on the stage, perhaps it didn't matter anyway.

As she walked through the quiet town, the little white church came into view, and she suddenly remembered Pastor Gregg's sermon yesterday. "Forgive and you'll be forgiven," he'd said so many times that it had actually stayed in her head. Oh, she'd heard those words before. From Delia and then from Aunt Lilly. Sure, they sounded good, but they'd never fully registered with her. For starters, there was a man from her past she was resolved to never forgive. Marcus had been a lying, murderous snake of a man who didn't deserve forgiveness. And yet Delia had managed to forgive him. And Delia had forgiven Miranda too.

She'd pondered on those things during church yesterday, and she'd thought perhaps she really was ready to learn about forgiveness. After all, she had much to be forgiven for…the list was long. And if that meant she needed to forgive others, well, perhaps it was time to try. But how?

31

For three days, Miranda tried not to think about Jackson. But each afternoon, as she returned from helping out at the school, she looked for him along the street. She looked for him outside of the hotel. She looked for him in the lobby. But Jackson was never there. This only served to convince her that he was truly done with her. It was like Sadie continued to say. "If he really cared, he would come."

So, on Wednesday night, despite her reluctance, Miranda took the stage with Sadie. She refused to paint her lips and insisted on a slightly longer skirt, but she did her best to smile and laugh. And perhaps she was becoming a true actress, because the audience, smaller than the weekend crowd, seemed to believe her.

"You were wonderful," Sadie told her afterward. "Thank you."

Miranda just nodded. Hopefully the weekend crowd would be as accepting. And hopefully she'd be able to save up enough money to go home by summer. She'd checked on ship fare and learned there was a ship passing through on Saturday. A ship she felt certain Jackson planned to board. That was what AJ had told Sadie. Miranda was getting resigned to this by now. If Jackson didn't care enough to even come and speak to her, why should she care?

Except that she still did. Sometimes it felt like his rejection of her only made her love for him increase. Of course, that seemed ridiculous. But maybe love wasn't supposed to make sense.

The highlight of Miranda's life the next few days was helping at the school. By the end of her first week, she knew each child by name. And the children seemed devoted to her. Whether it was reading aloud or solving arithmetic problems or playing at recess, the children completely embraced her. For a girl who'd experienced a fair amount of rejection and judgment, the children's acceptance felt surprisingly good.

Polly seemed pleased with her too. Although she was apologetic when she explained that Miranda's salary was only twelve dollars a month. "I wish it could be more, but that's the most we can afford right now."

Still, twelve dollars combined with her performing salary meant that she might be able to afford ship passage and train fare by the time school let out for summer. There was only one fly in the ointment. Miranda still wasn't sure how Polly or Pastor Gregg might react when they discovered she was half of the Sailor Sisters act. And for that reason, she decided to come clean on Friday. If it cost her the teaching job, she'd just have to live with it. She stayed until the end of the school day, which meant she'd be an hour late to practice with Sadie, but she knew it was worth it to get this out in the open. And when she explained the situation to Polly, she even forced herself to use the despicable word *burlesque*. For some reason she just couldn't get comfortable with that word. And then she braced herself for the older woman's reaction.

"Oh, I know all about that," Polly told her.

"What?"

"When I told my husband you worked evenings by singing at the hotel, he felt it necessary to look into it. We're aware of how some of the dancehall girls make their living. And we try to get them to come to church, but it's not easy."

"So you don't have a problem with it?"

"Oh, don't get me wrong, Miranda, we wish you had a better way to earn money. And we wish we could offer you better pay. But we understand. You have told me that you are only providing musical entertainment. We believe you."

Miranda couldn't stop herself from hugging her. "Thank you, Polly. That means so much. If I could quit singing with Sadie and still make enough travel money to go home, I would."

"Pastor Gregg and I are praying you will be a good, wholesome influence on Sadie and any other girls you meet while working at the Nugget. And we were both so glad to see you in church on Sunday. We hope you'll encourage others to join us too."

"I will." She nodded eagerly. Then, feeling greatly relieved, she slowly walked through town. As usual on Fridays, it was already getting busy. Worn out miners were lined up at the bathhouse and barber shop, others loitered around the various saloons. As she walked past a clump of dirt-encrusted men, wearing her school teacher dress, she wondered if they realized she was the other half of the Sailor Sisters. She hoped not. But she wouldn't be surprised if some of these men found their way to their burlesque show tonight.

As she went into the hotel, she thought about Jackson. Was there any chance he'd come to their show tonight? Sadie said that AJ claimed Jackson planned to leave by ship. Tomorrow morning. Miranda had watched a large boat sail into the harbor on her way to school. How she wished she could afford passage to go home too. But that was impossible. She glanced around the hotel lobby, curious as to whether Jackson might be nearby right now. If so, would he make any attempt to see her? Or was he too coldhearted? And could she really blame him?

Miranda had tried to disguise the bitter disappointment that Jackson made no effort to contact her when she and Sadie went to bed last night. But as a result of her broken and aching heart, Miranda had barely slept a wink. Instead, she tossed and turned and eventually conjured up a crazy scheme.

Before the sun rose, while Sadie still slept, Miranda got up and quietly dressed. She shoved what she could fit into her valise and then went to the bureau drawer where she and Sadie had put their earnings just last night. Feeling like a criminal, she took it all and, after scrawling an apologetic note, tiptoed out of the room.

As she hurried downstairs, she rationalized that Sadie would have food and shelter—and one week from now she'd get paid again. Sadie would be angry, but she would be all right. Meanwhile, Miranda would never be all right again if she didn't get one last chance to salvage her relationship with Jackson. Somehow she had to make him understand.

Down at the docks, Miranda realized her plan would not be easy. She knew she didn't have enough fare for passage and, for that reason, she planned to stow away. It was outrageous and risky, she knew, but she was desperate. She would reveal her presence on the ship after it was well on its way. The captain would be angry, but she would cry and plead with him and offer him what little money she had. Hopefully he would be merciful. But getting onto the ship looked more difficult than she had imagined. From a safe distance, she watched the busy gang plank. Several sailors were loading and unloading. And others just milled about, both on and off the ship. She had no way to sneak on board without being observed.

As she stood behind a stack of crates, she noticed a lone man standing toward the front of the ship. Wearing a bulky tan jacket and a brown felt hat pulled low on his brow, he didn't appear to be a sailor. About Jackson's height and build, but looking out toward the water, as if eager to be on his way, his face was not visible. Still, she felt certain it was Jackson. For that reason, she stepped out from behind the crates and walked closer to the ship. She would stand there, out in the open, in the hopes he might look back…might recognize her…might regret his decision to leave like this.

But soon the sailors were pulling in the ropes and shouting to one another and then, just like that, the ship was moving away from the dock. With tears streaking down her cheeks, Miranda waved and even called out, although she knew he couldn't hear her, but he never turned around. Never looked back.

32

ALTHOUGH DELIA HAD BEEN GREATLY REVEALED TO GET A LETTER from Miranda last month, she still felt concerned. She wished there was something they could do, but Wyatt insisted this was a journey that Miranda needed to make on her own.

"You're sure we shouldn't send money?" Delia asked him as they sat on the porch, sipping coffee and enjoying the sunset after a warm spring day.

"I just don't think it's wise. Like I keep telling you, she's made her bed, and we should let her lie in it."

"And you're sure that she's not in any danger up there?"

He chuckled. "Well, I'm not saying Juneau doesn't have its share of troubles. But there are plenty of good people up there too. And plentiful jobs for girls who want work. There were always 'help wanted' signs posted about. Businesses looking for maids and waitresses and store clerks. I doubt she's had any trouble finding a job. And maybe hard work is just what she needs."

"You're probably right. And you did write to AJ about her?"

"Yes," Wyatt reminded her.

"Because last time I saw Jackson's mother, she sounded fairly certain Jackson was coming home. He was done with Alaska."

"And no mention of Miranda." Wyatt sipped his coffee.

"Not a word. And I was afraid to ask. Maggie is an open-minded woman, but I'm not sure how she'd react if she thought Miranda was chasing after her son."

"Aunt Lilly and Uncle George sure didn't take that news too well."

"I hope they can forgive her." Delia sighed. "And I hope they'll still come out to visit us. Maybe not this summer since there's no need to ride out on the train with Miranda."

"No, that girl's proven she can travel on her own steam." Wyatt chuckled. "I knew she was strong-willed when I first met her, but I never would've guessed she'd head off to Alaska like that. Gotta admit that takes spunk."

"I can't help but believe your aunt is right and her friend Sadie has a lot to do with it. And after speaking to Sadie's father, he seemed to agree."

"And he cut Sadie off from any funds," Wyatt reminded her. "Which makes me even more sure we're doing the right thing not sending Miranda money."

Delia nodded, but she wasn't as sure as Wyatt. In fact, if Miranda wrote them, asking for help, Delia felt fairly certain she'd cave.

"Looks like the twins." Delia waved to what looked like Julianne and Julius walking toward the house but concealed in the long shadows of the barn. "Wonder what're they doing over there?"

"Julius wanted to show Julianne that bum calf he's been caring for," Wyatt said. "That boy's got a real good hand with ailing animals."

"And a tender heart," Delia added. "Although I never would've guessed this when we lived back in Pittsburgh. Back then my little brother would rather torture animals than help them. I still remember the time he tied a tin can to old Mrs. Lakewood's cat's tail."

Wyatt laughed. "I never heard that story."

"The kids have really grown up a lot since coming out here."

Delia sighed. "Julianne even more so than Julius. But that's probably because girls mature faster."

"She really is turning into a young woman," Wyatt agreed. "She's almost as tall as you now. Must be this good country food and fresh air."

"When I took the kids to town last Saturday, a full-grown boy acted overly interested in Julianne. I almost had to set him straight on her age. But I think she enjoyed the attention." Delia chuckled. "She'll be thirteen this summer, but sometimes she acts like an adult. Then other times, like when she's riding Dolly, she's just a kid again."

"I heard her arguing with your mother the other day," Wyatt lowered his voice since the twins were getting closer. "It was hard to tell who was the grownup and who was the child."

Delia laughed. "That's nothing new."

Suddenly both the twins were on the porch, excitedly telling about the progress of the new calf. "She's standing up really well," Julius proclaimed.

"And Julius let me feed her with the bottle," Julianne added. "She's such a sweet little calf. Such pretty eyes, and her coat is as soft as silk."

"So you think she's gonna make it?" Wyatt asked Julius.

"Yep." Julius nodded. "She's going to grow up to be a real good milk cow. And since she's red, I named her Rusty."

"Good for you." Wyatt patted Julius on the back.

Delia leaned back in her rocker, listening as the children talked with enthusiasm about the upcoming summer and all they wanted to do, peppered with Wyatt's comments and suggestions. All of this scene—with the background of the ranch and the Colorado sky now blazing with color—well, life felt just about perfect. She just hoped and prayed Miranda was safe up there in Alaska…and that she would figure things out and come home soon.

Miranda never told anyone about how she'd almost stowed away on the ship in an attempt to be with Jackson. By the time she returned to the hotel that day, Sadie had still been asleep. Miranda had sneaked the money back into the drawer, tore up the note…and pretended she'd never cooked up such a foolish plan.

During the following week, she also pretended to be fine. Whether she was performing with Sadie or working at the school, she covered her broken heart with bright smiles and sunny lightness. Her goal was to forget about Jackson O'Neil, once and for all. The same way he'd forgotten all about her. And imagining him back in Colorado seemed to eradicate any desire she'd had to go back home. The last thing she wanted was to bump into him in Colorado City. No, she was resolved to remain in Juneau for as long as Sadie wanted.

Unfortunately, that resolve was shaken just one week later. It was midmorning Saturday and, although Sadie had declined a stroll through town due to a headache, Miranda later discovered her tucked in a corner of the hotel lobby. Sadie appeared to be having an intimate tête-à-tête with a well-dressed young man. But upon closer inspection, the young man was none other than Jackson's old mining partner, AJ!

Miranda knew her aggravation wasn't rational, but for some reason it just irked her. Of all the available young men in Juneau, why would Sadie go for someone so closely associated with the very man who'd broken Miranda's heart? And why do it in such a clandestine manner? It was selfish and mean.

Miranda went up to their room and, after pacing and stewing, she was determined to confront Sadie. She was just trying to think of the right words when Sadie burst into the room, making her jump.

"Sorry." Sadie's grin looked sheepish. "Didn't mean to spook you. I was just in a hurry."

"In a hurry?" Miranda frowned. "Why?"

"I, uh, I'm going somewhere."

"What happened to your headache?"

Sadie shrugged, gathering up gloves and hat. "Gone, I guess."

"I want to talk to you first." Miranda stood in front of the door.

"Is this going to take long?" Sadie pinned her hat into place. "Someone is waiting."

"AJ?"

Sadie looked surprised, but simply nodded. "How did you know?"

"I saw you two down there." Miranda got closer to her, peering into her eyes. "What is going on?"

"Nothing is going on." Sadie tugged on her gloves.

"What are you doing with him?"

"I was simply talking to him. I don't see why it's any of your business."

"AJ was Jackson's partner, Sadie. Can't you imagine how that makes me feel?"

She shrugged. "Sort of. I guess that's why I was trying to be sneaky about it. Now, if you'll please get out of my way, AJ is waiting."

"I can't believe you're doing this." Miranda didn't budge. "I mean, why AJ? There are lots of other—"

"I like him, Miranda. I liked him from the start. Even before I knew he was Jackson's partner. Are you going to fault me for that?"

Miranda felt confused. "I don't know. It's just upsetting."

"He's a good guy. And he likes me. I'm sorry I tried to hide it from you, Miranda, but I had my reasons."

"What reasons?" Miranda demanded.

"Nothing." Sadie stubbornly folded her arms in front.

"If you don't tell me, it proves you're not really my best friend, Sadie. And if we're not best friends, then I'm quitting the burlesque show. Starting tonight."

Sadie's blue eyes widened. "Tonight is supposed to be a really big night."

"I know. But if you don't trust me with whatever's going on with you and AJ, I don't trust you as my partner. I've been wanting to quit anyway." Miranda stepped away from the door. "So go ahead, if you like. We'll just call it quits right here."

Sadie bit her lip. "All right, I do trust you. But if I tell you what's going on, will you swear to tell no one?"

"You don't think you can trust me?"

"Yes, I know I can. It's just that AJ swore me to secrecy about this."

"What is it?" Miranda's curiosity was exploding.

"AJ confided to me that he's hit the mother lode, Miranda. He is rich. Really rich. It's so exciting."

"Oh?" Miranda let it sink in. "So his partner is gone for just two weeks and AJ suddenly strikes gold. Go figure." Part of Miranda felt sorry for Jackson, but another part of her thought he probably deserved this for being such a coward and leaving.

"AJ doesn't want anyone to know. There are claim jumpers all over the place. I guess this is the worst time of year for it. So don't say a word to anyone."

"If he's so worried about claim jumping, seems he'd be out there protecting his claim. Instead of parading around in a brand new, store-bought outfit."

"He's got someone watching his claim."

"Right. So that he could come here and show off for you." Miranda shrugged. "Well, don't let me keep you two."

"Are you going to hate me just because AJ is—"

"I don't hate you." Miranda felt guilty. "I'm just, well…I guess I'm a little out of sorts. I'm sorry."

Sadie hugged her. "And I'm sorry you're still getting over Jackson. I honestly don't know what's wrong with that guy. You're such a dear person, Miranda, it seems like he would've been happy to see you."

"He might've been." Miranda sighed. "If he hadn't seen me up there on the stage like that."

"Yeah, AJ tried to talk sense into him, but sounds like Jackson is a pretty stubborn guy."

"Well, I hope he's happy back in Colorado."

"Colorado?" Sadie frowned.

"Yes. I assume that's where he was headed. Although I suppose he could be anywhere."

"Yes…anywhere." Sadie gave her a sad smile. "I better go. AJ has arranged for a carriage and a picnic. I told him I'd be right back down."

"Have fun," Miranda said, but her words sounded flat to her. After Sadie left, Miranda went to the window that overlooked the street, waiting until she saw AJ helping Sadie into a carriage…and the pair happily rode away.

Miranda didn't want to feel jealous, but she couldn't seem to help herself. Why did everyone but her got what they wanted? Was she such a miserably bad person that God was determined to shut her out forever? As she paced back and forth in the stuffy hotel room, she thought about Polly Gregg. Just yesterday Polly had commented on how wonderfully Miranda was doing with the children. "You're truly a godsend," she'd said once again. "I don't know what I'd do without you."

Miranda needed to talk to her.

An hour later, after confessing all her troubles, Miranda was helping Polly work in the little vegetable garden behind their house. "Thank you for listening," Miranda said as she pulled a large weed. "I actually feel better for just telling someone everything."

"I'm glad." Polly stood up straight, adjusting the brim of her sunhat. "But you need to remember that God is always there to listen too. I'm not saying it wasn't good for you to come talk to me, but sometimes—when you don't have someone right there—you need to remember that God is always listening, Miranda."

"But I feel like God ignores me," Miranda confessed. "As if His ears are deafened to any prayer that comes from me. Like I'm talking to the walls."

Polly just smiled. "I remember feeling like that…I was probably about your age. But over time, I learned my problem was that I wanted God to do what *I* wanted. Not what *He* wanted. Once I realized that God's ways really were higher than my ways, well, it got better."

"But sometimes I wonder if God is ignoring me because of something else. Something I've done…or haven't done."

"What do you mean?" Polly sat down on the garden bench.

"It's something Pastor Gregg has said. And others have told me this too. But I have a hard time with it." She looked earnestly at Polly. "I know that I haven't forgiven everyone. Not like I'm supposed to do. But I have people who've hurt me deeply. People I've sworn to never forgive."

"Well, unforgiveness can be a barrier between us and God." Polly pointed to the wall that her husband had built from the stones extracted from the garden. "Imagine if each of those stones represented a time when you refused to forgive someone. They pile up and up. And although that fence is good for my garden, to keep rabbits from my cabbages, I'm sure the rabbits wish it wasn't there." She laughed. "I don't know if that quite makes sense. But my point is that when we don't forgive others, we do build a wall. A wall that separates us from God and all the goodness He has in store for us."

Miranda sat next to Polly and began to pour out her story, confessing her childish foolishness and various people who had hurt her—everyone from the conniving Beatrice Phillips at the academy to the evil snake Marcus Stanley who murdered her stepfather. "I swore to never forgive that man."

"Some people are easier to forgive than others," Polly admitted. "Some people you give up to God once and that's it. Others take time. And we can't properly forgive anyone without God's help. Jesus said we need to forgive seventy times seven, Miranda. And even though that equals four-hundred-ninety, the number seven is supposed to represent eternity. So Jesus was really saying we need to forgive for as long as it takes."

"It might take me eternity to forgive Marcus," Miranda confessed.

"I hope it doesn't." Polly sighed. "Because that means Marcus has a hold on you. By not forgiving him, you give him power. Do you really want to do that?"

"No!" Miranda shook her head. "That's the last thing I want."

"Then you need to ask God to help you forgive." Polly reached for Miranda's hands. "Let's pray together, dear." And just like that Polly led Miranda in prayer. She helped Miranda to confess her mistakes to God and ask His forgiveness, as well as to ask to forgive others. Finally Polly said, "Amen."

"Amen," Miranda echoed. She opened her eyes. "I think that is the first time I've ever really truly prayed. I mean, prayed and meant it. Thank you so much."

Polly reminded her about seventy-times-seven and then, seeing it was getting late in the afternoon, Miranda had to excuse herself to meet up with Sadie for a rehearsal. But as she walked back through town, her feet felt lighter. It was as if a weight had been lifted. And now she felt that if she wanted to talk to God—about anything—He really would be listening. So she asked Him to help her to get out of performing with Sadie, and to make a way for her to do it without hurting Sadie too badly.

33

Two weeks after Miranda's garden lesson on forgiveness with Polly, Sadie returned from another Saturday carriage ride and picnic. She was wearing a huge smile. And a diamond engagement ring. "AJ has proposed marriage," she happily told Miranda.

Miranda was too astonished to respond.

"Aren't you happy for me?"

"Yes—of course. I'm just shocked." Miranda hugged Sadie.

"To be honest, I wasn't all that surprised. He's been hinting about it every Saturday. But I didn't expect him to get to it so soon."

Miranda sat down on the bed, trying to take this all in. "So when is the happy event?"

Sadie sat down on the chair, explaining in detail their plans. AJ felt that the big strike was winding down and that in a month's time it would be mostly mined out. "But the claim can still sell for a fair price. Apparently AJ had a chance to do this about a year ago, when he and his other partner, Wyatt—"

"Wyatt is my stepsister Delia's husband," Miranda interrupted, surprised at how just mentioning their names sent a wave of homesickness rushing over her.

"Yes, AJ has mentioned that. Anyway, it seems that Wyatt had the good sense to quit while he was ahead, but AJ stuck around and made some costly mistakes." Sadie giggled. "Although we're both thankful he did. Otherwise I wouldn't have met him. And, Miranda, isn't it wonderful that he was just a poor miner when we first met? And I liked him anyway. No one can say I'm marrying him for his money." She threw up her hands. "Although it's nice he has some."

Miranda just nodded. "I'm happy for both of you. So you don't plan to marry for a month? Will you continue performing?"

Sadie pursed her lips. "I'm not sure. I know you want to quit. To be honest, I'm a little tired of it too. Maybe I should tell Margaret to look for another act."

"Yes, that sounds good to me."

"And you don't need to worry about money to go home," she said quickly. "I'll give you my share of the earnings. That should cover you ship passage and train fare. If not, AJ has offered to help too."

Miranda sighed in relief. "Thank you. I think I'd like to go home."

"AJ wanted to get married here in town, but I suggested we do it aboard ship. Captains can perform marriage ceremonies, and I've always dreamed of being married on the high seas. And you will be my maid of honor."

"And hopefully I won't be seasick."

"No, we'll be on the top deck. And we'll get staterooms on top too. AJ is already looking into it. We will be traveling in style."

"Wonderful." Miranda tried to infuse more enthusiasm than she felt. It wasn't so much that she was jealous now. But a little sad. Still, she reminded herself. She was going home. That was something to be truly happy for.

"And do you know where we're going to live?"

Miranda considered this. "On the high seas?"

"No, silly. I've had enough of that. AJ's family is from Oregon. And his friend Wyatt offered to sell him some property there last year. AJ turned him down then, but now he's wired Wyatt to see if the offer is still good. If so, we will become ranchers right next to his parents' property in Oregon. Doesn't that sound exciting?"

"I guess so. Although it's hard to imagine you as a rancher's wife."

Sadie laughed. "I mentioned that to AJ, and he assured me that if we don't like it, we can move someplace else. He's like me, Miranda, an adventurer."

"Sounds like a match made in heaven." Miranda forced a bright smile. "I am truly happy for both of you."

"So one month from now, we will be embarking on a whole new life."

"One month?" Miranda considered this. "That's actually perfect for me. I will be able to finish out the whole school year with Polly."

"You really like that, don't you? I remember you back at the academy. Who ever would've guessed you'd be a good teacher?"

"It's because of the children. I love them. And they really respect me. That feels pretty good."

"Maybe you'll be a teacher when you get back to Colorado," she suggested.

"That wouldn't be so bad." Miranda picked up a piece of hotel stationary. "Speaking of Colorado, I'm going to write to Delia right now. I want to tell her I'm coming home." She grimaced. "I just hope I'll be welcome there. But if not, maybe I could get a teaching job somewhere else."

"You could come out to Oregon and live with us. And if there aren't teaching jobs, you could always sing at the local saloon," Sadie teased.

Miranda groaned. "No, thank you!" As she began to pen her letter, Miranda felt that she'd rather wear rags, go hungry, and live under a box than to perform in a saloon. Oh, sure, it might be an entertaining story to tell her grandchildren someday—not that she'd ever have any children or grandchildren…and perhaps that was for the best.

Jackson couldn't remember ever being so completely exhausted, as if every bone in his body was screaming out in pain. Every day was the same as the one before. Up before dawn, working the mine for up to twelve hours a day, then collapsing at night. Still, it was worth it. For one thing, the mine had been producing these past few months. But besides that, the hard work helped to block everything else from his mind. Plus it provided a good excuse to avoid any lengthy conversations with his increasingly obnoxious partner.

And lately AJ's lectures were even more longwinded than usual. Of course, that was because he'd been smitten by his dancehall girl. Not that Jackson dared call Sadie McGuire that. AJ would leap to her defense, claiming she was a singer and performer. "Not a dancehall girl!" Well, whatever you called it, Jackson suspected AJ planned to waste all his gold money on her once Jackson left Juneau.

Not that Jackson particularly cared. His only plan was to gather his share of the gold, sell his half of the share to AJ, and get out of Alaska for good. To that end, he'd already booked passage. Just one week from today, he'd be aboard the *Lady Heloise* and bound for San Francisco. After that...well, he wasn't even sure he cared.

"You're going to listen to me tonight," AJ insisted as Jackson unfurled his bedroll. "I mean it, Jackson. If you don't hear me out, it might come down to fisticuffs."

"Right." Jackson grimly shook his head. "You know I can take you, AJ."

"Maybe, but I can still make you sorry for it." AJ refilled Jackson's coffee cup. "Come on, buddy, sit down and just listen. Please."

"I know what you're going to say, AJ." Jackson accepted the cup. "You'll tell me that Miranda is a *nice* girl. That she's only working at the saloon to earn enough money to go home. I've heard it all before."

"And what about that she works at the school during the—"

"So you say. But I'm not buying it. For one thing, Miranda has never been the academic type. Besides that, she didn't want to go away to school and didn't even last a full year there. But that's not what really gets my goat. For the life of me, I cannot imagine that girl as a schoolmarm by day and dancehall girl by night."

"She's not a dancehall girl!"

"That's your opinion. Just the same, I can't fathom her teaching little children by day and singing to a roomful of drunken miners at night. Can you?"

"I'll admit it's a bit farfetched, but Sadie claims it's true."

"Do you seriously believe that parents would cotton to the idea of their little ones being taught by that kind of a woman? Juneau is a small town. Word gets around. Dancehall girls are not teachers, AJ. Get that through your head."

"So, you're saying Sadie's lying to me?" AJ challenged him. "Because those are fighting words, man."

"I'm saying it doesn't add up."

"Then why don't you go see for yourself?" AJ shook his fist at him. "You haven't been to town in months. We're running low on supplies and—"

"And you were going on Saturday so as you could meet up with your fancy woman."

"She's not a fancy woman, Jackson. I swear if you keep going on—"

"Settle down. All I'm saying is you've been getting our provisions."

"Not this time. And we're almost out of coffee, sugar, and flour. You go to Juneau this weekend. Find out for yourself."

"No school on Saturday." Jackson's smile was smug.

"Don't wait for Saturday. Tomorrow's Friday. Go tomorrow."

"I don't want to go."

"Well, you're going to need some things for your boat trip, Jackson. Your clothes are rags, your hair is down to your shoulders, and your beard's a mess."

"Doesn't bother me."

"Come on, man. You don't have to go home looking like a bum.

And I'll stick around and keep watch on things here. I can still go to town on Saturday if I want. In the meantime, you'll find out for yourself if Sadie's telling the truth or not."

Jackson considered it. "You know, I might just do that if it'd shut you up. I wouldn't mind having my last week here a little more peaceful."

AJ's eyes twinkled. "And if you find out it's true? What then?"

"I'm still leaving here next week. Nothing will stop me." Yet he wondered. What if he had misjudged Miranda? Still, he didn't think it possible. Dancehall girls were not schoolmarms.

"You mean you won't even talk to her? You'd just take your leave without a single word?"

"Why not?"

"Because, like I keep telling you, Miranda is pining away for you."

"That's hogwash."

"She is. Sadie is always telling me how sad Miranda is—"

"She sure didn't look sad that night I saw her singing and dancing at the Nugget. She was grinning and laughing. I don't think I'll ever get those red-painted lips out of my head. And that awful dress. And those horrible stockings." Jackson ran his fingers through his hair. "Trust me, that is not the Miranda I knew back in Colorado."

"Well, I've been to the Nugget to see their act since that night," AJ argued, "and Miranda doesn't paint her lips now. And her dress is more respectable. According to Sadie, Miranda's never liked performing. But they needed the money."

"So you've said. The way you tell it, besides being a schoolmarm, Miranda probably sings in the church choir on Sundays." Jackson tossed the remains of his coffee onto the fire.

"As a matter of fact, Sadie told me Miranda goes to church every Sunday."

Jackson laughed. Not a sincere laugh, but enough to let AJ know he wasn't falling for any of this nonsense. "Now if you'll excuse me, I'm going to bed."

"That's right. You have a big day tomorrow. Fetching our supplies in town. Getting yourself cleaned up, and stopping by the schoolhouse, which is actually in the little white church on the edge of town. But I'll warn you, Jackson, if you don't go see for yourself, I will give you one last week of some mighty strong lecturing."

"Like I said, I'm going by the schoolhouse just to shut you up." Jackson got into his bedroll with a loud warning growl. Hopefully AJ would heed it and stop running off at the mouth. It was bad enough to have a fool in love for your partner, but having him force his romantic notions was just plain insufferable.

Despite being bone-tired, Jackson didn't sleep well that night. The idea of possibly crossing paths with Miranda made him feel sick inside. The next morning, after setting out early with Rosie, he didn't think he'd bother to stop by the school. He could always just tell AJ he had. But what would he say?

By the time he reached town, he decided to just get it over with. So after tying Rosie to the Mercantile hitching post, he meandered across town. It was just a little before noon and his belly was grumbling, but he wanted to put this—whatever it was—behind him. He realized how nasty and grubby he must look as a couple of saloon girls gave him a wide berth on the boardwalk. What did he care if they turned up their noses?

As he got closer to the white clapboard building that housed the church and the school, he could hear the happy shrieks and sounds of children's voices. It was a pleasant, hopeful sound that almost brought a smile to his face. Until he remembered the purpose of this mission. Well, best to just get it over with. Hopefully his appearance wouldn't frighten anyone. When he got to the building, he could catch glimpses of children running around in the green grass behind the church. Feeling like an unwelcome intruder, and not wanting to be observed, he skulked around the side of the building, hoping to get a good look at the play area.

Jackson felt his jaw drop when he spied her auburn hair, pulled neatly back into a bun, shining in the sun. She was helping a little girl onto a wooden swing, laughing as she gave her a gentle push and then stepping back out of the way.

"Miss Williams," a girl on the other swing called. "Push me too."

"Come on," Miranda encouraged. "Pump your legs like I've been telling you. In and out, in and out. There, Elisa, now you're getting it."

"May I help you?"

Jackson turned to see an older woman peering curiously at him. "I'm sorry, ma'am," he muttered. "I must look like a thug, but I swear, I'm not."

"Why don't you tell me what you're doing?" She led him around to the front steps, studying him closely.

"I—uh—I used to be a friend of Miranda's. Someone said she was a teacher here. I just came to, uh, see if that was true."

The woman's eyes narrowed. "You *used* to be a friend?"

"Well, yes. I mean, it's a long story."

"Are you a miner?"

He nodded. "Name's Jackson O'Neil. I, uh, I knew Miranda back in Colorado. Actually, since we were kids."

"You're the man she followed here?"

"She told you that?"

"That and a lot more." The woman frowned. "But she said you'd gone home to Colorado."

"I'd planned to go. I still do."

"But you wanted to talk to her first?"

"I...I don't know for sure. Right now, I'm not too sure of much." He glanced around uneasily. "But, please, don't tell her you saw me here like this."

"Why not?"

"Well, it just doesn't seem right. So I'm begging you, ma'am, please, don't say anything."

"You say you're going home to Colorado? When do you plan to leave?"

"Just a week from now. Booked on the *Lady Heloise*."

Her pale brows arched. "Really?"

"Yes. I already paid my fare. I want to go home."

"I see."

"Can I ask you something, ma'am?"

"Yes, of course."

"Is Miranda a good teacher?"

"Oh, my, she is a wonder. I keep telling everyone she is my godsend. As you can see, I'm getting a little old for this. My husband worries about my health. But Miranda stepped right in and helped so much. You should hear her handling our music lessons. It's such fun. And the children adore her. I'm so glad she could stay until the end of the school year."

He slowly nodded, trying to absorb this information. "Thank you, ma'am. And again, I apologize for sneaking in like this. And please, don't mention it to Miranda."

She nodded. "Your secret is safe with me, Jackson. God bless your journey home."

He thanked her and, eager to escape before being spotted by Miranda, he hurried back to town. Taking AJ's advice, he got some new clothes then bathed and visited the barber, all the while being careful not to tip his hand regarding his recent mining success. After gathering supplies at the mercantile, he and Rosie headed back up to the mine.

Thanks to Alaska's long summer days, it was still light when he reached camp, but AJ was waiting for him by the campfire. "So?" AJ questioned as he helped to unload Rosie's saddle bags. "Is Miranda a schoolmarm or not?"

Jackson tugged out the sacks of flour and sugar. "Yep. You were right. Sadie was telling you the truth."

AJ slapped Jackson's back so hard he almost lost his balance.

"Did ya talk to her?"

"Nope." Jackson set the sacks inside the metal food locker. "She didn't even see me. Probably good because I hadn't cleaned up yet."

"Ya look real good now." AJ grinned. "Ya should've gone to see her."

"I needed time to think." Jackson put the last of supplies in the locker then closed it and sat down by the fire.

AJ poured a cup of coffee and handed it to him. "Ya hungry? I save some stew and biscuits for ya."

Jackson nodded. "Thanks."

"So ya needed time to think." AJ handed him the loaded tin plate and sat down. "Have ya finished your thinking yet?"

"Maybe. One thing I know. I'm not leaving Juneau on that ship next week."

"Hold on a minute, you—"

"Hear me out, AJ. First of all, I don't like leaving you here alone on a hot claim. Town was crawling with newcomers, and I'm sure there are some claim jumpers in the mix. You aren't safe out here by yourself."

"But I won't—"

"Listen to me, AJ. My concern for you is just part of my reasoning. The other part is that I need to talk to Miranda. I reckon you're right. I judged her too harshly. It'll take some time to sort it all out. And I can't do that if I'm shipping out of here."

"That's true, but you don't need to change your travel plans."

"How am I supposed to talk to Miranda if I leave?"

"Because she's leaving too."

"What?" Jackson was confused.

"I wasn't supposed to tell you," AJ explained. "It was Sadie's idea, and it sounded like a good plan to me too. But we wanted to keep it secret from you."

"What are you talking about?"

"I asked Sadie to marry me, and we plan to wed on the *Lady Heloise*—"

"The boat I'm booked on?"

"Yep. I booked it too. And Sadie was bringing Miranda with her."

"On the same boat?"

"That's right. And Sadie hasn't told Miranda that you'll be on that boat. In fact, Miranda thinks you're already back in Colorado. Sadie said that was the main reason she's been so sad. She went to all this effort to find you up here and then you took off without a word."

"Except that I didn't."

"Can't blame you for that. We hit that big vein just a few days before you were gonna ship out. I reckon you're glad you stayed."

"Yeah…." Jackson scratched his head. "So we're all leaving here on the same boat?"

"Should be interesting, huh?"

Jackson glanced over to the opening of the mine. "What about our claim? I thought you were staying on, you said you'd buy out my half of the share?"

"I already talked to Apple Jack. He wants to buy the whole claim. I was going to tell ya about that later this week, before we shipped out."

Jackson slowly shook his head, still trying to make sense of everything. "So we're all leaving on the *Lady Heloise* on Saturday morning."

"Yep." AJ looked pleased. "Me and Sadie wanted to surprise both you and Miranda, but now it'll just be her."

They talked awhile longer, finalizing the details and agreeing that they would pack everything up and leave camp on Friday morning. It was a little hard for both of them to realize they could be leaving a fair amount of gold behind. But Apple Jack was a good man who'd been looking for a strike for years. And both AJ and Jackson were finished with Alaska. Both of them wanted to move on…and start a new life.

34

Miranda had mixed feelings as she packed her trunk and bags on Friday afternoon. On one hand, she missed Colorado and Delia and everyone at the ranch. On the other hand, she had enjoyed her time with Polly and the children and would surely miss them. Yesterday had been the last day of school before summer vacation. And, during their little celebration party, complete with cake and punch, Polly had presented Miranda with a parting gift.

"This is both for your upcoming eighteenth birthday," Polly had announced ceremoniously as the children looked on, "as well as to thank you for helping at the school these past few months. You were truly our godsend, Miss Williams."

Miranda had been touched to see the gift was a golden heart-shaped locket with a tiny cross embossed into the front of it. Later on, Polly explained it had been her graduation present many years ago. But since she'd never had a daughter to pass it down to, she wanted Miranda to have it.

Miranda fingered the delicate locket hanging around her neck. She's promised Polly she would treasure it always. A memento of Polly and Miranda's time here in Juneau…and all she had learned.

"Are you ready to rehearse for tonight?" Sadie asked brightly. She laid out their sailor girl outfits and chuckled. "I won't miss wearing these things."

"I, uh, I have an idea, Sadie."

"What's that?" Sadie flopped down on the bed that was still strewn with clothes to be packed.

"Well. . . ." Miranda considered her words. "You have been calling the shots for the Sailor Sisters all this time. And other than asking for a more modest costume, I've pretty much agreed with you, right?"

"Well, we have had a few arguments," Sadie reminded her. "But for the most part, you're right, I've been in charge."

"Well, I'd like to be in charge tonight."

Sadie's brows arched high. "Really?"

"Yes. In fact, if you don't agree with me, I think I shall refuse to perform." Miranda crossed her arms in front, taking on her stubborn stance.

"But Margaret has already put out a special sign. It's all glittery and fancy. It says the *Sailor Sisters Farewell Performance Tonight*. You don't want to ruin our final performance, do you?"

"No. But I think my idea will make it even better."

Sadie's smile seemed amused. "Well, I suppose it can't hurt anything. It's not like we'll lose our jobs. And Margaret already paid us."

"Then we'll do it my way?"

"Sure. Why not? The worst that can happen is they'll throw rotten tomatoes at us. Although I doubt the miners will have any produce on them. But they could throw boots or beer mugs. You ready to do some ducking?"

"That's how much confidence you have in my plan?" Miranda frowned. "Thanks."

"Actually, I'm quite curious. What do you have in mind?"

Miranda took in a deep breath. "It will be more of a classical concert, Sadie, we'll wear out prettiest gowns with our hair nicely done up. And you can't paint your lips. And we will sing pretty songs and moving ballads. I thought we could do 'The Dawning of the Day' and 'The Rock Beside the Sea' and 'Where are the Hopes I Cherished' and..." She pulled out the list she'd made this morning. "And these other ballads you taught me back at the academy."

Sadie looked over the list. "Well, I happen to love these old Irish songs. I learned them as a child. But I'm not sure what the miners will think of it."

"Like you said, it doesn't matter." Miranda clasped her hands together as if to plead. "Please, Sadie, do this for me. I'd like to leave Juneau holding my head high. You know?"

Sadie nodded. "I like it. This is exactly how we'll do it. But I better get our list down to Charlie. I hope he knows some of these tunes. Otherwise, we might have to sing without accompaniment."

As Sadie got ready to go downstairs, Miranda reminded her they used to sing unaccompanied all the time. After Sadie left, Miranda returned to packing. But for the first time since the Sailor Sisters act first came to Juneau, she was looking forward to tonight's performance.

By the time Jackson and AJ had wrapped up all their business in Juneau, it was past seven o'clock. And after the last few twelve-hour days of scraping out every last bit of bullion they could find, they were both exhausted and ravenous. Although Jackson had booked their room at the Kodiak, because he wasn't ready to see Miranda, AJ insisted they dine at the Nugget.

Jackson threw up his hands in protest. "I do not want to go to—"

"I reserved us a table, Jackson. I want one last good steak dinner in Juneau, and Beulah's has the best in town. Come on, man, I'm starved!"

"But I already told you, I don't want to see Miranda. I'm not ready to—"

"Don't worry about that." He gave Jackson a firm shove toward the hotel entrance. "Sadie and Miranda always take supper in their room before a performance."

Jackson wasn't so sure, but once they were inside the restaurant, he didn't see either of the girls anywhere. And while they dined on what really was the best steak dinner in Juneau—and should've been, based on the expense—he was relieved to see the Sailor Sisters never made an appearance.

"I noticed that sign outside the hotel," Jackson said as they finished up their apple pie for dessert. "'The Sailor Sisters Farewell Performance Tonight at Eight.'"

"Wanna go?" AJ asked eagerly.

"No. Thank. You." Jackson wiped his mouth with a grim expression.

"Aw, come on, man. It's their final time on stage. Aren't ya curious?"

"Nope." Jackson firmly shook his head. The last image he had of Miranda was in the schoolyard with the children. She'd been dressed modestly and looked like a sweet, wholesome country girl. The kind of girl he'd fallen in love with back home. The kind of girl he'd written letters to while she was at finishing school. He had no desire to see her as the dancehall girl with painted lips and a risqué dress. No thank you very much!

"Well, then I reckon I'll meet up with ya back at the Kodiak." AJ winked. "But ya don't know what you're missing, my friend."

Jackson thought he did. He checked his pocket watch to see it was just past eight. "Better hurry, AJ. Don't want to miss a minute of your fancy-fiancée-dancehall-girl in her last burlesque show." He elbowed him. "At least you hope it's her last, right?"

AJ's scowl said it all as he stormed off. If they weren't in a public place, Jackson felt pretty sure AJ would've socked him in the jaw. And maybe he deserved it. But the idea of those girls parading that stage with drunken miners gaping at them…well, it was more than a little upsetting. In fact, it hurt his head. For the life of him, he could not reconcile the sweet schoolmarm to the sleazy dancehall girl. And as he glanced at a couple of similar *fancy* girls, both of them smiling his way, he wasn't sure he ever could. It was too much to ask of a God-fearing man.

As he walked past the entrance to the saloon, he paused for a moment. Just to listen. Expecting hoots and whistles and bawdy music, he was surprised to discover it was rather quiet in there. In fact, it sounded as if the girls were singing a sweet old-fashioned song that his mother used to sing to him. Curious as to what was happening, Jackson slipped into the back of the saloon and, standing in the shadows, took a peek at the spot-lit stage.

To his shock, Miranda and Sadie were both dressed in perfectly decent long gowns. No striped stocking or brightly painted lips! And unless he was mistaken, Sadie had on the same dress she'd worn for Delia's wedding almost a year ago. He blinked and pulled out a chair and, feeling dumbfounded, he sat and listened to the girls singing sweet old ballads and Irish folk songs. One after the next. As stunned as he felt by their performance, he was almost more surprised that the rough tough miners in the barroom seemed to be enjoying the music too. Sure, a few drunken rabble-rousers protested, but they were quickly cleared out by the burly bouncer. And when the girls sang "The Dawning of the Day" in perfect harmony, Jackson wasn't the only miner with misty eyes.

The girls invited the crowd to sing along with an old Civil war song, and then Sadie announced they were going to sing their last number. "But before we do, I have to tell you that my partner Miranda Williams is the one who put tonight's program together. The truth is, Miranda has never been that happy doing our burlesque show, but she has been a real encouragement to me, and I want you to all give her a big hand." The room erupted in enthusiastic applause, but Jackson thought he clapped the loudest. Now Sadie nudged Miranda forward, as if she wanted her to speak.

"Thank you all," Miranda said in a shaky voice. "For our final song I have chosen one of my—my favorite hymns." And then she stepped back beside Sadie and grabbed her hand as they began to sing "Amazing Grace." They sang all the verses and then invited the crowd to join them as they sang the first verse one more time. After the song ended, there was a brief silence…and then everyone clapped and cheered. Sadie and Miranda smiled and bowed and, blowing kisses, they rushed off the stage.

As Jackson stood, he felt slightly dizzy. Or maybe just off-kilter. But something was definitely cockeyed. Like an earthquake going on underfoot—hadn't Alaska had some recently? But he knew this was no earthquake. It was simply that everything in his world had been shaken up lately. And it would probably get worse tomorrow. As he hurried back to the Kodiak, hoping to sneak in before AJ so he could feign sleep, Jackson wondered if he'd even be able to board that ship tomorrow. Could he face her? And if he did, what would he say? Maybe the best thing would be to just let the three of them sail away tomorrow. Jackson could catch the next southbound ship.

The last time Miranda had been down to the ship docks was that day she'd watched Jackson sail away, but she tried not to think about that. In fact, she felt relieved she hadn't stowed away like she'd wanted to that morning. Like she'd told Sadie yesterday, it felt good to depart Juneau with her head held high.

As they boarded the ship, she felt worried. "I hope I don't get seasick again," she whispered to Sadie.

"Don't worry. AJ reserved us a stateroom on the top deck. You'll get your sea legs and be just fine."

Miranda shifted her valise to the other hand and nodded. She hoped Sadie was right. And if she did feel queasy, she would go up to the bow like Sadie had shown her last time. She'd breathe in the fresh air and look out over the ocean. That would help. And before too long, she'd be back in Colorado.

"AJ said our stateroom is number three and the best one on the boat." Sadie told her. "And our trunks should already be in there."

"And I'm wearing my money belt." Miranda remembered how Sadie's money had been stolen from her trunk. "Where it will stay."

"AJ has his money in a safe place too," Sadie whispered. "I've decided that unless I'm on one of Papa's ships, I don't trust anyone." She waved enthusiastically toward the front of the ship. "Oh, there's my bridegroom. There's AJ!"

"I'll take your bag," Miranda offered. "You go join him." She watched as Sadie ran up to the front of the ship, practically stumbling into AJ's open arms. Miranda was happy for them, but it was hard not to feel like a third wheel. Her plan was to stay out of their way. Polly had given her a thick book to occupy her shipboard time. She suspected she'd have it completely read by San Francisco.

Miranda stayed in the stateroom until she felt the steam engines rumbling down below and the ship began to move out of the harbor. She was tempted to remain inside but, worried she might not have her sea legs yet, she decided not to take any chances. And so, wrapping the rose-colored shawl Delia had made her around her shoulders, she went outside to breathe in the fresh ocean air. And to think happy thoughts like Sadie recommended.

Tomorrow was the summer solstice, the first official day of summer and longest day of the year. But today would be nearly as long. It was almost noon, yet the sun would be out for more than ten more hours. Even when it set, it would remain twilight for awhile before it got darker. And not long after that, in the wee hours of the morning, the sun would rise again. It was actually rather exciting. And she thought it was romantic that AJ and Sadie's wedding day would be on the summer solstice.

As Miranda strolled the ship's deck, she spotted AJ and Sadie sitting on a bench next to a lifeboat. They were so enthralled with one another, they seemed oblivious to anyone or anything else. And that was fine. Miranda hoped they would just ignore her as she slipped past them. She knew they were both excited about tomorrow's festivities. The wedding ceremony would be performed at seven o'clock tomorrow evening. And AJ had even arranged with the captain to have a special wedding feast prepared. Miranda squinted out toward the clouds on the horizon, hoping the weather would hold out until then.

As the boat left the inlet out of Juneau harbor, moving out into more open waters, the sails were hoisted and the ship began to rock and roll with the motion of sea. Feeling just slightly queasy, Miranda decided to go nearer to the bow. It wouldn't be the same without Sadie by her side encouraging her, but it was time Miranda got used to it. She not only needed her sea legs, she needed to learn to stand on her own two feet. And she felt certain she could. She found a spot not far from the bow and, clinging to the brass railing, she gazed out over the sea, watching as the ship sliced through it, curling the water over in a sleek, shiny wave as it went. So beautiful!

It was refreshing and exciting to stand here with the wind rushing across her face and billowing her hair out behind her. She wrapped her shawl more snugly around her shoulders and laughed out loud. She was going home! To beautiful Colorado. Not that it wasn't beautiful here. It certainly was. She looked all around her, admiring the sapphire-blue of the sea and the emerald-green landscape of the islands surrounding this inlet. Why had she not noticed how lovely this all was on the way up here? Perhaps she'd been too focused on not getting sick. But Alaska really was gorgeous. And it was a gorgeous day.

Suddenly Miranda felt so lighthearted and happy that she couldn't help but break into a song. She didn't even feel self-conscious since she knew that the whooshing wind would sweep away the sound of her voice. And so she began to sing another beloved hymn, "Glory to God on High." When she got to the third verse, she felt a tap on her shoulder. Thinking it was Sadie sneaking up from behind, Miranda whirled around with a huge smile—then nearly fell overboard!

"Careful there!" Jackson caught her, holding her close for a moment and then at arm's length as if to study her.

"Wh—what?" She felt lightheaded. Was she imagining things? Was this a dream? Was this a stranger who resembled Jackson? What was happening? She closed her eyes tightly for a few second then opened them. "Jackson?" she whispered in disbelief.

"Sorry," he said gruffly. "I didn't mean to frighten you, Miranda. Certainly didn't want you to fall overboard."

"It's really you?" Her knees felt like jelly, her hands shook uncontrollably, and her head was woozy.

"Yes. It's me."

"But what—how—why are you *here*?"

"Let's go sit you down, Miranda. You look like you're about to faint." He took her firmly by the arm, leading her over to a nearby bench. "I shouldn't have come upon you like that."

As she sat down, she took in a slow, deep breath then looked at him again. "What is going on? How did you get here? Why are you here?"

Now he began to explain the whole story, saying he'd been in Juneau the whole time, confessing that he couldn't stand the idea that she'd become a dancehall girl. He paused, slowly shaking his head. "But then I realized that you really weren't like that."

She didn't say anything.

"I realize that I misjudged you, Miranda. I thought you'd become a saloon dancehall girl, and I didn't like it. Not at all. Even when AJ tried to straighten me out, I was too mule-headed and stubborn. I made up my mind about something I didn't fully understand."

She frowned. "And now you do?"

"I'm trying to." He told her about seeing her at the school. "I spoke to Mrs. Gregg. She told me what a fine job you'd been doing."

She pursed her lips, still trying to get her bearings, trying to understand what he was saying...what it really meant.

"And I saw you and Sadie performing last night at the Nugget."

He ran his fingers through his hair. "I was so surprised. I mean, it was really nice."

"Thank you." She tipped her head to one side, trying to gauge her feelings toward him. Part of her was thrilled and wanted to just fall into his arms and stay there. Another part was uncertain. What was he really saying?

"Do you forgive me?" he asked hopefully.

"Forgive you?" She studied his eyes. "For what?"

"For being stupid." He shook his head. "Miranda, I'm really sorry. I should've spoken to you the first time I saw you in Juneau. I shouldn't have judged you like I did. I should've found out the truth."

She barely nodded.

"I shouldn't have stayed away like I did. But there was another reason too. I was discouraged. Remember, I told you I was going to strike it rich? Well, I hadn't. And I reckon I was embarrassed. And maybe even a little mad at myself. And when I saw you, I don't know, it's like something in me just snapped. After that, well, I was a mess."

"What do you mean?"

"I mean I was so angry I just started taking it out on the mine. And on AJ. Ask him if you don't believe me. I'm sure he felt like he was living with a wild animal."

She really wanted to reach out and touch his cheek just now, to tell him that it was all right, but she kept her hands in her lap. She wanted him to finish.

"In my craziness, I wound up striking a real big vein. I should've been happy about it, but I wasn't. Still, AJ talked me into staying longer. That's why I wasn't on the boat like you thought I was."

"I remember that day…I was so sad when I thought you'd left."

"I can't believe you still cared for me."

"I did."

He took both her hands in his. "I never quit loving you. I tried to make myself believe I did, but that just made me act crazier."

"I never quit loving you either." She sighed. "But you did hurt me deeply."

"I know. That's why I want you to forgive me. For being so stupid and for hurting you. Can you forgive me?"

She considered this. "Yes, of course, I forgive you. I know that to be forgiven, one has to forgive. But do you forgive me?"

"I absolutely forgive you, Miranda."

She smiled, and then he leaned forward to kiss her. And as they kissed, she knew that it was true. They really had forgiven each other.

"I love you, Miranda." He pushed a windblown strand of hair from her face.

"I love you too." She touched his cheek.

"Will you marry me?"

She didn't even have to think about it, but she didn't want to sound too eager, so she waited, watching his expression as she did. Then she grinned. "Yes, of course, I will!" And they kissed again.

June 21, 1885

A shipboard double-wedding was held out in the Pacific, on the first eve of summer, and the weather was perfect. Miranda Williams and Jackson O'Neil were joyfully united. And Sadie McGuire and AJ Robinson both said a hearty "I do." Both couples were extremely in love and happy and, during the next few days of their nautical honeymoons, they discussed the exciting plans for their futures.

After anchoring in San Francisco, the two couples enjoyed more celebrating in the big city. And they didn't neglect to wire their joyous wedding announcements to their loved ones. After San Francisco, all four of them traveled by train to Colorado City.

There, a big wedding reception awaited them at the Double W Ranch. Jackson and Miranda's family and friends all gathered to celebrate with good food and good music. The guests soon became acquainted with AJ and Sadie as well. Although AJ struck a deal with

Wyatt Davis to purchase some Oregon ranch property adjacent to his family's ranch, Sadie winked at Miranda and said she thought they would eventually settle near the Double W.

Jackson happily informed his parents that he wanted to invest in the family's failing mines. He hoped to develop a new section of mountain that he felt certain was rich with silver. With Miranda by his side, he felt anything was possible. And for the first time since she could remember, Miranda felt that she truly belonged. Not just to Jackson and his family, although that was wonderful. But she still had Delia and Wyatt and her Double W family. And perhaps best of all, she knew she belonged to God.

Westward to Home
Book 1

Delia and the Drifter
Available Now!

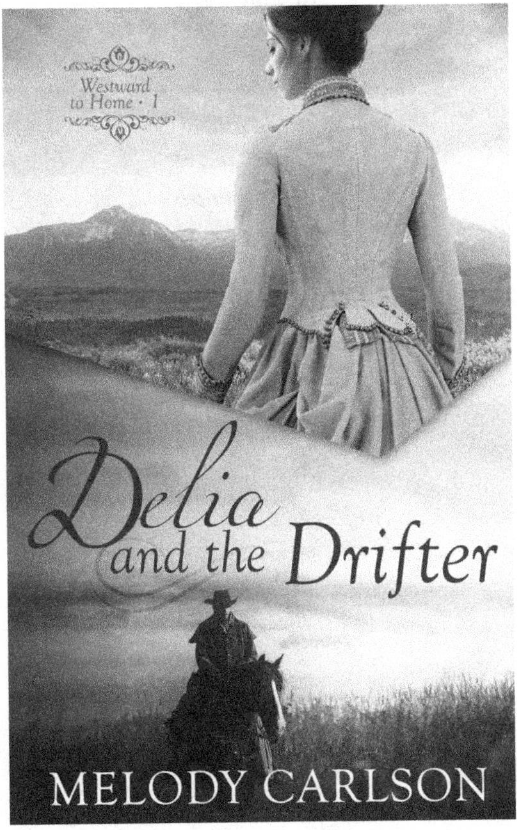

Also by Melody Carlson

The Legacy of Sunset Cove

Harbor Secrets

Riptide Rumors

Surf Smugglers

Turning Tides

The Mulligan Sisters

I'll Be Seeing You

As Time Goes By

String of Pearls

We'll Meet Again

Dear Daphne Series

Home, Hearth, and the Holidays

A Will, a Way, and a Wedding

Whispering Pines

A Place to Come Home To

Everything I Long For

Looking for You All My Life

Someone to Belong To

Second Chances

Heartland Skies

Looking for Cassandra Jane

Shades of Light

Armando's Treasure

Thursday's Child

Built with Love